STEEL-PLATE SUBVERSIVE

Oisín McGann

Steel-Plate Subversive

First published in 2025

Text, illustrations and cover design © Oisín McGann 2025.
The author has asserted his moral rights.

Cover designed and illustrated by Oisín McGann.
ISBN: 978-1-0687545-2-4

Oisin would like to thank the Arts Council of Ireland for
providing funding for time spent researching and writing this book.

Also by Oisín McGann

Novels from Open Road Books (US)
Ancient Appetites: The Wildenstern Saga – Book 1
The Wisdom of Dead Men: The Wildenstern Saga – Book 2
Merciless Reason: The Wildenstern Saga – Book 3
Strangled Silence
Rat Runners

Novellas from Open Road Books (US)
The Vile Desire to Scream: A Companion to
The Wisdom of Dead Men
The Need for Fear: A Companion to *Strangled Silence*
Spoil the Kill: A Companion to *Rat Runners*

Novels from Penguin Random House (UK)
All the novels available from Open Road plus:
Small-Minded Giants
Kings of the Realm: War's Harvest
Kings of the Realm: Cruel Salvation

Novels from The O'Brien Press (Ireland)
The Gods and Their Machines
The Harvest Tide Project: The Archisan Tales – Book 1
Under Fragile Stone: The Archisan Tales – Book 2
Race the Atlantic Wind

Non-fiction from Little Island (Ireland)
A Short, Hopeful Guide to Climate Change

Indie Novels
Cut Off at the Throat
The First Fire of Halloween

For a full bibliography of his work,
please visit his website at: oisinmcgann.com

Praise for Oisín's Books

'A sinister, shadowy world of conspiracy theorists, political double-dealing and media distortion. McGann, in his most accomplished young adult novel to date, handles all of these (and more) with an excellent pace and occasional flashes of ironic humour. The result is an impressive and highly intelligent political thriller.'

Robert Dunbar *The Irish Times Weekend Review* for *Strangled Silence*

'Richard Morgan blasted on to the bookshelves with his hard-hitting tech-noir *Altered Carbon*, a book so in yer face you could smell its toothpaste. Oisín McGann has done the same thing in young adult form with *Small-Minded Giants*, a debut novel so powerful it all but explodes off the page . . . What's astonishing is the confidence with which McGann describes his world, from the workings of the mammoth machinery powering the city to his evocative descriptions. Acts of terrorism give the plot a *V For Vendetta* feel and the tone is just as uncompromising. In short, this book isn't content to sit on your shelf; it's too busy screaming at you to pick it up and READ IT!'

Jayne Nelson, *SFX Magazine* (gives *Small-Minded Giants* five stars out of five)

'The internal turmoil of this multi-generational
family is intense and resembles the powerful Russian
sagas written by Fyodor Dostoyevsky and Leo Tolstoy.
Thankfully, the spunky characters, accessible dialogue,
and nonstop action make this novel enjoyable for
contemporary teens who already enjoy the
[steampunk] genre and are willing to tackle
a dense and complex story.

Sunnie Lovelace, *School Library Journal*
for *Ancient Appetites*

'Four criminally inclined teenagers in future
London are on the run in this fantastic dystopian
thriller . . . Teens will relish McGann's nonstop action,
full of intrigue and heart-pounding excitement. Fans
of Cory Doctorow, particularly the Orwellian
surveillance-themed *Little Brother* (2008),
will find a lot to love here.'

Stacey Comfort, *Booklist* (Reviews journal for
American Library Association) for *Rat Runners*

'This excellent novel is a fantasy, yet every word of
it has direct and understated relevance for our own
political world ... The novel is chiefly a fast-paced,
tense and highly convincing thriller. But McGann's
impeccably fair-minded and intelligent hints at
parallels with Israel and Palestine, or America and

the Middle East, or the secular west and Islam, are
impossible to miss, and his even-handed narrative is all
the more effective in consequence.
Exciting as fantasy adventure, thoughtful in present-
day relevance, the book is a fine achievement and
is strongly recommended.'

Peter Hollindale, *The School Librarian* magazine for
The Gods and Their Machines

'With this book, Oisín McGann has contributed a
compelling and complex work about people who have
suffered and been scarred by the war attempting to use
the airplanes that were once instruments of war in a
way that will inspire instead of destroy . . . McGann
offers a view of humanity as something that is flawed,
ingenious, passionate, wounded, terrifying, and
ultimately, hopeful that it might be possible to change.'

Tony Flynn, Inis Magazine for Race the Atlantic Wind

Contents

Pronounced 'Uh-Sheen' – Biography

Oisín McGann was born in Dublin, Ireland, and spent his childhood there and in Drogheda, County Louth. He studied at Ballyfermot Senior College and Dun Laoghaire School of Art and Design, and went on to work in illustration, design and film animation, later moving to London to work as an art director and copy writer in advertising.

He has since become one of Ireland's most prolific and best-known writer-illustrators, and has produced dozens of books for all levels of reader, including fifteen novels.

He is a winner of the European Science Fiction Society Award, Children's Books Ireland's Children's Choice Award and has been shortlisted for numerous other awards, including the Waterstones Children's Book Prize in the UK, le Grand Prix de l'Imaginaire in France and Locus Magazine's Best First Novel Award in the US. He is married with three children, two dogs and two cats, and lives somewhere in an Irish countryside that no longer hides armed rebels.

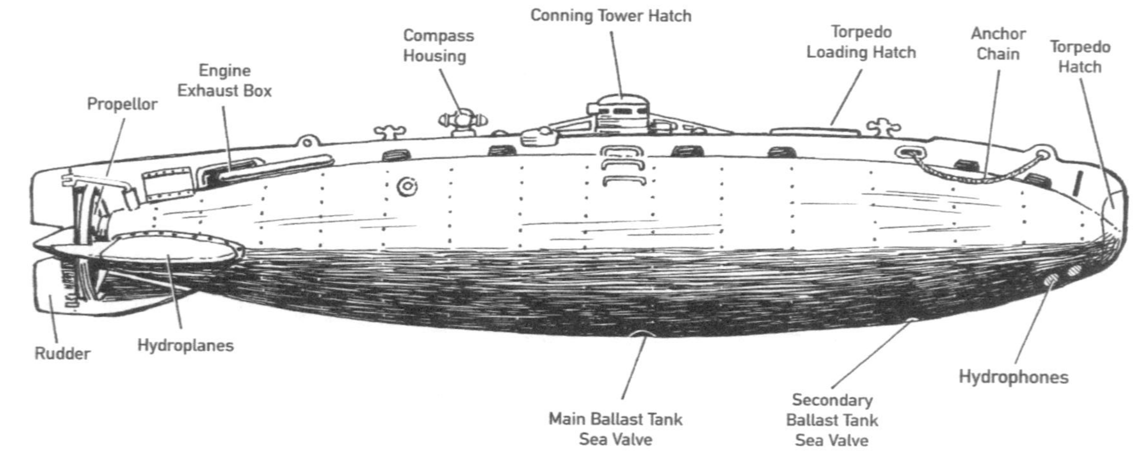

Subversive Exterior – Periscope and Air Intakes Retracted

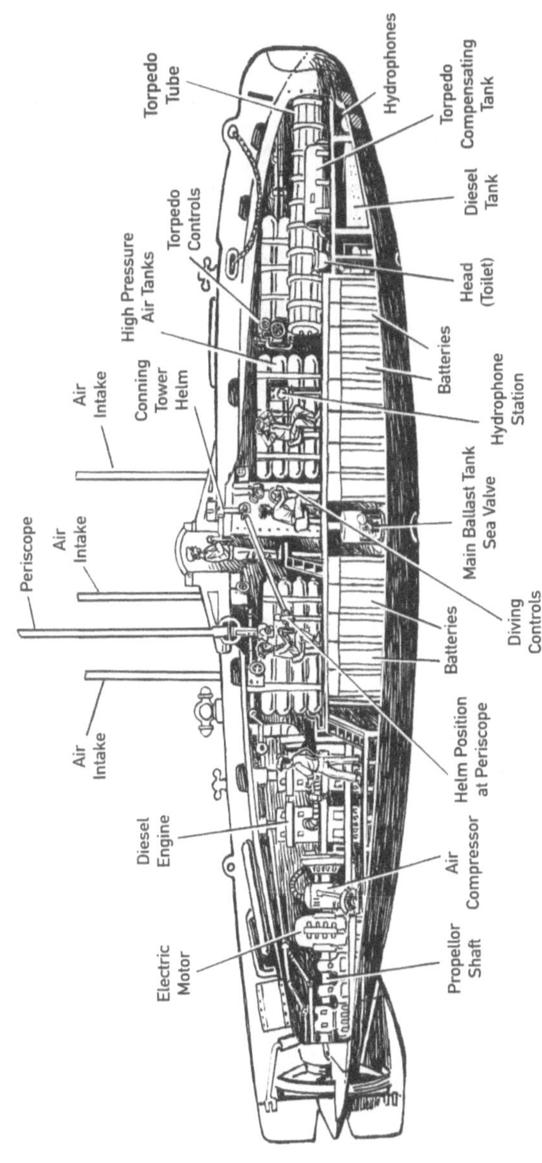

Subversive Cutaway – Periscope and Air Intakes Extended

We could indulge our vanity if we were foolish enough to waste public funds in such a manner by having an infant navy that could never mean anything at all to the British sea power, but we could not have one submarine. Submarines are cheap to build and require few men to operate them. Submarines are a real menace to England.

I fought my best to try to argue the point.

'After all,' I said to the British Prime Minister, 'Ireland could never hope to wage an aggressive war against England.'

Restricting our offensive armament seemed to me on a par with muzzling a Skye terrier.

'Submarines,' replied Mr. Lloyd George, 'are the flying columns of the seas.' He looked at me straight as he said this, and slowly a twinkle came into his eyes. Then he spoke again. 'And I am sure,' he said, 'there is no need for me to tell you, Mr. Collins, how much damage can be inflicted by flying columns! We have had experience with your flying columns on land!'

There was nothing to be said then. He knew what he was talking about. More than that, he knew that I knew.

From Michael Collins' Own Story – Told to Hayden Talbot

They are afraid of Irish submarines and it was on that Mr. Lloyd George based his Carnarvon speech, that Irishmen with submarines would block the channels, that they would cut Empire communications of Great Britain. We would give them a guarantee that we would not build submarines unless by the common defence arrangements that would be entered into by this. There was agreement that we should do so.'

President Éamon de Valera.
Transcript from Dáil Éireann debate
on the Anglo-Irish Treaty.
Thursday, 15th of December 1921

Chapter 1

One Sunday in November

'They know who you are. They're coming. You have to get out of there.'

With a click, the man's voice was gone and Esther was left listening to the buzzing of the dial tone as the terse message triggered a chilly, sickening sensation that spread out from her gut. She placed the receiver back on the fork of the candlestick-style telephone, exhaled slowly, and handed it back to the receptionist. Not *today*. This couldn't be happening *today*. Her hand went instinctively to the tooled leather handbag slung from her shoulder, already knowing her gun wasn't there. She'd left it in her room before going out. After the murders this morning, if she was caught out in the city with a weapon, she was as likely to be shot as questioned. Dublin City was a bomb waiting to go off.

With a relaxed motion, she turned, leaned back against the counter, and took off her bell-shaped cloche hat. She began to adjust the pins that held her long, auburn hair, as if they'd been dislodged while she was walking. It gave her a chance to look around, first through the glass of the double doors to her right, and the street beyond, then taking in the rest of the room, which suddenly exuded a more threatening atmosphere. She needed to compose herself and think. The message at reception had been waiting for her when she'd arrived back at the hotel. Three words: 'Call your uncle'. Her handler, Faulkner, was never supposed to contact her directly. How had her cover been blown? Was there someone watching her right now?

Along with the gun, Esther had a small suitcase packed and ready too, in the event that she ever had to leave in a hurry. Now, her mind boiled with rushed thoughts. Did she have time to go up to her room? Or should she leave immediately, before she could be cut off? Straight out the front, or out through the kitchen, to the back door into the alley? She had routes planned in either direction.

There were six other people in the small lobby of the hotel, apart from the receptionist. Esther had chosen the place carefully; cheap enough to be anonymous, but not grotty. Appropriate lodgings for a young woman living alone, within walking distance of the centre of Dublin. The lobby had a smoke-yellowed ceiling and walls, and a carpet that had seen better days. Gas lamps on the walls, rather than electric ones. She suspected the old place hadn't done much business since the Rising four years earlier.

On the far side of the room, in the corner to her left, the young barman was washing glasses, discussing the afternoon's news with a sozzled, middle-aged customer in a rumpled suit. In the other corner, near the line of windows that provided a view onto the street, a chambermaid, no older than Esther, was polishing one of the wooden-framed mirrors. In the light from one window, an older man was sitting alone in a green velvet armchair, reading a newspaper and smoking a pipe. A mature couple were playing gin rummy at one of the round tables in the middle of the room. They tapped their cigarettes into the glass ashtray between them, intent on their cards and showing no interest in her.

Her sea-green eyes swept back again, and, she met the maid's gaze in the mirror. The girl had been polishing the same spot when Esther had walked in. She glanced away quickly now, seeing she'd been noticed. That settled it for Esther; she didn't want to leave the building without her gun. Pushing off from the reception desk, she picked up her hat and hurried to the stairs. The bloody chambermaids – they saw *everything*. The Secret Intelligence Service could learn a great deal about spycraft from Dublin's hotel staff. Esther started climbing, and once she was out of sight of the lobby, she ran, taking the steps two at a time, thankful that the current style of skirt was short enough not to get in the way of her feet.

Halfway up the third flight of stairs, she caught the toe of her shoe on a frayed piece of carpet and nearly went sprawling forwards. 'Less haste, more speed, Esther my girl,' she thought, as she regained her balance. 'No point falling down the stairs and doing the scoundrels' work for them.'

Reaching the second floor, she approached the door

of her room cautiously, wary that someone might be waiting for her inside. She placed her hat and bag on the floor, took her key and a penknife from the pocket of her trench coat and opened the blade. Putting her ear to the door, she listened for a few seconds before inserting the key and unlocking it. Then, holding the knife ready, she listened again before swinging the door open and rushing in, blade held up to slash at anyone who came at her. One look around the compact, bland room confirmed that there was no one there. Anyone small enough to fit in that miserable wardrobe would pose little challenge. Exhaling in relief, she picked her hat and bag off the floor, hung them on the hook inside, closed the door and locked it behind her, folding the knife and tucking it away.

The overnight case was under the bed, and the pistol was in a hidden pocket in the long wool velour overcoat in the wardrobe. She quickly retrieved the gun, leaving the coat where it was – her trench coat was adequate for the day that was in it, and it had been a present from her friends, the Regans.

She gave a start as three sharp bangs sounded from out on the street. Gunshots. Stepping over to the side of the window, she peered out, the revolver held down by her thigh. Below her, a Crossley Tender truck was driving past, carrying six men from the Black and Tans in their mismatched uniforms. Despised by the Irish, these were the former British soldiers newly recruited into the Irish police force. One of them was firing his rifle into the air to clear a group of people out of their way.

Across the street, the building directly facing her was a burnt-out shell. She didn't know who had set the fire; it could have been the rebels or the Tans. The man below fired off another shot, and Esther drew back away from the window. Everything was starting to fall apart. 1920 was turning out to be a very bad year for Ireland.

That morning, Irish rebels had shot twenty people in a synchronised series of attacks – a mixture of intelligence officers, soldiers, policemen and civilians. They had taken their enemies where they lived, showing no mercy. They were trying to purge Dublin Castle's intelligence network. Esther had not heard anything confirmed yet, but there were reports of at least fourteen deaths.

She tried to remind herself that the Irish Republican Army's General Order No. 13 on 'Women Spies' was that they should be exiled from the country rather than executed, but found little comfort in it. Esther knew that other women had been attacked or 'disappeared' and her particular betrayal would be considered a deeply personal one.

It was time to leave.

Out of habit, she broke open the revolver, checked the load and snapped it closed again. It was a Webley .455 calibre. Used by Irish police officers, it was a common weapon, popular on both sides of the conflict – issued to policemen and stolen by rebels. Its weight felt reassuring as she laid it on the bed and knelt down to pull out the suitcase.

'Leave that shooter where it is, Miss Sinclair,' a man's voice said. 'Stay down on your knees and move away from the bed.'

A man stood in the doorway, wearing a flat cap low over his brow, the bottom half of his face covered by a scarf. Even so, she knew immediately who it was, from his build, his posture and those eyes. Michael Regan. He too had a Webley revolver, and it was aimed at her chest.

Chapter 2

Passing Sentence

Behind Regan was the girl from the lobby, a key in her hand. Bloody chambermaids. Years of practise in opening and closing these doors quietly. The girl had the decency to look ashamed, though it didn't show much in her eyes. She pulled out of sight, and Esther could see there were two other men in the landing behind Michael, with their caps still on, dressed in drab, forgettable clothes and with their faces covered.

'Off you go now,' Michael said to the maid.

He and his companions stepped into the room, the last one closing the door behind them. The two with Michael were young men, as so many of the rebels were, barely more than boys, already hardened by violence. Fresh faces that hid a splintered innocence.

Michael, on the other hand, was a spry man of fifty-six, with a physique built on years of working in shipyards, now a wealthy businessmen returned to his homeland. And running guns for the Irish republican movement, Esther was convinced, though she'd been unable to find evidence of it, until this moment. She had heard whispers that he was the commander of the secretive unit known as 'the Selkies'. Named after the mythological creatures that lived in the ocean as seals, but could shed their skins to appear human, this rebel group smuggled guns across the Irish Sea, and also specialized in attacking targets along the coast, before disappearing back out to sea. It spoke volumes that he would come here himself. Up to this point, he'd always been careful to avoid being connected to any crimes.

'I know it's you, Michael,' she said in a tight voice.

'Yeah, I thought you might,' he grunted, pulling the scarf down from his face, revealing weathered cheeks and a greying beard. 'I suppose it doesn't matter now.'

The words sent a shudder through her. If he wasn't concerned about her being able to identify him, it did not bode well for her future.

'So it's true then,' she said, shuffling back from the bed as she'd been told to. 'You're one of Collins's lot.'

'And you're a back-stabbing witch,' he replied. 'I took you in, girl. My sister thought the world of you . . . she thought of *you* as a little sister. My daughter idolizes you. You ate at our table. You slept under under our roof, and you were a rat all along. Who put you up to it? Your father, was it?'

Esther didn't answer. The man wasn't here for answers. He was here to see her punished. Michael's accent was as much American as Irish, and it seemed to make his accusing tone all the more harsh. Though he'd been born in Cork, he'd grown up in the industrial city of Paterson, New Jersey, and his voice seemed to have the most aggressive qualities of both. From blue eyes set deep under a broad brow, his stare was corrosive, his gun still raised but trembling slightly, and she was sure then, that he wanted to kill her.

'The murders this morning, were you part of that?' she asked.

'No, but I won't be crying any tears for them,' he said. 'They picked their side and took their chances. They were enemies of the Irish State, killed in occupied territory.'

'Shooting men in their homes? In front of their families? That's what you call a *war*, is it Michael? A bit of cold, calculating murder on a Sunday morning, and then you can pop off to Mass, and clean the slate by confessing your sins to the priest?'

'When it comes to spreading a lively terror, we learned from the best, didn't we?' he snapped back. 'They've been paid back in their own coin. The lads probably even used British guns for the job. And I keep my sins to myself. They're nobody else's business.'

Esther thought she now detected some doubt in his words. Could it be that Michael wasn't as committed to the revolution as he made out? It gave her hope. Maybe she could talk him round. And these two men with him. Were they fanatics, or would they show restraint if their superior officer did?

'So you're happy to put your name to all this, are you?' she pressed him. 'To all this death? And how would Kathleen have felt about it, do you think?'

'She's nothing to do with this,' he growled. 'And you're not fit to say her name. Were you ever her friend, or did you just use her to weasel your way in? We treated you as family! Akiko *loved* you. You know I had friends there today, in the crowd when your brutes showed up at the match? They could have been killed!'

'The . . . the *match*?'

Esther was puzzled. The attacks this morning had all taken place in homes and hotels. She'd heard no mention of a match. And what did he mean by *her* brutes? Though she'd grown up in Ireland, Esther had little interest in Irish sports; she'd been raised on hockey and tennis. She remembered mention of a Gaelic football match taking place in Croke Park today, between two county teams, despite the fact half the country would be keeping their doors shut against the violence. Dublin versus Tipperary, wasn't it? There would be agents and detectives watching the crowds there, to see if they could spot known republicans, who frequently attended these games. Had something happened?

'Look at her,' one of the younger men said, with a strong Cork accent. He had eyebrows like hedges, and above the scarf that masked his face, his grimace revealed premature lines down his cheeks. 'She doesn't know.'

'Know what?' Esther demanded, looking from the two youths to the older man.

'What happened in Croke Park,' the second fellow prompted her, his voice flat and cold. He had a long face, with cheeks pockmarked by chickenpox, and was tense with suppressed fury. 'How can you *not know*?'

'*Know what?*'

Esther just shook her head, and seeing the blank look

on her face, Michael lowered his gun.

'A reprisal for the attacks this morning,' he told her. 'It happened an hour ago, just after the match started. Tans and some Auxiliaries, truckloads of them drove up to the football ground. An armoured car with a machine-gun. They started firing into the crowd. Ordinary people, just there to watch the game. Word is there's a dozen dead, maybe more, including two boys. Just *children*. And scores more people wounded. It was a massacre.'

Esther began trembling and hung her head. That was it, then. There would be no more restraint shown now, on either side. And there'd be none shown in this room either. They meant to execute her . . . and she wasn't inclined to let that happen without a fight. Michael had still to raise his pistol again. Settling onto her hands and knees in a posture of defeat, she braced her toes against the floor.

'Esther Sinclair,' Michael said, 'you've been found guilty by the Irish State of being a British agent. Do you have anything to say before sentence is passed?'

'You're criminals and killers and I don't have to justify a damn thing to you!' she hissed, glaring up at him. 'Just stop bleating and get on with it!'

He raised his gun and this time his hand was dead steady. But he only held it there for a matter of seconds before lowering it again.

'To hell with this,' he replied, that glimmer of doubt showing again. 'I don't need another death on my conscience. Give her a trim, lads.'

'Those aren't our orders, Mister Regan,' the one with

scars muttered. 'Our commander said we were to–.'

'And your commander told you who I was, didn't he? *I'm* giving the orders here, son. Do as I say now.'

'She can identify you now, sir,' the man with the eyebrows said. 'You can't let her live.'

'That's my decision to make. Get on with it.'

Chickenpox Scars shrugged and took a horse clippers from his jacket pocket and Esther felt a rush of relief that she was not to be executed after all. Even though she could identify him? They clearly had a very different punishment in mind for her, but even so, she was not going to make it easy for them. As the man reached for her hair, she lunged up and drove her elbow into his groin. He folded in half with a wheezing yelp. Eyebrows went to grab her and she twisted free of his hands and rammed the heel of her hand into his nose. He stumbled back, and Esther was turning to follow up her attack on Chickenpox when a hand seized her shoulder and she felt the cold barrel of a gun against her right temple.

'Settle down now, girl, or I might change my mind,' the older man said, but he gave a chuckle and shook his head. Then, to his thugs, he added: 'Are you right there, lads? I think this little girl is done beatin' up on ya, so if you don't mind, I'd like to be gone before the peelers show up.'

Esther locked eyes with Michael Regan, her face bunched up in defiance. The two other men pulled out a chair and forced her down onto it, and then as Eyebrows held her arms from behind, close enough that she could smell his breath, Chickenpox yanked the clips from her hair. Then he began cutting close in to her scalp, shearing away her thick auburn locks. He was rough about it, deliberately, tugging at the hair and jerking her head, making it hurt, but she kept her eyes on Regan, determined to show that she was not beaten, and that they would not make her cry. The hair began to litter the floor around her, and she could feel blood running from cuts in her scalp, and Regan stared right back at her the whole time.

But they would not make her cry.

Chapter 3
Dangerous Currents

Liam O'Leary stared down into the crystalline grey water, working up the nerve to plunge in. It didn't help that the small sailboat was rocking violently, a stark demonstration of the strength of the current and the wind. Akiko was doing everything she could to hold the boat on a safe course, and even with him shifting his weight around to help, it still wasn't enough to keep things stable. She'd have to turn about soon, or risk the boat being thrown against the rocks.

'Don't do it,' she said again. 'You're being an eejit. If you're so desperate to go in there, then go down by the cliff.'

He'd kill himself trying to climb down that cliff, he knew that. Though he was a good climber, he was a much better swimmer. Gripping the gunwale, he shivered as he was drenched in another burst of spray, the crest of a wave slapping off the side of the boat. His sandy-coloured hair looked dark brown, and his skin, prone to flushing pink, had a definite blue tinge at the moment. Akiko, who had one hand gripping the tiller, the other holding the rope for the mainsail, was dressed for sailing, wrapped up against the elements in wool and oilskins. Her waist-length black hair was bound up under a broad-brimmed sou'wester. Liam, on the other hand, had already stripped down to his silk one-piece swimsuit, and the brisk breeze was quickly chilling his damp skin.

'Liam,' she called to him, louder this time, over the snapping of the sail as it tugged at the boom. The sharp gusts were getting stronger. 'Come on, give it up. Or at least wait until it's calmer.'

'So we'll have no wind for the sail?' he replied. 'You want to try rowing against these currents? There'll never be a right time. If I keep putting it off, I'll never do it!'

'I'm sure you'd get over the disappointment,' she assured her cousin. 'There's no shortage of other ways to risk your neck, that wouldn't leave me explaining things to Otosan.'

'Otosan'. Although Akiko had spent half her life in America and half in Ireland, she still sometimes referred to her Irish father by the Japanese term. She called her mother 'Okaasan'. There were traditions to be upheld, particularly when she wanted to take a stern tone with her cousin. It still felt strange to Liam sometimes, who had grown to think of her more as a sister. Liam and his mother had been living with Akiko's family for years, a bond that had only strengthened after his mother had died a year and a half before. He lifted his head to stare at the high, menacing rock face that loomed over them, about seventy yards away, with ridges reaching out on either side of them. This was the Devil's Drain, a small cove whose shape made for unpredictable currents and swirling winds, dangerous for swimmers and sailors alike. There were supposed to be caves at the base of that cliff that swallowed boats and spat them out in pieces. This was what Liam wanted to explore.

'Can you get me in closer?' he asked.

'Not on your life. I'm staying clear of the selkies.'

'Aki, there's . . . for Heaven's sake, there *no such things as selkies*! That's just stories!'

Sometimes his cousin seemed so clever, and then she'd talk like this, like a fool who believed in the local fairytales. It was only to be expected, he supposed, when her only friends were storybooks. Not for the first time, Liam wondered if she'd turned out odd because of her Japanese features, and her accent, which was a mixture of American, Japanese and Irish. The children in her rural Cork convent school used to tease her because she was different. Maybe being *treated* as strange *made* you strange. Or perhaps she'd have been odd no matter where she'd ended up.

'It's not selkies dragging people into the sea,' he told her. 'It's more likely smugglers who murder anyone who finds their stash.'

'That's *so* much better,' she snorted defensively. And then added: 'Anyhow, there are also lots of very big rocks, so this is as far as I go.'

'Never mind, so,' he said huffily. 'I'm going in.'

'Off you go, then.'

And so he did. He stood up, put one foot on the gunwale and launched himself into the grey, November sea. The water engulfed him, so cold it hurt. He straightened his body as his chest went tight, his hands out in front of him like the head of an arrow. As his muscles got over the shock of the cold, he surfaced, looked around to get his bearings, and started swimming.

He rose up and down with the waves, sometimes able to see the foam of breakers on the rocks, other times in a trough, with slopes of water in front and behind. His main concern was to find a way to shore that didn't involve him getting hurled against a boulder or the face of the cliff. His uncle would have a fit if he saw what he was doing. As he got closer to the shoreline, he could see a number of small hollows. Sea caves. They probably weren't even visible at high tide. One was larger than the others and he aimed for that.

Despite Akiko's claims, he was not a complete eejit. This place was called the Devil's Drain for a reason. He knew that the current could be taking him in faster than it seemed, that it could well carry him into the cave, and could be powerful enough to keep him in there until he became too cold and exhausted to keep his head above water, or the tide rose and trapped him in there. But this was the only part of the coast around his home that he had not explored, and he was no longer willing to be frightened away from it by his uncle's warnings, or the tales of the superstitious. He was a strong swimmer, he had plenty of experience at swimming in coastal currents, and he was going to see what there was to see.

To his surprise, the waves lost some of their force as he reached the shallows approaching the cave. While the rocks rose higher further out on each side, there seemed to be a long trench beneath him, where the water kept its depth, and it was calmer than it had appeared from farther out. Still dangerous for a large boat to to get caught in, but manageable for a smaller boat or a swimmer.

As he came closer still, he saw there was a nearly horizontal line along the base of the sandstone cliff that ended at the mouth of the cave. It was a path, leading from the cluster of rocks to his right. Was there another way down here after all – one that wasn't visible from above? With long, confident strokes, he swam into the cave, brushing his hand along the wall on the right-hand side. The waves washed in, but not so forcefully that he wouldn't be able to swim back out.

There was a path along here too, and he pulled himself up onto it. It was only narrow at the start, little more than a foot wide, a line of footholds and flat areas chipped out of stone. The roof of the cave mouth was low enough that a tall man would have to stoop to walk in, though Liam guessed the opening extended deep under the water. When the tide was at its highest, it might be completely covered. Further in there was a series of steel girders to walk over, bridging gaps between the protruding rocks along the wall, and a chain strung along at chest height to hold onto, attached to steel pegs driven into the stone.

Liam felt a flush of excitement. Somebody had put a lot of work into providing a route into this place, considering no one was ever supposed to come here.

And the land above was his uncle's property. Though he'd heard stories about his uncle as he was growing up, of Michael's life both here and in the States, Liam could never be sure what was true and what was a heap o' nonsense.

He stood on the narrow ledge, shivering and holding onto the chain. He stepped onto the first girder. The chain and the steel rail were badly rusted, spotted with barnacles and slimy with algae from the time they spent submerged at high tide, so he worked his way forward with care, afraid of cutting open his hands or feet. About twenty yards inside the mouth, the ceiling started to rise higher, and the path did too.

Liam hadn't gone far when he realized it was growing darker and he had no torch. He couldn't go much further in. He'd have to come again, and bring one, along with a pair of shoes and some gloves. The water was getting higher too. Next time, he'd come when the tide was lower.

Liam was about to turn back, when he spotted something, just at the point where the last of the light from the cave mouth faded out. There was a wider shelf of rock, several feet higher than the ledge, and on the wall above that was a metal cabinet with a cable coming out of it that stretched horizontally off into the cave. From the lack of damage to it, the tide didn't reach that high. The roof of the cave was higher here too. He made his way to the shelf, climbed up onto it and studied the box in the low light. It was the size of his uncle's briefcase and made of a dull green painted metal. There was a locked door on the front, and a lever on the side.

Liam pulled the lever, and suddenly two lines of small lights came on, on either side, running along the walls of the cave, placed every couple of yards from that point inwards. While they were faint, probably barely visible to the outside, they revealed a channel of deep water and a wider path down the right-hand side. Enough light to navigate a small boat in through the cave. This, he felt, was as good an invitation as he was ever likely to get to explore further. With his heart thumping so loud he was sure it would echo through the cave, he started along the path . . .

* * * *

Akiko had been zig-zagging back and forth across the cove, trying to stay as close as she could to the cliffs without being slammed up onto the shallow rocks that littered this section of the coast. When Liam finally emerged from the cave, the current in the channel of deep water was slow enough for him to swim out past the breakers, but after the first twenty or thirty yards, he had to fight to make progress with every stroke.

By the time he reached Akiko, he was exhausted. When he tried to grab the side of the boat as she slowed it down, it rammed into him, knocking him back, and then was swept away. His cousin circled around again, and this time she threw him a rope so that he could catch it a few yards out and pull himself in. Hauling himself up and over the side, he flopped into the bottom of the boat and groaned, wet, cold and worn out.

'Well?' Akiko asked him impatiently, an amused scowl on her angular features.

He needed a minute to get his breathing back to normal, so she concentrated on tacking the craft and heading back out of the cove. It was a relief to get out onto the open sea, where the water was more settled. Liam pulled a lump of oilcloth from out of his swimsuit and laid it on the thwart next to where Akiko was sitting. It made a clunk, as if it there was something heavy wrapped up in it. Taking her hand off the tiller, she unwrapped it, then drew back with a sharp breath, leaving it on the seat beside her.

It was a Mills Bomb, a hand grenade. Liam knew she'd seen pictures of one before.

'Holy God, Liam! Where did that come from? And why did you bring it onto *my boat*?'

She picked it up and went to throw it overboard, and he seized it off her.

'Give it here, that's mine!'

'Be gentle with it, do you want to blow us up?' she snapped. 'Get rid of it! Did you find it in that cave? What kind of godawful fool are you? You found a mouldy old bomb in a cave and you brought it onto my boat?'

'It's not mouldy, it's fine. It won't blow up unless you pull the pin out of it. There was a box of them in there. There was *loads* of boxes. And I can tell yeh, that wasn't even the half of it.'

'Is that right, is it? ' Her eyes narrowed, interested. 'What do you mean?'

Her cousin flashed her a savage grin, sweeping his dripping hair off his face.

'You know all that mad stuff that people say about

this place? About how people disappear around here? Well, it's not selkies, and it's not smugglers neither, Akiko. It's *your father*.'

Chapter 4

There's No Putting Out That Fire

Michael Regan could not find the map he was looking for. He was sure it was one of the charts he'd saved from the fire, and yet it was nowhere to be found in his study, or in the cupboard under the stairs. He didn't actually need it – it showed the features of a section of shoreline less than a mile from the back of his house, so he knew the area intimately. But it was old and beautifully drawn and he was thinking of having it framed, to start replacing those that had been lost when fire had ravaged half of his home two months before. He loved hand-drawn originals of coastal charts.

And so did his nephew, Liam. Liam lived with the family, and his bedroom had been one of those destroyed in the blaze, so Michael had cleared out a small room on the other side of the house for the boy, but Liam had a grim fascination with his burned-out room. After all the debris had been removed, he had laid out a couple of tattered rugs and put another chair and desk in there, where he did his homework . . . and studied sea charts. The roof, walls and floor were damaged, but still intact, and the shattered window had been boarded up, so Michael had indulged the lad's quirks, telling Liam he could leave the desk where it was, as long as he didn't track soot through the rest of the house, and went to bed back in his more civilized, less charred bedroom.

The light fixtures no longer worked in this part of the house. It still irritated him; electric light was a rare luxury in rural Cork in 1921 and it had cost him a small fortune to have the cables run out to the house. However, the rebuilding work was still ongoing, there was no light to be had through the boarded up window, so Michael brought a torch with him into the room. There weren't many places to search. The rest of the room was bare, powdery surfaces of grey and black in streaked patches, with sections of plaster on the ceiling and walls missing, so he looked through the loose leaves of paper on the desk, checked in the couple of card folders Liam had left on the floor beneath it, and then pulled open the two drawers in the front.

Something moved in the right-hand drawer with a solid thunking sound, and he frowned, finding a heavy object wrapped in an oilcloth. It felt damp, and smelled of seawater. He was going close the drawer again when he stopped and gazed at the oilcloth. There was something about the weight of it that aroused his curiosity. Picking it up, he unwrapped it . . . and then carefully laid the Mills Bomb on the desktop.

He knew immediately where the 'pineapple'-style grenade had come from. He'd painted a little yellow dot on the few Mills Bombs in the box that had been fitted with their detonators – he kept meaning to dismantle them, but hadn't got around to it. This was one of them. Michael rolled his eyes, sighed, sat down on the chair and put a hand to his face. Dear God in Heaven, the boy must have swum to the cave. If he'd found that box, then he'd seen *everything*. And then he'd picked up the bloody hand grenade and swum back out. And he couldn't have swum all the way around the headland, not in the weather they'd had over the last few days, so that meant he'd sailed. And there was no way Akiko would have let him take her boat out there alone, so that meant *she* knew now too. And his daughter and his nephew had sailed back to the jetty behind the house with a live hand grenade on board.

'Looks like your chickens have come home to roost,' a voice said.

Michael turned to stare at the man who now stood in the room with him. His slight figure and pallor hinted at someone who had suffered ill health for much of his life. Even so, there was a restless energy in his manner. He was dressed in an unremarkable, overused brown suit, white shirt with a large green cravat under his winged collar, and black bowler hat.

'I couldn't have known,' Michael said. 'Nobody goes near that cave now – hardly anyone alive even knows it's there. He risked his life swimming out there. He could have drowned, just for wanting to look around. How can you account for that kind of pigheadedness?'

'You look at the kind of man his father is, and his uncle. And you look at his mother.'

'Kathleen was a live wire,' Michael shook his head,

'but she was never reckless like this.'

'And what about you? Were *you* any different when you were sixteen years-old?'

'I . . . that wasn't the same,' Michael said. Then he sniffed, and added: 'Growing up poor on the docks? I was worse, if anything. You know that.'

'Well, then.'

The man's shrewd, short-sighted eyes were partly hidden by the gleam off rimless spectacles, perched on a small nose over a large walrus moustache of grey hair. His accent was that of a Clare man whose consonants had been flattened and his vowels drawn out by years of living in the US state of New Jersey.

And he had been dead for seven years. It worried Michael. If he was having visions of his old mentor again, then how else might his mind be playing tricks on him? He wasn't sleeping properly either, and when he did, he often had nightmares and woke exhausted. Those nightmares were creeping into his waking life. He had not killed many men in his life, though he had hurt quite a few more, but he suffered visions of some of them now, and dreamed of dozens of drowned bodies floating in the sea. It was a terrible thing for a man, not being able to trust his own brain. And one of the most common hallucinations was the ghost of John Philip Holland.

'Why do you keep turning up, John?'

'Why are you asking me, Michael? I couldn't explain the workings of your mind, not even if if it was built of pipes and motor parts. We both know I'm not a ghost.

We're neither of us the type to give much credence to the supernatural.'

'And yet here you are once more. I should get blind drunk, and blot you from my mind.'

'By all means, if you think that would work . . . but first, I think you should disarm that bomb.'

Michael regarded the hand grenade reluctantly, then he gently took it up and unscrewed the cap in its base, drew out the cylindrical detonator, and placed both back on the desktop. As he did so, he heard Liam coming in downstairs, shouting a greeting to their three dogs. The boy could sneak well enough when he put his mind to it, but otherwise, he entered a place the way he did everything else, with all the energy he couldn't keep in check. A herd of cows moved with more subtlety. So unlike Akiko, who seemed capable of arriving unseen, the quiet one that nobody noticed, but who was equally untameable in her own way.

'What am I going to with him?' Michael asked his old mentor.

'Is there something *to* do?' John replied. 'You can't put an old head on young shoulders, Michael. Do you remember how it felt to be that age? Remember how you blazed through life? There's no putting out that fire, and you'd be foolish to try.'

Michael nodded. Sure, didn't he know it? For years, he had lived by the words, 'Ní síochán go saoirse' – 'No freedom, no peace'. He and his comrades would burn everything British but its coal . . . and yet he could no longer feel that raw passion. He thought back to that day the year before, when he'd passed sentence on Esther Sinclair. He recalled the defiance on her face, the fire in her, fierce and self-righteous, with the unquestioning conviction that she was on the side of justice. Whereas for him, life seemed to be an increasing mess of compromises and blurred lines.

After all the killings that day last year, it was now known as Bloody Sunday. In the year that followed, the country had been mutilated in an increasingly bitter guerilla war.

He had been a fool to go to her hotel himself, and it was no surprise that she'd recognized him, even with his face covered. He'd expected the Crown forces to come after him once he'd let her go, but nothing happened. She must not have reported him to the Castle, but *why*, after what he'd done to her? Was it because he'd chosen to spare her life, or out of loyalty to his sister Kathleen and their childhood friendship? Or had she done it for Akiko? Those two had become very close last year. Esther had connived her way right into the Regan family, and though he wanted to hate her for it, he couldn't. All of his emotions were a muddy mix these days.

God, sometimes he wished he could feel that pure, untempered passion again. What a dazzling spark Esther had grown up to be! So like Kathleen at that age. His face twisted up as he remembered his baby sister, Liam's mother, and part of him was grateful that she had not lived to see how much worse things had become – a distortion of her dreams for Irish freedom.

'That young passion can burn those around it,' John

added. 'In fact, perhaps *that's* why I keep showing up.'

'What do you mean?'

'Perhaps you're afraid that Liam or Akiko will make your mistakes. That they'll hurt *you* the way you hurt *me*.'

'Christ, John. How many times can I say I'm sorry?'

'A few more wouldn't hurt.'

'I have to do something.' Michael gestured towards the hand grenade. 'What if Liam ends up like his father? He could be killed if he keeps going the way he is.'

'What you can't stop must be steered, Mick. He's been to the cave now. You have to give him a compelling reason to stay quiet. You can't have him telling anyone, can you? And what are you going to do about Akiko? You're not paying enough attention to how she's changing too. You must do for them what I did for you, Michael; channel the passion into something productive. Besides, you've been sitting around too long yourself. It's time to get back out to sea, don't you think?'

Liam's feet stamped up the stairs.

'Liam!' Michael shouted. 'Get your ass in here!'

'Yes, sir!' came the immediate reply.

The boy arrived in the doorway, flushed and breathing hard. He'd cycled back from school, and had probably belted it the whole way. It was Monday, and since the violence across the country had been put on hold, Michael had started taking the children to the café in the nearby town of Ballinashort on Monday afternoons. The eager expression on Liam's face dropped however, as his eyes fell on the dismantled hand grenade. There was a sudden nervousness in his manner, but there was something else too, a hint of a challenge. He was ready for an argument . . . *hoping* for it. Well, Michael wasn't going to give it to him.

'I know where you got this,' he said to his nephew, tipping his head toward the desk. 'I'm going to get rid of it now. You understand that we can't have it in the house? I know you were just being curious – it's only natural, I suppose. I want you to go downstairs and put the kettle on. Then you're going to go and fetch Akiko, and we'll all have a chat about what you saw.'

Chapter 5
A Search for the Truth

Akiko had her ear pressed against the wall, listening to her father, who was having a conversation with someone when there was no one else in the room. She heard Liam come in downstairs with all the restraint of a bull breaking through a fence, his entrance announced by the excited barking of their three wolfhounds. Papa continued talking, and she was certain that it sounded like one half of a conversation. He was in Liam's burnt-out old bedroom. The only telephone in the house was downstairs in his study. *Who was he speaking to?*

She had been worried about her father for months now, and she knew her okaasan was too. This was not the first time Akiko had heard him talking to himself, and there were nights when he woke up shouting, or even screaming, as if from terrible dreams. Papa was a rock of security in Akiko's life, and these sounds were frightening to hear. Sometimes he would walk back and forth along the hall downstairs at nights, unable to sleep at all.

Liam's feet pounded up the stairs, and her cousin was greeted by her father's shout:

'Liam! Get your ass in here!'

'Yes, sir!'

Liam was in the damaged room now. Papa had found the hand grenade. Akiko listened anxiously through the wall for another minute, but when she had assured herself that her father – for some reason – did not seem angry, she pulled away. They had defied his warnings by sailing into the Devil's Drain, placed themselves in danger, and whatever he had planned, it wasn't going to be a straightforward rebuke.

Her room was a similar size to Liam's, though it had only suffered minor damage in the fire, which her father had soon fixed himself. She had less space than Liam for her bed, desk, dresser and shelves, and not just because she had far more books than she had shelves to hold them. One corner of the room was given over to the tiny dark room Papa had built for her the year before. Seeing her growing passion for photography, he'd said that if she was going to do it properly, she'd need a dark room to develop her film. He'd even bought her a photo enlarger to make prints, with its own electric bulb.

Akiko had been wrestling with some deeply troubling thoughts since Liam's discovery in the cave the day before. Standing by her carved, elegant writing desk now, she stared at the wall above it. Pinned to a board were numerous scraps of paper; notes, clippings, drawings, maps and photographs. This had been the focus of her attention for the last year. She had gathered newspaper articles on people who had gone missing in the area, of strange weather and accidents off the coast. All of it had been an attempt to prove that there were supernatural goings-on in this region of Ireland, particularly around the shores near her home.

And placed at the centre of the whole display was a photograph of Esther Sinclair.

Akiko's Aunt Kathleen, Liam's mother, had died of the flu in March the previous year. Papa came from a large family – there were *ten* children – he was the eldest and Kathleen was the youngest. Fierce, sharp-witted and curious about the world, she had been by far Akiko's favourite aunt. Akiko had felt the loss almost as much as Liam.

And then this young Englishwoman named Esther had shown up at the funeral. She had lived nearby as a child, Papa said, and adored Kathleen as much as Akiko did, looking up to the older girl as a role model. Akiko was almost immediately smitten. Her Asian looks and mixed-American accent made her an oddity at school, and as Liam was keen to point out, her penchant for saying strange things did not help her win friends. But Esther did not care about any of that stuff. The Englishwoman was clever and attractive and easy to talk to, and wore stylish clothes the like of which were not be seen here in rural Cork, and she had been to university and spoke four languages, including Irish. An *Englishwoman* who spoke *Irish*!

Esther had only recently moved back to Ireland. She was living in Dublin, and Papa, who was conscious that his daughter needed the influence of educated young women, had invited her to come and stay with them.

She became a friend to the family again, and a regular guest, and Akiko had relished every minute she'd spent with her. It was Esther who had inspired her passion for photography, who had taught her about lighting, and how to use the chemicals to develop film and make prints. It was Esther who'd listened to her fantasies of being a photographer and a pirate and of fighting for women's rights and . . . and so many other things. When she was with this amazing woman, she had felt she could aspire to being anything.

And then, in November, when she was due for another visit, Esther vanished without a trace, and the Regans never heard from her again.

Other people had started to mysteriously disappear in the area over that period too, and ever since, Akiko had been trying to prove that there were supernatural forces at work. Ireland had a deep and strange mythology, so different from the Japanese stories her mother told her, and many people still believed in things like the evil eye, selkies, changelings and faerie rings. The grown-ups' refusal to talk about the disappearances with their children had made her all the more convinced that they were protecting their innocent young ones from the truth about the dark forces from the otherworld that haunted Cork's coast.

But it was all a load of rubbish, wasn't it?

What Liam had discovered in the cave had shattered her illusions about her father, and about Esther's disappearance. Papa was actively involved with the Irish Republican Army, and must have been for years. What else did Akiko not know about him?

She let her eyes wander along the prints she had hanging up, pegged on a string to dry. These were her most recent shots. They showed the damage to the house, and the builders who were working on the repairs. A group of 'policemen' had been attacked down the road one evening a few months before and, in response, two trucks full of armed officers had pulled into the driveway the following day and set fire to the Regans' house.

She had thought that the arson was a random reprisal, the type they committed all the time now, where they would show up and burn the buildings of innocent civilians in revenge for rebel ambushes. But perhaps this hadn't been so random? Did they suspect her father worked with the rebels? He had certainly never been shy about sharing his political opinions.

It was something that fascinated her about the culture of this land, how some of it lay out in the open, while much more had to remain hidden beneath the surface of a seemingly 'British' society. The revival of the language, for instance, had been a key tool of the independence movement. As that slogan her father used sometimes put it: 'Tír gan teanga, tír gan anam' which translated as 'a country without a language is a country without a soul'.

This half-hidden character was one of the reasons that recording people doing ordinary jobs was one of her favourite subjects for photography, and the builders had been funny and kind about it, happy to pose for her as she took her pictures. Standing on her chest of drawers however, were older photographs that she had saved from the ashes, set in charred or smoke-damaged frames. These ones were of her father, taken by other people. He was not very open about his past, and so she had treasured these images.

The first was of Papa as a young man in New Jersey, beside his mentor, John Philip Holland, the little man with his big moustache and ever-present bowler hat. Papa looked a much rougher type back then, fresher-faced, with wild hair and no beard. Though he was not much taller than the older man, his strong, ropey figure in those rolled-up shirt sleeves contrasted starkly with Holland's slight form in its rumpled suit. Behind them, still in dry dock, was the sleek shape of the famous *Holland VI,* which was to become the first vessel of the US Navy's submarine fleet.

The second picture was her most favourite photograph of all; Mama and Papa standing with Jiji and Baba, her grandparents, in front of their house in Japan, when she was still a bump in Mama's tummy. In 1904, the Imperial Japanese Navy had purchased some submarines off Holland's firm, to be used in their war against Russia. And though they never saw action, Akiko's father had moved to Japan for a couple of years, to work with their engineers, helping them to build their own submarines. Her grandfather had been an engineer on the project, and that was how Michael had met Akiko's mother.

The third photograph was of her father, looking older now, standing with Éamon de Valera in 1919, not long after the rebel leader had escaped from prison in England. A tall man with a long, wily, sharp-nosed face and an imposing manner, de Valera had returned home to be elected the President of the newly declared Irish Republic.

Akiko was seeing these pictures with new eyes. Her father, her beloved otosan, was not who she'd thought he was, and the realization was intensely disturbing. Had she been fooling herself all this time? He was stern, certainly, and willing to use violence to defend his family – she had seen that for herself – but he was always kind too. Could she still believe he was a decent and civilized man? After all, he had spent his early career building weapons of war; in true American style, he often carried a gun, and had a collection of firearms. He'd started training her and Liam to shoot when they were twelve.

She knew that the Irish rebels exiled and even killed people they suspected of being spies or informers. Allowing a single informer to operate in their ranks could result in an entire company of men being captured or killed. *That* was why people in the area sometimes disappeared in mysterious circumstances. Had Papa been involved in any of those killings? And what about the accidents that had occurred off the coast? Could they all be blamed on the currents and the rocks? She no longer believed it could be the deliciously creepy selkies, the seal people that she'd fantasised about. Harsh reality had truly set in.

With tears in her eyes, she started pulling the pieces of paper off the board on the wall, and tore each one into small pieces, methodically destroying all the 'research' she'd gathered. Soon, the floor at her feet was littered with this confetti of information, until only the picture of Esther remained whole in her hands. Having been made aware of her ignorance, Akiko felt humiliated – and worse, for the first time, she realized that she was scared of her father.

Because now she knew that he was one of those men of violence, men who would kill to keep their secrets. She knew that Esther, an intelligent and curious Englishwoman from a military family, had disappeared after she'd become close to Michael Regan's family. Akiko knew that he had a cache of weapons stored in that cave in the Devil's Drain that he had to protect. And she knew about his most dangerous weapon, the most shocking of all his secrets.

She knew her father had a submarine.

Chapter 6
A Missing Horror

Esther Sinclair tucked a lock of hair behind her ear. Her hair was long enough that she could do that again now, a year after Michael Regan's thugs had cut most of it off. She'd taken to wearing a wig for months afterwards, to hide her humiliation. Now that it had regained some of its shape, she'd decided to keep it this length, a fashionable bob that her mother despaired over. That said, her mother had been despairing ever since her father had roped her darling daughter into the world of espionage. Not that Esther was in any danger these days, sitting in this gloomy basement office in London, surrounded by transport records.

There had been times when she'd regretted not reporting Regan for the assault, but the Crown forces had been out for blood at the time. If an order for his arrest had been put out, he would most likely have been shot for what he'd done to her. She did not want to see him dead, and more to the point, she couldn't do that to Akiko, of whom she'd become so fond, so she had claimed she could not identify her attackers.

Daddy had been something of a big figure in what

was now the Secret Intelligence Service, but Esther had started with Army Intelligence during the war, after putting her university studies on hold to join the Women's Auxiliary Army Corps, or 'WAAC'. Adept in mathematics and fluent in German, she was assigned to a small unit of women who'd been sent to France in 1917 to help break German codes. Because of the secrecy of their work, they became known as the 'Hush' WAACs.

After the war, she'd finished her chemistry degree, only to find that her country still had need of her. This time, 'the tap on the shoulder' came from the Secret Intelligence Service. They recruited her because of her skill with languages; not for her German or French, but for her *Irish*. Esther's family had lived in Ireland when she was a child, and curious and sociable as she was, she had learned Irish from speaking with her neighbours in Cork, particularly a young woman named Kathleen, whom she had absolutely idolized. Michael Regan's youngest sister. Given that there were very few British intelligence operatives who spoke the language with any fluency, her superiors felt that Ireland was a natural posting for her.

She had been disappointed, knowing other agents were being sent to more far-flung places like Germany, America, the Middle East – or even Russia, now that the Bolsheviks were spreading their Communist tentacles out into the world. Esther had big plans, and Ireland, in comparison to those more . . . *significant* locations, offered little in the way of excitement.

Or so she'd thought. In the end, of course, there had

been rather more than she'd have liked.

She took a sip of her tea and continued tracing the finger of her left hand down the endless lines of entries in the ledger, matching them with her right hand to other lines in other ledgers, laid out on the desk around her. Despite the lamp on the utilitarian, army surplus desk, and the bare light bulb above her, the office full of metal filing cabinets and glass-fronted shelf units was never anything but dull, damp and dreary. And the work . . . the work, she was convinced, was pointless, checking information that had already been checked and checked again.

Under the Treaty of Versailles, the Germans had been forced to dismantle their military machine after they lost the Great War, which only served them right. This process was overseen by the Disarmament Section of the League of Nations, but the British, among others, were distrustful of the process, and so they had their own people going over everything. She was one of them and, to her dismay, found the work was more akin to accountancy than intelligence analysis.

Three years on, it was clear to Esther that Germany was not being entirely cooperative in relation to its obligations – to be frank, it was pulling a fast one here and there – though she was sure Britain would have done exactly the same thing in its place. It was also clear that there were no *men* down here in this cave, doing this mind-numbing work, apart from her supervisor, that she might well die of boredom, and some days, it grew so tiresome that she'd rather have been in Dublin, fighting some ham-fisted oaf who wanted to chop off her hair. Anything to raise the heart rate.

If anyone asked, of course, it was an absolute honour to serve her country in any way she could. It was just a pity that it had to be *this* way.

Her finger stopped on an entry in the left-hand ledger, searching for the matching one to her right. Two months ago, a truck carrying a consignment of mortar shells containing chlorine gas had left the depot on the west coast of France where they'd been stored and, from what she could see, had failed to arrive at the site where they were to be destroyed. These were part of the stockpile that had been gathered from surrendered German strongholds after the war, and stored in a warehouse until they could be disposed of.

Both sides in the war had used chemical weapons and they were generally regarded as being truly vile. It was estimated that 125 million tons of toxic gases were used during the war, in artillery shells, grenades, bombs, mines and canisters. At least forty-six different types of chemical. Chlorine was not the deadliest of them, but it was still a horror, eating at the eyes, nose, throat and lungs of victims. Death occurred when the gas was concentrated enough to suffocate you.

Esther went over to the one telephone shared by everyone in this small department and made a couple of calls. This could, after all, be a simple clerical error. Instead, it confirmed what she had read. A truck had left the storage depot and had never arrived at the French army base where the mortar shells were to be destroyed.

She clicked her tongue and tapped the ledger with her pen. She knew how this would go. The war had left an almighty mess behind it, and every country that had taken part was struggling to get themselves back in order. There had been military equipment left lying around all over the place. Despicable as poison gas was, she was sure that if she took this upstairs, it would end up filed under 'This-Is-Somebody-Else's-Job' and would most probably go nowhere. It was a detail in a haystack of details. As a chemist however, she understood the effects of chlorine gas better than most, and she couldn't bear the thought of a mislaid truckload of the frightful material becoming a footnote in a report that nobody would read.

Edward Faulkner, the man who'd been her immediate superior in Dublin Castle during that grubby Irish war, now worked on Winston Churchill's staff. Churchill had recently been made Secretary of State for the Colonies, and the Colonial Office was in Whitehall, only a few stops away on the bus. It had been Edward who'd telephoned her on the day the Irish called 'Bloody Sunday', to warn her Regan was coming. He was a cold fish, but like her, he was detail-driven and devoted to the service. Also, she thought he had a soft spot for her, and might share her concern about the missing horror. Taking her little black notebook from her handbag, Esther looked up his telephone number.

Perhaps she could persuade him to take her to lunch. Anywhere would be better than the rat's nest of a canteen they had here.

Chapter 7
A Night at the Opera

Akiko was reliving the worst day of her life. Again. She was in that shallow sleep, on the edge of waking up, when the dream is so convincing it can leave you confused when you first open your eyes. It was nearly a year ago, the 11th of December, 1920, and her parents had taken her to the opera. Papa had been in a low mood ever since Bloody Sunday and the mysterious disappearance of Esther Sinclair. Mama had insisted they needed an evening out; they both loved the comic operas of Gilbert and Sullivan and *The Gondoliers* was playing in the Cork Opera House.

Liam was there too, bored and restless as he always was when they went to a show. Sitting still for a couple of hours was not in his character, and he was bothered by the feel of the fabric of the theatre's seats. Akiko was between him and her parents, and his fidgeting was a constant distraction.

She could not remember much about the plot of the story, except that it was set in Venice, and some princess was supposed to marry a prince, but he'd secretly been raised as a gondolier, working the city's canals, to keep him safe from his enemies, and there were two of them and everyone was confused, and anyway, the princess was in love with someone else. It was something like that.

Not for the first time, Akiko was pondering Esther's disappearance. The English woman had vanished around the time of that infamous Sunday in Dublin, without a hint of where she might have gone, and while Akiko feared for her friend, the whole thing was like something out of a book. She loved old bloodthirsty mystery stories featuring characters like Dick Turpin, Spring-Heeled Jack and Sweeney Todd, though her favourites were the ones about pirates, voraciously consuming tales of Blackbeard, Ann Bonny, Captain Kidd, Henry Morgan and the mightiest of them all, the Chinese pirate queen, Zheng Yi Sao. Akiko was especially fond of the gruesome stories that described gory scenes of terror she had to hide from her okaasan.

She enjoyed the songs of the *The Gondoliers* that night, despite its gore-free storyline, and she rather related to the prince's situation, as she often felt as if she'd been born into the wrong family, and as a result, it always seemed as if there was something wrong with the world.

That evening, on the 11th of December, she would experience some very real horror, and no story in a book could ever have prepared her for it.

During the performance, she was sure she could hear bangs outside, over the sound of the music. She noticed Papa turning his head from time to time and thought he heard them too. The show ended at 9.30pm, and since the Royal Irish Constabulary had imposed a 10pm curfew because of all the republican attacks, there wasn't enough time to drive home. Papa had booked two rooms in a hotel instead, so they only had to walk a few hundred yards along the quays. As the crowd began to descend the steps from the doors of the theatre however, it was clear that something was going on outside.

Gaslights illuminated the road, but over the roofs of the buildings beyond the opera house, bright flames were reaching into the sky. Part of the city centre was on fire. From the back of the theatre, they could hear shouts and then shots were fired. In the distance, men in uniform could be seen crossing the street, some of them carrying what looked like cans of petrol. Then Akiko was struck by the strange sight of the show's cast streaming out of another door around the side of the building. They were still in costume, dressed for the warm splendor and canals of Venice, and despite the cold, only a few of them were wearing coats.

'Hey, you there!' Michael called to a gondolier who was striding past. 'What's going on?'

His loud, American-Irish voice commanded attention, and the man came to a halt.

'I'm told the army have set fire to half of Patrick Street!' he called back in a London accent. 'Someone attacked some soldiers up near the barracks and the whole lot of 'em are back for blood! There's people bein' shot all over the place! You need to get off the streets!'

Michael immediately turned to head down the waterfront for their hotel, only to see Crossley-Tender trucks full of gunmen coming up Lavitt's Quay towards them. Reaching around inside his jacket, he pulled an automatic pistol from a holster on the back of his belt, and waved at his family to follow him. Taking her mother's hand, Akiko rushed after Liam and her father into a narrow alleyway.

'Okaasan,' she asked in a low voice, 'why did Otosan bring a gun to the opera?'

'Because in America, many people carry firearms and say it makes them free, Akiko-chan,' her mother replied. 'And your otosan wants the Irish to be more like Americans.'

She said this with a slightly disapproving tone. Though it was not Midori Regan's way to openly criticise her husband, especially to the children, she could say a great deal with her tones. They were still walking, and Akiko could not help noticing that the route they were taking was *towards* St Patrick Street, not away from it. She was sure Liam was loving this, the idiot. He was so keen to join the rebels and start running around in the hills, shooting people. There were others from the theatre with them in the alley now, all trying to stay out of the way of the policemen on the street. Though they were not actually policemen, she reminded herself.

There was a time when there had been more than a hundred police barracks dotted all over the Cork countryside, a constant presence to keep an eye on the rebellious county. However, faced with constant attacks by the rebels over the last few years, the Royal Irish Constabulary had abandoned many of their rural stations and retreated to larger, more fortified barracks in the bigger towns. From there, they had resorted to trying to maintain control with patrols in trucks and armoured cars.

All over the country, more and more Irishmen were leaving the constabulary out of fear of the rebels, no longer willing to risk their lives to serve their British masters. Some were even *joining* the rebels. To replace them, the government had brought in thousands of new reserve constables, most of them from Britain.

Little more than mercenaries, these ex-soldiers became known as the Black and Tans, the nickname inspired by their appearance. Due to a shortage of uniforms, they had improvised with what was available, adopting a mix of the dark green of the RIC, which looked black at a distance, and British Army khaki.

Fresh from a war where they'd faced a uniformed enemy across an open battlefield, they were unprepared for a conflict against guerilla fighters who would attack without warning and then melt back into the civilian population. With little or no police training, these men were prone to using violence to get things done, and quickly developed a reputation for brutality.

Many of 'the Tans' were deployed to the southern counties. And most of those came to Cork. And while the republicans ruled the countryside, the Crown forces still reigned in the city.

The smell of smoke hung heavy in the air of the alleyway, and in the sky above them the orange light from the fires glowed against the undersides of the low clouds. The group from the theatre had been joined by others seeking shelter from the violence. Every now and then there was a distant bang of a gunshot, and they were close enough to St Patrick's Street to hear the crackling roar of flames and the smashing of windows, and smell the smoke on the breeze. Michael led them down to the corner and peered around. There were a dozen or so in the alley, and by unspoken assent, he had become the de facto leader of the group. Akiko wondered if this was just because he was the one with a gun.

She peeped around the corner below her papa's shoulder. Some men had pulled up in a truck and were questioning some of the other people from the theatre.

'Damn it,' Michael muttered, pulling his head back from the end of the wall and turning to the others. 'It's a squad of Tans. They've blocked off the road. They're between us and the river now. Anyone know what happened? How did it start? That fellow back there mentioned an ambush.'

'There was an attack at Dillon's Cross earlier,' a woman told him. 'We were there when it happened. A convoy came out of Victoria Barracks and the Volunteers ambushed them. Shootin' and throwin' grenades, they were. Only a few hundred yards from the barracks! The Brits got away, but a lot of them were injured. I'd say that set them off.'

Akiko nodded to herself. Arson was a favourite reprisal of the Black and Tans. Cork was already littered with burnt-out buildings. If the Crown forces couldn't get back at the rebels, someone else had to take the punishment. And sometimes *anybody* would do.

'They're out of control this time, Michael,' Midori asked in a hushed voice. 'They're liable to shoot anyone they think is a republican.'

'All right, here's what we're going to do,' Papa said. 'We have to–.'

It was at that moment that another truck roared past the mouth of the alley behind them and someone fired a machine gun down the narrow lane. Bullets smacked off the brickwork over Akiko's head and she screamed. Another one ricocheted off the ground at her feet and, in blind panic, she started running.

'Aki! Stop! Come back!' her father bellowed. 'AKI, NO! *STOP!*'

But it was too late. Her sprint had taken her straight out of the alley, across the street and down another lane and then she was right there, out in the open, staggering to a stop. She stared up, awe-struck and unable to move. Like her okaasan, Akiko practised the Japanese religion of Shinto – though she could never admit to this in school – and so she did not believe in the Christian Hell. If she had, she imagined it would look like this.

The tall buildings in front of her were being consumed by fire, to the point where only the fronts stood, like the sets of a film, as the structures behind them slowly collapsed. Smoke and embers swirled across the street and ash rained from the sky. The noise was overwhelming. She and her family had been shopping here earlier in the day, strolling through Roches Stores, Grant's and Cash's department stores, the Munster Arcade. Now they had all been destroyed. She knew some of the staff of these places lived upstairs in the buildings. Had they escaped? How many had died already tonight?

This war wasn't being fought on battlefields; it came to your streets. It came to your home.

Nearby, crews of firemen were trying to fight the blaze, but the Black and Tans were blocking the way, hurling insults and threats and slashing the firemen's hoses. A section of wall crashed down onto the street a few yards from Akiko, making her jump and bringing her to her senses. She saw one of the Tans crossing the street carrying a petrol can and a half-empty bottle of whiskey, a rifle slung over his shoulder. He was unsteady on his feet and looked drunk. Looking over, he spotted her and turned in her direction.

She spun round, but there was only the wreckage of the wall and a pall of smoke behind her, a nearby fire spitting sparks. Which direction should she run? Where was her father? Where was her family? The man was coming at her faster now, dropping the petrol can. Akiko went to scramble over the rubble beside her and her foot caught on some charred wire. She had seconds to pull it free before the man reached her.

And in that moment, everything became very clear. She would not get her foot free in time, and she was quite certain that this man meant her harm. There were no decisions to make.

Feeling she had time to take things in, she blinked, and glanced around. None of the other soldiers were paying her any attention. The entire place was in a state of chaos. The man was almost upon her. She stooped, picked up a brick and hit him over the head with it as hard as she could.

It knocked him sideways, and he barely stayed on his feet, a look of shock on his face. Stumbling back, he snarled and fumbled for the rifle hanging from its strap on his shoulder. Akiko heard a shot and something plucked at the man's heart. He dropped onto his knees and fell on his face. Then Papa's arm was around Akiko's shoulders as she began trembling violently. His beard brushed the side of her face and he spoke into her ear:

'There's my girl. There's my good girl, Akiko. We have to go now. Come on, we have to go.'

She shuddered awake on the sofa, her book on her lap, still hearing her father's words. 'There's my girl.'

She always felt tired after that nightmare. Who *was* her father? She had always known that he was a secretive man, but she had never seen him like that, before or since that day. Perhaps she was finally going to find out. After he'd learned that Liam had discovered the sea cave, Papa had promised that he would share its secrets, but only if *they* promised to keep them from *everyone else*.

She blew out her cheeks and sighed. The weather had been too wet to take the dogs for a walk after school, so once her homework was done, she'd started reading. And then she'd ended up taking a nap, because she'd stayed up reading for hours the night before. Looking out the window now, she could see it was still raining. Gah! Why was there so little sun in this country? She missed America, where she had spent the first half of her life. She dreamed of Japan, though she had only visited twice. Flopping back on the sofa, she picked up her book again. It was *The Mysterious Affair at Styles*, a detective novel by a new author named Agatha Christie, and she was soon absorbed in the story.

And she tried to forget that day nearly a year ago, on a burning street, when her father had killed a man without hesitation, right in front of her.

Chapter 8
A Smell of Bleach

Oberleutnant Wolfgang Zürn, formerly of the Imperial German Navy, was returning to Belfast Harbour after a rare break from work, a little lighter in the wallet, but with his spirits refreshed. Though he had heard reports of political violence continuing across the city, he had seen little of it, having spent most of the three days in the library and a series of pubs, cafés and hotels with his crew. That said, there was no shortage of dark green Royal Irish Constabulary uniforms in the city centre.

A compact, sinewy man, Wolfgang was not overly concerned with his appearance. He had not changed out of his rough work clothes to go out on the town, and there was several days' growth of beard on his high-boned cheeks, the same red-tinged blond as the untidy locks that protruded from under his cap. He had the type of eyes that turned people's heads though, a striking green, lined with near-invisible lashes, over a long patrician nose and an expressive mouth.

He was returning to the boat later than the others after a very enjoyable afternoon at the cinema. They could do such wonderful things with storytelling in film, and the technology was advancing so quickly. Wolfgang had been rather depressed since the crew had been told the news about their boat, and spending that Tuesday afternoon at the flicks had been just the tonic he needed. The boys had decided to go back and finish unloading their personal belongings from the vessel and checking into a hotel, before ending the day with a few more drinks at their local pub on the docks.

Their time here was coming to an end, and when they were done, the mixed group of German and British men would all be going their separate ways, having become *kameraden* over the last six months. He would miss them very much when they were gone.

On the way back to his temporary home, Wolfgang sat upstairs in the bright red and white double-decker tram so that he could take in as much of the city as he could. The vehicle's electric motor gave off a loud hum, following the rails north to the harbour. Even from the centre of the city, he could see the shipyards on the skyline and he had come to love the sight. The small forests of towering cranes were visible from miles away, and the sounds of ship's horns carried through the smog of industry, which was ever-present in the air. That pungent smell would thin out somewhat as he got closer to the fresher sea air. Ireland was such a small country, and yet the shipyards of Belfast were a match for anything he'd seen in Germany; indeed, they were more impressive than most.

Wolfgang was feeling the cold that November evening, despite his heavy coat and cap, though he did not mind.

Cold was a familiar companion. His war service at sea had left him looking older than his twenty-seven years, but it had honed his mind and taught him resilience. He'd now be considered quite old for the U-boat service, where young men were favoured for those weeks-long hunting expeditions, enduring mind-shredding stress in sweaty, claustrophobic spaces. While submarines had been the terror of the seas during the conflict, Wolfgang had learned later that if you served on a U-boat, you had a seventy percent chance of being killed. It was the most dangerous job in the war.

All that was in the past now. There were times when he'd loved the life beneath the waves, the men he'd served with and the boats he'd served on; now he had left the Ubootwaffe behind and it was time to move on. After tonight, it was possible that he would never set foot on a U-boat again, and if that meant never again facing a nightmarish death in a metal coffin at the bottom of the sea, that was fine by him.

The tram continued on its journey, its bell ringing at a junction as a stream of people, wrapped up against the chilly sea wind, walked across the road in front of him, heading home from the yards. The minutes passed, the vehicle rolled on, and the city's buildings were giving way to goods sheds and other harbour infrastructure. Railway lines ran alongside the tram lines here, glinting in the tram's single headlight. Though there was less activity as darkness fell, there were still people at work under the harbour's electric lamps. This was a landscape of large, functional structures, tall chimneys, heavy machinery, open tracts of land – yards and wasteland – and deep and dirty stretches of water. Hills swept up on either side, cupping the long shape of Belfast Lough and the harbour that occupied its south end.

From somewhere nearby, he heard the sounds of gunshots, and he leaned his head over close to the window, in case there was anything to see, but whatever was happening was down one of the darker side-streets.

It was three years after the end of the Great War, the city was only slowly recovering and now this new conflict was raging through the country. And while the peace talks in London offered hope to those in the south of Ireland, here in Belfast, things seemed to be getting worse.

The city boasted some the greatest shipbuilding yards, the birthplace of some the world's largest ships. As the tram made for the docks, Wolfgang could see vessels in various stages of construction. One of the boats on the stocks was said to be 32,000 tons, and some areas of the harbour could accommodate ships of up to 48,000 tons or more. The place fed his imagination, and he liked the people – most of them, anyway. This was a city of the future, and though he missed his family terribly, he wanted to be part of it. Perhaps, when he had made enough money, he could bring Edith and the children over, and they could spend the rest of their lives here.

But the violence was unsettling; he would not bring his children here while that persisted, and it did not seem to be getting any better. His mind darkened as he was brought back to his own situation. Up until now, he'd been left alone by the unionist mobs on the harbour because he was working for the Royal Navy. How would he be treated when he was just an unemployed German in a city full of British war veterans?

He had been proud to serve his country in the Great War, knew he'd been lucky to make it through alive, and had been entirely pragmatic about the outcome. It was a bitter fact that they had fought and they had lost. He had been working on his father's fishing boat before he'd joined up as a young lad, so despite the rank he'd achieved, he had never truly been one of the officer class; he had little time for a warrior's honour or his blaublütig superiors.

Things were desperate now in Germany, and his youngest son Günther, who was recovering from polio, required regular, expensive doctor's visits. About two years ago, Wolfgang had learned that the Royal Navy were looking for Unterseeboot engineers to work on the vessels the Germans had surrendered to the British. They were offering to pay a lot more than he had been earning gutting fish in a factory – the only work he'd been able to find back home. And so he had endured the disgust of his friends and relatives, and had left home to go and work for his enemy.

There came the sound of police whistles then, and more shots, this time from somewhere behind him. He twisted and tried to peer out the back windows, as did others on the top deck, but though they could hear shouting, there was nothing to be seen. Wolfgang rubbed his hand over his mouth, eager now to get back to the safety of his boat. If the republicans were out and about, there might still be more trouble on the streets tonight.

In two days, his contract would be up, and he would have to find another job, or go back home – and there wasn't much to go back to. After the disastrous end to the war, the Treaty of Versailles had established what Germany's defeat would cost them. His country had been forced to reduce its armed forces to a fraction of what they'd been and pay enormous sums of money in reparations to the Allied powers. Germany was broke, there was little work to be had back there, and because of the war, Germans were not very popular in Belfast – but then neither were Catholics and what were known as 'rotten Prods', the socialists or labour activists.

In fact, anyone who might be considered disloyal to the newly created territory of Northern Ireland was made to feel decidedly unwelcome by some of the more hostile of the British Irishmen. That had been the start of the violence here. In the last year, thousands of these undesirables had been driven from their jobs in the shipyards, pelted with 'Belfast Confetti'; the nuts, bolts and rivets used in their millions in the yards. Many had been driven from their homes too. Catholic businesses had been looted and fire-bombed.

Wolfgang was still some way off from his dream of buying his own fishing boat and building a business he could hand on to his children. Between the money he sent home to Edith and the cost of living here, it could be two or three more years before he had saved enough – assuming he could find another job.

He heard a revving engine, and once more, he leaned

in closer to the window. A group of Harbour Police drove past at speed in a truck and a motor car, heading off in the other direction. There were normally a lot of police around the quays, though he wasn't seeing many out on the port roads this evening. With everything that was going on, their presence must be demanded somewhere else.

The tram pulled up at the last stop, close to the dock where his boat was moored. He descended to the lower deck, hopped off the back step, and took in the way the harbour's electric lights picked out a brick-brown smudge of smog-stained sky over the lough. He considered joining the boys in the *The Prince of Orange*, the pub a few streets from their dock, but decided it would be nice to take one last look around the boat while it was all quiet. Their Royal Navy mooring was not far from the electric power station on the Musgrave Channel, and he could see that stevedores were still unloading coal from a ship, cranes on rails using 'grabbers' to lift the black fuel out of the hold. From there it was dropped onto the horizontal, mechanical conveyors that ran into the great box-like slab of a building, its walls lit by the lamp-posts at ground level.

This is the world we are building for the future, he thought. I *must* find a way to stay here.

For some reason, the lamp-posts along his jetty were not lit, which was odd. The Navy prided itself on keeping its equipment in good order. At the end of the pier, the sleek shape of a Type U93 lay moored. An ocean-going, diesel-powered torpedo attack vessel, it was one of the

U-boats that had terrorised Britain and its allies in the Great War. From where he stood, only the submarine's conning tower was visible. Her deck gun had been removed long ago. He could, however, see two faint columns of light shining up from the hatches fore and aft, so at least one of the others must have left the pub early to pick up their things.

As he started along the jetty, Wolfgang saw a man standing on one side, about twenty yards from the boat, gazing at the dark water lapping at the stonework below. He looked up when he heard Wolfgang approaching.

'A'right there, mate,' he said, in a local accent. ''Ave you got a light, by any chance?'

He held up a cigarette, but something in his manner put Wolfgang on edge. The submarine did attract curious visitors; the main reason it had been brought to Belfast was as a trophy, a public symbol of Germany's defeat, but it had been here for six months, long enough that it no longer drew much attention, and there wasn't much to see in the dark. Dressed in a navy knitted hat and a black wool coat with rope and peg fasteners, the man was shorter than Wolfgang, but wide and solidly built. He had a jutting jaw, a bullish face and an expression that was friendly and interested, apart from the eyes, which seemed overly intent on Wolfgang. He was a somewhat menacing figure on that gloomy dock.

'I am sorry, I do not smoke,' Wolfgang replied. 'I have work to do here. Can I help you with anything?'

'Nawt at all. Just takin' in the air,' the man said. He gestured at the scene around him. 'Out for a walk, y'know.

It's quite the fish, this thing. Are you crew on this boat?'

Wolfgang was about to reply when he heard high-pitched shouts coming from the submarine. At first, he thought his kameraden must have brought some beer back to the boat, to continue the party on board. But then he caught the faint scent of bleach on the breeze. For a submariner, that was like a fire alarm. His friends were screaming. He immediately turned and started running towards the vessel. As he came close enough to see the rest of the U-boat's deck, lower than the level of the pier, his fears were confirmed. Rising from both of the open hatches were wisps of greenish-yellow gas, illuminated from beneath in an eerie glow from the lights inside the boat. The smell was much stronger here.

His immediate thought was that the vessel was taking on water. When seawater came into contact with the huge bank of batteries in a submarine, a chemical reaction created chlorine gas. It was one of the many horrific hazards of sailing on these boats. From inside, there were the sounds of strangled cries and coughing.

'*Oh, mein Gott!*' he gasped.

He was starting down the ladder to the deck when he hesitated, miserably torn as the reality of the situation hit him. If the poisonous gas was thick enough to see, he couldn't get close to the hatches without a gas mask. All their gas masks were on board the boat. How was there *so much* of it? What had happened? Was it sinking? It didn't look any lower in the water. He felt a sob rise in his throat. How many of the crew were in there? Stefan, William, Karl . . .

He had to get help. Some of them might still be alive in there, if they had managed to get some of the watertight doors sealed. Climbing back up onto the pier, he pivoted to see a figure rising up from one of the hatches, in the gas-tinted light. From his size, Wolfgang immediately knew that it was not one of his crew. He was too big for a submariner. He barely fit through the hatch. He was wearing a gas mask . . . and he was holding a large knife in one hand. The figure looked up at Wolfgang, who felt a presence close to him and spun to find the man from the jetty right behind him.

This man too had a knife, and it was only pure luck that Wolfgang had turned in time to see him, narrowly avoiding the blade that was meant to drive between his ribs. He pivoted again as the man came at him a second time, and Wolfgang's foot slipped off the concrete edge of the pier. He cried out, fell, tried to grab the edge, hit his face off it with a painful smack, and tumbled into the narrow gap of water between the submarine's hull and the wall of the pier. The clamp of the cold river closed around him and then he surfaced, gagging and coughing up salty, oily water.

He was dazed from the blow to his face, his head throbbing, but was still conscious enough to hear booted feet clattering towards the edge, and people speaking in low voices above him. A blurry image of more men in gas masks. Not knowing what else to do, he ducked beneath the water again before a torchlight shone down in his direction. There were more noises that suggested a group of men were taking turns climbing down the steel ladder and jumping over onto the deck.

Staying underwater for a long as he could, Wolfgang fought his way out of his heavy coat and swam around the end of the submarine and across to a small tugboat anchored further upstream from the dock. Putting the barnacle-encrusted hull between him and the U-boat, he hung on to the anchor chain, barely keeping his head above water. Shivering in the piercing November chill, he continued clinging on even as he heard the familiar sound of his vessel's two diesel engines start up . . . then he must have passed out. When water rose up around his face, he jerked awake. Somehow, he had managed to hold onto the chain. There was silence again. With a groan, he let go and swam back out from behind the tug and raised his gaze to the end of the jetty. He must have been out of it for longer than he'd thought.

The submarine was gone.

Chapter 9
A Modest Shipment of Arms

The sun was dragging itself up off the horizon that morning as Liam cycled along the road to the farm where his father was waiting for him. Although he was excited about seeing Da, he did not look forward to delivering his news. That was why he was not pedalling as furiously as he often might, even though this detour meant he would be late for school, and it was usually in his nature to travel as quickly as he could.

At a point where the road dipped and turned, he slowed down even more. This was Ned's Boreen, and just beyond the corner, there was a wide trench across the uneven, gravel road that had only recently been filled in. The new earth and gravel had sunk, creating a wide, nasty pothole that could buckle the wheel of a bike or even throw you off, if you hit it too fast. The trench had originally been dug to stop a truck of Black and Tans as part of an ambush a few months back – one of the last before the truce was called. It was a good spot. There was a hedge of hawthorn offering concealment on the high bank on the right, facing a dry stone wall on the left. As he always did, Liam stopped at one of the high rocks along the right side of the road, to run his fingers over the bullet scars that had been left there. Three Tans had been killed that day, another four wounded and taken prisoner, and their weapons seized. One Volunteer had died.

The Ned's Boreen ambush had been the work of the local flying column – a small company of full-time guerilla fighters led by his father, Lar O'Leary, who was considered a true republican hero in these parts. It was Liam's ambition to join the column some day soon. Or it had been, at least. He started pedalling again, uphill now, the last stretch before Sheehan's farm, a place of thirty acres a few miles from the town of Ballinashort.

Descending the slope on the other side, he saw there was a buzz of activity in the farmyard below, at the end of the boreen. There were six horses and carts and a motor car in the yard, with people coming and going, including a lot of familiar faces. Drawing closer, he realized that there were more IRA men here than he'd seen together in the last year. Twenty at least – most of Da's company. And there were as many women, Cumann na mBan members, who organised much of the support for the men who lived on the run. Something big was happening.

As he swung in through the gateway, he could see rifles and revolvers being carried across the yard, with no attempt to keep them concealed. In the field next to the yard, groups of young men were running from one piece of cover to another, guns in hand, kitted out with haversacks, and belts and bandoliers lined with pouches.

Some were being instructed by the older hands on how to throw grenades – they were practising with stones – and how to lay the company's homemade landmines. In a kitchen in Ballinashort, Liam had once watched his father mixing the basic ingredients to create these explosives, new formulae with unlikely names like 'War Flour' and 'Irish Cheddar'. Preparations were being made for some kind of operation. It was a dramatic sign that, despite the truce, the Volunteers were still active, and Liam took it all in with an excited energy building up inside him. *What was going on?*

This kind of gathering, out here in the open, would have been unthinkable at the height of the conflict, when one well-placed spy could result in the whole company being imprisoned or shot. However, it had been months since the last real fight. With the violence becoming increasingly savage, the British government and the Irish rebel leaders had finally agreed that it had to stop, and in July, they had agreed a truce. Since then, a troubled peace had reigned across the country, as people gradually began to believe that an end to the violence might be within sight. The British had decided that this blight of an island was more trouble than it was worth. Much to their distaste, they had declared themselves willing to sit down and negotiate with the Irish upstarts.

Incredible as it seemed, Ireland might be on the verge of winning its independence.

Liam had mixed feelings about the truce. If he was honest, he wasn't sure what he'd prefer, to see Ireland freed from its centuries-long colonization by Britain, or to have Britain rule for a while longer so that he could go into action with his father, shooting Black and Tans. He noticed with some annoyance that there were new lads training with the veterans. His Uncle Michael had started teaching him to shoot a few years ago; he was a much better marksman than most boys his age, and yet his father still wouldn't accept him into the column.

'Liam! Get your arse over here!'

And there was Da, waving him over to the motor car – not a car, actually, but one of those Fordson tractors, bright red with great, yellow steel wheels that had no tyres, which the column must have stolen from some rich landowner. Based on the Ford Model T and built in Cork, there was hardly a farmer in the county who could afford one, so it only added to Liam's excitement. He cycled across the yard, bumping over the holes in the muck left by cow's hooves.

Lar O'Leary was an older version of his son, a horse of a man, with a lively, handsome face prone to smiling or scowling to an equal degree, and a coarse shock of sandy hair that was somewhere between straight and curly and was as untameable as the man it was attached to. His troops loved him. Uncle Michael said of Lar that he had 'enough fight in him for two men', and that if he didn't have a war, he'd have to find one.

Leaning against the red tractor, Lar grinned at his son, reaching out to give him a hearty slap on the back.

'You're just in time, son. I have a job for yeh.'

Liam nodded eagerly. There had been a lot of 'jobs' over the last year; delivering messages or medical supplies or even hiding guns sometimes, or keeping watch while Da and some of his lads broke into some Brit's farmhouse looking for weapons. He was always happy to do it, though he considered it women's work, when he really wanted to go out on operations. But then he remembered his promise to his uncle and his smile lost some of its enthusiasm. Still, one more time wouldn't hurt, would it?

'What's the job?' he asked.

'I need to you to go into town and pick up a bag for me. Nell Flanagan has packed up some sandwiches and apples for the leds. They're famished.'

Liam lost the last of his smile. Fetching sandwiches and apples wasn't how he'd imagined fighting for Ireland.

'I thought maybe I could help with the guns,' he said.

He gestured toward the thatched stone-block house. Out the front of it, sitting at a table, Mrs Sheehan and her two daughters were stripping down and cleaning some Lee Enfield rifles. If the Cumann na mBan lot could do it, why couldn't he?

'That's taken care of, led. It's the sandwiches we need.'

Suddenly, Liam's mood had turned entirely, and he was glaring at his father, feet planted, fists bunched by his sides. He wasn't so reluctant to deliver his news after all.

'You'll have to send someone else to fetch your lunch, Da. I came out here to tell yeh I'm done running errands for you. I made a promise to Uncle Michael.'

Lar's manner abruptly became a mirror of Liam's.

'Oh, did yeh indeed? And how is it you're making promises to *him* to disobey your *father*?'

Liam bit down on his reply, afraid of getting Da's

blood up. He'd been forbidden to talk about what he'd seen in the sea cave, and the truth was, Michael had long been the father that Lar had failed to be. Liam idolized his da, but the man had left to join the British Army in 1915 to fight in the war against Germany, when Liam was just ten years old. When he'd come back, he'd almost immediately got involved in the campaign for Irish independence. Over those years, Liam had hardly seen him. Da hadn't even shown up in the church for Ma's funeral after the flu took her a year and a half before, because the RIC had been watching, hoping they could catch him. Lar had come to the grave later. It was the last time he'd hugged his son.

Liam hated to admit it to himself, but he hardly knew his father. The man was a warrior and a hero . . . and he never came home.

'Yeh'll do as I say and go off to Nell's,' Lar told him, a familiar hardness in his voice. 'Or you'll feel my boot up your backside.'

He eyed his son for a few seconds, then he pressed his lips together, and relaxed, throwing his hands up in the air.

'Ah, look . . . don't mind me now, I can send one of the leds,' he sighed. 'I don't want to be fightin' with yeh. Sure, I hardly see yeh these days. Here, what d'yeh think of the tractor?'

'It's a marvel,' Liam replied with relief. 'Where'd you get hold of it?'

'We were up at Malone's place. He hasn't paid his levy and we thought he might have some guns we could take as payment. He didn't, so we took his tractor. Y'know, as a *loan*, like.'

The republican campaign was funded by a levy, a sum everyone in the area had to pay based on how much property they owned. Thomas Malone was one of the biggest landlords in the county. Lar was smiling, but Liam couldn't match the expression as he gazed at the modest shipment of arms. He wondered how Britain's military forces would fare if they had fund themselves by collecting at the church gate.

The tractor had been hooked up to a flatbed trailer, which was being loaded with blocks of turf. Between the layers of peat, some of the men and women were laying rifles and revolvers wrapped in blankets and sacks. Each bundle of firearms was quickly covered by the turf. Liam's eyes widened as he saw one of the men wrap up a Lewis light machine gun before placing it on the trailer.

'Da, you promised me you'd let me shoot a Lewis gun if you ever got one!'

'I would, son, if we could spare the bullets, but we're terrible short,' Lar had a regretful look on his face. 'We don't even have enough for practice – and God knows some of the new leds could do with some.' He dropped his voice, so that only Liam could hear. 'Some of them couldn't hit the side of a house. The only chance they'd have of out-shootin' a Tan or an Auxie is to stand next to him and put the gun to his hid.'

The Auxilaries, or 'Auxies' were even more dangerous than the Black and Tans. While the Tans were hated and feared for their random savagery, most were ordinary former soldiers, hired to make up numbers; hurried replacements for lost police officers. The Auxilaries were not just veterans of the Great War, they were decorated officers, and their squads included British, Canadians, Americans and other nationalities. What mattered most to their masters was their combat experience. These were small, mobile units of men who had forged their lethal skills in the worst war the world had ever seen, and had been tasked with hunting down the rebels like Lar's father wherever they could be found.

'It's shockin' ironic, but we're victims of our own success,' Lar went on. 'We've driven the Brits out of the countryside, but sure most of our guns and ammunition came from the small police stations, and the trucks we ambushed. Now we can't git at them in those big barracks, and when they come out, they do it in great big convoys, armed like battleships, so we'd need *artillery* to take them down. I mean, *look at us*. We've backed them into a corner all over the country, forced them to declare a truce, to recognize we're a nation in our own right . . . and here I am, just hopin' the blackguards don't realize we've cut off our own supply of arms.'

'So where's all this lot goin'?' Liam asked, pointing at the stack of turf.

'North, up to the new "border". We'll take it to the city first, and put the guns on a whiskey truck bound for Belfast, while we take the train. We may have a truce down here, but it's all goin' to Hell up there.'

Liam nodded. He so desperately wanted to go with his father. The unionists in the north considered themselves true Brits. That lot were as dead set on *staying* in the empire as the republicans were on *leaving* it, and the British were inclined to let them have their way. The Brits had already drawn a random border around the northern counties, and were planning to keep the bit they wanted and rid themselves of the rest. The swines were going to split Ireland in two. As his da had said, Belfast was all going to Hell as a result. That would be a mighty scrap though, taking on the unionists. They were a hard lot, committed, well organised and better armed.

Lar regarded his son thoughtfully, biting the side of his tongue, which was a habit of his.

'Here, tell me this, and tell me no more: What's your uncle givin' yeh to make you give up on the struggle?'

'Ah Jaysus, Da. For God's sake,' Liam groaned. 'I haven't "given up on the struggle".'

'But you don't want to do jobs for me.' Lar stared at Liam, eyes narrowed. 'He's promised you something, hasn't he? What would turn your head, I wonder? You never knew much about what he got up to, did yeh, Liam?'

'I knew a bit.'

'But I think you know more than a bit now, don't yeh? How much have you found out? Is he active again, yer uncle? Is that why you're coppin' out on me? Is he tryin' to drag you into his outfit? Not that he's got much of an outfit left, from what I hear. They're most of them dead, y'know.'

'I'm not *coppin' out* on yeh, Da!' Liam protested. 'It's just . . .'

'It's "just",' Lar said, nodding, with a hint of sneer.

'Yeah, he's got you under his thumb good and proper, hasn't he? You know, he was was one of our best gun-runners back in the day. A real operator. Could handle hisself in a fight too. So you're workin' for the Selkies now, eh? It'd be good to get him back in the water. Maybe he could bring us in some ammo.'

Liam said nothing. Michael had warned him not to. And yet if Da told him to mount up and come north with them, he didn't know if he could refuse. He'd give anything to be going to Belfast with his da, but if he showed that he couldn't keep a promise – or a secret – he'd be no good to the cause and he'd lose the respect of both his father *and* his uncle.

'Howaya, Liam!' one of Mrs Sheehan's girls called, a playful smile on her face. 'You stayin' for some tea? Our ma's made a fruitcake.'

Mary was her name. A round-faced, ginger tomboy with bright eyes, she was a bit older than him, and courting with Mad Francie Devlin, last he'd heard. Devlin was one of Da's toughest lads, a fruitcake of a different type, and if he saw her aiming that smile at Liam, there'd be trouble. She was holding two Winchester pump-action shotguns and a Thompson submachine gun to her chest. The shotguns would have been supplied by the Royal Irish Constabulary or the Tans, while the Tommy gun had come from America. They were bound for the stack of turf on the trailer, though it was clear the girl wanted to stop and chat.

'All right there, Mary,' he said. 'No, I'll be headin' off, I'm afraid. Sorry to be missin' the cake.'

'Sure, I'll wrap some up for yeh.'

She looked completely at ease with the weapons. Liam had to remind himself that, while the men of the flying columns had been living on the run for the last few years, constantly moving from place to place to avoid being caught, they couldn't have survived without all the people who supported them, many of them women. Food and billeting, gathering intelligence, storing weapons and delivering them to the sites of ambushes, providing hiding places and medical treatment. The newspaper headlines were always about the men who did the shooting, but the network was so much wider than that.

Mary swept on past him, giving his arm a nudge with her elbow, before laying out the guns on the trailer. Lar had moved away to talk to one of his men. Liam ran his fingers over the fibrous roughness of the peat and the coarse fabric of the sacking, enjoying the feel of them. As Mary tucked the weapons into a blanket, he picked up some blocks of peat from a pile on the ground, and covered up the bundle, but not before he'd slid his hand along the form of the Tommy gun under the sackcloth. The weapon they called the 'Chicago typewriter', because of the noise it made.

'He's some man, yer father,' Mary murmured to him. 'D'you remember what he said, that day they took the coffins through town?'

Liam nodded, noticing how close her hand was to his as she leaned on the trailer. After the Ned's Boreen ambush, the truck carrying the coffins of the three dead

Black and Tans had gone through Ballinashort, and a small crowd had gathered to watch them go past. From the middle of the crowd, Lar had shouted:

'Good riddance to yeh! Sure, send back the empties, and we'll fill them agin!'

Mary chuckled and shook her head.

'"Send back the empties and we'll fill them agin",' she sighed. 'He's some man. Here, will yeh be headin' north yerself, Liam?'

'No. No, I won't,' he replied reluctantly.

'Ah well, probably for the best. I'd say it'll be awful dangerous. Best to wait until you're grown up a bit more, eh?'

She flashed him another smile, and set off across the yard to where her mother had finished reassembling the last few rifles. Grinding his teeth, Liam decided he wouldn't wait around for that piece of fruitcake after all.

Chapter 10
A Depressing Lack of Alarm

Edward Faulkner did not have time for lunch, but he did grant Esther an audience at the Colonial Office in Whitehall, where he held a senior position on Winston Churchill's staff. Though he had come up through the intelligence service, Faulkner was an expert navigator of the political world, and Esther was not quite sure where his intelligence work ended and his political work began, or if there was even a distinction between them. Certainly, his boss, Churchill, had a reputation for being one of the most cunning and influential figures in the government.

Faulkner's office had the feel of power about it; old and worn, not altogether grand – quite small, actually – but with an archaic style that harked back to the glory days of the British Empire, before everyone started trying to leave it. The high-ceilinged room was a working space, but it was also a statement, full of bookshelves and filing cabinets, all centered around a carved teak desk and complimented by oil paintings on the walls of prominent figures from the nation's colonial history. It smelled of tobacco smoke and faintly of Faulkner's cologne.

The surroundings were fitting, as he now occupied the kind of position where one could reasonably expect to retire with a knighthood, as her father had, though most people would never know what he did to earn it. Esther had been there less than ten minutes, and had already explained her concerns about the missing chlorine gas. Her former superior was showing a depressing lack of alarm.

'My supervisor, Buckley, is a decent sort, but I suspect if I leave it to him, it will be stuck in a pile of reports and forgotten about,' she told him.

'Well it's not the first time weapons have gone missing over there, is it Esther?' Faulkner pointed out. 'I mean, would anyone even notice? Except for you, of course. France and Belgium are positively littered with the ruddy things. A fellow can't walk around out there without tripping over a machine gun or some artillery shells. There are whole fields that one can't stroll across without blowing oneself up. They'll be digging the stuff up for years!'

'But we had possession of these particular weapons before they disappeared,' she said.

'No, *the Disarmament Section of the League of Nations* had possession of them,' he corrected her, his finger raised like a schoolteacher to a recalcitrant student. 'It was *they* who misplaced them, and the responsibility for finding them is *theirs*, nor ours. And let us not pretend that their record on these matters is exemplary. I would even go so far as to say that they are bumbling clods.'

He sat back and lit one of his cigarillos, the thin cigars

he had taken up smoking during a short posting in America before the war. He was a trim man, well put together, with neatly oiled, black hair, a pencil moustache and narrow, aristocratic features. Exhaling smoke as he lounged back in his leather swivel chair, he cut a svelte figure in his navy, bespoke, Savile Row suit.

'But no one has ever had to clear up after a war like this,' Esther argued. 'It's everyone's responsibility to help. This gas could be a nightmare if it has ended up in the wrong hands. Half the states in Europe are unstable at the moment. Think of all the groups we're trying to monitor! How many of them would be willing to use this weapon against our forces? Or against civilians. You'd only steal this frightful stuff if it was your plan to commit *mass murder*! We must *do something*, Edward!'

'Esther, my dear girl, it simply is not our concern,' he said, shaking his head. 'And as you rightly point out, we have enough on our plate, what with these difficulties in India, Egypt, Turkey, Mesopotamia, and the bloody Bolsheviks spreading out all over the place . . . the list goes on. We cannot act as the policemen of the world – others must take some responsibility. We are stretched thin, just as the empire finds itself on shaky ground.

'For pity's sake, we have reached so low a point, we've extended a cordial hand to Ireland's murder gangs, inviting them to the negotiating table. The very thought of it . . . a cut-throat thug like Michael Collins meeting with the Prime Minister himself! It's an embarrassment.'

Esther wanted to retort, but didn't. It worried her when some of the senior officers spoke like this. They constantly made the mistake of underestimating the Irish nationalists. These were no mere 'murder gangs'. They employed skillful propaganda on an international level and had funding from America. Their elected politicians had formed their own parliament in Dublin. The country was setting up its own system of courts.

And it was ridiculous to dismiss Michael Collins as a simple thug. Apart from being the Minister for Finance in their self-declared government, the 'Dáil', he was the director of intelligence of the Irish Republican Army, its most respected leader and a brilliant strategist. Britain could boast the most effective intelligence service in the world and yet, despite a reward of a thousand pounds offered for his capture, Collins had managed to evade them for years – to the point where he was regarded as some kind of phantom. Not only that, but his own network, and his small gang of assassins known simply as 'the Squad' or sometimes 'the Twelve Apostles', had put the fear of God into the British agents working out of Dublin Castle.

There was a definite element among the higher-ups in the British government who still thought of the Irish as inferior wretches who could be made to kneel if only sufficient force were brought to bear. She suspected Faulkner was one of them, only dying for a chance to unleash the full might of the British military on that obstinate little island.

'I think I'll talk to my father, at least,' she said at last, picking up the ledgers she'd placed on Faulkner's desk. 'He knows people in the Disarmament Section, and

I'm sure he could draw some attention to it.'

Faulker lifted his chin at that. Though her father had retired from the Secret Intelligence Service after the war, he was still very well connected.

'Oh, there's no need to do that,' he said casually, though a little too quickly. 'I'll tell you what; leave it with me and I'll put out some feelers. You're right, of course. We can't let this kind of substance wander off willy-nilly. Let me see what I can do. In the meantime, would I be right in thinking that you'd like to get out of Buckley's little basement? Perhaps even get back in the field?'

Esther didn't even try to hide her eagerness.

'Oh Edward, I'd be ever so grateful. I'm going quite out of my mind down there.'

'You deserve better, it's a waste of your talents. I'll pull some strings with the chaps down at HQ. Given that the Irish have got their feet under the Prime Minister's table, we could do with as much information as possible about the goings-on across the water. It is my suspicion that they are using the truce to build up their forces again, and unless I miss my guess, they mean to cause more mischief in the north.'

'I'm sorry . . . you . . . ,' Esther stammered. 'You want to send me back to *Ireland*?'

'Yes,' he regarded her with an expectant expression. 'We need more eyes and ears in Dublin.'

'But I was marked, Edward. Exiled. They . . . they know who I am.'

'There's a *truce*, dear girl. You'll be quite safe, I'm sure.'

Esther was feeling numb as she walked out of Faulkner's office a couple of minutes later. Edward had refused to hear her protests, insisting this would be the best thing for her, to 'get back on the horse, so to speak'. She closed the door behind her and stopped, putting a hand to her face. She remembered Michael Regan's face, the certainty that she was going to die as she stared down the barrel of his gun, before she was held down and his men chopped off her hair.

'Are you all right, Miss Sinclair?' a voice asked.

She gave a start, and looked at the man sitting behind the desk to the right of the door. It was Edward's aide, Captain Nigel Moore, who occupied the outer office and helped manage Faulkner's affairs. His office was, in every respect, smaller and more modest than Edward's, and some would have thought the man himself more insignificant still. His frail-looking, underweight frame belied his background, however. Moore was a highly decorated war veteran, a once-fierce soldier who had been celebrated in newspapers and on the radio for his acts of heroism.

But the war had taken its toll.

She had seen early photos of him, when he had been a handsome man in his prime, with strong square features. Now, three quarters of his face was raw and misshapen, with terrible pink and yellow burn scars over some areas, and sections of flesh grafted on by surgeons to cover holes where the skin had been lost entirely. It was hard to look at. The left sleeve of his jacket, empty below the elbow, was folded and pinned up. She knew that damage to his left foot caused him to walk with a limp, requiring the assistance of a cane. He gazed up at her, and his ravaged face looked attentive, sensitive.

'I am to go to Ireland,' she said simply. She was surprised to hear a tremor in her voice.

'I . . . I could not help overhearing,' he replied. 'I wonder if you've seen this morning's *Times*? I'm finished with it, if you'd like to read it.'

'No,' she said in an absent-minded voice. 'No, but . . . thank you.'

She was feeling very tired, and disheartened, and had no interest in reading the news.

'I rather think you'd find this story interesting,' Moore said, his tone a little firmer.

Frowning, she looked down and saw that he was tapping an article on the front page.

'Edward gave me a job after the war,' he added, fixing his eyes on hers. 'I was a ruined man, but we'd been in university together, and he saw to it that I was looked after. I could have ended up on the street, like so many others who came back. It would be a *great dishonour* for me to betray his confidence.'

His finger was still resting on the article. She glanced down, and then back to his face. Tentatively, she reached out and picked up the newspaper. The headline read: 'U-BOAT HIJACKED FROM BELFAST HARBOUR.' A photo showed a man identified as a German member of the skeleton crew, and the only witness.

'I was at Loos in France in 1915,' Moore said quietly. 'Our engineers were ordered to use chlorine gas against the enemy. But the wind changed direction, and blew the gas back over our lines. Our gas masks were only rudimentary things back then. They did not provide adequate protection. It seeped in around our faces. I was lucky.' He gave her a rather contorted smile. 'That time, anyway. I only spent three days in hospital, and was back in action within two weeks. Some of my friends were not so fortunate.'

She wasn't quite sure what to make of it, but she remembered how quickly Faulkner had changed his tune when she'd mentioned going to her father with the files. Something wasn't right here, and Moore was trying to tell her . . . without telling her.

'I wish you the very best of luck in your new posting, Miss Sinclair.'

Esther gave him a slight nod of thanks. Minutes later, she stepped out onto Whitehall and started walking, her briefcase with the ledgers in one hand and the newspaper in the other. She read as she walked. The journalist writing the article seemed skeptical of the lone witness to the hijacking of the Type U93 U-boat, probably because the man was German. Oberleutnant Wolfgang Zürn, formerly of the Imperial German Navy, had claimed his crew were not involved in the crime, and what was more, that they had been murdered using chlorine gas. The writer pointed out that such a gas could be released by accident in a submarine, if the batteries came in contact with seawater, and that the witness was almost certainly mistaken. He was still being held by the Royal Irish Constabulary in Belfast, and was being questioned by detectives.

Esther decided that she would like to talk to this Oberleutnant herself. She was coming up on Downing Street and was surprised to find her way blocked. The entire path was occupied by a large group of people, forty or more, not counting all the journalists and photographers who waited with them. They were all here because of the negotiations going on in Downing Street, between the government and the Irish nationalists. Some of the people in front of her were singing a rousing Irish song, but most of them were praying.

They had gathered in the street to pray for an end to the war in Ireland.

Chapter 11
The Subversive

Michael stood in what had once been the living-room of their house. Like Liam's old room, it was now a burnt-out ruin. In the months since the fire, Michael had done some of the repair work on the house himself, but sections of the structure had to be demolished and completely rebuilt. It required a team of men, and builders were hard to come by at that time in Cork. The conflict had left a lot of buildings in need of repair across the county, and after the tens of thousands of men lost to the Great War, the 1918 flu and ongoing emigration, there were fewer fit men of working age to take on the work, even for the wealthy owner of an engineering company, who could pay over the odds.

Liam and Akiko were standing in front of him, a few paces away, and Midori was off to one side, the expression on her wide-boned, but delicate features showing that she was not happy with what he was doing, though he would not have done it without her consent. Like him, she had to accept the reality of the situation. She normally dressed in elegant kimonos at home unless she was doing housework, most of which she made herself.

Today, however, she wore the same kind of clothes as her husband; a shirt, a warm woollen jumper, trousers and boots. In addition, her hair was tightly bound up in a bun under the traditional, white *ama* headscarf, which Midori had worn as a young woman, working as a pearl diver back in Japan. Akiko kept staring at the odd combination, as her okaasan was dressed for sailing rather than swimming.

Michael regarded his daughter and nephew, and gestured at the ruined room, with its burnt collapsed plasterwork, the charred wooden beams in the ceiling.

'You know what happened here,' he said to them. 'Just before the truce, a gang of the local lads took some shots at a squad of Black and Tans down the road, and then did a runner. The Tans came and found the nearest house, and set fire to it, to punish us for allowing rebels to wander around in our area. We had no part in the attack, but their attitude is, if we're not reporting the flying columns to the police, then it stands to reason that we must be supporting them.

'Liam, I know you've been helping your father. Akiko, I know you've been reading my James Connolly pamphlets. Also, your growing obsession with violent pirate stories is . . . of concern to us. However, you're both getting to an age where we can't control you any more, we understand that. What you can't yet fathom are the risks you're taking.

'This is what the British do to us just for *being here*,' he said, waving at the room again. 'If they knew who I was, *what* I was, I could be imprisoned without trial, tortured or killed – maybe all three. Midori would most likely be imprisoned too.'

'But what about the truce, Papa?' Akiko asked. 'Isn't the war over?'

'The truce is a temporary ceasefire,' he replied. 'The shooting could start again at any time, if the talks fail, and there are too many people on both sides just waiting for that to happen. In the meantime, we still live under a military power that can and does use vast resources and overwhelming force against us if it identifies us as an enemy. We have no such power. Our only defence is *invisibility*. Do you understand that?'

Akiko and Liam nodded.

'You remember how Esther Sinclair came back from England for Kathleen's funeral?' he continued. 'Esther grew up down the road from here, a neighbour, a friend of Kathleen's . . . and when we met her at the funeral, we trusted her, invited her to our home, and back into our lives. Well, Esther was *a British intelligence agent*—.'

'I KNEW IT!' Akiko shrieked, making them all jump.

It was so rare for her to raise her voice, they all stared at her for a few seconds, and she dropped her eyes, clasping her hands behind her back.

'I *knew* it,' she said again, ever so softly.

'I only discovered this months after we welcomed her into our circle,' Michael continued, acknowledging his daughter's announcement with a nod. 'Over a dozen key men and women ended up in prison because she infiltrated the organisation in Cork. She cut off half of our supply routes for weapons from Britain. It was only luck that she never got anything on me. Luck . . . and extreme caution.'

Akiko and Liam glanced at each other, both looking suitably shocked.

'Is that why she disappeared?' Akiko asked hesitantly. 'Did you kill her?'

'No, she was exiled, with a warning never to come back,' Michael replied. 'And to the best of my knowledge, she never has. But I need to be sure that you are clear on this. Hardly anyone among the Volunteers knows what you're going to learn today, and I want to keep it that way. The more people you involve yourself with, the greater the risk. For this family, secrecy is a matter of life and death. We must remain unknown to our enemies. *Do you understand?*'

'We understand,' they replied together.

Michael looked to Midori, who nodded.

'Right,' he said. 'Let's go.'

He and his wife led the two teenagers out of the house, onto the wild ground beyond the garden and then followed a line of trees and bushes not far from the cliff edge that marked the coastline. They walked for fifteen minutes, cutting across the rough ground of the peninsula to the cliff overlooking the Devil's Drain. They came to a gnarled old Monterey Cypress, a few yards from the edge of the cliff. Michael took them round behind it, and there in the ground was a crevice that descended down through the cliff. He started clambering down.

Liam and Akiko were both able climbers, and were

surprised to find that the way down was relatively easy, compared to the sheer cliff face itself, and where no hand- or footholds occurred naturally, bolts had been driven into the stone to provide purchase. The crevice ended behind some high rocks close to sea level, and from there, a narrow ledge offered a route along the base of the cliffs to the sea cave Liam had found two days before.

Michael paused outside the low mouth of the cave, conscious of how much was going to change now – not least of all was the fact that he was breaking his oath of secrecy to the Brotherhood. But if he was going to share his secrets with Akiko and Liam, then they needed to know everything.

They had heard about some of his past, of course; how he'd grown up along the river in Paterson, New Jersey, where the labour movement had taught him how to organise, and facing the police and employers' hired thugs during protests had taught him how to stay alive in a street fight. They knew that he'd worked for John Philip Holland, but they didn't know he had joined the Fenians at their age – the secretive organisation known as the Irish Republican Brotherhood on this side of the water. It was with this organisation that he'd learned his Irish history, how to run an underground network, and how to handle firearms.

If he could not protect the children from the world, he could at least teach them to navigate it.

These caves had formed as the sea had worn away the near-vertical slabs of dark shale sandwiched in tectonic folds between the layers of tougher, purple-tinged grey sandstone. Inside the mouth, Michael pulled the lever to turn on the lights and then made his way across the rusted rails and stepping stones to where the cave opened out into a much wider cavern. The air was damp but still, and thick with the smell of the sea. Several wooden platforms had been constructed, set at slightly different heights as they followed the shape of the walls. Positioned around these decks were stacks of crates, a large steel fuel tank standing on stone blocks, a few metal barrels and some mechanical equipment like winches and a small crane. Against the furthest wall was a steel rack holding a dozen torpedoes in sealed crates, each one more than ten feet long. A short jetty jutted out into the deepest part of the water.

And at the end of the jetty, there was the *Subversive*.

Compared to the submarines now used by some of the world's navies, it was very small; about seventy feet in length, and not much more than ten feet wide. The bow was higher in the water than the stern, and unlike more modern designs, its conning tower was little more than a low hump and a turret on its back. The highest points were the three extendable air intake pipes and, tallest of all when it was raised, the periscope, Even so, its sleek shape, painted slate grey, gave it the feel of the future about it. Exchanging smiles with Midori at the teenagers' astonished reactions, Michael strode out onto the boards of the jetty and jumped down onto the narrow steel deck-plates that ran along the top of the hull. He tugged on the lever to unlock the hatch.

'Get in,' he said, pulling it open. 'Have a look around. Don't touch *anything*.'

They descended the narrow ladder, and he grinned again as he heard their excited exclamations echoing around the interior. Though this craft was an unusual sight to them, their reaction was a thin shadow of his, the first time he'd seen a submarine. He had been younger than these two, and back then, most people had never even heard the term 'submarine', though history had already witnessed some earlier versions of this strange vehicle – and their often disastrous failures.

On the 22nd of May 1878, on the right bank of the Passaic River in Paterson, New Jersey, he had jostled his way through the growing crowd for a place to try and see what was going on. Workmen stood each side of a large wagon harnessed to eight pairs of stallions. Beside a boathouse near the Spruce Street bridge, the driver backed the wagon's load into the water. It was a boxy, lozenge-shaped metal craft with a kind of circular turret on top. At fourteen feet long, it was barely large enough to hold one man, and Michael would learn later that the propellor at the back would be spun by foot pedals. One of the lads beside him had commented:

'I see that the professor has built a coffin for himself!'

John Philip Holland was not a university professor, however. He was a schoolteacher and self-taught engineer, and that day, when it was slid into the water, the first Holland 'wrecking boat' began to sink. And despite the claims being made about this craft, the sinking was not deliberate. Even so, the young Michael Regan found himself spellbound.

He watched, in the days that followed, sneaking into the machine shop of JC Todd and Company to see Holland tinkering with his contraption, before testing it in the river, having it hauled back out and making changes and testing it again. The schoolteacher tolerated the interest of the local brats on the dock, and would let them look around inside the strange boat.

'And I noticed you, or course,' John said from behind Michael, his voice sounding insubstantial in the cave. 'Your curiosity, your intelligence. How intently you followed everything that was happening. I recognized that passion.'

Michael nodded, trying not to look at the other man, the one who wasn't there. Why did he keep appearing like this? What did it mean?

'I imagine it's *guilt*, Michael,' John replied, as if the question had been asked out loud. 'You have a fierce problem with guilt.'

Chapter 12
Death on the Pier

Watching his nephew raise his beaming face up through the hatch, Michael's mind drifted back to the last operation Liam's mother, Kathleen, had been part of in the *Subversive*; an assault on a coastguard station on the Kerry shore, back in early 1920. These stations, along with lighthouses and lightships, were administered by the Admiralty, the government department that also controlled the Navy. There were hundreds of them around the coastline, keeping watch, mostly to prevent smuggling. For the republican rebels, they were prize targets. It was a chance to strike at a symbol of British rule, and most of the stations were small outposts with firearms that could be seized. They were often so isolated that even if they could call for assistance from the nearest RIC barracks, it would arrive too late.

'You know, of course, that my *father* was a coastguard,' John reminded him.

'Yes, I was aware of that, thank you,' Michael gave a muttered reply.

The smells in the cave brought him back to that night on the pier; wet rust particles on the skin of his hands, the seawater, and the sulfur scent of algae. They normally didn't bring the submarine in close to where they were going to land, preferring to keep it out of sight in the darkness and row in to shore in an inflatable dinghy. Michael never wanted the vessel to be seen, both to protect it, and to reinforce the legend that was developing around his squad, 'the Selkies'. But there were strong riptides along this stretch of stoney beach. He had decided that the menacing ceiling of cloud and lashing rain would offer enough cover, and besides, if the local IRA company did its job, nobody would be looking out off the coast.

They surfaced in the rough swell, slowing as he sighted on the stone jetty. Michael peered in every direction through the two-by-six-inch deadlights in the turret, but he couldn't see much through the heavy rain. He pulled over the lever in the thick steel, counter-weighted hatch and lifted it open. Though it gave him a better view, enough to see that there was no one in sight on the beach, visibility was still down to little more than fifty yards. Now that they were on the surface, he could drive the boat with the controls in the turret.

Swinging the craft in to the side of the pier, where it was protected from the wind, he jumped out with a coil of rope, tied it off to a cleat on the bow and jumped onto the pier to tie it to one of the corroded iron mooring rings. Kathleen had already climbed out and she secured the stern in the same fashion. The boat's low profile meant that it couldn't be seen from the coastguard station, a hundred yards up the slope.

His squad followed him out. Joe Goat, Del, Paddle and Shay were all armed with either shotguns or Thompson submachine guns, recently imported from America. They all carried pistols too. If there was any shooting to be done, it would most likely be close in. As well as his weapons, Joe had a sledgehammer. Kathleen would stay and keep watch from the pier. If things went badly wrong, his sister would pull the *Subversive* away and take her out to sea to keep her from being captured, and scuttle her if necessary.

The first part of the raid went as planned. The local IRA company cut the telephone and telegraph lines to the station, then took up positions in the bushes, opening fire on the building from the front. Their shots were sparse; they did not have much ammunition to waste, so Michael and his squad had to move fast. They expected the station to be staffed by five men, and knew that it had reinforced doors and windows. It consisted of a two-storey house with a watch tower, an equipment shed and a boathouse down on the shore.

Someone in the house fired off a signal flare, the bright flame arcing into the sky, before fading and falling into the sea. Then another was fired. Who did they hope would come to their rescue?

Distracted by attackers at the front, and in the darkness and the rain, the men in the station never saw the squad coming. Joe Goat stood ready by the back door with his sledgehammer. Paddle went round the side and tossed a grenade out in front of the house, timing it so that Joe smashed open the back door as the bomb went off.

With hats on and scarves pulled up over their faces, they came in quietly, guns raised. They caught four men in two different ground floor rooms, disorientated by the blast and aiming their rifles towards their unseen enemies out front. One turned and got off a shot, the round buzzing past Michael's ear as he fired a burst from the Tommy gun in return; three rapid barks, loud in that small space. The man collapsed to the floor, clutching his belly. Michael stared, his lips pressed together. The man might live, or he might not. The others surrendered, laying their weapons on the floor, and were herded together with the wounded man, where Del kept his own submachine gun levelled at them.

Paddle and Shay hurried up the stairs to search up there, and in the watch tower, as Michael and Joe finished searching downstairs. Coming to the last door at the end of the hall, Michael kicked it open. There were shrieks of terror, and he found a woman and three young children huddled together on the floor in what must be a storeroom. Michael pointed his gun at them for a moment, and then turned it away, feeling a sudden sense of shame at the fear on their faces. He saw bullet holes in the tiny window that faced out to the front, with matching holes in the wall above their heads. How many stray rounds had passed through this room? He silently cursed the intelligence he'd been given. There weren't supposed to be any families in the house.

'Stay put, and you won't be hurt,' he growled at them, and backed out of the room.

They didn't find the fifth man, but his colleagues

said he was out patrolling on horseback along the coast.

For the scale of the operation, it wasn't a big haul – six rifles, four shotguns and five pistols – but there was ammunition, and that was something. A hundred and fifty shotgun shells and a thousand rounds of .303 inch calibre ammunition, suitable for Lee Enfields and the Lewis machine guns. Keeping his scarf over his face, Michael waved up the local commander and his men, and they split the weapons and ammunition between them. As far as the locals were concerned, Michael's group had come ashore in a motor launch. Saying their goodbyes, he and his squad hurried back towards the pier, carrying their haul. Behind them, the coastguards were being dragged out of the house, and the woman and her children were hurrying after them, as the rebel company poured petrol out in the rooms and set fire to the building. Another symbol of the Crown's power destroyed.

The rain was heavier now, falling in thick sprays and blotting out the way ahead. Michael lagged behind the others. He kept thinking about the expressions on the faces of the children, and he grimaced in shame as a shuddering nausea came over him. He'd been assured there were only men in the station. He stopped abruptly, stepped off the path and threw up. He stayed there, bent over and dry-heaving for a minute. Then, taking some deep breaths, he wiped his mouth and continued on. Thankfully, the others had not seen his lapse in composure. They had reached the pier, and were striding out to where the *Subversive* was moored.

Michael rubbed his sleeves across his eyes, thinking he saw lights out on the sea beyond the pier. Were there some fishing boats coming in? This late, in this weather? He stared until the pattern of lights formed a vague shape. No. No, it wasn't several small boats, it was one large one with most of its lights extinguished. Out there, in the gloom, he finally made out the silhouette of a Royal Navy destroyer, bulging with gun turrets.

They must have been just out of sight offshore, and had seen the flares fired from the coastguard station. Slinging his gun over his shoulder, Michael stared running down the path, tripped and almost fell, forcing him to slow down. The others had seen the ship now, and were rushing to get on board the submarine. They did not carry torpedoes, so they were no match for a British warship. If the lookouts on the destroyer spotted the *Subversive*, they could shell it at the pier or ram it as it tried to get out to sea. He had to get his crew beneath the surface, and fast.

Less than a minute later, he was sprinting along the pier as searchlights pierced the darkness, turning the rain into a curtain of shining splinters. Kathleen was waiting for him, crouching by the hatch. He untied the lines from the mooring rings and threw them down to her. She was already untying them from the boat's cleats.

'They'll see us!' she cried out as he tossed his gun to her and climbed down from the pier onto the narrow ridge of deck on the bow of the boat. The light swept over their heads again. 'Mick, they're going to see us!'

'No, we have a chance,' he gasped, pointing up. 'The

beams will reflect back off the rain. They're blinding themselves. They're coming in on the far side of the pier, and they won't see fifty yards across the water!'

He was about to order her below when her face set suddenly with a hard resolve, she raised the submachine gun and pulled the trigger. Michael twisted round to see a man with a revolver standing above him on the pier, dressed in a coastguard's uniform. The fifth man. The .45 calibre rounds of the Tommy gun punched up into his chest, lifting him off his feet. He staggered across the cobblestones of the pier and toppled into the water near the bow of the boat. Michael stared numbly at the coastguard officer as he rose to the surface, face down, the life draining from from his limp body.

Kathleen was shaking, one hand to her mouth, as the smoking barrel of the gun dropped toward the deck. She had never shot anyone before. Michael grabbed her arm and pushed her towards the hatch. The rain on the sea and on the boat's steel plate was blotting out other sounds, but there was a dull rumble and through his feet, he felt a trembling that told him Joe Goat had the engine started. As soon as Kathleen was inside, he climbed down himself, slamming the hatch shut over his head and locking it. Standing on the small platform, he looked through the turret's deadlights and took the helm. He reversed the submarine away from the pier and turned her toward the open sea.

The destroyer was turning side on to the beach, over the only area with any depth. Michael would have to take the *Subversive* right underneath it. The beams of the searchlights still swept back and forth overhead, but they were focussed on the coastguard station and had missed the figures on the pier. They could not have guessed that there was an Irish submarine within thirty yards of their hull. Joe had already disengaged the diesel engine. Its rough rumble was replaced by a powerful, throbbing hum as the electric motor took over. Michael gave the order to dive, the intake pipes were retracted, the exhaust was shut and Kathleen pushed on the levers that tilted the hydroplanes down, driving the submarine beneath the surface.

Michael came down out of the turret into the cramped interior; curving steel walls, rows of air tanks, pipes, dials and cables illuminated by red-shaded lamps, which helped retain the crew's night-vision. Shay had control at the other helm now, sitting at the periscope, below and behind the turret, but he had to quickly lower it. Once they were deep enough to slide under the destroyer, they'd be all but blind. They navigated by chart and compass. There was no way to see at any distance underwater. They all raised their eyes as they passed under the destroyer, hearing the pounding sounds of its much, much more powerful engines . . .

Coming back to the present, there in the cave, Michael still remembered Kathleen's muffled sobs as she covered her mouth with her sleeve. Liam never knew that his mother had been an active member of the Selkies, and that had been the last time she took any part in the squad's operations. The death of that man on the pier had smothered something inside her. And only two months later, she would become a belated victim of the influenza that had already killed thousands in Ireland.

'Michael!' Liam shouted, his voice echoing around the cave. He was sitting on the edge of the hatch opening. 'Are we gonna take her for a spin, like?'

Akiko was standing inside the conning tower, her head barely visible in the turret, a giddy smile on her face. Michael smiled back, but his eyes were drawn to the shadowy figure in the bowler hat who stood behind them now, hands in his jacket pockets.

'Not for a while yet!' Michael replied to his nephew, forcing a chuckle as he stepped up onto the jetty. 'First things first. We need to get you trained in. And besides, this lady needs a crew of five . . . and we're one short.

'C'mere to me now, listen up both of you.' He waited until they were both standing in front of him. 'For most of the world, this submarine does not exist. There's a couple o' dozen people in the whole movement who knew about it, but when things were at their worst, there were a few heads who wanted to take the boat off me and use it to torpedo ships – and I wasn't having it. As far as *they* know the *Subversive* was *sunk*. Me and the crew scuttled it not long after Bloody Sunday, when we were nearly caught by the Royal Navy, and that was the end of it, do you understand? If any of the Volunteers come asking about it, the wreck of this boat is lying at the bottom of the Irish Sea, you got that?'

They gave him wide-eyed, earnest nods and with a flick of his head, Michael let them off to explore again.

'Look at them . . . that joy of life, the sense of wonder,' John said to him. 'This is how you do it. There's hope, I think, that these precious souls won't follow you down the path you took.'

Get off my back, old man, Michael thought sourly. I'll live with my choices. You're an Irishman who built a boat that could sink a dreadnought and sold it to the *bloody British*. I don't need any lessons in morality from you.

The brim of John Holland's hat was casting a shadow over his face at that moment, so Michael could not see his old mentor's expression as he thought this, but he was sure the ghost took on a greyer, more drained look.

And Michael felt foolish then, for if John was a figment of his imagination, then what was he doing, but arguing with his own mind?

Chapter 13
Contact with the Enemy

Esther took the train from Euston to Holyhead, to catch the mail boat which would take her across the Irish Sea to Kingstown Harbour, and her new posting in Ireland. Under Faulkner's direction, she was being transferred to Dublin Castle. Faulkner had seen to it that she was booked on the same train and boat as the Irish delegation, who were returning to Ireland to report to the 'President of the Irish Republic', Éamon de Valera, on the peace negotiations. Edward had told her to get close to the delegates and report anything interesting.

Esther was not convinced that this idea had any merit. Really, what did he expect her to learn? The republican peace delegates weren't likely to discuss the negotiations with some woman they'd just met, and it wasn't as if they'd be trying to take a shipment of guns across the Irish Sea, though the IRA had found other ways to smuggle arms into the country during the conflict, including one involving the Germans and a U-boat ahead of the Easter Rising in 1916.

That made her think of the incident in Belfast again. She had spoken to a contact of hers in the city, who had told her that there were no police anywhere near the moored U-boat when the hijacking took place. A squad of B-Specials, Ulster's part-time police reserves, had been attacked not far from the harbour and every policeman in the area had rushed to their aid. Which conveniently meant that there was nobody on the quays to react when an armed group was using poison gas to steal a U-boat.

The fact that the B-Specials had been targeted was noteworthy. They only operated in Northern Ireland. Formed because of the ongoing violence up there, these reserve constables were almost entirely Protestant and unionist men; enthusiastic amateurs with official arm-bands who had been given firearms and police powers, and tended to use both against Catholic nationalists. They were despised by the republicans. If the attack on the B-Specials had been carried out by the rebels as a diversion, did that mean that the republicans had been involved in the hijacking?

The idea of the Irish Volunteers stealing an *unterseeboot* was incongruous, to say the least.

The submarine was one of those that had been surrendered to the British at the end of the war. They had been considered so dangerous that, under the Treaty of Versailles, Germany had been forced to give up all of its U-boats and was forbidden to build any more. They had transformed warfare at sea, starting in September 1914, when a single submarine had sunk three of Britain's large cruisers in a single day, the *HMS Aboukir*, *Hogue* and *Cressy*. These new weapons would go on to sink 5,000 more ships over the course of the war.

Moored in the port of Harwich, most of the U-boats had been scrapped or sold to other countries. The one in Belfast had been used by the Royal Navy for training their sailors – both to learn how a U-boat worked, and how to sink one. It had been due for destruction on this very day, scheduled to be towed out into the North Sea and used as target practice for Royal Navy warships. Had the hijackers known this? *How* would they know?

If a person wanted to smuggle arms onto an island, a submarine was the best way to do it. In fact, both the unionist *and* republican paramilitaries had a history of doing secret arms deals with the Germans. But stealing a *U-boat*? Did they intend to smuggle guns, or attack British ships? This question was of particular interest to her as she crossed the gangplank onto the boat to Kingstown. During the Great War, three mail boats that she knew of had been sunk by the U-boats that prowled the Irish Sea.

However, stealing poison gas in France in order to steal a U-boat in Belfast, with the intention of sinking ships in the Irish Sea felt needlessly complicated. Irish extremists tended to stick to more direct means of murder, so she put her half-baked theory aside until she could gather more information. It was imperative that she make her way to Belfast at the earliest opportunity.

She had already spotted the Irish group gathered on the quay in the chilly, early morning gloom, and stayed as close as she could when they boarded. Accompanying the delegates were at least four lean young men with wary eyes and jackets that were heavy enough to conceal a shoulder holster or carry a pistol in the pocket. The Irish negotiators travelled with their own security, some of whom were part of Michael Collins's infamous gang of assassins, the Squad, who had been involved in the murders of the intelligence and army officers on the morning of Bloody Sunday.

Esther had only packed a small case, having already decided she would not be staying in Ireland more than a week or two. If she was forced to commit to a longer visit, she would have what she needed shipped over. Apart from the possible threat to her life, she was reluctant to commit to this transfer because it was starting to feel as if she was being sidelined. She suspected that Faulkner was sending her to Dublin to keep her out of the way, though she wasn't sure why.

This suspicion was reinforced when, within ten minutes of boarding, she spotted two other agents on the main deck, keeping watch on the Irish. She didn't know them, but they were not being very subtle. It seemed that she was surplus to requirements. But then, this whole thing was a game. It was common knowledge that the delegation were followed by British intelligence wherever they went; it was yet another way that the Prime Minister, David Lloyd George, was trying to intimidate his opponents, demonstrating the overwhelming power of Britain's empire.

As the ship rumbled away from the dock and headed out to sea, Esther regarded the busy but rather dreary port of Holyhead, noting the infrastructure built up to service the mail boats. In the darkness of early morning, the buildings' forms were defined by their lights. It got her thinking: What did one need to service a submarine? Fuel tanks, spare parts, cranes to do any kind of heavy work out of the water . . . she had seen the U-boat pens in Bruges in Belgium before they were destroyed at the end of the war. Where in Ireland could one moor a stolen Type U93 submarine without being detected? For a small country, it had a lot of coastline.

Though the country's coastguards had the most intimate knowledge of that kind, most of their stations had been attacked and burned in the conflict. The service no longer had control over Ireland's shores. How sublimely fortunate for the hijackers of that submarine.

The cold sea air made her shiver, and she wished she'd bought a better coat before she'd left. The Irish group had booked cabins, and some of them made their way inside. Two stayed out on deck, and Esther noted that they were the leaders of the delegates. There was Arthur Griffith, founder of Sinn Féin and one of the father-figures of the organisation; the moderate of this group and its most senior member. A short, stout, square-faced man with glasses and a thick moustache, intelligence reports suggested that he was doing his best to bring the violence to an end. Esther had encountered him a couple of times the year before, and she was struck by how much greyer his hair had become.

The second man was Michael Collins, younger and more ruthless, a pragmatist. He was also taller, more handsome and more charming than his colleague. He had a newer and less impressive moustache, and a relaxed posture as he leaned back against the rail, talking quietly with the older man, regularly casting his gaze out at his surroundings. His men called him 'the Big Fella', and he was the orchestrator of much of the violence in question, at least where the murdering of Dublin Castle's agents was concerned. It was so strange to see him out in public like this. Until recently, he had been one of the most wanted men in the British Empire. The service had spent so long grasping for him as if he was some ethereal, malevolent spirit, it seemed almost disappointing to see that he was a man of flesh and bone.

If Esther's enemy could be represented by just one man, it would be Michael Collins. And much as she hated what he was, she felt a thrill of danger just being this close to him.

Griffith took his leave, saying he was retiring to the cabin. He looked exhausted; no doubt drained by the stress of weeks of tense talks, the responsibility of keeping the war from starting again. Collins nodded to him. It would be a short rest, Esther knew, as the crossing would take less than three hours. Collins drew a cigarette from a pack and lit it with a match, casually touching his homberg hat in salute to the two intelligence agents who were maintaining a feigned lack of interest in the Irish men, while lingering intently.

'Alright there, leds,' he said, speaking with a Cork lilt and flashing a rakish smile. 'Give my best to Mr Churchill! Tell him I'd be awful lonely without your company.'

Esther narrowed her eyes, resenting the man's confidence, taunted by it – which was surely the intention.

To hell with it, she thought. My cover's blown in Ireland anyhow, they'll know who I am. I may never get this chance again.

Taking a cigarette from her silver case, she strolled up to Collins and leaned against the rail beside him, the cigarette held up in her left hand.

'Could I trouble you for a light?' she asked.

He hesitated for only a moment, before pulling the box from his pocket and striking a match. She cupped his hands in hers, inhaled, nodded her thanks and smiled at him through the smoke.

'Michael Collins, isn't it? The infamous scourge of Dublin Castle?'

'You get that from the newspapers, did yeh?' he asked.

'Not exactly.' She held out her free hand. 'I'm Esther Sinclair, Mr Collins, of His Majesty's Secret Intelligence Service. I'm here undercover. Would you care to join me for a stroll around the deck?'

He stared her for just a few moments, and she wondered if she'd misjudged it, then he laughed and shook her hand. Turning out his left elbow, he let her hook her arm into it, and they began walking down the deck as if they were old friends. She waved to the two intelligence agents as she passed them.

'They trail me all over London,' Collins grunted. Then slightly louder, for their audience: 'They even follow me to Mass. Isn't that right, leds? Give me enough time, and I'll make Catholics outta ye yet.'

As he left his shadows behind, he added:

'Miss Sinclair, we have a mutual friend, I believe.

Michael Regan? Though I heard you two had a bit of a run-in last year.'

So he was marking her card right at the outset. He knew who she was, and what she'd done. Then a thought hit her, and she wondered if she'd been a complete bloody idiot, missing something so obvious: Michael Regan, who was without question a member of the IRA, and possibly one of that smaller group of secret manipulators, the Irish Republican Brotherhood. Regan, whom she was sure led the Selkies, a squad that specialised in raids along the coast. A marine engineer who was very familiar with Belfast's shipyards, and who, as a young man, had trained under John Philip Holland. Holland, who had made his name at the turn of the century, building *submarines*. She wondered if Regan had travelled to France recently.

How many Irish republicans had the skills necessary to steal a U-boat? It was possible that some had served in the Royal Navy during the war, but . . . after she'd spoken to Oberleutnant Zürn, perhaps she should turn her attention to Michael Regan.

Chapter 14
Hostile Territory

Wolfgang Zürn walked along the quays on the east side of the River Lagan in the settling twilight, miserably considering his future. When his boat had been stolen, he had not only lost a submarine, but also his friends, his job and his home. The small crew had continued to live on board while in port, and when the vessel had been hijacked, most of Wolfgang's possessions had gone with her.

He felt an unsettling vulnerability now. He'd once thought that the war had numbed him to any grief he might feel again, but the loss of his friends had hollowed him out. His heart yearned for Edith and die kinder. He had only been released from police custody that afternoon, and though there was no evidence against him, it was clear that the Royal Navy no longer wanted anything more to do with him. Wolfgang was a German submariner, and that was reason enough for suspicion. A *former* German submariner, he corrected himself. His contract was up and they had washed their hands of him.

Things did not look good. How was he to find work? He had his last pay packet, and his savings in the bank.

Perhaps he should just walk straight over to Donegall Quay and catch one of the cross-channel steamers to Britain, and make his way back to Germany. Everything about this place felt different to him now – tense, and even dangerous.

The closer Ireland came to separating itself from Britain, the more the unionists – those in the north who considered themselves *British* as much as they were Irish – believed they were being betrayed by the empire. In their minds, separating Ireland from Britain was like trying to slice off Essex or Yorkshire. They were being cut off from their own nation.

Now that Ireland as a whole was being offered Home Rule, the right to have a government of their own, the unionists were feeling abandoned and desperate. They feared they would become a British minority in a land full of Brit-hating, Catholic nationalists, ruled from the Vatican by the Pope. From what little Wolfgang had seen of the south of Ireland, he could not disagree. But they had developed a siege mentality, striking out at *anyone* they considered a potential enemy. And the nationalists struck back.

Now, in a port city full of veterans of the Great War, no one was more of a potential enemy than an ex-officer of the Imperial German Navy. Anyway, this was what it had come to; Irish people shooting each other in Belfast, and he was stuck in the middle of it.

Even so, Wolfgang could not help feeling a smidgeon of satisfaction at how Britain, the glorious victors of the Great War against Germany and all its allies, was so comprehensively cocking up its affairs at home.

He made his way to *The Prince of Orange*, the pub that had become his local while he'd lived in Belfast. Josie Porter, the owner of the pub, had left him a message at the Harbour Office, saying she might have a line on a job for him. His curiosity was piqued, though his hopes were not high. He was half an hour early for the meeting, but in truth, he had nowhere else to go. Josie greeted him from behind the bar as soon as he walked in, and he was grateful for the warmth in her smile. There was a table by one of the windows, and she arrived with a pint of lager before he'd barely sat down.

'Bout ye, Wolfgang, my love,' she greeted him. 'I'm so sorry for your loss. That was an awful thing altogether. How are you holdin' up?'

'I have . . . known better days, Josie, but thank you for asking,' he said, though he tried not to show the depths of his dejection.

The woman's concern was genuine. Although Belfast had become a divided city, and Josie was a staunch unionist, she maintained that she was 'a mother to all sailors', regardless of their creed. A big-bosomed, blonde woman with a bigger personality and a voice that could put manners on the drunkest lout, she reminded Wolfgang of some of the characters in operas back in Germany. She was the type of woman stories would be written about, formidable and protective of all 'her lads', and her pub was sacred ground for the sailors who worked out of Belfast.

'That wee fella I was tellin' you about will be along

now in a while,' she told him, wiping wet hands on her apron. 'Bless my heart, you look like you're in a right state. Just let me look after these lads here and I'll come over and sit with ye for a bit.'

The man would not necessarily be a 'wee' fella, Wolfgang knew. This was just something people said here. Anything in Belfast could be 'wee', no matter what size it was. Josie moved with drama, a whoosh of arms and skirt, and was pouring more drinks within seconds, for a group of men at the other end of the bar.

The place was a shrine to those who sailed the oceans, the smells of the harbour mingling with the boozy, smoke-filled air. Apart from the nautical prints and the usual enamel signs advertising drinks, cigarettes and tobacco, there was various ships' paraphernalia hung on the walls, like anchors, bells and navigation instruments. The tables, chairs and benches were a hodge-podge mix, as the furniture in the *The Prince of Orange* went through an ongoing process of being broken and replaced. It was a rough establishment, despite the profound respect the customers had for its owner.

Wolfgang's English was nearly fluent now, though he still found anyone with a very strong accent hard to understand, and this included many of the people in Ireland. The pub was busy that evening, and as he sipped his beer, he half-listened to the conversations going on around him, most of which had to do with the shootings and bombings that were taking place across the north, despite the truce in the south and the peace negotiations in London. The hostilities had started a little over a year ago and seemed unlikely to wind up anytime soon.

If Home Rule was going to happen, unionists like Josie wanted to keep the northern counties in the Union, as part of Britain. To keep their *loyal* subjects happy, the British government had introduced a law that separated out six of the northern counties, drew out a new border, and gave them their own parliament.

On the 3rd of May 1921, the territory known as Northern Ireland was officially created.

Drawing a legal line on a map was one thing, however; trying to break a country in two was another thing entirely. After centuries of struggle, both political and violent, Ireland's nationalists were not inclined to settle for three quarters of their island.

'Some **IRA** monster threw a hand grenade onto a tram!' Josie declared, settling onto the chair opposite Wolfgang. 'Ach, can you believe it? Has everyone lost their humanity? Dear Lord, a bunch of workin' folk just tryna get on with life and someone throws a *bomb* at them. These lads really need to catch themselves on. It's a disgrace!'

Wolfgang gave a tired nod, but he had no appetite for discussing violence that evening.

'This man you mentioned, you said you know him well?' he asked.

'Aye, he's been comin' here for years. He's a *Taig* mind you, from the south, so I'd only trust him so far, but a friend all the same.'

A 'Taig' was a Catholic, or an Irish nationalist. It was not a friendly term.

'He's well regarded in the yards anyway,' Josie added. 'A parful smart man, they say, and I've always known him to be civil.'

'And he asked specifically for me? I don't understand. How does he know me?'

'He's very well informed – almost as connected as *I* am, my love! And besides, you're something of a celebrity now. Have you not seen the papers?'

She reached over to a discarded newspaper lying on the windowsill and dropped it on the table in front of him. It was yesterday's copy of *The Belfast Telegraph*. He had been in police custody for the last two days, so he hadn't seen any papers. On the front page was an article about the hijacking of his boat, along with a photograph of Wolfgang being led away from the dock by the Harbour Police. He was clearly identified in the article.

'Mein Gott,' he muttered. 'Everyone in the shipyards will see this.'

'Aye, they've put you in a right spot, so they have,' she replied, shaking her head at the stupidity of the world. 'Anybody who knows you, knows you're telling the truth, Wolfgang. And they'll sympathise with your loss. You're a sound bloke, but the peelers don't have a heap o' sense when it comes to dealin' with anythin' unusual. And if this Home Rule rubbish goes through, I wouldn't want to be the copper tryna keep order in this town. If you get a chance at workin' somewhere else, I'd take it, my love.'

Wolfgang nodded glumly. Even if you took Britain out of it, the Irish were at risk of going to war with *each other* – and he was stuck in the middle of it. He couldn't stay here any longer.

It was at that moment that a man walked into the pub. Aged somewhere in his fifties, he was of average height, in good physical condition, with a greying beard, deep-set blue eyes and square cheekbones. He was dressed in a tailored grey suit, herringbone coat, a fedora hat, and expensive but practical shoes. He was accompanied by a boy and a girl, both in their teens. The boy bore some resemblance to the man, but with sandy coloured hair, and while the man appeared fully at ease with his surroundings, the boy had the look of one who had too much energy and something to prove. Wolfgang had known many such boys in the Ubootwaffe. The military was fuelled by young men like this.

The girl was a complete contrast, Chinese or Japanese perhaps, shorter than the boy, with straight black hair in a very long plait. She had a different kind of energy to the boy too; attentive, but restrained. She had perceptive eyes, and there was no attempt to hide the curiosity on her pert, angular face. Wolfgang guessed that she'd never been in a place like this before, and she was finding the whole experience very exciting. Like the man, the boy and girl were dressed in good quality clothes and shoes.

Josey waved to the man, who took off his hat as he came over to the table, his young charges following close behind. She stood up to throw her arms around him and kiss him on the cheek, and then gestured at Wolfgang as if he was some new exhibit that gave her immense pride.

'There y'are, my love. As promised.'

Wolfgang rose slowly, and shook the hand that the other fellow offered.

'Oberleutnant Zürn,' the man said, using the proper German pronunciation, 'my name is Michael Regan. This is my daughter, Akiko, and my nephew Liam. We would like to offer our condolences on the loss of your kameraden. Mein tiefes Mitgefühl.'

Wolfgang nodded his thanks, unexpectedly moved to hear the German words spoken so sincerely.

'I apologize for my opportunism,' the stranger went on, 'but when I heard of your misfortune, it occurred to me that we might be able to help each other. I understand your contract with the Royal Navy has finished up, and I happen to be in need of a marine engineer – and I have the greatest respect for the high standards of practice in the Ubootwaffe. Josie here vouches for you; she tells me that you're a man of principle, and you were well respected by your crew, and I've never had reason to doubt her judgement.

'Oberleutnant, if I could have a few minutes of your time, I'd like to find out if you're the man I'm looking for.'

Chapter 15
The Wrong Kind of Shoes

It was already getting dark when Esther stepped out of the guesthouse that was to be her home while she was in Ireland. It was a well appointed, four-storey terraced building whose front door opened straight onto Upper Pembroke Street, one of the better parts of town. Though she was not due to report in to her superiors in Dublin Castle until the morning, she thought she would walk over and refresh her memory of the layout of the area.

She had not informed anyone of her plans, so it came as a surprise when a black Talbot motor car pulled up at the kerb just as she stepped onto the path. A man opened the passenger seat door and hopped out, tipping his hat to her. He was about her age, dressed in a smart suit and coat, with an alert, confident manner and a face that could have done with some more flesh to soften its hard, bony edges.

'Miss Sinclair? Good evening! I'm Sergeant Dennehy, Dublin Metropolitan Police,' he said in what she thought was a Louth accent, though it sounded a little off. 'Sorry to turn up out of the blue like this. Mr Eccles has asked if you'd come in this evening. There've been some developments today that he'd like to get your view on. We're to drive you up there now.'

'Developments, you say?' Esther asked, frowning. 'What developments? Relating to which situation?'

'He declined to tell us, ma'am. We're just following instructions.'

Eccles was Faulkner's man in the Castle, but she was not supposed to report to him; he didn't run any of the service's active agents. He ran a desk, across which reports passed, which he read before passing on. Nothing he did was urgent or important.

There were two other men in the car; the driver and a man in the back behind him. Like Dennehy, they were dressed in civilian clothes, rather than police uniforms. Perhaps they were from G Division, Dublin Castle's 'political crimes' section, whose remit was rebel extremists. It would be just like Eccles to send G-Men to run an errand for him. Sending three of them was overdoing it somewhat.

'Thank you, Sergeant, but I'm happy to walk,' she said. 'It's a fine evening and I was on my way over anyhow.'

'He's keen to bring you in as soon as possible,' Dennehy insisted. 'He said it was important.'

Esther chewed the side of her tongue for a moment. There was no one else in view on the street. She absent-mindedly touched the left pocket of her camel's hair polo coat, which she'd only just picked up in Clery's that afternoon. The pockets were delightfully deep.

'Very well, then. Let's not keep him waiting.'

Hooking her handbag over her right arm, she nodded

her assent and let him open the back door of the car for her. His coat was unbuttoned, and as he stretched out his arm, she caught sight of the butt of a pistol in a shoulder holster. She looked him up and down before she climbed in, and then ran her eyes quickly over his companions. They were not as smartly dressed as he was; in fact, they looked a little rough, though that could be true of some policemen.

The fellow in the back beside her was built like an ox, with wide, lumpy features and scars on his knuckles that she suspected came from bare-knuckle boxing. He had a homberg hat and a trench coat like Dennehy, though neither were worn with the same flair. From the bulge on his left side, it appeared that he too had a concealed weapon. The driver was a squint-eyed, dull-faced chap in a flat cap, and his prematurely grey hair was rather long and unkempt for a constable of the Dublin Metropolitan Police.

While the Royal Irish Constabulary enforced the law in the rest of the country, Dublin had its own police force, and unlike the RIC, they were not usually armed with anything other than a baton. They were modelled on their counterparts in London. However, since Michael Collins had started waging war against G Division, she presumed they were now being issued with firearms. Which was fine . . . assuming that these *were* G-Men.

Dennehy climbed back into the passenger seat in front of her and the driver set off.

'Only a few minutes away,' he said, turning to look over his shoulder at her. 'A bunch of us are heading to the Cairo Café after, if you're interested in joining us. First time in Dublin?'

'Yes,' she replied, in a breathy voice. 'This is my first posting abroad, actually. It's all jolly exciting.'

If they didn't know anything about her, she would give them the innocent young novice act. Most men had a natural tendency to consider a woman incapable, and Esther was always happy to use that to her advantage. The more helpless she seemed, the more they'd be likely to drop their guard.

It was Dennehy's shoes that bothered her most. If he was, as he claimed, a sergeant in the DMP, then he had spent years walking the beat as a uniformed constable – hours on his feet every day. Every experienced police officer Esther had ever met considered a pair of sturdy and comfortable shoes one the most important tools of their trade. You walked in them, ran in them and kicked with them.

Even if Dennehy was no longer on the beat, his stylish but cheap wingtips were too thin and inadequate for police work. They wouldn't last long kicking in doors or giving chase over walls. No self-respecting copper would wear those on the job. Even her own shoes had been chosen because she could walk for miles in them and still look presentable.

Also, the route the driver was taking was not in the direction of Dublin Castle. Perhaps it had been a mistake to get in the car with three armed men, but she was curious, and wanted information. They could easily have ganged up on her out on the street, and this way, she had lulled them into a false sense of security. And if a struggle was to ensue, the car would restrict their movements, what with two of them being in the front seats.

Even so, she could not help casting her mind back to the year before, on Bloody Sunday, when republican gunmen had arrived at locations across Dublin to murder British officers – and Michael Regan had shown up at her hotel.

Esther had not been issued with a weapon before leaving London, but she was not unprepared. She was carrying her own FN Model 1910 in her coat pocket; a small .380 ACP calibre, automatic pistol with a six-round magazine.

Manufactured in Belgium, it was no longer than her hand, but useful in a pinch, particularly at close quarters, and this type of gun had the rather dubious honour of having started the Great War. One of these pistols had been used to assassinate the Archduke Franz Ferdinand of Austria. Esther's had been a Christmas present from her father. Her mother had come over all faint at the sight when Esther had unwrapped the box and yelped with delight.

'Are you G Division?' she asked, eyes wide and, as if she found it ever so impressive. 'I heard there weren't many Irish G-Men left.'

'There's a few of us still hangin' in there,' the mound beside her replied, in a bass Dublin voice, though there was something off about his accent too.

'Do tell me, is Peggy Snodgrass still working on the Athlone desk?' Esther inquired. 'She's been there for years, I believe. She's a cousin of my aunt's.'

'I believe she's still there,' Dennehy said, after a beat. 'I know the name, but can't say I know her personally.'

She thought she saw his shoulders tense slightly, suddenly unsure of himself. Esther nodded, and then slipped her left hand into her coat pocket and drew out her gun. The brute beside her was the most immediate threat, so she pointed the weapon at him. He pulled back instinctively, but a cynical sneer spread over his face. Dennehy glanced back and then did a double take at the gun.

'Gentlemen, I think we must be frank with each other,' she declared. 'There is no "Athlone Desk" in the Castle, and Peggy Snodgrass is Eccles's pet parrot, so she is not in the service . . . and neither are you. Now, I'd like to know who you are and where you *think* you're taking me.'

'Or what?' the brute asked. 'You're going to shoot us with your girlie gun?'

Esther pursed her lips and, feeling that she needed to be taken seriously now, shot the man in the thigh with her girlie gun, avoiding any major arteries. Probably. He let out a very high-pitched squeal for such a big man, almost as loud as the shot itself, and when she raised the gun as if to shoot him somewhere higher up, he fumbled with the door handle, threw the door open and fell backwards out onto the road with the car still moving. Which was unexpected, but satisfying.

One down.

Dennehy snarled and lunged over the back of the seat, reaching for her gun arm. He was trying to throw his full weight onto her, so she drove her arm up, raising her elbow, and let him crunch his own nose against her forearm. He jerked back, one hand clutching his face, but kept his wits and went to punch her. She hit him first, across the cheek with the butt of the automatic, and shoved him onto the front seat. Then she pressed the muzzle against the back of the driver's head and said in a low, venomous voice:

'Turn right here, and drive down to end of the street.'

He did as he was told, and stopped on Camden Street, where she got out, keeping the gun trained inside the car.

'Now drive away, and don't look back,' she said. 'If I even see one of your faces turned my way, I'll put a bullet through it. And I can assure you, I am a crack shot.'

There were other people on the street, but if anyone thought it odd that a young woman would exit a motor car and point a pistol at the remaining occupants, they kept it to themselves. Dennehy and the driver behaved themselves, and drove away. She was sure they wouldn't go far before they tried to double back, so she pocketed her weapon, ran in the opposite direction, and waved down a taxi. Straightening her hat, she slouched down in the back seat, clutching her handbag, and let herself catch her breath and think, muttering quiet little curses as she did so.

They weren't G-Men, but they knew who she was, where she worked, and that Eccles was one of her contacts. Which meant, at the very least, that they had spies in Dublin Castle. Who could she trust now? She couldn't go there, and she didn't have anywhere else to go. What *was* all this? She needed somewhere to lie low, to work out her next move – somewhere no one in the Castle knew about. Then she smiled to herself.

'Miss? Where do you want to go?' the driver asked, having waited expectantly.

'Harcourt Street,' she said.

The man, a slumped fellow with a hangdog face, gave a reluctant wince.

'Miss, that's . . . that's two minutes walk down that lane there. I couldn't take your money for that.'

Esther thought of Dennehy and his men, probably still prowling around the area.

'I'm not in a rush,' she said. 'Take the scenic route.'

Chapter 16
Cultural Differences

The conversation between her father and Oberleutnant Zürn was likely to take some time, so Akiko asked if she and Liam could go out for a walk on the docks.

'Yes, you can, but c'mere to me,' Papa said. 'You see that fellow out there?'

Looking out through the window to where he was pointing, they saw a young man across the street, leaning against a lamp-post which was already casting a yellow glow as dusk set in. He was dressed in overalls and a flat cap, was perhaps two or three years older than Akiko, and was smoking a cigarette. His face seemed set in a faint but permanent smirk.

'He's been standing out there since before we got here,' Michael told them. 'Looks like an unsavoury character. Steer clear of him. Stay within sight of the pub. And don't let anyone hear your accents.'

'Yes, Otosan.'

'And definitely do not speak Japanese.'

'Yes, Papa.'

Akiko was intrigued to know what was so particularly unsavoury about the young man, but didn't want to ask about it in front of Zürn, and appear unworldly.

Her father often used work trips as an excuse to do some sailing with his family, and on these trips with her parents, Akiko and Liam had spent enough time in harbours around Ireland and Britain to know they could be rough places. At the same time, they could be both familiar and exciting too, and were unusual in Ireland in that you could find all manner of races and nationalities coming off the ships. Belfast was the most important port in Ireland, she had not been here since the violence had started in earnest more than a year before, and she and Liam had never had the chance to wander around on their own.

Her father's attitude towards the two cousins had changed noticeably over the last week. Though Akiko could tell that it was taking some effort on his part, and Mama was not altogether happy about it, it was clear that her parents had accepted that she and Liam had to be allowed the take some of the same kinds of chances that their folks had when they were young. They were finally realizing that the best way to keep their children safe was to let them learn how to deal with risks. Akiko had been waiting patiently for this realization, and as her okaasan was currently far away in Dublin, she intended take full advantage of the situation.

She had a passion for photography, and the camera her parents had given her for her last birthday was a gem. A Vest Pocket Autographic Kodak Special, it was small enough to fit in her handbag when folded up and could produce excellent quality photographs. Opening it, she extended the lens out like an accordion. Each film reel had eight shots, and she had a particular interest in taking pictures of everyday scenes of people, especially at work. It was her conviction that the work of ordinary people was not recorded and celebrated as it should be. She always sought out the people and occupations that were overlooked, and Belfast offered a wealth of possibilities. She had taken a dozen pictures already today, a roll and a half of film, though with the light fading, she might not get many more.

The harbour was split into three main channels, the middle one leading from the River Lagan. *The Prince of Orange* pub was near the river, and looking north-east along it, she could see out past the docks and the ship-building yards on the Victoria Channel, to the lough with its sloping sides. Beyond that was the sea. It was getting dark, and lights were already on, both gas and electric, across the port. Not far from them, a dredger was deepening the channel, emptying the mud into a long barge – earth she knew would be used to reclaim land – but all around them, activity was starting to wind down as the work day came to an end. She paused to take a photo, knowing it would be little more than an outline in this light, but might still make for a dramatic image.

'If we walk further up, we'll get a better view of the yards,' Liam said.

She agreed, so they set off in that direction, walking past shop fronts and warehouses. When she glanced back, the 'unsavoury' young man was still standing by the lamp-post. On the far side of the river, they could see two huge hulls in the yards, and another ocean liner already on the water, being completed and fitted out. Smaller ships and boats could be seen up and down the channel, the polluted stink from the river mixing with the ever-present smell of coal smoke.

'I keep thinking about the cave,' Liam said. 'It's mad that there was a secret cave right there near our house, big enough to hold a submarine. What were the chances of that?'

Akiko raised an eyebrow at her cousin.

'I think, that maybe Papa found the cave *first*, and then bought the house and land because of it?'

Liam's face made an 'Oh' expression, and nodded.

'Right, yeah. That would make sense. Da told me once that there's loads of smugglers' caves along the coast. And the locals always know to steer clear of them.' He was quiet for a moment. 'If Ma was one of the crew of the submarine, Da must have known about it. He *definitely* knows more than he's ever told me. Maybe he even helped Michael find the cave.' He made a face and kicked a stone into the river. 'They kept us in the dark the whole time. And now we're hiring a *German*. A complete stranger. I wonder how many other people knew?'

'Not many, from what he said,' Akiko replied.

She stopped to take a photograph of some slogans painted in white paint on a high brick wall. Illuminated by a streetlight, it was possibly just bright enough for the film to capture the lettering. One line was 'ULSTER WILL FIGHT AND ULSTER WILL BE RIGHT', while another said 'HOME RULE IS ROME RULE'.

One of the Protestant unionists' fears was being part of an Ireland they knew would be ruled by the Catholic church. Akiko, who only pretended to be Catholic for school, and had suffered in Ireland for her 'pagan' beliefs, had some sympathy with the sentiment.

'It must have been a hard secret to keep,' she added. 'Papa says a lot of the republican leaders didn't even know about it. Sure, if the British found out that the rebels had a submarine, they would have turned the country upside down looking for it. Like he says, the more people know, the greater the risk. Even now, when everyone thinks the submarine was sunk, someone might still let it slip. I do think he's taking a big chance, trusting a stranger.'

Liam grunted in agreement. Akiko noticed that he was staring at something and followed his gaze. Across the road, two men were walking in the same direction past an ironmongers shop, at a pace that suggested that they did not have a destination, that the walk was the reason they were here. They were looking about them in a way that gave the impression that this duty was both important and boring. Though they were in civilian clothes, they wore police caps and a band on their arms.

'B-Specials,' Liam muttered, scowling. 'Look at them, the louts.'

Akiko did look. She could see nothing particularly sinister about them, but knew that, like the Black and Tans, these men of the 'Special Constabulary' were not real policemen. With almost no enforcement training, they had been armed and rushed into service in response to the violence in the north – and had made things worse. They had all been recruited from the unionist side of the community; in fact, many were also members of the Ulster Volunteer Force, the unionist equivalent of the Irish Republican Army. And Britain, instead of treating them as criminals as they did with the Irish Volunteers, had given them uniforms, guns and police powers. As part-timers, they tended to patrol in the evenings. Still, they were part of Belfast's story, and Akiko went to take a photograph, but then hesitated. There wasn't enough light, and there would be no point anyway, while they were moving. She considered going over and asking them to stand under a light so she could take their picture.

To her astonishment, Liam stooped to pick up a stone and then hurled it at the men. As it hit one of them on the back, she thumped his shoulder.

'Oh. My. God. Have you *lost your mind*?!'

The men spun round and came running towards them. Akiko and Liam only hesitated for a second before they turned and started sprinting away. The men were both much older than the teenagers, though they could certainly run well enough. *The Prince of Orange* was a few hundred yards away, and though the two cousins were extending their lead, they could hear the beat of the men's boots behind them, a long blast on a whistle and the order to stop where they were.

'Idiot!' Akiko snarled at her cousin, as he started to race ahead of her. 'Is there anyone you *won't* pick a fight with!'

'I'm sorry-I'm sorry-I'm sorry,' he panted. 'Can you not run any faster?!'

Not for the first time, she wished Liam's brain worked as quickly as his hands and feet, but Akiko was still paying enough attention to her surroundings to see that the lad who'd been standing by the lamp-post had tossed his cigarette and was striding away, hands in pockets, hat pulled low and head hunched down.

Her father must have spotted them through the window, because he emerged from the door of the pub, a stern look on his face, his hands loose by his sides, and started striding to meet them. The German came out behind him.

'What's going on here?' Michael asked, and Akiko immediately noticed that his accent was now entirely American, without a trace of his usual Cork lilt. 'What have you kids been doing? Can't I let you out on your own for ten minutes without you makin' trouble?'

Liam opened his mouth to reply and Michael took his shoulder, squeezed it hard, and murmured:

'Not a word, son. Don't say a word.'

Akiko was a few yards behind Liam, and she darted around behind her father, leaning back out to look back at the B-Specials. Michael had his hand up, greeting the two constables as they came running up.

'Are these your kids?' one of them demanded. He was a tall fellow, with a long handsome face, but bad teeth.

'They are, sir,' Michael replied. 'Can I ask why they're being pursued by the law?'

'One of them threw a stone at us,' the other replied. This one was the same size and shape as her father, with a pointy face and bushy, mutton chop sideburns.

'A grievous act indeed,' Michael declared. He slapped the back of Liam's head, nearly knocking his hat off. 'That would have been my nephew here. My humblest apologies, gentlemen. He'll be suitably disciplined. As God is my witness, I won't have my family showing disrespect for officers of the law.'

'You're American?' the fellow with bad teeth said, giving Akiko's father the eye. 'Are you *Fenians*, is that it? Some Yanks are. What brings you to Belfast?'

'A mixture of business and pleasure!' Michael assured him. He pulled a business card from his breast pocket and handed it over. Regan Marine Engineering had a factory in Ireland and two in the United States and, from the cream colour of the card, Akiko knew this was one with the American addresses on it. 'I'm Michael Regan, gentlemen, marine engineer. My company makes engines and pumps for boats, and there's no better place to do that kind of business than your fine city. And since I was coming here, I thought it would be a chance for my children to see one of the world's greatest ports!'

'And let them peg stones at police constables?' Mutton Chops growled.

'Is this true, darlin'?' Michael asked Akiko. 'Was your simpleton of a cousin at it again?'

'He didn't mean anything by it, Papa,' she replied, also giving her American accent full rein. 'You know how he can be. Hasn't the sense that God gave a horse.'

Liam opened his mouth to protest, only to be silenced by another squeeze on the shoulder.

'The boy's not right in the head,' Michael explained,

nodding sadly. 'And a dullard to boot. And he's *mute*. Doesn't speak a word. Hasn't been right since he fell out of that tree some years ago. Breaks my heart. But what can I say? He lost his parents some time back and he's my responsibility now.'

'Well simpleton or not, he needs to learn some respect,' Bad Teeth retorted. 'A man's got to take responsibility for raisin' his children right.'

'Quite so,' Michael replied, and Akiko was surprised by his submissive manner. 'Quite so. I apologize again, constables. As I say, he'll be disciplined. My thanks for your understanding.'

He was turning away when Mutton Chops held up his hand.

'Hold on a second. Who's this other fella? I know him from somewhere.'

Bad Teeth stepped to the side to see past Michael and get a better look at Zürn.

'Aye, it's that German fella. The one from the U-boat.' He addressed Michael. 'You got business with this man?'

'They've got business together all right. They were discussin' it in the pub,' another voice said from behind Zürn. It was an older man, also dressed in the police cap and armband of a B-Special. 'And I'd surely like to know what that business was . . . and why they were discussin' it in *German*.'

This man had an air of command about him, a hostile look on his hard, leathery face, and he was pointing a Webley revolver at Wolfgang Zürn.

Chapter 17
The War Hero

Liam twisted round to lay eyes on this third constable. The boy was already fuming because of his uncle's comments about him, and though he'd been sensible enough to hold his tongue and let Michael handle this situation, something told him that it would take more than a bit of bluster and a business card to deal with this new threat. This older lad had a look about him that Liam knew all too well, because it was an urge he constantly had to control in himself.

This fella wouldn't be happy until he got to lay into someone.

The aggression was written deep into the hateful lines in his face, displayed in the tense stance of his body. Here was a man for whom a cap and an armband was a dream come true; a license to bully, and to use a baton or a gun on the flimsiest excuse.

'I didn't spend my best years fightin' the bloody Krauts at sea, only to come home and listen to that swine's language spoken right here in my local,' the man hissed, his left eye twitching slightly, but his gun-hand dead steady. 'Thought you were keepin' it quiet, you did, but I could hear well enough. And days after someone stole a German submarine right from off our docks. Somethin's goin' on here. You're an American? And how it is you speak German, eh?'

'A smattering only,' Michael said carefully, raising his hands. 'I grew up among immigrants in New Jersey, sir. I speak a bit of German just as I speak some Italian, Spanish and French. Because that's what people spoke around me. And I have some Japanese, thanks to my beloved wife. In this case, I have business with this man, and I wanted to put him at ease. It's nothing more significant than that.'

'*I'll* decide what's *significant*. Put your hands up, the lot o' yez!' His twitch got worse when his temper flared. He jutted his chin at the other two constables. 'You two, search them.'

'Yes, Sergeant!'

Mutton Chops and Bad Teeth were quick to obey. Liam was frisked briskly, but out of modesty, they left Akiko alone. Then Zürn and finally Michael himself. In a holster underneath the back of Michael's herringbone coat, Teeth found a .45 Colt automatic. Liam's eyes widened when the constable pulled out the gun, and the B-Specials immediately reacted with suspicion.

'What are you doin' carryin' a gun?' Twitch asked, taking the weapon.

'I'm an American abroad, gentlemen,' Michael replied, spreading his raised hands as he shrugged. 'Why would I *not* have a gun?'

Mutton and Teeth both chuckled at this, but Twitch

was not amused. Without warning, he lashed out, catching Michael across the side of the head with the handle of the gun, heavy with a magazine of lead bullets. The blow was enough to knock Michael to his knees.

'This ain't the wild west, sunshine. We don't care for cowboys walkin' round our city with loaded weapons. Between your lot and the Krauts, those Fenian bastards have got themselves a right wee arsenal, and I reckon you're here for more of the same business.' Hefting the Colt in his left hand and the Webley in his right, he pointed the other two constables towards Zürn. 'You two lads hold that Boche swine, while I knock some answers out of this bawbag.'

His fellow officers did not look comfortable with this.

'The lad only chucked a wee stone, Sarge . . .' Mutton Chops began to say.

'That's enough outta you!' the sergeant snapped. 'See to that Kraut!'

As Michael raised his hand in defence, trying to stagger to his feet, Twitch pulled the Colt back with his left, to deliver another blow . . . and Liam swung a punch over the man's right arm, driving his fist with all his might into the man's face. It caught Twitch on the cheekbone, just below the eye, and the sergeant's head rocked back and he stumbled sideways under the force of the strike. Liam didn't give him a chance to recover. In a fighting rage now, he slapped the Webley out of the man's hand and shoved him before he could regain his balance, sending him sprawling to the ground. The Colt clattered away, and the other two constables fumbled for their own weapons.

'Liam, *NO!*' Michael bellowed at him.

But the boy's blood was up, and he wasn't to be stopped. He went after the sergeant, not giving him a chance to get up, laying in punches to his head and chest. The older man might have overpowered the teenager if he'd had a chance to recover, but Liam didn't give him that chance, and the man was bleeding from his nose and a split lip as he scrambled backwards. Mutton Chops was drawing his gun from his holster when Michael grabbed his gun-hand and held it down, coming up from his knees to shoulder-charge the man, ramming him into the wall behind him and knocking the wind out of him.

Meanwhile, Teeth had pulled out his gun, letting go of Zürn to level the pistol at Liam. There was a loud crack. Liam spun round in fright and the constable flinched, for it was not his gun that had fired. Instead, Zürn was standing there with the .45 Colt in his hand, and a red stain was blossoming on the policeman's white shirt over his collarbone and Akiko screamed.

'Wha . . . ?' the man gasped, before taking a few faltering steps back and sliding down against the wall, hand pressed to the wound. 'God, lads. I'm *shot* . . .'

'Jesus, that's done it,' Michael rasped, snatching the gun off Zürn. 'Run. *Run, all of you!* We'll have the whole bloody city down on us in a few minutes.'

And then they were running, though Liam had no idea where they were supposed to run to, and was sure nobody else did either. Behind them, a police whistle sounded, and he knew it wouldn't be long before the two other constables would be able to give chase, assuming they didn't stay with their comrade. So the four fugitives ran, crossing a railway line and sprinting down one alleyway after another, trying to keep to the shadows. Zürn took the lead, as he knew the place best, though the police would know it even better. The darkness would help, but not for long. The docks blocked their way north and the river blocked the west.

'Regan!' a voice called out from a doorway as they passed it. 'Regan, in here!'

Michael paused for just a second, and the others slowed down to the see a young lad leaning out and waving to them. It was the same fellow, his full-cheeked face lifted in a smirk, who'd been watching them across the street from the pub, the one in the flat cap and the overalls. Michael nodded and headed for the door. They all slipped inside and the door was closed behind them.

'It's Seán, isn't it?' Michael asked, and to Liam's surprise, the boy nodded. 'Right then, lead on.'

They were in a short hallway that opened into a couple of offices, but Seán took them through another door that led into a large goods shed. Walking down an aisle between stacks of wooden crates, they came to the far side of the building, where Seán motioned at them to wait while he checked outside. Liam's curiosity was tormenting him. How did Uncle Michael know this lad? Had he recognized him outside the pub? Why hadn't he said so then?

'I didn't want this,' Michael growled, as if guessing

his nephew's thoughts. 'We were supposed to stay out of all this.'

'Stay out of what?' Liam asked.

'I shot that man,' Zürn was saying, holding his hands up to his face. 'I *shot* him.

'In the shoulder,' Liam said. 'He'll live.'

'It won't matter to them,' the German retorted. 'They still have the hate from the war. There will be no prison for me. They will kill me for this.'

'You probably saved that boy,' Michael told him. 'We're in your debt, sir.'

'Someone's coming!' Akiko hissed.

But it was only Seán returning. He gestured at them to follow him again, and he took them across the road to the cobblestoned dock beyond, where a small steam freighter was moored.

'Here, wait a moment,' Michael said, touching Liam and Akiko, and waving to Zürn to go ahead. 'Now listen, you're not to utter a word about the *Subversive*, y'hear? Remember, anyone else who knew about it thinks it was scuttled, and I want to keep it that way.'

'Yes, Papa,' Akiko said, but Liam frowned. Who were they about to meet?

They hurried after Zürn, up the gangplank and onto the deck, where a small group of men was standing waiting for them.

'Mick Regan, as I live and breathe!' the foremost man said, in voice that hailed from somewhere in Tipperary. 'What brings ye to Belfast?'

There was something familiar about this fellow. He

was tall, well over six foot, and solidly built with it. He had a pipe in his hand, and as he barked the words, smoke billowed dragon-like from the small, thin-lipped mouth barely visible beneath the thick handlebar moustache. His long face was cut into trenches, deep vertical lines that also gathered in the area between his bushy eyebrows, though Liam guessed he was no older than his forties. The grey eyes were small and far apart, and opened a little too wide, bestowing an intense look, and a receding widow's peak gave him a high forehead. His dark hair was oiled back, but still managed to be untidy, and Liam sensed from the earnest directness of the man's gaze and the way he held himself that this was not a fellow to be trifled with.

'Hello Jim,' Michael replied. 'I don't suppose I need to ask why you're here?'

'I don't suppose yeh do! And look at you Mick, same as ever; never *quite* managing to be respectable. Come aboard there, folks! Let's get you out of sight before that Prod rabble set eyes on yez. Get yourselves below decks there, and we'll cast off.' Addressing the young man who'd led them aboard, he added: 'Good man, Seán. Tip up to the captain there, and let him know we've got some additional passengers. Tell him that's us now, he might need to set out a little earlier than planned.'

It was only then that Liam recognized this fellow, for he'd only ever seen the one photograph of him that was used in all the newspapers. A man who was only slightly less infamous, and hated by the British even more, than Michael Collins himself.

'Holy God,' he gasped. 'You're Grim Jim Gorey!'

The man laughed, and some of the other lads behind him smiled at the boy's reaction.

'Jaysus, are they still using that nickname? I'd thought they were done with that,' Gorey grunted, and leaned in close to Liam, making an exaggeratedly hurt expression. 'Tell me now, do I seem all that "grim" to you?'

Grinning, he didn't wait for an answer, and Michael pushed Liam towards an open door. They needed to get off the deck before the police spotted them.

'You're getting under way? Where are you headed?' Michael asked as he came up to Gorey and shook his hand.

'We're bound for Southampton, so we can drop you at Howth if you want,' the Tipperary man replied. He had a flat cap in his hand, and now he pulled it on and slapped Michael's back. 'But sure lookit, we should get you below and brew some tea – or coffee. I know you're into that foreign stuff. It's good to see you again, me oul' segotia! It's been too long.'

'That it has.'

'Who's your friend?' Gorey tipping his head towards the German.

'A man who needs to get out of Belfast in a hurry. I'll tell you all about it.'

As they were herded through the doorway, Liam was still trying to get his head around the fact that his uncle knew Grim Jim Gorey. In fact, he didn't just know him – they were *friends*.

Gorey was a living legend in the movement and a hero to Liam's father. There had been dozens of news articles, of course, but Lar had told Liam stories only shared among the Volunteers, about the man who was a veteran of the Great War and the 1916 Rising. After forming one of the first flying columns in the country, he became one of the most prominent leaders in the IRA, conceiving of ever more devious ways of attacking the occupying forces. The authorities had managed to find him three times because of informers, and sent in the Auxilaries, only for him to escape every time. Gorey had been wounded in action at least six times in his life, and it was said of him that he had so many bullets and pieces of shrapnel in him, that he rattled when he walked.

He had built a reputation for being fearless, cunning, ruthless and downright impossible to kill. He was a kind of Robin Hood figure, often described as wielding his distinctive C96 Mauser in action, the machine pistol nicknamed 'Peter the Painter'. He was loved by the Irish and hated by the Crown forces. And now Liam was on board a ship with this hero, his own fists still bloody from a fight with the B-Specials. He felt a warmth in his chest, his heart beating hard. He rubbed his eyes, wondering if he was going to cry.

This was turning out to be the best day of his life.

Chapter 18
Undervalued, Underestimated and Undercover

After spending half an hour being driven around the city in the taxi, Esther got out and knocked on the door of a house on Harcourt Street. Like the guesthouse she could not return to, this was the kind of Georgian, four-storey terraced building that was common in the centre of Dublin. She had only been here once before, and it had been a short visit. She expected this one to be somewhat longer.

The door was opened by a rather shrivelled woman whose greying hair was tied back in a bun so tight, it suggested she was trying to pull her wrinkled face taut. It was a severe, but not unkind face, and the woman regarded Esther with interest, probably wondering why a young lady was calling here alone after dark.

The landlady was polite enough, though there was a wariness about her towards this stranger that you often found in a proprietor whose tenants were all women. After Esther introduced herself as a friend of Lizzy Noonan however, the woman let her in. The door she was looking for was on the top floor. That floor was divided into two small flats, taking up the width of the building. She knocked on the right-hand door, and it opened quickly. No doubt the occupant had heard her footsteps on the creaky stairs.

The woman who stood there was shorter and older than Esther, though her slim frame and soft white face of rounded shapes made her look younger than her thirty-four years. There had been an expectant expression on those features that stiffened instantly into a scowl as she saw who was at her door. Esther realized she'd probably have to get used to this reaction from people she'd known, now that she was back in Ireland.

'What do you want?' the woman demanded

'And a very good evening to you too, Lizzy. How have you been? Aren't you going to ask me in?'

'I asked what you *want*, Sinclair.'

'I've had a spot of bother, and I need your help. Don't worry, your secret's still safe with me . . . for now, at least.'

The implied threat got her some cooperation, and Lizzy Noonan stood aside to let the British intelligence agent into her flat, patting down her mousey brown hair, which looked recently released from tight bonds. It was a small place; a square little living-room, with an even more compact bedroom leading off it. In one corner was a gas stove and a cupboard that together served as the kitchen. There was no bathroom. Instead, there was a basin and jug of water on a pine sideboard. The building had started off as a house before being broken into flats, so presumably they all shared the one bathroom, with perhaps another lavatory in the back yard. She wondered how many residents there were in total.

Despite being a modest affair, the flat was neat, warm and civilized, and though the furniture was cheap and somewhat ragged, Esther had stayed in much worse places. She was confident of Lizzy's hospitality, because Lizzy was in her debt, as was her daughter Agnes, a girl of fifteen who sat at the table next to the stove, studying a schoolbook. They had not met before. The lass had her mother's baby-faced looks, and the same suspicious stare. She'd heard the English accent. Esther gave her a smile, which was not returned. The girl was watching Lizzy's reaction.

Esther's decision not to report Michael Regan for his assault on her could have landed her in hot water with her superiors, but it had not been the first time she had chosen to omit key facts from a report. When she had last been posted in Ireland, she had infiltrated Cumann na mBan, 'the Irishwomen's Council'. Women were not permitted to join the Irish Volunteers, so they had formed their own organisation in 1914, which performed all of the same roles as the Volunteers, short of actually shooting people or blowing them up, though some women stepped across that line too, during the Rising in 1916. They were messengers, smugglers and thieves. They provided safe houses, food, clothing and weapons to men on the run, as well as tactical information and medical treatment.

And they engaged in espionage.

It was a woman's eternal curse to be undervalued and underestimated by the men in their world, but Irish women had turned that to their advantage. Lizzy Noonan was just such a woman. When she'd got a job as a typist in the garrison adjutant's office in Dublin Castle, she had been recruited by Michael Collins to pass on any intelligence information she came across. For more than a year, Lizzy had worked as an agent for the rebels, right at the very centre of British military power in Ireland.

Esther, who had no illusions about the threat that women represented, had discovered this unlikely spy . . . and then had chosen not to expose her. Though it was not her habit to defy her superiors – on any *significant* matter – she had learned all about Lizzy and her situation.

The young Irishwoman was married, but her husband had run off years earlier, leaving her to raise their daughter on her own. They had no other family. If Lizzy was arrested and imprisoned, her daughter would mostly likely end up in an institution, and Esther had heard discussion about these places in Cumann na mBan meetings. They were, by all accounts, truly ghastly, particularly for young girls. Taking pity on Lizzy, she had visited the woman and laid out the facts to her. She could give up her job in Dublin Castle and avoid any further work that brought her into contact with the Crown forces, or Esther could report her, and she could face the wrath of the G-men. The same fate would befall her if she mentioned this conversation to anyone.

Lizzy had no choice but to agree. She quit her job and found a new position in a printing company with no access to anything important. The two women had both assumed they would never see each other again.

And yet now here they were, face to face once more.

'What. Do. You. Want?' Lizzy asked for a third time.

Esther glanced towards Agnes, and Lizzy gave an impatient flick of her hand.

'You can talk in front of her. She knows.'

They started training their revolutionaries early in Ireland.

'I need a place to stay for the night,' Esther replied frankly. 'I need to know if I've been targeted by the Dublin Brigade or by Collins's lot. I need help finding someone. And I could absolutely murder a cup of tea.'

'Why don't you just go to the Castle?'

'Because three men just tried to kidnap me on my way to the Castle. They might even have been out to kill me, I don't know. The place is clearly as compromised as it has ever been. I've only just come back to Dublin, and I don't know who to trust.'

The Irish woman frowned at the mention of the attempted kidnapping. This was why Esther had been confident she could trust the ex-spy. Lizzy had a particular contempt for men who were violent towards women. There were limits to what she would tolerate for the cause.

'They can't have been Volunteers. The lads are abidin' by the truce.'

'Now Lizzy, let's not pretend that every republican marches to the beat of the same drum,' Esther said. 'You have everyone from communists to fascists fighting for different dreams of Ireland, and the only thing holding them all together is their hatred for the British. You have splinter groups and you know it. These particular chaps were posing as G-men. I know they weren't, but they put on a good show. I've been here for one day and they knew who I was and where to find me. Lizzy, this is important. I'm investigating something that could lead to the death of a lot of people if I don't find out what's going on.'

'What do you mean? Somethin' our lot are doing? Where did you hear this? Sure, the truce is on. The negotiations. Jesus, we've been years tryin' to get you to listen to us. Why would we want to balls that up now?'

'*I don't know*, Lizzy. That's why I'm here. What about up in Belfast . . . and Derry? Nobody's listening to anyone up there at the moment.'

Lizzy sighed and shook her head in exasperation, and in truth, Esther didn't know enough about anything to work out who had taken the poison gas or why. If it was connected to the hijacking of the U-boat however, it could be a rebel group with the expertise and resources to carry out two very different kinds of large scale operation, and that in itself was worth investigation. Because if they were defying the truce, then anyone connected to the British forces or the government could be a target. If Lizzy was to be of use to her however, the Irishwoman needed a reason to get involved.

Esther saw that she was already unsettled; things were still very fraught in Dublin between the two sides, and having a known British agent show up at her home must have shaken her badly. The woman had worked directly for Michael Collins; she knew what happened to informers . . . though Esther suspected she had been rather infatuated with that charismatic scourge, and probably still was. And Collins would be heading back to London after the weekend, the heart of enemy territory, negotiating for Ireland's future.

'If there's a major attack, it could break up the peace talks,' Esther said, breathlessly. 'It can't be sanctioned by your commanders. It could all go to Hell, Lizzy. I have to get to Belfast, there's a man I need to speak to there. I'll be getting the train tomorrow. I just need somewhere to stay tonight. I can sleep on the floor. I don't suppose you have a telephone?'

'Listen to this one! A *telephone*, indeed! I'm a secretary in a print shop, darlin'. How could I afford a telephone?'

'Never mind. There's one more thing; I need to find out if a man named Michael Regan is currently at home in Cork. His wife is a member of Cumann na mBan, and a major donor. Members down there will know about her – she's Japanese.'

'You're talking about Midori Regan?'

'You know her?'

'She came to Dublin to run swimmin' classes for our members a while back. She was a pearl diver when she was young – an extraordinary woman. Swims like a seal. Like you say, it's not every day you meet someone from Japan . . .'

Yes, thought Esther. Michael met Midori in Japan while he was working with her father there . . . assembling *submarines* built for the Imperial Japanese Navy by the Electric Boat Company in the United States. After they married, she had moved back to America with him, and then to Ireland, where Midori had taken up her husband's cause with a passion.

'. . . But listen, I'm not about to start reportin' on our members, if that's what you're askin',' Lizzy went on. 'I kept out of the spyin' like you told me, but I'm drawin' the line there.'

'This isn't a *request*, Lizzy,' Esther said sharply. 'There are lives at stake here. You still work in that printing company, you say? The one on Crow Street? Why, that's just down the road from the Castle. I don't imagine a *police raid* would be good for business, would it? What do you think? Are any of your friends still active? I seem to remember Kitty O'Doherty having her fingers in quite a few pies. Probably wouldn't be too happy to have a visit from the peelers, would she?'

Lizzy blanched, and cast an embarrassed look at her daughter, who was studiously fixed on her book. Then the woman shuddered and shook her head submissively, and Esther felt rather like a bully at that moment, conscious of how she appeared to that young girl. But she did not have time for niceties.

'I just want to know if the Regans are currently in Cork,' she pressed the woman. 'They travel to America most years, and they often go away on sailing trips. After Belfast, I have to find Regan, and I don't want to venture into that wasps' nest of a county only to find they're not home. And the sooner I find out, the sooner I'll leave you alone.'

'How am I supposed to find that out without someone gettin' suspicious?'

'You're an eminently resourceful woman, Lizzy. I have faith in you.'

Lizzy looked close to tears, though there was only hostility in her stare as she took her coat from the hook on the wall. Esther removed her own coat, but instead of hanging it on the hook, she draped it over the back of the armchair where she sat down, so that her gun remained within easy reach, and dropped her handbag on the floor beside it.

'I'll see what I can find out,' Lizzy muttered as she opened the door. Then to her daughter, she added: 'I have to go out for while, love. Mind what you say to this woman. Don't trust her an inch.'

And then she was gone, the door slamming behind her. There was a tense silence in the room as Esther was left alone with Agnes, before the girl stood up, her hands clasped in front of her.

'Would you like a cup of tea?'

'That would be splendid, thank you. One sugar and a drop of milk.'

'Are you really a British spy?' the girl asked, as she opened the cupboard by the stove.

Esther arched an eyebrow at her.

'A real spy never tells, my dear. What about you? Still in school?'

'Yes. Well . . . durin' the week. Mam says every girl needs an education . . .'

'She's right too,' Esther said.

'. . . But on the weekends I work in a hotel. I'm a chambermaid.'

Esther recalled that day the year before, when Michael Regan had appeared at her hotel door. Oh, *of course* you are, she thought sourly.

Chapter 19
Keeping Out of the Way

Akiko, Michael, Liam and Oberleutnant Zürn had to stay below decks until the ship, the *Medusa*, was under way and had left the port behind, gushing smoke from its single funnel. As they cruised out into the lough, making for open sea, Michael told his daughter and nephew they could go out on deck, but they were not to get in the way of the crew. Jim Gorey added that parts of the ship were out of bounds, as they were not safe for children, and that they should check with the sailors before wandering anywhere beyond the main deck or the galley. And though he was not a member of the crew himself, he spoke with the tone of a man used to deference and obedience.

Akiko was keen to do some wandering and take some photographs if she could, but Liam was clearly intent on staying put, mesmerised as he was by the presence of this infamous warrior. Nor was the oberleutnant in the mood for exploring. Shooting that policeman had left him in low spirits, and one of Gorey's men had offered him a drink of rum down in the galley to help settle his nerves. Being left alone didn't bother Akiko; she was used to doing things on her own.

She made her way forward to the foredeck, leaning against the gunwale, listening to the dull, booming chug of the steam engines and feeling the gentle motion of the water under the hull. She loved the sea air on her face, so tangy and fresh after the smog of the city. The sky was overcast, and looking ahead, to the north, there was nothing but darkness. There was little to see below her except the white foam where the hull cut through the water. She had sailed with her father along this stretch of coast and had studied it on maps. Out of sight to her left, as they emerged from the wide mouth of Belfast Lough, was the much more enclosed inlet of Larne Lough. There was nothing out in the gloom that she could photograph.

It was clear that the men she'd seen with Gorey when she'd come aboard were not part of the crew. A ship's crew tended to be busy when leaving or entering a harbour, and the six men she'd seen with Gorey had played no part in the work. Instead, they were scattered around the main deck, staring out to sea, like her, or sitting in the galley, drinking with Oberleutnant Zürn. She thought about Grim Jim Gorey, and how it was a strange thing to be passing the Larne headland in the company of what must be a whole squad of republican guerilla fighters and a German sailor.

It was at Larne that one of the defining events of this conflict had taken place. Back in 1912, before the Irish Volunteers had existed, the unionists of Ulster had reacted in shock as the government in London offered

Home Rule to Ireland. It would mean a limited kind of independence and a government sitting in Dublin, but with Britain still holding most of the power. Those loyal to King and Country in the north still felt bitterly betrayed by the politicians in Westminster, however. Declaring that they would not be ruled from Dublin or separated from Great Britain, 100,000 men signed up to a new organisation founded by a man named Edward Carson in 1913, called the Ulster Volunteer Force, swearing to take up arms against the government if they had to, to resist Home Rule.

It was an extraordinary thing. The first paramilitary threat towards the British government in this century came not from republicans, but from *unionists*. It was only after this that the Irish Volunteers were formed in response.

The UVF quickly backed their words up with actions, and started smuggling in weapons. Then, over the night of the 24th and 25th of April, 1914, they pulled off a massive operation led by Major Frederick Crawford. The unionists landed a shipment of 25,000 rifles and three million rounds of ammunition at Larne and at two other ports. The arms had been bought in Germany, and when they were unloaded, they were distributed onto six hundred cars, lorries and horses and carts.

Despite Britain's control over Ireland, the ship was not stopped by the coastguard or the Royal Navy. None of the men or vehicles on shore were seized by the police or the army.

In the sea, in the darkness, Akiko imagined the excitement of that night; the daring, the sheer scale of the operation and how many people it would have taken, all to prepare a paramilitary army formed to resist its own government. It had been a great propaganda success too, reported across the newspapers afterwards, and it made the newly formed Irish Volunteers conscious of just how woefully under-equipped their men were in comparison. That day in Larne was an omen that, sooner or later, violence would burn its way into Irish politics once more.

And now she was wondering if there were any arms being smuggled on board *this* ship. It wouldn't make sense, of course. They were heading *away* from Belfast, where the guns would be needed, so surely whatever might have been here had already been delivered. Still, though . . . Gorey and his men were on their way somewhere, so it was worth a poke around. Learning of her father's hidden history had only fed her appetite for uncovering secrets.

The darkness helped, with most of the deck lit only by the running lights and portholes. She floated around until she saw a chance to slip in through a door unnoticed, so that no one would be sure if she was up on deck or not. Her father's company made pumps and engine parts for ships, and she had been on several commercial vessels in her short life, so she was familiar with the basic layout. Finding herself in a passageway, she headed aft. It was much brighter here, with the regularly-spaced electric lights. On the way to the stern, there would be the boiler room, engine room, gear room, and the steering gear compartment, in that order. She decided to go right to the end, start at the steering gear and work her way forward.

Twice, she had to duck out of sight into doorways as men came striding down the passage. Then, as she was passing the door to the engine room, it opened and a man stepped out. He was wearing stained blue overalls, and his sweat-soaked, cherubic face was grubby, creased with paler lines around his eyes and mouth where the grime had not rubbed in. He was wiping oil off his hands with a cloth, and froze when he saw her, staring at her with wide, panicked eyes. Her first instinct was to run, to try and avoid getting into trouble, and then she recognized the face beneath the dirt.

'Mr Gogarty?' she said. 'It *is* you, isn't it? Joe Goat? It's me, Akiko. You're a friend of my father's?'

This was one of Papa's old squad, the man who had once helped run the *Subversive*. Her father had said he'd quit and found a job on a ship. If he was working on this ship, he evidently hadn't given up on the fight for Ireland. He didn't strike her as rebel material, however. The man was still staring, and turning his head as if wishing he could look away, but was unable to. He seemed genuinely scared of her.

'Are you real?' he asked in a hushed voice.

'Of course,' she replied. 'Why would I not be real? Didn't you know we were on board?'

Joe Goat held out his hand, tentatively, as if needing to confirm that she was solid, and yet was fearful of touching her. She took the hand and shook it, as she would if they were being formally introduced. He pulled away when he saw his filthy, oily hand touching her clean pale one, and winced an apology.

'Akiko? Dear girl, is that really you?'

'Yes, it is,' she assured him again. 'Why wouldn't you think I was real?'

'And Michael, your . . . your otosan . . . he's *here*, on the ship, pet?'

'Yes. Do you want to come up and meet him? He'll be so happy to see you.'

'No. No, I don't think I will.' He twisted the cloth tightly in his hands. 'I don't really go on deck. I prefer to stay down here. What are you doing here, lass?'

'I'm sorry, I was just having a look around. I'm . . . I'm a sailor. I'm interested in ships.'

His expression relaxed, and he gave her a welcoming smile, instantly more comfortable as the subject turned to the vessel.

'She's an old girl, taken a beating over the years, but still up for anything. Nearly two thousand tons, two triple expansion steam engines . . . here, do you . . . do you want to have a look?'

His manner was that of a man who was introducing a prospective bride to his parents, all nerves and pride, and it seemed like a perfect opportunity for a bit of in-depth exploring.

'Yes, I'd like that very much,' she said, with a grin.

Through the door, she was immediately struck by the heat, the noise, and the smell of steam and hot oil. It was a typical engine room, all pipes, taps and valve wheels centered around the two massive engines. They descended some steel stairs to the deck and, as if performing some religious ritual, Goat brushed his hand against the wheel that controlled the steam pressure in one engine, its throttle lever, and then touched a finger to each of the pressure gauges.

'Can I take photographs?' she asked, unfolding her camera. Her voice was lost in the noise of the engines.

'What's that?' he replied.

'Can I take some photographs?' she shouted.

'Eh? Why, yes . . . em . . . if you like.' He appeared quite chuffed at the idea.

She pointed the lens at him, and he was at a loss for moment, and then he stuffed his cloth in his pocket, put one foot up on a step by the port engine and struck a manly pose.

Taking another couple of snaps, she moved past him to climb the steps to the top platform of the engine, to get a better view. There wasn't much in the way of storage space anywhere here. From the rear of each engine, a shaft ran inside a large tubular structure, through the aft bulkhead where it would eventually lead to the propellor. The machinery took up most of the room. There was no likely hiding place for weapons, but she kept looking for anything unusual or out of place. She didn't want be rude to her father's old friend, but she couldn't stay too long, as she wasn't sure what effect all the heat and humidity would have on her film. Also, she wanted to get on with searching the rest of the ship.

There were two other men in the room, both busy with maintenance. Proper sailors, not hangers-on like

Gorey's lot. One of them was at a workbench, fixing some small, barrel-shaped piece of equipment she couldn't identify. This was the kind of everyday work she loved to record, and she took a picture. He saw her do it and rounded on her, a stern look on his face. He wagged his finger at her and shook his head.

'Right, right, that's probably enough photographs,' Joe Goat said hurriedly. 'Sorry Akiko, but we need to leave the lads to their work. Want to take a quick peek in the boiler room?'

There was a door that led forward into an even hotter compartment, where the oil-fired furnaces heated the water in boilers to make steam. In ships that burned coal instead of oil, she knew, these could be hellish places; dark, coated in soot and roasting hot. Even here, she found it uncomfortable. She was curious about the way she'd just been scooted out however, and she noticed that Joe was looking anxious again. She was sure she was right; they were keeping secrets on this ship. It was quieter once he closed the door behind them, and the two could speak in normal voices. There was only one man in here, and he was busy mopping the floor.

'We run a clean ship,' Joe Goat declared proudly. 'The surfaces, the bilge, the furnaces, they all have to be kept clean of oil, to avoid fires.'

'Mr Gogarty,' she asked. 'What did you mean when you asked me if I was real?'

'Oh, don't mind me. Just the old noggin playing up on me!' he gave a forced laugh. 'One too many hits on the head, probably, but . . .' He glanced at the other man, who carefully kept his eyes on the floor. Then Joe's face took on a more vulnerable expression, and he kept talking, blurting it out like a confession. 'Sometimes I . . . I see things sometimes that aren't there. Like ghosts, except . . . except sometimes they're people who are still alive. And I hear things. I hear screams from inside the engines, like . . . Like, as if there's people in there. And gunshots, sometimes.'

Akiko stared into his eyes, and at that moment, she thought they were the saddest eyes she'd ever seen. He sounded like some of the men who'd come back from the Great War, but she knew he'd never served on the front. He'd only ever served in Otosan's squad, and they were guerillas. They hadn't been in a *real* war, had they?

'You should talk to someone,' she said firmly. 'I always find that talking helps the head. You should come up on deck and talk to my father. It would do you good, and he'd love to see you.'

Joe Goat moved back from her, his face slumping, his eyes going dull and it gave the effect of a fading spirit.

'I don't go up there much,' he muttered, raising his eyes to the deck above them. 'It's worse outside. There's more of them can see you outside.' He managed a dismal smile. 'You go on back to your father, love. Tell him I said hello. And . . . and ask him not to come down. He'll only bring the bad stuff down with him.

'You do that for me child, would you? Tell your father old Joe's all right down here. You tell him to stay away from me, that's a good girl. It's for the best, y'understand.'

Chapter 20

'It's Not Over Till We Say It's Over'

Michael knew he could not hold Liam responsible for what happened in Belfast, but he fervently wished the boy would learn to show more sense. He had hoped to avoid any drama. The few people in the movement who knew about the *Subversive* thought it had been scuttled out at sea nearly a year ago to avoid having it captured, so talking to Zürn had involved enough risk without complicating things by crossing the B-Specials. Throwing a stone at them for no reason! And then attacking them! What had possessed the boy? Michael shook his head. Now they had his name and Zürn's, and it was likely a warrant would be put out for their arrest for the shooting of a policeman. He was sure he could have talked their way out of it without starting a fight . . . or could he? That sergeant had been hell-bent on giving him a beating. If he had been in Liam's place, at his age, would he have acted any differently?

He knew the answer already, of course. More than once, he'd been involved in street fights against the police who had been deployed to beat up strikers on the docks in Paterson.

It was bad enough for him, but worse for Zürn. If he was caught, a German could not expect fair treatment in Belfast for shooting a copper, even a dodgy part-time one. Michael was surprised that Holland hadn't appeared on the deck beside him to chide him about that, though it was likely he wouldn't come out while Michael had Jim Gorey standing right there beside him. The ghost tended to choose his moments.

'You finished in Belfast then, Jim?' Michael asked.

'For now,' Gorey replied. He had just tamped the tobacco down in his pipe and was relighting it. He took a few short puffs to bring it to life, and the top of the pipe bowl glowed in the dark, the smoke he exhaled swirling away in the breeze. 'It was gettin' too hot. We were there to back up the local lads, but the Prods have control in the city. We weren't doin' much but helping people defend their homes, and once they knew I was around, I was drawing trouble wherever I went. It was time to get out for a while.'

'Price of being famous, Jim.'

'Don't I know it. My face is up on posters in every peeler station in the north, and every one of the beggars wants to put a bullet through it.'

'Yeah, well . . . "heavy is the head that wears the crown", as they say.'

Gorey laughed, turned his back to the gunwale and looked down at Liam, who had adopted his own lean against the rail, hoping to look casual.

'You're Lar O'Leary's lad, ain't yeh?'

'Yes, sir,' Liam replied.

'He's a good man, Lar,' Gorey commented. 'A good leader. We'll need men like him in the new republic. And from the sounds of things, you have the same spirit.'

Liam gave him a tip of the head in response, but Michael could tell he was lighting up inside. He looked like he'd just achieved an Irish republic right there in front of them. Staring back out to sea, Michael could not help but be amused at Liam's reaction. The boy was awestruck. And it was hard to blame him, for Gorey's life was almost mythological in nationalist circles.

'So how about it son? An tírghráthóir tú?' Jim asked.

'Is ea! Éirinn go brách!' Liam exclaimed.

'Oh, is sea, Éirinn go brách!' The veteran chuckled. 'Tiocfaidh ár lá, sin é lomchlár na fírinne. Here, Liam lad, go down to the galley and fetch us up a cup o' tea there, would yeh? Strong with a sup of milk, there's a good boy.'

Liam nodded, and set off eagerly to comply.

'And a coffee Liam, más é do thoil é,' Michael called after him, receiving a distracted wave in response.

Gorey leaned back and puffed on his pipe, his eyes turning to regard his old friend.

'Does Joe Goat still run the engines on this old girl?' Michael inquired.

'He does, though he tends to stay out of sight,' came the reply. 'The boy's safe enough with machines, but otherwise . . . well, his head's still not right. He doesn't come up on deck much. Not sure if he'd be that happy to see you, to be honest. Easily rattled, he is. Emotional. Not keen on walks down memory lane – he has enough of that already.' Gorey tapped his temple. 'Sees things that aren't there. I'd call it shell shock, like we saw on the front, but he's never even seen an artillery barrage. It's much the same though. A sad case.'

Michael nodded, and resisted the urge to look around for any sign of Holland. Some lights caught his eye, and he recognized the distinctive, formidable shape of a Royal Navy destroyer less than a mile away, off their port side. Even off her coasts, Ireland was surrounded by symbols of British control.

'We've got company,' he said, pointing. 'You got anything on board you don't want found?'

'Ahh, the Navy ain't searching ships much at the moment,' Gorey grunted. 'They're honourin' the truce, more or less.'

'I take it that's a "yes" then?'

'Gotta keep busy, Mick!' Gorey said, grinning around his pipe. 'And nobody saw you come on board. We'll be all right.'

It was the roguish smile of a man who lived for risk. This daring, this steel nerve in the face of a massively more powerful enemy, tempered by a keen intelligence, was one of the qualities that inspired so much respect in his men.

'So that fella you brought on,' Gorey went on. 'That's the German, ain't it? From the U-boat that was stolen. Now, what would you be wantin' with a U-boat engineer, Mick? I thought your submarine was sunk?'

'It was,' Michael replied. 'But he's got expertise none of my other engineers have. I've lost some of my best over the last few years, Joe Goat included. Zürn'd be a good man to have on the factory floor. And . . . and well, between you and me, Jim, I've been thinking I might build another boat when I get the business back on its feet, if this war is finally over. For exploring this time.' He nodded to the darkness beyond the ship. 'There's so much we've never seen, that we don't know about the sea, and I'm of a mind to learn what I can in the time I have left to me.'

'It's not over,' Jim snorted.

'What?'

'The war, Mick. Think what you like about this truce, but the war's not over till *we* say it's over. What, you think Griffith and Collins and them are going bring back a republic from London? Is that what's going to happen?'

'I'm sure you've read the same newspapers I have, Jim.' Michael turned to face him. 'Whatever they bring back will be a hell of a lot better than what we have now. Our own government? Control over our laws and finances? Our own army and police force? Can you imagine having all that? That's more freedom than we've had in centuries. Give us that, get the British out, and we'll take the rest eventually.'

'A piss-poor, half-hearted effort,' Gorey declared. 'With that treaty, we'll never be rid of the Brits. They don't call that Lloyd George "the Welsh Wizard" for nothin'. He's a divil, running rings around those lads. They've been sold a pup! If they get their way, we'll still be swearing an oath of allegiance to the Crown! *Loyalty to the Royals*, Michael! Still a part of their bloody empire!

Did I do a runner from the British Army only to find myself back in it?

'And what about the North? "Chaps with maps" cutting the island up like it's a cake they can dish out onto different plates. All the good people in those six counties; we're just to let them go and hang are we? They're no longer part of our nation, is that it?'

'Look at all the people who *gave their lives* for this cause, Mick. My two brothers and my sister, killed by the Tans and the Auxies, seven of my own men . . . and all the others around the country. Think of the years we've put in, all the folks whose houses or businesses were burned, all the ones who went to prison. Look at all the people *we've* killed for this, for God's sake! Was all that just for a mealy-mouthed compromise? So we'd get the best price we can for the cow?'

He took his pipe from his mouth and poked Michael in the chest with the stem.

'I won't have it, Mick. It'd be like strangling our new state at birth. I won't betray the northern counties, and I tell yeh, after all the Brits have done to us, I'll let Hell take my soul before I see my lads swearing an oath of allegiance to *the bloody King*!'

Michael didn't reply at first, because he knew his friend was right. Everything he said was true. The peace agreement that had been leaked to the newspapers fell well short of the Ireland the nationalists had dreamed of, and if the various armed groups didn't accept it, it could tear the country apart.

The *Medusa* was turning east now, and it would follow

the coast south to Howth, just this side of Dublin. Out off the port side of the ship, the destroyer was cruising closer, following a course alongside the *Medusa* that was almost parallel, slanted enough to dovetail in the next few miles. It was close enough to make out some details between the lights; nearly three hundred feet long, the three funnels hinting at the mighty steam turbines below, and armed with four-inch guns. The vessel was an awesome display of power.

'The British were always going to insist on loyalty to the Crown,' Michael said at last. 'It's how they think. And the Unionists in the north are their people. They were never going to let us leave the empire completely. They . . . they can't conceive of it. If the world sees they can't even control this little country off their coast, they could lose *India*, and all those other places trying to get free. It would be the end of their empire – you might as well ask them to cut off their own heads. We've been fightin' the Brits since God was in short trousers, so I'll take the treaty as a stepping stone to something more, Jim. The people want peace. I think they'll accept the price.'

'The *people*!' Gorey blew smoke from his nostrils. 'Mewlin' sheep, most of 'em. Pay no mind to those pearl-clutchers, *we're* the men who matter, Mick. The ones who put our lives on the line. Do you think Brugha will stand for this? Or Markievicz, or Lynch, or Barry down in Cork? The lads from Tipp? Half the fighting men in the country will spit on that deal.'

'What about our good President?' Michael said, trying to lighten the tone. 'Dev sent the party over to London.

You don't think he'll hold it all together?'

'Huh! He's too slippery to hold anything. The Devil himself couldn't get a straight order out of de Valera – and then he'll have the nerve to lecture us all like we're schoolchildren on how he knows best. I've no more faith in the man.'

Michael gestured towards the warship, whose captain was making no attempt to hide his interest in the *Medusa*, though he showed no sign yet of acting on it.

'You see that out there? That's an R-class destroyer. Our new republic couldn't afford to build *one* of those. The British built *sixty-two* of them over a few years, during the war. They can draw on the resources of an empire. You fought in that war, you saw the way they sent thousands to die on the front. Tens of thousands of troops, chewed up in the mud. The army defeated the Rising in *six days*, and it was barely a distraction from that slaughter in France. They have artillery, tanks . . . if the British went all out on us, they'd crush us. And they would have already, if they weren't afraid of the headlines. They know the rest of the world is watching us now.'

'And we've nothing at all to take on their navy. Nothing. We can't beat them, Jim. We can only convince them that Ireland is too much hassle to keep.'

'Who needs sixty-two destroyers?' Gorey retorted. 'Drop a few of your submarines in the Irish Sea for a fraction of the cost and you'd put the fear of God into them. They wouldn't dare come near us. Look what the Germans managed to do, even though the Royal Navy had them completely outmatched at sea. Nobody knew what was hiding under that water. It nearly paralyzed the British swines! You could *cut them off* from their empire.

'The submarine is the guerilla fighter of the sea, Mick. You proved that, you and your Selkies. Strike when they're least expecting it and blend back into the environment before they can use their superior power against you.

'Look at the how those Germans stole that U-boat in Belfast. *That's* how you take on an empire . . . with guile and nerve, using their own resources against them. God, what I'd give for some of those fierce machines! I'll never understand why you never torpedoed any ships. I know you had the means to do it.'

'And you know why I didn't,' Michael answered him quietly. It was interesting that Gorey seemed sure that *Germans* had stolen the U-boat, but he didn't press his friend on it. 'Where do you think you're going to get the money for a fleet of submarines, when we can't even get bullets for the guns that we have? The country's broke, man. This war has nearly put my Irish factory out of business, and there's many like it. The fight is done, Jim. We have to do a deal, or we'll end up waiting another generation. I think we've waited long enough. And I'll be honest with you, I don't have the stomach for it any more. I can't see an end to it. One side committing murder, so the other always has to kill in return – it'll just keep on getting worse. You know as well as I do, if you invite the British to use violence, they will always oblige.'

'And as God is my witness,' Gorey said in a grating voice. 'I'll make the bastards pay for every drop of blood they spill.'

Michael didn't answer, his eyes drawn out to the sea again. Gorey's capacity for violence had always been far greater than his. The man was fifteen years his junior of course, and had fought in the Great War. He had seen slaughter on an industrial scale, and that had changed him, damaged him forever. For a few seconds, Michael caught a glimpse of dead bodies scattered across the surface of the water, before he blinked and looked again and saw only the glittering of the ship's lights reflecting on the low waves.

Chapter 21
The War Machine

When he went down to make the tea for Gorey, Liam found a couple of his men in the galley with Oberleutnant Zürn. They pressed Liam to recount what had happened on the docks with the B-Specials, and he proudly told them the story, without embellishing his part in it too much. He noticed the German growing increasingly uncomfortable, until he stood up and left altogether, but Liam was enjoying the glow of the rebels' attention too much to pay him any mind.

That glow did not last as long as he'd thought it might however, and after he brought up the tea and coffee to the two men on deck, he decided to go looking for Zürn. As the excitement of the fight, the chase and meeting the famous commander subsided, Liam began to feel a little queasy. It was the first time he'd seen anyone shot up close, and for all his bravado in talking about the fight, he was finding himself troubled by the memory of it. He supposed that was to be expected, it being his first time, but Zürn couldn't be having the same problem, could he? The man was a war veteran; he must have seen plenty of people die over the years.

He found the German inside a doorway off the main deck, at the top of a brightly lit flight of steps. He was peering through a porthole in the door, his face tense with fear.

'Those men in the galley,' he said, when he saw Liam. 'They are Irish Republican Army, are they not? The man your uncle knows, he is their leader, yes?'

Liam couldn't see any point in lying. The lads in the galley hadn't exactly been discreet.

'Yes,' he replied. Then, seeing a chance to impress the man, he added. 'We're *all* with the IRA, in one way or another. And my father commands a column too. I haven't joined them yet, but I do other jobs for them.'

Zürn nodded grimly, his suspicions confirmed. His face was damp with sweat.

'*Das ist eine Katastrophe!* Your uncle said nothing of this when he offered me the job. And the crew of this boat, they are also sympathisers? This ship is used for smuggling arms?'

'I don't know . . . probably.' Liam shrugged. 'If they're loyal to Jim Gorey, yeah, I'd say they do some gun-running for him.'

Smuggling weapons into the country was an ongoing challenge for the rebels. Ever since the Ulster Volunteer Force had landed that huge shipment at Larne, the Irish Volunteers had been playing catch-up, never managing to achieve the same success. Their first real attempt had been in 1914, by two groups, the main one led by Erskine and Molly Childers, who used their yacht to land nine hundred very old, heavy, single-shot Mauser rifles and 29,000 rounds of ammunition at Howth. Arms that, like the UVF's, had been purchased in Germany.

In stark contrast to the much bigger operation at Larne however, the authorities had taken action, despatching the police and the army, only to be met by hundreds of Volunteers. Some of the Irish-born police refused to use force against them, and the stand-off attracted a crowd. In the confusion, the rebels managed to escape with the weapons, but the army overreacted and three civilians were shot dead, one was killed with a bayonet and thirty-eight were wounded.

In terms of landing weapons, that had been the movement's greatest success, and those clunky, obsolete weapons had gone on to be used in the Easter Rising. They had become part of those legendary few days in Dublin, and Liam had often fantasised about being there, fighting in that doomed battle alongside James Connolly, Éamon de Valera and Michael Collins, his face blackened by gun-flash residue from his old Mauser rifle.

'What *did* Uncle Michael tell you?' he inquired.

'Not much. He said he might have a job for me in his factory. Mostly, he asked questions.'

'Yeah, that's his way. Keeps his cards close to his chest, if you know what I mean.'

'What have I done?' Zürn was running his hands through his hair, his face creased with anxiety. 'Gott im Himmel, das ist eine Katastrophe! I've shot a policeman, in *Belfast*, and now I'm . . . I'm running off with Irish terrorists instead of trying to explain myself . . . on a . . . on a ship that is used for gun-running, after . . . after being questioned about the hijacking of a U-boat from the Royal Navy. They are bound to think I am involved now! *Gott!* Das ist eine Katastrophe! What's going to happen to my family? My children? The British will hang me for this . . .'

'Here now, it's all right,' Liam said, wanting to reassure him, but starting to feel more on edge now, as if Zürn's panic was infectious. 'You're away from it now. We're headed south. No one knows you're here . . .'

'Look!' the German said, pointing frantically through the porthole. '*Look!* You see? They are coming for us!'

Liam stepped up beside him and peeked out the porthole . . . and saw a Royal Navy destroyer cruising alongside the *Medusa*, only a few hundred yards away. He gasped and stepped back, his heart pounding.

'You see?' Zürn exclaimed.

'You think they're here for us?' Liam asked.

'You think they are not?'

'How would *I* know? You're the one who served on a warship.'

'A submarine is not a *ship*, it is a *boat*. And it was a *German* boat. You are the ones who break British laws and fight British police. Is this what happens? Is it normal for your ships to be followed by destroyers?'

'No!'

'Well then!'

Seeing the heavily armed vessel out there, Liam felt the first genuine chill of fear at what this could mean. He had thought that once they'd got away from Belfast, they were home and dry. But the RIC, the B-Specials, the Auxies, the Black and Tans, the Army, the Navy . . . they were all branches of the same titanic, imperial might. Would the British send a massive war machine after a few fugitives like this, just for shooting one man? He had never really appreciated how much the odds were stacked against the rebels, and the risks they took. The scale of the power they faced, while they stole pistols and rifles from police stations and transported them hidden in cartloads of turf. That one ship out there had more destructive power than the IRA's entire arsenal.

He found himself trembling, feeling sick with fear, and hated himself for it. Was this who he was? His father never spoke of being afraid, and the idea of someone like Grim Jim Gorey feeling scared was unthinkable. Perhaps Liam was not like his heroes, as he'd thought. Perhaps he was small and ordinary after all. Perhaps he was a coward.

Zürn, still considering the bleakness of his future, had not registered Liam's terror.

'Do the British put young boys in prison?' he asked. 'Do they shoot them, do you think?'

He turned to look at Liam and, seeing the boy's face, realized his mistake.

'Oh, I am sorry. That was insensitive. I am sure they won't shoot you.'

'They hanged a lad named Kevin Barry last year. He was only a couple of years older than me.'

'I . . . I am sure it will be fine.'

Liam didn't think he sounded very sure. He put his hand against the wall, feeling suddenly short of breath, a sob rising in his throat. He drew in some long breaths. Oh God, was he going to cry? Was he really so scared he was going to cry?

'Would they . . . would they sink the ship, d'yeh think? If they knew we were here?'

'No, no, that would be totally unnecessary,' Zürn assured him. 'They would send a party of Royal Marines to board us.'

Liam shuddered. What should he do? There was nowhere they could hide on this small tramp steamer. There was nowhere to run. It was a miserable moment, discovering he was *not* like the fearless heroes he'd heard so many stories about. He just wanted to escape. Where was Michael? He'd know what to do. Liam was staring through the porthole again. He was trying to decide if he should go out on deck to find his uncle or just give in to the panic, run to the other side of the vessel and jump overboard. And then Grim Jim Gorey strolled into view, stopping to lean on the gunwale and contemplatively puffing smoke from his pipe. He regarded the great British war machine with the cool and casual air of a man on a pleasure cruise.

This was the kind of man who, undaunted by any challenge, would win freedom for Ireland, no matter what the cost was to himself. Liam gazed out at him in awe. *This* was everything he wished he could be.

As a career soldier in the British Expeditionary Force in 1914, the Tipperary man had seen action on the Western Front before being wounded and sent back to Britain. While recovering, he had taken the secret oath of loyalty to the Irish Republican Brotherhood and eventually deserted, no longer willing to fight for the British Empire. He went on to take part in the Easter Rising in 1916 in Dublin with the Irish Volunteers.

The Rising was the biggest armed revolt against British rule in centuries, with most of the action taking place in Dublin. A small army of uniformed men, marching in under flags and using conventional warfare tactics, had occupied positions around the city. It was a heroic disaster. They put up a good fight, but they were hopelessly outgunned and outnumbered. In six days of fighting, nearly five hundred people died. Gorey was wounded again, and sent to an internment camp in Frongoch in Wales with most of the other defeated rebels.

However, the British made some serious mistakes after the Easter Rising. With so many Irishmen serving with the British in the Great War, most of the Irish public did not support the rebellion; in fact, about a third of the British Army troops who'd responded had been Irishmen themselves. But because of the army's use of artillery in the middle of Dublin, most of the casualties were civilians. Forty children were killed. And when the army then executed the rebel leaders for treason instead of treating them as prisoners of war, like the Germans, opinion started to turn against the rulers in Dublin Castle.

At the same time, the British foolishly gathered one thousand eight hundred rebels together in one place – a gathering the republican leaders had never been able to achieve. Frongoch internment camp became known as 'an Ollscoil na Réabhlóide' – 'the University of

Revolution' – Gorey and other new leaders like Michael Collins emerged, helping to organise the Volunteers, and setting up training in military and guerilla tactics. In Frongoch, Gorey took on an assumed name, as the army would have executed him too, if they'd identified him as a deserter.

By the time the prisoners were released later that year to try and show some good will to an increasingly hostile Irish public, the British had missed their chance. Grim Jim Gorey was gone, disappearing back to his home county of Tipperary, and the Irish Volunteers were on their way to becoming a more disciplined and effective organisation, which would later be renamed the Irish Republican Army.

Liam pressed his brow against the cool glass of the porthole. What was he, compared to a man like this? He saw Gorey spit into the sea, in the direction of the destroyer, then jabbed his middle finger up in a gesture of defiance.

'We are doomed,' Zürn groaned, fretfully. 'Das ist eine Katastrophe! We are doomed! We are . . . Oh. Oh no, wait. No . . . they are heading away.'

'Are you sure?' Liam wheezed.

'Yes, yes, I am sure. They are accelerating, and taking a divergent course. We are safe.'

They both sagged in relief, and in that moment, a sharp voice shouted:

'*Hey*! LOOK OUT!'

They both twisted round in fright and found Akiko standing on the steps below them, aiming her camera up at them. Snapping her picture, she lowered the device, pointed at them and giggled.

'Sorry, but you should see your faces! You look like you just had electric shocks up your bums!' She climbed the steps, still smiling as she stepped past them to push open the door. 'Oh, that's very funny! I hope I got that, I'm going to get it framed.'

The door slammed behind her and the two of them jumped again.

'I am sorry to say, Liam,' Zürn commented, 'that meeting your family has not been good for my nerves.'

Chapter 22
Connections

It took Lizzy Noonan more than three hours to come back with the information Esther needed, during which time she had taken the opportunity to lie down in the corner of the room and catch up on some much-needed sleep. Midori Regan was not in Cork, she was actually here in Dublin, staying in the Gresham Hotel, and Lizzy had discovered that she had a meeting there in the morning with Constance Markievicz, or to use her proper title, *Countess* Markievicz, as her husband was a member of the Polish nobility.

Esther thanked her, and went back to sleep, letting the exhaustion of the last few days overcome the discomfort of the bare floor. As she drifted off, Lizzy tutted and laid a blanket over her. Even a British spy needed a cover while they slept.

What little hospitality Esther's host was willing to offer expired early the next morning. It was Friday, and Lizzy was getting ready for work and her daughter for school.

'That's all you'll be getting from me,' she told her unwanted guest. 'You can have a cup of tea, then you may grab your hat and coat and be on your way.'

Pleased with the intelligence she'd obtained, Esther took the dismissal in good grace. She used their small mirror to straighten up her hair and touch up her make-up, said goodbye to Agnes, and then she and Lizzy parted on the same difficult terms that they'd met, neither one wishing to see the other again.

Watchful for any sign that she was being followed, Esther took an electric tram across the city centre to the Gresham, which was on Sackville Street, Dublin's widest and busiest shopping street. She intended to look in on Midori's meeting with the countess before catching a train to Belfast. It was an opportunity to observe them both, and perhaps she could learn something useful.

She found some comfort in the crowds that filled the paths as people headed to work. The lobby of the hotel was busy too, and Esther was early. It was a very grand place, not the equal of the fine London hotels, but close, with its high ceilings, fine fabrics, elegant furniture, gold-framed mirrors and deep plush carpets. Conscious of the opulent surroundings and the fact that she did not look her best after her rough night, she sought out the most inconspicuous corner of the lobby. It was best to keep a low profile anyhow. Then she treated herself by ordering a capital breakfast. She was famished. She was still finishing her coffee when Markievicz came in. Esther had been in the same room as her a couple of times before at Cumann na mBan meetings, and there was the possibility of being recognized, so she lifted a newspaper to hide her face as the other woman sat down on the far side of the lobby.

Constance Georgine Markievicz, born Gore-Booth, was by far the most famous member of the Irishwomen's Council. As a founding member of the Irish Citizen Army, the worker's rights organisation, she had taken part with the Irish Volunteers in the Easter Rising, one of the women who had fought alongside the men. She had been sentenced to death for her part in the rebellion, only have it commuted to life in prison because of her gender. She was later released along with others in the Rising, but would be imprisoned again later for campaigning against introducing conscription in Ireland.

She was also the first woman ever to be elected to the House of Commons, though like other members of Sinn Féin, she refused to take her seat in London. She was the current Minister for Labour in the Dáil; which would be another political first, if Ireland eventually became a nation in its own right and the role became official. While Markievicz was undoubtedly an enemy of the Crown, Esther had a lot of respect for her as a woman of consequence and a self-confessed troublemaker.

Midori arrived soon after, coming down the stairs from her room and waving to the countess. She ignored the heads that turned to look at her Japanese features, a rare sight in Dublin. Her long, glossy black hair was pulled back from prominent cheekbones, and skin coloured by years spent on or near the sea, and pinned up with a comb in a style she called *'yakai maki'*. Again, Esther was careful to avoid being spotted, feeling a pang of regret on seeing Midori's characteristically placid, controlled expression loosen into a smile as she let her guard down with her friend. Michael Regan's wife would never smile at *her* like that again.

Esther was surprised to see that Akiko was not with her mother. That girl was a budding revolutionary if she'd ever met one, and would have relished the chance to meet the famous rebel countess. She must not have come to Dublin with her mum.

They were clearly settling in for a good chat, Esther couldn't get any closer to listen in without being seen, so now that she had the lie of the land, she decided it was time to make a telephone call. Perhaps she could move to a better position when she came back. Staying out of the women's eyeline, she made her way to one of the glass and dark wood booths next to the reception desk. Closing the door of the small booth, she dropped some coins into the slot and asked the operator to connect her to a number in London.

She was relieved when it was Captain Nigel Moore, Edward Faulkner's secretary, who answered.

'Miss Sinclair,' he said. 'I am very glad to hear your voice. We've been worried about you. When you didn't return to your guesthouse last night, the landlady called in to report you missing.'

'I'm quite all right, Captain Moore,' she replied, 'though my return to Dublin has proved to be more eventful than I'd expected.'

She told him about the men who'd tried to kidnap her, but did not explain where she'd stayed the night, and he didn't press her on it, as if sensing she needed to show discretion.

'A frightful business,' he responded. 'We must get you to the safety of the Castle as soon as possible.'

'Actually, I think I might steer clear of the Castle for a bit,' she said. 'Frankly, the place was a sink of jobbery and corruption when I left, and I doubt things have improved much. I rather think I'll pop up to Belfast, to speak to the German chap about that U-boat.'

Moore was starting to say something in return, when another voice called for the receiver, and Faulkner came on the line:

'Esther, is that you girl? Thank heavens you're all right! Now look here, if things are still that dicey in the city, we need to get you to a secure location. What's this bunk you're talking about going to Belfast? That's like jumping out of the frying pan and into the ruddy bonfire!'

'I'm following a line of enquiry, Edward,' she told him. 'I want to know if the chlorine gas used to kill the crew on the U-boat was from the shipment that was stolen in France. It's possible that a local rebel group was involved, and if so, they are a resourceful bunch. That would only have been small fraction of that gas shipment. They could do much, much worse with what they have left.'

'Stuff and nonsense, girl!' he exclaimed. 'There was no *gas* used in that hijacking. There was gas released from the batteries, because it's a Boche lump of scrap that would have gone to the cutter's torch if the Navy hadn't been planning to use it for target practice. And as for the *Irish*, what are those oiks going to do with the bally thing? *Paddle* it into battle?

'No, I just spoke to our man in Belfast an hour ago.

We have it on good authority that it was stolen by a bunch of Krauts – some of those paramilitary Freikorps fellows. Not that it will do them a lot of good; the clapped-out piece of junk will probably sink on the way back to Germany.'

'Who told you it was the Freikorps?' she asked, feeling a little let down that nothing might come of her theory.

'The investigation is well in hand,' he assured her. 'The last fellow left alive is still in custody, a chap named . . . eh . . . what was it, Nigel? Yes, that's it, *Zürn* . . . well, he's giving the Harbour Police all the answers they need. The whole thing will be wrapped up in a week, there's no need to bother your pretty little head about it.'

Esther slumped, overcome with disappointment. A dead end. Had Moore steered her wrong, when he'd shown her the newspaper? That gas was still missing though. Perhaps she could ask to be transferred to France to try and track it down there? No, she could tell from his voice that she'd already tested Faulkner's patience. He was not inclined to accommodate any more of the theories conjured up in her 'pretty little head', and if they cooped her up in the Castle, she'd spend the rest of her time in Dublin typing up the reports of people who were doing *real* intelligence work. She had to take advantage of what little good will he might still have towards her.

'There was something else I wanted to follow up, from my time here before,' she said, in an offhand manner. 'You remember Michael Regan? We suspected him of involvement in the IRA, but could never pin anything on him. He has a lot of the right associations, and his wife is in Cumann na mBan. It's always felt like unfinished business, and I'd like to take another look at him. Could you square that with the chaps in the Castle, do you think?'

There was a pause on the line, and then Faulkner exhaled, as if humouring an overly-enthusiastic child.

'Regan? The American in Cork? Oh, by all means, go on. Have at it.'

'Thank you, Edward.'

As she was talking, she kept glancing out into the lobby, where she could see Midori's back and had a partial view of the front door. Something caught her eye, her mouth fell open and she nearly dropped the receiver.

'Well, I must be going,' Faulkner said. 'Stay on the line there; Nigel has a contact that may be of use to you.'

'Sorry? Oh . . . yes . . . eh . . . thanks again.' She was still staring out into the lobby.

'Miss Sinclair?'

'Oh please, call me Esther. I think we should be friends, don't you?'

'I would heartily agree. And please, call me Nigel. Esther, if you're heading down to Cork, I have a friend down there who might be of use to you. His name is Lieutenant Krishnan Chowdhury, and he's with the Royal Engineers, posted in Victoria Barracks. He's a good man, and you should look him up if you're down that way.'

'Krishnan Chowdhury, Victoria Barracks,' she repeated, trying not to sound too distracted. 'Thank you very much for that. I'll speak to you again soon, Nigel.'

'I shall look forward to it, Esther. I wish you best of luck in your endeavours.'

She nodded, forgetting that he couldn't see her, and hung up the telephone. Across the lobby, a small group had just walked in through the front door. Much as she had, they looked out of place, arriving in a somewhat dishevelled state, as if they'd been out all night, or had slept in their clothes. There was Michael Regan, his daughter Akiko and his nephew Liam, Kathleen's son, who lived with them.

The fourth person with them seemed in even worse shape, dressed in shabby, badly creased work clothes, with heavy bags under his striking blue eyes, and several days' growth of reddish-blond beard. And unless she was very much mistaken, this was the man whose picture she'd seen in the newspaper only a few days before: Oberleutnant Wolfgang Zürn, formerly of the Imperial German Navy, and until recently, the engineer on the Type U93 that had been hijacked in Belfast Harbour.

Stunned as she was to see this man walk into a Dublin hotel with Michael Regan, where he was being introduced to Midori and the countess, a more pressing question was blotting all other thoughts from Esther's head. Edward Faulkner, a man who prided himself on being informed and up to date on all matters relevant to his brief, had just told her that Zürn was still in custody, still being questioned by the police in Belfast about the hijacking. To be standing here now, the German must have been released hours ago, most likely yesterday evening. Hadn't Faulkner said: 'I just spoke to our man in Belfast an hour ago'? How could he not know about this? Or had he just lied to her? The very idea of it baffled her.

Why would he lie?

Chapter 23
Hard Choices

Wolfgang had heard that Cork was one of Ireland's major ports, though he had never been there himself. Arriving by train at Glanmire Road Station, near the River Lee, he followed the Regans out onto the street. They had a late lunch in a restaurant, for they still had some way to go, and then the rest waited while Michael fetched his car from a nearby garage. A 1914 Benz Tourer; Wolfgang noted with approval, a sound choice of German automobile.

While Cork was an industrious place, it could not compare with the scale of Belfast's harbour and shipyards. He did not feel the same excitement about it as the five of them squeezed into the car and drove along the river, across a bridge and headed south out of town. There was evidence of fire damage to some of the buildings, and Wolfgang could not get his mind off the fact that he was now in the heartland of the republican paramilitaries.

Situated on the south coast, the opposite end of Ireland to Belfast, the city's port relied mainly on stop-offs from transatlantic traffic, the mail boats, and the fact that it was a major base for the Royal Navy. That last point made him anxious. He had travelled the length of the country, but he would not escape for long if the Navy and police thought to look for him here.

Then he saw a convoy of three trucks full of uniformed men go past. These were the RIC, or perhaps the notorious Black and Tans, he thought. He was struck by the sight. These were not like the police in Belfast, confident in their control of the ground. Each truck had high armoured sides, the open tops covered by wire mesh to prevent grenades from being thrown in. Liam had told him that the locals called these 'chicken coops'. Even with the truce keeping the peace down here in the south, the men in these trucks were moving fast, hiding behind armour . . . For them, the very city they lived in was enemy territory.

'As long as you stay out of their way, the peelers won't come looking for you here,' Regan said, as if guessing his thoughts. 'They have enough on their plate already, and the wounding of a B-Special up north will be of no great concern to them.'

They had done some shopping in Dublin, staying the night in the hotel before catching the first train the next morning. Michael and the children had been forced to leave their luggage in Belfast. Wolfgang had lost all of his possessions when the U-boat was stolen, except for his bank book, kept in a waterproof oilskin wallet, which he always took with him when he wasn't on board. Michael had generously bought him a couple of changes of clothes and a new coat and shoes, so he looked a bit more respectable, though he'd kept his old seaman's cap. He had never stayed in such a fine hotel, and he'd been unable to sleep very well on the voluminous hotel bed, though he'd made up for it on the hours-long train journey. Now he tried to sleep in the car as they drove on for hours more, but the roads outside Cork were atrocious – some were hardly fit for a car at all, and there were many more horses, carts and wagons out here than motor vehicles. He was taken aback by the signs of desperate poverty he saw when they went beyond the city. It would have been rare to see such squalor in his own country. These were the people the British Empire could not tame?

When they finally reached the Regan's home on the coast of West Cork, it was well into the evening, and the last of the sun was gone, though with a bright moon and clear sky, there was still enough light to take in some of the land around them. A manor house lay at the end of a long driveway, the kind a wealthy farmer might own. The left side had been damaged by fire and was being rebuilt. The tended gardens were small enough for a property of this type, and beyond them, the terrain was rocky and wild. The place spoke of money, but fell short of boasting great wealth.

Three giant Irish wolfhounds came bounding out to greet the family and sniff around Wolfgang. The dogs were friendly enough, but alarmingly large. Their master clapped his hands and told them to go back to the house.

'Let's take a walk,' Michael said to him, as the others brought their things into the house.

They strolled along a path of beaten earth out of the

garden and towards the sea. The path followed the edge of a cliff, and Wolfgang relished the refreshing scent and the sound of the surf washing against the rocks nearly a hundred feet below.

'You told us what happened with the U-boat,' Michael said as he walked, 'but do you have any idea who those men might have been?'

'As I said, I hardly saw anything before I ended up in the water,' Wolfgang replied. 'But . . . I didn't say this to the police, but I'm sure I heard German voices. The man I spoke to was from Northern Ireland . . . I am not good at recognizing accents in English, but I know that one well enough. The other voices I heard were speaking German, and fluently.'

Michael nodded, not saying anything for a minute.

'And the police told you a squad of B-Specials was attacked by some republicans near the harbour, and that was thought to be a diversion, to draw other constables away from the docks?'

'Yes.'

Wolfgang saw that they were heading directly away from the house, out along the dark coast. If Michael was a republican, was this some kind of set-up? Was he drawing Wolfgang into the gloom in order to kill him, and throw him off the cliff? In a belated moment of realization, it struck the German that this man could be working with the hijackers, and this could be a ploy to get rid of the last witness. But no, it would have been a ridiculously complicated way of doing it, surely . . . ?

'I ask this because it's no coincidence that we ended

up on the ship, Wolfgang,' Michael went on. 'That young man who was hanging around outside the pub was one of Jim Gorey's lads, and he wasn't there for us. I think he was watching *you*. Which makes me wonder if he was involved in the hijacking. It wouldn't be the first time that Volunteers have worked with Germans.'

'Do you think they intended to finish me off?'

'I don't know.' Michael stopped and cast his eyes out at the sea. 'Gorey wouldn't kill you unless you were a threat to him, though he might think you know more than you do. He could have done it on the *Medusa*, but it's possible he held off to see what I wanted with you. He's hoping for my help with something.'

Wolfgang's spirits sank. If the rebels wanted him dead, he'd made it easy for them by coming down to Cork. Michael raised his hand sharply as if in response to something, an irritated expression crossing his face.

'Yes, I'm getting to it!' he muttered.

'I'm sorry?'

'Nothing, just thinking aloud,' Michael said.

But that wasn't what it had looked like. It looked like Michael Regan had been talking to someone who wasn't there. Wolfgang had seen this kind of thing before, and it was disturbing to witness, alone out here in the dark with this man, with a long fall to the rocks below.

'Look, I must confess that this hasn't gone the way I wanted,' Michael added. 'I had planned to offer you a position in my factory, and wait for a while . . . see how things worked out, because I wanted something more from you, but circumstances have forced my hand. I'm normally slow to trust people, Wolfgang, but you shot that man to protect Liam. I think I saw something of your true character in that act. Now, you have a hard choice to make, and I am willing to place a lot of trust in your decision.

'The way I see it, you have three options. Option One: I can take you to the barracks in town, where you can throw yourself on the mercy of the police, tell them what happened and hope they don't arrest and prosecute you.'

'I think we both know what would happen if I did that,' Wolfgang said dourly. 'I would not expect kind treatment when they got me back to Belfast.'

'Indeed. Option 2: I give you some travelling money to compensate you for your inconvenience, and put you on a ship tomorrow that will take you to France or the Netherlands, so you can make your way back to Germany. You'll be a free man, but you'd have to forget any thought of a life here or in Britain.'

'I could live with that, though I have little enough to build a life upon back in Germany,' Wolfgang replied. 'The situation is not good there now. The war has ruined many things. Am I to take it, Michael that you have another option for me?'

'I have. And this is where I will be gambling my future, and the future of my family, on the strength of your word. I would like to employ you on a private vessel of mine, as an engineer, and with a view to making changes to its design. I'll help you lie low, to stay clear of run-ins with the law, or Gorey's people. I'm offering you double what the Royal Navy were paying you, and a year's contract. There are two catches: the first is that this will not be a conventional role, or a conventional craft. The second is that I will need your complete discretion. If you take this on, you cannot tell people the true nature of your work.'

'I am sorry, Michael. I will not be part of this . . . this political conflict,' Wolfgang said, waving to the general world around them and shaking his head. 'All these groups, your UVF and IRA and IRB and Auxilaries, your Black and Tans and B-Specials and all the rest. I cannot . . . I cannot even keep it in my head who they all are. I must provide for my family, I've had enough violence in my life and I have . . . what's the saying? I have no dog in this fight.'

'No, no, it's not to do with that. In fact, I'm of the same mind. I want to be free of that too, though it's . . . a complicated situation. What I'm doing is for Akiko and Liam, and I promise you I won't ask you to do anything you have a moral objection to. But I am serious about keeping it secret. I would need your solemn oath.'

Wolfgang stared out at the sea, the foam of the waves faint white lines on a moving, iron-grey plain.

'It is useful to you,' he said, 'that I am wanted by the police, and maybe even the republicans too.'

'I won't lie,' Michael replied, 'it doesn't hurt my position . . . though it does force me to trust a man whose character I haven't had time to judge. I'm not trying to railroad you here, but I'm in a bind. You're a wanted man now, but there are precious few people in Ireland with your skills and experience. And now, you either need to leave the country, or find someone who can offer you protection.'

Wolfgang nodded. That was a fair assessment of his situation. He thought about this man, whom he'd only spent a couple of days with – a man with a troubling background. But he had seen Regan under pressure, seen him in a fight, seen how he behaved with his family and how he treated strangers. Years of facing death in confined spaces with men driven close to insanity had taught Wolfgang to quickly recognize a man of substance.

'I will agree to your terms, but only if I can see this boat of yours,' he said at last. 'If I'm not happy with what I see, I will take my leave and board a ship tomorrow. But I give you my word now that, if it is not harming anyone as you say, I will at least keep your secret.'

After some hesitation, Michael nodded.

'I can't ask more than that. I'll take you to her now. There's enough light, I think, for the climb down.'

Wolfgang peered over the grassy edge of the cliff.

'The . . . The *climb down?*'

Chapter 24
Hopes for the Future

Just as he had watched the young ones' faces as they entered the cave, so Michael made sure he was turned to see Wolfgang's as the German came into the echoey space. Wolfgang's eyes drifted around the room, taking it all in, but quickly came to rest on the slate-grey submarine moored at the jetty.

'*Mein Gott!*' he gasped. '*Unglaublich*! That's a *Holland* boat! How old is it?' Wolfgang hurried over to have a closer look. 'Is it British? American?'

Michael was impressed. In his experience, not many of the men who crewed navy submarines knew the history of these vessels, or that the submarine fleets of the United States, Britain, the Netherlands, Japan and Russia had all been first established with submarines designed by the Irish engineer. It was possible that they'd also influenced the creation of the first U-boats.

'No, no, it's not one of the originals,' he called, as he followed the other man over the boards to the dock. 'I built this one, based on John's final designs, with some modern modifications of my own. I trained under him; he was my friend . . . my mentor. This girl is only a few years old. I installed more intuitive controls, a throttle at both helms, and we don't use the torpedoes now, so it needs a crew of just five. There's a modern diesel engine instead of the original petrol one – which is safer, as you'll know – and I added a periscope. A German one, the best. And hydrophones, of course. You must have your ears.'

'I've never seen one of these in real life.' Wolfgang gaped at the narrow channel that led into the cave. 'You drove it in here?! What is it, sixty feet long? Seventy? It's so *small*. What speed can it do? How deep can it dive?'

And now there was Holland himself, standing on the narrow deck behind the hatch, hands behind his back, chin stuck out with pride as the German climbed down to stand in front of the turret and look around. The slight-figured ghost glanced over at Michael, who allowed himself a hint of a smile. They knew that passion, that curiosity all too well. It was in Wolfgang's eyes, in his excited tone. It was a lead-pipe cinch – they had him. Their new friend wasn't going anywhere. Michael stepped down beside him and opened the hatch for him.

They descended the ladder, sliding past the small platform that allowed the commander to stand in the turret, and into the submarine's interior. Unlike a U-boat, there was only one compartment. Everything from the diesel and electric motors in the stern to the torpedo tube in the bow, were in the same long, narrow cabin. Less than ten feet at its widest, it was a cramped space, especially when you had the crew on board, with any equipment or weapons they needed on their raids.

The engines and propellor shaft took up the aft third

of the space. The rest of the cabin's deck was set two feet higher, and under that raised section of steel deck was the submarine's huge bank of batteries. Though he was not an especially tall man, Wolfgang could only stand up straight in the middle of the cylindrical space. The torpedo tube in the bow ran about a quarter of the entire length of the boat. Down alongside it, a heavy curtain was all that separated the toilet from the rest of the cabin. The cabin's seats were little more than stools with low backs fixed to the floor. All around the two men was the myriad of pipes, rows of cylindrical tanks, taps, dials and wheels whose functions Wolfgang would be so familiar with, once he learned what was where.

'She can do fifteen knots on the surface,' Michael said. 'And with my electric motor and improved screw design, she does twenty-two underwater . . .'

'Impossible! That is more than twice the speed of a submerged U-boat!"

'Yes, and most of the other navies' submarines too,' Michael grunted. 'All those admirals wanted a surface ship that could hide underwater. They sacrificed basic hydrodynamics in order to have a wide deck to strut upon, a deep keel, deck guns and high conning towers, all of which create drag. But John did not compromise on the shape. He based it on the form of a porpoise, designed specifically for travelling *underwater*. It is a true submarine, and the speed reflects that.' He grinned, and gave a wince. 'She handles like a pig on the surface, I'll grant you, especially in rough weather, with hardly any keel, but she can dive *much* faster, and when she's submerged, she can do up to twenty-two knots, and is still more maneuverable. She can turn in half the space your U-boat can, dive to a depth of two hundred and fifty feet, and can stay submerged for up to sixty hours, depending on the drain on the batteries.'

'A design this old capable of all that?' Wolfgang exclaimed. 'I'll believe it when I see it!'

'So . . . you do want to stick around then?'

Wolfgang hesitated, pent up with emotion, and then grinned and stuck out his hand and they shook on it. Behind him, near the lever controls for the dive planes, John Holland was clapping his hands in appreciation, giving Michael a nod.

'It is my aim to use it for exploration,' Michael went on. 'Shipwrecks, coral reefs . . . My wife is a professional diver, and she introduced me to a whole world down there most of us know nothing about. I want to see more. This is for Akiko and Liam, as much as for myself. To give them a greater sense of purpose, one that goes beyond all the strife that the country is facing.'

Having found a kindred spirt, he began outlining his plans for that future. He intended to put portholes in the hull, to allow observation, and powerful lights on the bow and sides. He was also attempting to design a mechanical arm that could be operated from inside, which Wolfgang snorted at, but Michael could tell that he was growing ever more enraptured by the possibilities. It was a future that offered more ambition and excitement than he could ever find on a fishing boat.

As they spoke, Michael noticed a dark look settling

over Wolfgang's expression, and he seemed to grow uneasy again.

'You used this to fight the British?' the German asked.

'Yes. For personal reasons, and to hide the existence of the boat for as long as possible, I made the decision not to torpedo ships. We carried out raids along the coast, and ran guns across from Britain, and we would meet that ship, the *Medusa*, out at sea sometimes to save them bringing the stuff in to port.'

'The men you said were watching me – this Jim Gorey. You think he was involved in the hijacking of my boat?'

'I don't know,' Michael admitted. 'You said yourself that you heard Germans. But it's possible that he and his men provided support.'

He was thinking now about what Gorey had said. How he'd mentioned, with such casual certainty, that Germans had stolen the U-boat. And the man was mighty keen to get his hands on a submarine. Had his company already made a start?

'They used chlorine gas, releasing it into the boat before . . . before going in with gas masks and knives. To . . . to kill my friends as quietly as possible,' Wolfgang said, the words catching in his throat. 'It was a strange thing. I don't know where they could have got this gas. Would your friend do such a thing? Would he murder people in such a way?'

There was another question there, unspoken. Would *Michael* murder someone like that? Avoiding Holland's hard gaze, Michael shrugged uncomfortably.

'Jim is a . . . a pragmatic man,' he said at last. 'He's

fighting a war against a much more powerful enemy. What kinds of things did you do, Wolfgang, during the war? What were you willing to do to defeat your enemy? How many men burned and drowned out there in the ocean, because of your torpedoes?'

'The war is over, Michael.'

'*Our* war isn't. Not yet.'

The mood had turned, and Michael felt the excitement of his plans for the future slipping away again. Had Jim been involved in the gas attack? Was he that intent on getting his hands on a submarine?

'It's an ugly business and no doubt,' he said at last. 'One I want to keep my children out of. I want their world to be different.'

Wolfgang nodded, and gave a solemn smile.

'I too, hope my children never go through what I have. Let us to do this then, my friend. Let us start to make this a better world. One where they never have to destroy another person's life for "a greater cause", eh?'

At that, Michael found his eyes straying to John Holland again. He placed his hand on the helm, the large steel wheel with its six protruding handles. There was a smaller version up in the turret, for steering while surfaced. He had done so much to refine his mentor's designs, but the essential features were very much the same as the early prototypes Holland had produced forty years before.

'"Young people destroying lives for a greater cause",' Holland said. 'A rather *optimistic* definition of war, don't you think?'

'Always have to have your dig, don't you?' Michael growled.

'Pardon?' Wolfgang said.

'Nothing. Sorry. Thinking aloud.'

And yet he could not help recalling that gloomy November night in 1883, when he arrived at the gate of the Morris and Cummings pier in the Canal Basin. He had been little older than Liam was now, and had been working with Holland long enough to have seen the inventor's signature many times. He had produced a decent forgery of it for the pass he had to show to the night watchman. Holland was known for being eccentric, so if it was odd that he had ordered his men to move his rather mysterious boats during the night, the watchman thought little of it. Michael followed his fellow Fenians onto the pier with quiet urgency.

Holland's first 'wrecking boat', the one Michael had seen tested that day in 1878, now lay at the bottom of the river, stripped of its parts and scuttled after the inventor had learned all he could from it. The two machines moored at this pier were his latest work. There was the now-famous three-man boat, known as the *Fenian Ram*, which was causing such excitement in the area, and a smaller, sixteen-foot model named the *Holland III*, built for navigation tests.

The Fenian movement had been funding the inventor's work in the hope of creating a weapon that could sink Britain's fearsome warships, but splits were forming in the organisation. Senior figures were fighting amongst themselves over how their money was being used. Some were taking issue with the growing cost of what was known as 'the salt water enterprise'. And though the Fenians didn't know it at the time, British intelligence agents, who had treated the strange boat as a harmless oddity at first, were starting to wake up to the threat it posed. They were secretly helping play each side against the other. Without consulting Holland, the Fenians made the decision to seize the boats and sell them, perhaps to Russia, in order to recover some of that money.

It was a painful decision for Michael to betray his mentor, but his first loyalty was to the movement. And so he produced the forged document they needed, and when the Fenians' tug drew up to the pier, he helped the others tie the towlines to the *Fenian Ram* and the *Holland III*. Then they towed the two submarines out into New York Harbour, around Manhattan, and started up the East River. Out in the open, the waters were choppy, and it was Michael who belatedly realised that the hatch in the *Holland III*'s turret wasn't closed properly. She had a low freeboard, and waves had begun slopping into the hatch. They watched helplessly as she took on water and began to founder, forcing them to cut the towline and she sank in a hundred and ten feet of water, leaving them with just the *Fenian Ram*.

Without its creator's expertise, the organisation was never able to operate the submarine properly, and they couldn't sell it. For a long time, Holland had no idea that Michael had taken part in the theft, and Michael would go on to work with him again some time later. The loss of years of his work was devastating for the Irish inventor, and it would take him a long time to recover, emotionally and financially. The *Fenian Ram* was left to rust in storage, and then in 1916, the hull was put on display in Madison Square Garden in New York, to raise funds for the victims of the Easter Rising.

John Philip Holland was the man Michael had admired most in all the world . . . and his was the first life Michael ruined for the cause of Irish freedom. It would not be the last.

Chapter 25
Rough Water

Five days had passed since Esther had seen Wolfgang Zürn with the Regans in Dublin. On that first day, she travelled down to Cork, found discreet accommodation in the city, bought a few changes of clothes, made an appointment to meet with Captain Moore's contact, Lieutenant Krishnan Chowdhury – he was away until later in the week – and hired a car from a garage. Cork was a large county with little public transport outside of the city and larger towns, and the Regans lived right out on the far edge of it. That also meant that getting close enough to observe them without being spotted was a challenge, as she was finding out. Few enough people out here owned a motor car, and the sight of one along these potholed, rutted roads attracted attention. And in these thinly-populated places, people were quick to notice any new faces.

She had decided to avoid official contact with the authorities if at all possible, and to rely on her own resources. Like Dublin Castle, Cork's army and police barracks were likely to be riddled with spies – or at least the ones that were still manned. The dozens of deserted

RIC stations across the county were, according to The Times, 'tombstones of British supremacy in Ireland'. Thankfully, she always made sure she travelled with plenty of ready money and her cheque book. While attempting to find ways to get close enough to the family to gain new intelligence, she settled on a new angle of investigation.

On her visits to the house before her exile, it had been common for Michael, and sometimes Midori and Kathleen, to disappear off on walks along the cliffs. They'd go north, away from the steps down to the small, private dock where they kept their three boats, and might be gone an hour or more. One day, Michael returned from one of these walks and left his coat hanging on the hook in the hall as usual. Esther had searched the pockets earlier that day. She noticed that he had rust stains on his hands when he returned; it was clear to her that he'd been involved in some kind of work while he'd been out. She waited for him to go upstairs and went through the pockets again. The coat was damp with sea spray, even though the cliff path was well above the level of the sea. And it was heavier. She found a .45 Colt automatic in the one of the pockets.

It seemed that Michael was keeping weapons concealed somewhere beyond the house, in the wild land along the cliffs. She had never been able to find the stash. Now that she was in search of a stolen submarine, she wondered if she'd been thinking too small. If Michael really was one of the Selkies, was it possible that he was working out of one of the smuggler's caves that she had heard rumours of along this section of the coast? Was there some path down to the base of those cliffs that had escaped her notice? And if so, might this marine engineer have the means of operating a German submarine? It seemed highly unlikely, but if *any* Irishman was capable of such a thing . . .

And so, on that Thursday morning, her fifth day in Cork, having studied a chart of the coast and decided on a course, she purchased a dinghy she found advertised in an ad in the local newspaper. It was a modest little craft, small enough to handle on her own, but the seller assured her it was more than suitable for sailing in the harbour. He cautioned her against heading out into open water however, unless she knew the coast. These could be dangerous waters. Esther had taken her father's boat out alone many times on the lake at home, and she knew Akiko and Liam regularly went sailing out here together. And though she did not have a great deal of experience navigating at sea, she was certain that she was capable of handling anything that *they* could.

She took some time to practise, and learn the boat's idiosyncracies, but little more than an hour after she'd left the harbour, sailing south along the coast, she began to question her earlier assumption.

A journey that would take hours by road would, she hoped, take far less time by sea, but she was finding the steepening waves alarming as she struggled to keep control of the sail in the gusty wind. It was not a stormy day and yet, as she found herself facing out into the open Atlantic, the elements seemed intent on defying her attempts to stay on course. The waves knocked the boat back and forth, and one moment she was hauling on the mainsheet to stop the front edge of the sail from flapping, the next, she was frantically letting it out, giving it slack to avoid tipping over as a powerful gust hit her forcefully at a slightly different angle. Fit and strong as she was, she was finding it exhausting, her hands were cramping, and she was sorely tempted to turn about and head back, but that would have meant that all her efforts had been wasted. Perhaps she could find some stretch of beach along the base of the cliffs she where she could safely put in to take a break.

It was only when she sailed into the small cove known as the Devil's Drain, the setting for so many local legends about disappearances, that she finally accepted that she had made a horrible mistake. The waves grew higher, throwing the little craft around and carrying her towards the rocks, and the wind became even more unpredictable as it swirled off the high cliffs.

As she wrestled to control the motion of the boat, she spotted something in the water about fifty yards from her. It looked like a pipe, sticking vertically up from the surface. She gasped.

A *periscope*. There was a submarine out there. And they were watching her.

She was only distracted for a moment, but it was enough. The sail snapped taut with a bang as it caught a gust, the boom swung hard, and she nearly lost her grip on the mainsheet, instinctively grabbing at it with both hands . . . and letting go of the tiller. The boat spun and she found herself side-on to the wind. It caught the sail with all its force and the boom smacked into the side of her head. She slumped over, stunned, as the boat keeled over, capsized and threw her into the sea.

In the next second, she was swallowing salt water, thrashing for the surface while still only half-conscious. Reaching the air, she coughed and threw up, barely getting another breath before she went under again, weak and sluggish in her heavy sailing clothes. Every time she got her head up above the water, a wave clapped over her face, and she was down again. She heard her own desperate scream underwater, still dazed. She couldn't get enough air, she couldn't stay up. She was drowning.

And then she felt a hand grabbing her upper left arm, and another took her on the other side. There were two other people in the water with her, and they were pulling her up towards the surface. Barely conscious, she surrendered to their grip, looking from one to the other. It was Midori and Liam, suddenly out here, in the middle of the cove, swimming with the grace and power of creatures born for the water. In her last moments before blacking out, she remembered the Irish legend of the selkies, the seal-people, and there and then, it felt like it could all be real.

She experienced consciousness in muddled instants, blurred images: Being dragged up a coarse, wet, sloping metal surface. Lowered into the quieter interior of some vessel. A large boat rather than a ship, she thought, judging by the feel, the sounds. She was laid on the deck, her cold body shivering violently, her cheek pressing against some kind of matting over metal plating. Something was covering her eyes. There was the noise of water washing high against the outside of the hull, the deck tilting back and forth, rising and falling. The stuffy air smelled of diesel and oil on hot metal, and beneath that, she recognized the faint, fresh odour of ozone from some strong electrical current close by. Hushed voices around her. Three people at least, maybe more.

Someone wrapped a blanket or towel around her. She heard a strange machine sound that she couldn't identify at first . . . a deep and throbbing hum. It was a motor, but an electric one, powerful enough that she could feel the vibrations through the deck. Only one type of vessel of this size ran on an electric motor that she knew of – because an electric motor didn't need oxygen or an exhaust pipe. She was regaining her senses now, and realized that her hands were bound behind her, and she had been blindfolded. She was a prisoner.

And her suspicions had been proved right after all. She was with the Regans . . . on board a *submarine*.

Chapter 26
Questions

Although Akiko had been warned not to talk to Esther, her mother was on board the *Subversive*, busy refuelling the diesel engine, the long hose snaking down through the hatch. The noise of the pump would prevent her from hearing anything from inside the vessel. Papa always insisted that the submarine be kept in a state of readiness. It couldn't turn its seventy-foot length around within the cave without the help of two winches on opposite walls, and no matter how tired the crew were, they always ensured that was done, and the fuel was topped up before they went home.

Everyone else had left the cave, so it fell to Akiko to keep watch on the woman who sat bound and blindfolded on the jetty. Esther had a blanket around her, but she was still shivering in her sodden clothes.

'Who's there?' she asked again, her head turning even though she couldn't see. 'Where am I? Midori? Liam? I know it was you who pulled me out of the water. Midori, I heard you whispering in Japanese on the boat! Michael? Come on, *I know you're there!*'

She didn't seem to be afraid, just uneasy, and even

slightly excited. Lunging forward, she got herself onto her feet, the blanket dropping from her shoulders. Akiko was standing only a few feet away, and she darted forward before Esther could step off the edge of the jetty, pushing her back into a sitting position.

'Who are you? That's . . . that's Akiko, isn't it?' Esther said, nodding to herself. 'Are you involved in this too? Look, you don't need the blindfold. I saw Midori and Liam in the water, and you had green tea recently – I just smelled it on your breath. How many people in Cork drink green tea, do you reckon? And your okaasan only drinks it first thing in the morning. You always were such a quiet one. Come on, leave my hands tied, but take the blindfold off, at least.'

'Don't move,' Akiko said quietly. 'You're only a few steps from the water.'

Esther nodded again in satisfaction that her deduction had been confirmed.

'Thank you,' she sighed. She was keeping her voice low too, as if guessing that Akiko did not want them to be overheard. Tilting her head, she added: 'Any chance you could take this off?'

'No. You're not allowed to see this place.'

'It's a cave,' Esther told her. 'I can tell by the sounds and the smell. What else am I not supposed to see?'

'That would the be entire point of the blindfold,' Akiko replied tartly.

'Yes, quite.' Esther lowered her head, breathing slowly. Then: 'So . . . what's going to happen to me?'

'Otosan's gone to our dock to get the runabout. He's

going to bring you back to the harbour.'

'Ah. Well, I suppose you can't just waltz into Cork in a *U-boat*, eh?'

Akiko didn't answer. She wondered why Esther thought they had a U-boat. She assumed the woman meant the one that was hijacked in Belfast, but she wasn't going to offer up any information Esther hadn't worked out for herself. Happy as she was to see her former friend alive and well after all this time, it was awakening some uncomfortable emotions. Akiko could not forgive the Englishwoman for betraying her family's trust. And any word spoken to a spy might be something that could be used against you. Still though, she could not not help feeling a thrill to be up so close to this woman, whom she had admired so very much, and who had been revealed to be a cunning and dangerous enemy.

'You're sure your otosan isn't going to kill me, and just dump my body out at sea?' Esther's tone was light, but there was a tension beneath the words. She was scared it might actually happen.

'He's not a murderer!' Akiko snapped.

'No! Of course not! I'm sorry. I'm sorry I said that.'

Esther chewed on her lip, and Akiko realised the woman was afraid of contradicting her. She needed Akiko on her side. That was what she'd be trying to do now, to win her over. To convince her to help. Akiko had read enough kidnapping stories to know how this might go. But it was true enough that kidnapped victims were sometimes killed. Her books had featured some spectacularly gruesome examples. And was she really sure that her father wouldn't kill to protect his secrets? Perhaps he'd done it many times. How were they to stop Esther from telling what she already knew? She had already learned enough to expose them.

'I know Wolfgang Zürn is here too,' Esther said. 'Did he help your father steal the U-boat up in Belfast? Do you know what happened to the rest of the crew? They were all *killed*, Akiko. That's . . . that's why I'm scared. You weren't involved in that, I'm certain of that. I know you have a good heart. You wouldn't want me to be hurt, would you?'

You don't seem to know as much as you think, Akiko thought. She had witnessed Wolfgang's grief over the last few days and knew it was genuine and heartfelt. Although perhaps the English woman wasn't all that far from the truth. Papa thought that Grim Jim Gorey was having the oberleutnant watched. That was how they'd ended up on the *Medusa*. Was it possible that Papa's friend killed Wolfgang's crew?

'How could . . . could you do it?' she asked, a belated sense of outrage rising within her. She was embarrassed to hear the croak in her voice, as if she might start crying. 'How could you pretend to be our friend like that, just to spy on Otosan? We brought you into our home. Was everything you said a lie? Was *anything* true?'

Esther went to speak and then hesitated, appearing to give the question serious thought.

'Often, the best way to deceive is to lie as little as possible,' she said at last. 'To build a lie on the truth. Kathleen was a wonderful friend to me when I was your age. And I was . . . I am genuinely fond of you, Akiko. I think you're an outstanding young woman, who shows huge promise. I have the greatest respect for Michael and Midori. But your father is a criminal and an enemy of the Crown. He has funded terrorism and spied and smuggled arms and committed arson and assault. Of this, I am quite sure, as I'm one of the people he has assaulted. I firmly believe that he has killed men, Akiko, though I don't know how many. And he may be involved in something that could cause even more deaths. I must tell you that it's my duty to bring him to justice. And if that means lying to your family and others, then it is a far lesser sin than those that *he* has committed.'

'And I suppose none of these are sins when the *police* and the *army* are committing them?'

Standing over her, Akiko stared down at this woman, bound and blindfolded, and for one vicious moment, she was tempted to kick her into the deep water. But the urge passed quickly, and even as it did, she heard the throaty gurgle of the family's motor boat. A sleek mahogany, thirty-foot runabout with a muscular petrol engine, it navigated carefully down the channel and into the wider part of the cave, carrying two more barrels to resupply the cave's large tank of diesel. As it approached, Midori rose up out of the submarine's hatch with the end of the fuel hose and she waved to her husband.

'Well, you'd better hope Otosan's not the evil fiend you make him out to be,' Akiko said sharply to their prisoner, 'or this is going to be a very short boat ride.'

Chapter 27
Wounded in Action

Liam had been taken out of school early that Thursday morning for training in the *Subversive*, as Michael wanted to take advantage of the tide and sea conditions. They had spun a story about some Japanese religious holiday that his aunt was celebrating. However, some of the teachers in the Christian Brothers secondary school were active in the independence movement, and before Liam left, his maths teacher had slipped him a piece of paper in the first class. The boy had felt his heart clench when he'd read the words upon it.

He couldn't act on them because he had to join the others in the submarine as soon as he got home. Now, with everyone distracted by the reappearance of Esther Sinclair, he took the first chance to slip away after they docked in the cave, but not before sneakily slipping a couple of brick-sized cardboard boxes into a satchel to take with him. Racing back to the house, he changed out of his wet clothes and hopped onto his bike.

Now, twenty minutes later, he was cycling back along Ned's Boreen as the last of the afternoon light faded, heading for Sheehan's Farm. Wait till he told his da they'd caught a British spy!

Mary Sheehan greeted him at the door. There was no trace of her brash, flirtatious manner now, as she led him into the kitchen. She was all business, a bearing that matched her mother, who was busy changing the bandage on the bullet wound in Lar O'Leary's shoulder. He was sitting at the oilskin-covered table with his shirt off, and Liam was shocked to see the state he was in. All thought of Esther Sinclair was forgotten. The wound was just over his da's collarbone on the left side, and leaked blood when Mrs Sheehan peeled off the soiled dressing. Lar's face was grey and coated in sweat and he seemed weak and exhausted. Liam had never seen his father looking so vulnerable.

'Liam . . . ugh!. There . . . there you are,' he said, his face creasing up, and it was clear that taking a breath to speak was causing him severe pain. 'Thanks for . . . thanks for comin', led.'

'Da! What happened?!'

'It's all right, son. Looks . . . looks worse than it is. We had a run-in with some coppers up . . . up . . . in Derry. We ran out of ammo and got pinned down in a burnt-out house. One of them . . . got . . . got me good and proper. We were lucky to get away. Don't worry though . . . it'll be grand. I've survived worse than this.'

Even that seemed to take a lot out of him, and Mrs Sheehan told him to hush until she was done replacing the bandage. He gave his son a weary, sheepish grin. Liam took the opportunity to pull the two boxes from his satchel.

'Listen, Da. I got some ammo for yeh! From Uncle Michael. There's some three-oh-threes for the Lee Enfields, and some four-fifty-fives for the Webleys. Michael won't be usin' them, so I thought . . . I thought you could take them up the north.'

'That's marvellous, Liam,' Lar gasped. 'Good . . . led. Good led!'

Mrs Sheehan was finished, and she waved at Mary to come out of the kitchen to let the commander talk to his son. Lar put his hand to his shoulder, and then motioned to Liam to help him get his shirt back on. The material was stained with his blood, but it didn't show once he had his jacket on.

'You need to let a proper doctor look at that,' Liam said, feeling queasy at what he'd seen. 'It could get infected.'

'I'll live for the time bein',' Lar replied. 'C'mere to me now. I had a telephone call from Jim Gorey. He's . . . he's here in Cork at the moment.'

'He is?' Liam tried to hide his surprise. Why had Gorey's ship dropped them off in Howth, telling his uncle the *Medusa* was headed to Southampton? Had the rebel leader just been trying to get rid of them?

'He said he met yeh in Belfast.' Lar gave a chuckle and then groaned, rubbing sweat off his face. 'After me . . . after me tryin' to keep you out of it, yer uncle brings you right . . . right up into the lion's den . . .'

'I wish everyone would stop tryin' to *keep me out of it!*' Liam growled. 'I'm ready to get stuck in! I'm . . . I'm . . . I'm scared of it, like. I may not be a . . . a warrior, like you or him, but I can do me part!'

His father held his hand up defensively, and tried to sit straighter in his chair.

'Anyway, it is what it is. Gorey was impressed with yeh – said yeh had some neck on yeh. Smacked down a B-Special, no less! He liked what he saw in yeh. And . . . and he . . . he asked me to ask you for yer help.'

'Help?' Liam exclaimed, a buzz of excitement growing in him. 'How can I help *him*?'

For the first time in his life, he saw his father adopt a pleading expression, taking Liam's hand in both of his and squeezing it. Liam found this, along with the sweaty weakness, profoundly unsettling. Could one wound really have brought him so low, so quickly? He had always considered his father indestructible.

'Your uncle is a divvil for his secrets, always has been, ever since his time in America,' Lar said. 'And he's right too. It's kept him alive. And your ma was the same. But I know everything, Liam. When Michael came back to Ireland years ago, to build his new factory, Kathleen told me about the submarine he was making, and how he needed a place to hide it. It was me who showed him where the cave was, and me and the leds made sure people kept away from it. I helped him find a small crew he could trust. His Selkies. He even asked me to lead the raids on shore–.'

'What? Are yeh serious?' Liam piped up.

'Yeah, but sure I couldn't get into that thing! Trap meself in that tiny steel can, with nothing but tons of water above me? No, it'd be like a nightmare for me.

I've never been good with tight spaces.'

Liam didn't know that about his father. Another vulnerability – one that had been there all along.

'Your ma made me swear to keep that secret though, on my life and on hers, and I have, to this very day. Few enough in HQ in Dublin knew about it either. Mick put his foot down about that. He'd run his operations the way he wanted. And when he lost his nerve after Bloody Sunday, he told them he'd scuttled the boat because it was going to be captured by the Royal Navy. Sent it to the bottom of the Irish Sea. But he didn't, did he? It's the best weapon we've ever had, Liam, and it's still . . . still sitting there in that cave . . . *doin' nothin'*. Don't try and deny it – I've been down there. I've seen it. Might have helped meself to a box or two of that ammo an' all. Sure he wasn't usin' it, like you say.'

He wiped his sleeve across his face again.

'But I kept your mother's secret, like I promised, and I respected Michael's decision. Now Gorey's come to me, and he . . . he wants a submarine, Liam. He wants Michael to build another one, to use against the British Navy. He says there's years of fighting still left to do, and the future of the struggle rests on bein' able to strike at the navy the way we've done with their Tommies and peelers. It's time to start sendin' torpedoes up the arses of those arrogant swines. And I know he has those things, I've seen them in the cave.'

Years of fightin' still left? Liam thought. Who'd stand for that? Sure, the country's already in bits. And Michael had been right about using torpedoes. The first time they sank a ship, the British would know the Irish had a submarine. They'd have the entire Royal Navy combing the seas and coasts for them. His uncle had only survived this long because the British still had no idea the *Subversive* existed.

'Da, what are yeh askin'?'

'Gorey wants you to help persuade Michael to . . . to . . . to build a new submarine for us,' Lar wheezed, 'but there's already one right there, and . . . I can't tell him because of this promise. I won't betray your mother's memory. But you . . . you can *release* me from that promise. You can speak for your mother. Let me tell him. Michael's no good to us any more, he's lost his nerve. The man's mind is broken . . . you must know it! He's hearin' things and seein' things. Let me tell Gorey about the cave, and we can take that boat and start stickin' it to the navy. We can start building our own navy! What do yeh say?'

Liam unconsciously took a step back, pulling his hand out of his father's. Shaking his head, he turned away, then faced his father again.

'"Build our own navy?"' he said, embarrassed now, as tears welled in his eyes. '"We've years of fightin' left to do"? What are yeh ravin' about? You nearly got killed 'cause you and your leds *ran out of bullets*, 'cause you can't steal them from peelers any more. Yer sneakin' guns around in turf carts and gettin' wounds patched up by a farmer. Da, you and the Volunteers fought the Brits all the way to a truce! Got them to hold off on wreckin' the country just for a while, and make them *listen* to us. God Almighty . . . Collins and them are over there tryin' to cut a deal to get us free. If the Brits find out the state we're in, he and the rest of them will be laughed out of London!'

'Yer just a boy, Liam,' Lar snarled, hauling himself to his feet with a stiff, pained motion. 'Yeh've a lot to learn. Those pigs in London are just stringin' us along – lettin' out the leash a bit. There's no freedom to be had there! We won't get anything from them that we don't take by force. It's the only language they understand. And it's a language *Jim Gorey* speaks better than anyone. And we'll beat them one day, you mark my words!'

'What, like this? With empty guns and blind faith?' Liam retorted. 'We will in me hole!'

'Get out then, if that's how yer goin' to talk to me! Get out, yeh little cur, and don't come back until yer ready to show me some respect!'

'Maybe I won't come back! Liam bellowed. 'Maybe you better find someone else to . . . to . . . to fetch your bloody sandwiches! To Hell with yeh!'

And that was how he left it, slamming the door behind him.

Chapter 28
'You've Gotta Have Limits'

Michael drove the motor boat out to a point a couple of miles off the Old Head of Kinsale, beyond which lay the mouth of Cork harbour. There, he stopped the engine, and turned to Esther, who sat beside him, and pulled off her blindfold. Her hands were still bound behind her, and even though she was seated, she had to sway with the motion of the boat to stay upright.

'Why did you bother saving me from drowning, if you're going to dump me out here?' she asked sourly. 'Are you just trying to protect Akiko's innocence?'

'I'm not going to dump you in the sea,' Michael sighed. 'But this is a difficult situation, and I'm not sure how to resolve it. I know that you didn't identify me after Bloody Sunday, when you could have, and I'm grateful for that. My family is grateful. Perhaps you only did it for Akiko's sake, or to honour Kathleen's memory, but I want you to know that I ended my operations not long after that. A couple of my crew were killed, another went to prison, one lost his mind . . . and . . . and really, I just couldn't bear it any more. Everything we did seemed to be making things worse for the people we cared about. But I have hope now, with the truce and the treaty, that maybe we can make it work.

'I still support the cause, Esther, but I'm done hurting people. If you draw attention to my family, my children could suffer for it along with me. I'm asking you to . . . to just leave us be.'

Esther realised she could still live through this if she kept her mouth shut, but she could barely contain her anger now, finding herself at his mercy once again, after the terrifying, humiliating day in that hotel a year ago. She couldn't endure having to submit to this man, to pretend she was anything but herself; an Englishwoman who knew her duty. She was going to have this out with him, here and now, no matter what it cost her.

'You're done hurting people?' she scoffed. 'And what was that in Belfast, when you killed those poor men with chlorine gas? You can't fool me, Michael. I know that German, Oberleutnant Zürn, is here. You pulled me onto that U-boat, right there in the Devil's Drain. And there's something bigger going on, though I haven't figured out what yet. I'm grateful to you for saving my life, but how can you expect me to keep quiet about that?'

Michael regarded her for a bit, then pointed towards the headland that blocked the view to Cork Harbour.

'John Holland taught at a school just a few miles over that way, years back, before he moved to the States. He died just after the Great War started, and part of me is glad he did. He was, at heart, an idealistic dreamer. He believed that submarines would make warfare at sea so unworkable, they would effectively end it. He died before he could witness the nightmare he helped create.'

Michael pointed in the opposite direction, out to sea.

'And a few miles that way, is where the *U-20* torpedoed the *Lusitania*, less than a year later. That liner was one of the fastest ships on the sea, sailing from New York to Liverpool. It was 1915, so your family had moved back to England at that stage. I'd say you were in university? Up until then, the U-boats hadn't really been attacking civilian ships like that, without warning. The Allied navies were trying to strangle Germany's economy, cutting off access by sea, so Germany started using U-boats to do the same to Britain. At the start of the war, they used to send a signal first, to let people abandon a ship before they destroyed it. It was a matter of honour.

'But a year into the war, that kind of chivalry was over. It only took *one* torpedo, from *one* submarine. It hit the *Lusitania's* bow, then something else exploded, and the ship went down in eighteen minutes. It happened so fast, most people never got out. More than half the passengers and crew, over a thousand people, were killed. They either got dragged down with the ship, or drowned after they managed to get off. There were families with children. The poorest people, of course, were in steerage, the lowest part of the vessel. They had the furthest to run to get out on deck.

'I was home in Cork on the day it happened, and when the mayday call was picked up onshore, everyone who had a boat went out to try and help. The ship was still moving as it sank. It left a two-mile trail of debris and people in the water. We'd pulled out all the survivors in the first three hours. After that, it was just dead bodies. We were finding them for days afterwards.'

Michael didn't seem to be seeing Esther in those few minutes. It was as if he was witnessing the ocean on that day again, scattered with dozens of floating corpses.

'I'd . . . I'd never seen slaughter like it,' he said, grimacing bitterly. 'One torpedo, from one submarine, and it killed more than a thousand people. All civilians. The Germans justified it by saying the ship had been carrying ammunition for the military. That made it a legitimate target.

'I didn't hijack that submarine in Belfast, Esther. I built *my own one* years ago, from Holland's designs, in one of my factories in the States. That's why I've brought Oberleutnant Zürn to Cork. I brought it over here during the war, but I made a decision on that day in 1915 that I'd never use it to sink ships. You've gotta have limits to what you're willing to do, no matter what the cause.

'There were some who called me weak and a coward for that decision, but it was better that way anyhow, to keep a low profile. My critics were happy to use the guns and ammo I smuggled in for them. Our greatest advantage was that the Brits never figured out we had a submarine. I never became some admiral's white whale.

'But like I said, I'm done with the violence. And no one else will use my boat either, I'll swear to that on my life.'

Esther exhaled, groaned and shook her head, not sure how much of his claims she could believe – or if it even mattered.

'Michael, you might have drawn these lines for yourself . . . I don't know . . . but . . . but there are plenty who *haven't*. There are some who care nothing for the truce or . . . or . . . or anything short of complete victory over the British Empire. I didn't come here for you – I came looking for the U-boat. Because I think that whoever stole it, also stole a shipment of chlorine gas in France. They might have used a canister or two in the hijacking, but they have a whole *truckload* of it left, and they stole it to *use* it. And I don't think they're setting limits on what they'll do for their cause. If it wasn't you, then maybe you can help me. Help me find this stuff, Michael, before it's used to create a catastrophe.'

Michael gazed at her, unblinking, and then shrugged.

'I'm out of things now, I don't know what's going on any more,' he told her. 'I'm going to drop you back to the harbour. There's nothing I can do to stop you, short of killing you or keeping you captive, and like I said, I'm done with all that . . . So you go back to your masters, and do what you need to do. There's a truce on. Maybe we can leave each other alone long enough for things to work out. I suppose we'll just have to see.'

Taking out a knife, he motioned at her to lean forward and she still felt a spark of fright before he reached behind her and cut the rope binding her wrists. Then he sheathed the knife and took something from his pocket. It was her FN Model 1910.

'The clip's empty,' he grunted, 'in case you were thinking of trying anything.'

Her mouth was gaping slightly as she took the gun

back, realising that she would have been desperately disappointed if she'd lost the gun her father had given her. Michael switched the engine back on, put his hand on the throttle lever, and was about open it up, when he saw something that made him stop. There was a ship out on the water; a small freighter, about halfway between them and the wide mouth of the harbour. Opening a compartment beside him, he pulled out a pair of binoculars and peered through them, a frown on his face.

'What is it?' Esther asked.

'Nothing,' he replied. 'Just . . . someone I didn't expect to see around here for a while.'

He put the field glasses down on the seat between them, took the wheel and pushed the throttle forward. Picking up the binoculars, she aimed them in the same direction. They were good quality, the magnification just strong enough to enable her to see the name painted on the stern of the ship.

She was called *Medusa*.

Chapter 29
Photographic Evidence

Papa was taking Esther back to Cork. He'd have a chat with her along the way, and Akiko was sure they'd work things out. Liam had disappeared without a word as soon as they'd got back to the cave, and his bicycle was gone. Akiko guessed that he'd gone to meet his father. Mama had finished refuelling the submarine, and was taking a bath before dinner. Wolfgang was down in Papa's study, examining the maze of pipework, tanks and wiring on the *Subversive's* blueprints.

They were all calling him 'Wolfgang', now that they had spent hours with him, training in the *Subversive*.

Akiko had taken advantage of the peace and quiet to make some prints of the photographs she'd taken in Belfast. She had already made several, which were hanging on the line in her bedroom to dry. In the red light of her dark room, she watched carefully as a new image appeared on the sheet of gelatin silver paper, waiting for the edges to sharpen. It was a picture of the statements painted on the wall, taken in the light of the streetlamp, and though the low light meant it lacked proper definition, she was pleased with the image. The white words stood out starkly from the brick surface, framed by dramatic shadow:

'ULSTER WILL FIGHT AND ULSTER WILL BE RIGHT' and 'HOME RULE IS ROME RULE'.

Glancing at the little clock on the wall in front her, she used the tongs to take the sheet out of the tray of developer fluid, then bathed it in the stop and the fix trays, to finish the process. Then there was a final rinse in water to remove the chemicals. Hearing a distant knock on her bedroom door, she made sure the rest of her blank paper was properly wrapped up away from the light and then opened the door of her dark room, releasing her from the pungent, metallic combination of odours from the chemicals. She went over to open the bedroom door. It was Wolfgang.

'I'm sorry to disturb you,' he said, holding up a book, a copy of *The Clipper of the Clouds*, by Jules Verne. 'Do you think your father would mind if I borrowed this?'

'No, of course not,' she replied. 'I presume you've read *Twenty Thousand Leagues Under the Seas?*'

'I confess that I have not.'

'Oh my God.' Akiko ushered him in, her expression a blend of shock, sympathy and excitement, as if she'd just discovered a man who'd lived his whole life on a desert island. 'Stay right there, I have it here somewhere.'

And she quickly began searching through the books stacked on her floor because there was no more room on her shelves. As she searched, Wolfgang gazed at the prints hanging on the lengths of cord strung across that end of the room.

'Are you comfortable in your new room?' she asked

him. 'Is there anything else you need?'

'No, no, it is very fine. I am the son of a fisherman and a navy sailor. It is much better than I am used to.'

'I'm sorry about the state of the house . . . the fire damage and that,' she said, tutting as she knocked over a particularly unstable pile. 'It's taking such a long time to fix everything. It's the same reason Otosan thinks he'll be able to find you an empty cottage nearby soon. We've lost a lot of people over the last few years.'

'This is true all over.' Wolfgang nodded sadly. 'The fire in your house, that was the police, yes?'

'Yes . . . well, the Black and Tans. More like mercenaries than real policemen.'

The German continued to study the pictures.

'These photographs . . . You took all these while you were on the *Medusa*?'

'Yes,' she said, moving one stack aside to reveal another behind it, scrunching her face up as she glanced back at them. 'They didn't come out as well as I'd hoped. The light wasn't good enough in most of them.'

'Even so, I am very impressed,' he told her. 'You have great ability. I am interested in photography. I don't have your eye for it. I would love to work in motion pictures, but I am no artist.'

'Thanks! One of the things I'd like to do with the *Subversive* once we've added portholes is to see if we could fit a camera to it, so we could photograph what's in the water. Because . . . I think . . . If we're going to use it to explore . . . you know, shipwrecks and that kind of thing, we should find a way to take photographs, right?'

Do you think that would be possible?'

When the German didn't answer, she looked back at him. His gaze had come to rest on one particular print, and she saw a sickened scowl come over his face.

'Wolfgang? Wolfgang, what is it? What's wrong?'

'Where was this?' he rasped, pointing. 'This man here. Who is he?'

It was the photograph of the fellow who had been working in the *Medusa*'s engine room. The one who hadn't spoken, but warned her away with a wave, before Joe Goat had moved her on to the boiler room.

'I met a friend of Otosan's below decks. He showed me around the engine room. That man was working there. Why? What's wrong?'

'Because that . . .' Wolfgang said in a guttural growl as he pointed at the object the man was working on, '. . . *that* is an ocular box. You see these handles, the eyepiece? It is a part from a *Type U93* targeting periscope. So what is German submarine component doing on an *Irish cargo freighter*?'

Chapter 30
Right Under Their Noses

On landing at the harbour, Esther returned to the car she had hired, and drove back to the guesthouse where she was staying. There, she found a message had been left for her: Lieutenant Krishnan Chowdhury, Nigel Moore's friend, had returned her call, and wished to meet her at her earliest convenience. Shaking her head, she dropped the note on the bedside table when she reached the room.

She shed her wet clothes, put on a dressing gown, and then, sitting on the bed, she broke down her automatic pistol. It needed to be cleaned, dried and oiled to prevent any damage by the salt water. Then she reassembled it and reloaded it. When that was done, she went down the hall to the bathroom she shared with the other guests, and took a long bath, leaving the gun within reach, and took stock of her situation. She felt dejected, exhausted and drained of all motivation. It took a long time for the last of the chill to fade from her weary body.

She had nearly died. She had nearly died, and the Regans had saved her. If Michael had really had a hand in the attack on the U-boat, if he was involved in stealing the chlorine gas, then why would he rescue her, at the risk of being exposed? He should have left her to drown. Had it been to keep up appearances for his family? But then he took her back to Cork, when he could have dropped her into the sea, once they were out of sight of Midori and the two children. Nobody would have been any the wiser. No, she found herself forced to believe him. He had not taken part in the hijacking. And yet, he was far from innocent.

The Irish rebels had a submarine.

No . . . . *Michael Regan* had a submarine. He'd said that it was his, that nobody else could or would use it, now that he had developed this newfound respect for life. She snorted at that, and laid a hot facecloth over her eyes. A submarine. A *Holland* submarine.

She remembered when she'd spent time with the family, how Michael would sometimes talk about those pioneering years and his fondness and respect for his mentor, though she gathered that there had been some kind of falling out before Holland died. Michael had always maintained that he had put his work on war machines behind him, that he had left the company after the military started taking control of things.

Evidently, he had not put it very far behind him.

Even in those early days, British intelligence had taken an interest. A doctor named Thomas Miller Beach, also known as 'Henri le Caron', had worked for the service at the end of the last century, infiltrating the Irish nationalists in America. He had been one of the first to warn of the threat posed by the bizarre weapon the Irish inventor was building in New Jersey.

The contraption had been treated as a harmless oddity at first. Little did the intelligence service suspect at the time, but John Holland's oddities would eventually be commissioned as the first vessels in the US Navy's new submarine fleet.

There were other inventors working on the same challenge at that time, of course. Michael had talked about Simon Lake, Holland's main competitor in the US. The combined work of Thorsten Nordenfelt in Sweden and George Garret in England would eventually lead to the first submarines in the German and Ottoman navies. In France, Maxime Laubeauf was building his *Narval*, a potential match for Holland's craft.

But in 1897, the US Navy put the *Holland VI* through its tests and the 'submarine torpedo boat' proved its lethal abilities. In war games, this small boat showed itself capable of sinking the most powerful battleships, striking without being seen. The Irishman's creation was beginning to inspire fear. People were calling it the 'Sea Devil', the 'Monster Warfish' and the 'Hell Diver', as if it were some mythical creature. Eventually, even the Royal Navy felt compelled to buy his designs, despite their distrust of the inventor and his Irish republican loyalties.

Now, twenty years later, Esther had stumbled across one of these boats. She had been inside one, right here, in waters controlled by the Royal Navy. Surely though, it was hopelessly obsolete compared to more modern designs? And yet it had been here for years, right under their noses, and they had never even suspected.

She thought of the pistol that lay on the stool beside the bath, and cast her mind back to when she'd first been posted to Ireland, briefed with infiltrating the women's movement, Cumann na mBan. Her mission had been to find out where the rebels were obtaining their arms, and she'd learned that there was a whole range of sources, including corrupt British soldiers who were willing to provide Lee Enfield rifles at £3 a pop. A bargain at the price. Most weapons, however, were stolen in raids.

The intelligence officers in Dublin Castle had been particularly mystified by the success of the rebel groups operating along the coast. Crown forces had once exercised firm control of Ireland's shores, and yet coastguard stations, lighthouses and lightships were being attacked at night and seized without warning, the rebels always evading capture afterwards. She recalled too, whispers among Cumann na mBan members of caches of arms being brought into the country by means known only to a tiny few. And she remembered the rumours of the mysterious group they called the Selkies.

Now she had an explanation for so much of it. The missing piece. She dismissed Michael's pleas to be left alone. Truce or no truce, her superiors would have to act on this. After the destruction and terror that Germany's U-boats had caused in the Irish Sea during the war, the Royal Navy could not tolerate a submarine operated by Irish republicans.

Wait until Faulkner hears about this, she thought.

Faulkner. She pulled the facecloth off and blinked. She had to tell him that Zürn was here with the Regans.

Did he really think the German was still in Belfast? The more she thought about it, the more unlikely it seemed. She could think of no one in the service who was better informed on events in Ireland, and he was not prone to making mistakes. No, there was something he wasn't telling her, and she needed to know what it was. Ten minutes later, she was dried, dressed in fresh clothes and sitting in the guesthouse's cramped little telephone booth, with only a curtain to pull across to offer a modicum of privacy. Thankfully, the other guests downstairs were engrossed in a game of cards, and the shrill chatter from the living room would drown out her hushed voice.

It took a few minutes to get through to Faulkner, and from his tone it was clear that, as ever, he had more important things to do.

'Yes, Esther, what is it?'

'I'm down in Cork, Edward, following up that lead I was telling you about on Michael Regan,' she said, a little put out at his manner. 'There's a lot we need to talk about. For a start, Oberleutnant Wolfgang Zürn isn't in Belfast assisting the police in their inquiries, he's down *here*, assisting Regan in his–.'

'Oh for Heaven's sake, girl!' Faulkner cut her off. 'I've already told you that matter is well in hand! Look here, there's an operation in progress that . . . Oh, why am I bothering to argue with you?' He paused for a few seconds, and she heard him breathing, low and slowly; a sign he was thinking something through. Then he was back: 'All right, maybe it's just best to bring you on board. I have some agents down there already. I want you join up with them, and they can brief you on what's going on. Take this down.'

He gave her an address at the edge of town.

'You'll meet a man there named Dollmann. He'll be expecting you tomorrow evening at six o'clock. He'll brief you and – let me impress upon you the importance of this – *you are to obey his orders in every respect.* Do you understand?'

'Yes,' she sighed. 'But listen, Edward, there's so much you need to . . .'

There was only a dial tone. Faulkner had hung up. Sighing, Esther hung the receiver back on its fork. It was beneath her dignity to call him back, desperately seeking his attention.

Some day, she swore, I'll be the one giving orders to men like that. I'll be the one hanging up the phone.

Chapter 31
A Dangerous Game

The following evening, Friday, the 2nd of December, it was already dark by half five, with what little sun there was left hidden behind a curtain of cloud. Esther was striding out the door to where her car was parked, but before she could get in, another vehicle pulled up behind it.

It was a British Army staff car, a Vauxhall D-type, driven by a bearded Asian man wearing a Sikh dastār, the religion's distinctive turban. He stepped onto the path and waved her over. He was in the uniform of a sapper, a Royal Engineer, and he seemed agitated, even scared. Remembering the last time a man had pulled up in a car outside her guesthouse, she approached cautiously, careful to stay out of reach, with her hand clutching the gun in her coat pocket.

'Miss Sinclair? You must come with me, please!' he said in low, but dramatic tone. 'I am Lieutenant Krishnan Chowdhury, Nigel's friend. I left a message for you yesterday. You are in some peril, Ms Sinclair. You must come with me right now!'

'I'm delighted to meet you, but I'm afraid I'm on my way to a meeting,' she replied warily. 'Could we do this another time?'

'You must not go to that meeting!' he implored. 'It's a trap. Those men have been sent to capture you!'

He had a slender build, his face handsome, if a little gaunt, its lines exaggerated by his obvious anxiety. His accent was that of a man who'd been born and raised in India, but who'd been educated among the British officer class.

'Please, Nigel sent me,' he said again, a little calmer this time, holding his hands up as if she was a startled horse in danger of kicking him. Perhaps he'd noticed the shape in her pocket. 'If you make that rendezvous, you will be taken captive. If you *don't* make that meeting, the police will be sent after you. They already have a description of your car. There is a warrant out for your arrest . . . for treason.'

'I beg your pardon?' she exclaimed. 'What are you talking about?'

'I'll tell you everything, but we need to go!'

Esther hesitated, her eyes narrowing, suspicious of another lie, another attempt to hoodwink her.

'You say you're a friend of Nigel's. Where was he serving when he was injured in a German gas attack?'

'It was in Loos, in France, in 1915. But the gas was British,' Chowdhury told her. He gestured towards his car. 'Now . . . if you please?'

Reluctantly, she walked around the front of the car, and got into the passenger seat as he sat back behind the wheel. He accelerated off down the street, glancing back furtively from time to time, and grimacing as he saw a pair of headlights in the distance behind them.

'I think someone was watching your place,' he said. 'They weren't content to wait for you to show up for the rendezvous.'

'Can you please tell me what's going on?' she snapped at him. 'What do you mean, I'm been charged with *treason*?'

'Faulkner's had the warrant issued because he wants you picked up,' Chowdhury said. 'Look, I don't . . . I don't know anything about this, I can only tell you what Nigel told me, and he doesn't have all the details. But apparently . . . Hang on . . .' He swerved round a corner, took another, tighter bend at speed, and looked back at the car behind them. 'No, they're still there. All right, so . . . Faulkner . . . Faulkner has an informant in the Irish group that were involved in the hijacking of that U-boat in Belfast. Nigel says you were right about that – they did use chlorine gas in the attack . . .'

'I bloody knew it!'

'Yes, well . . . that's only the half of it. The Irish were just there in support. It was a bunch of Germans who did the actual hijacking, a Freikorps company, and it was they who stole the gas canisters in France.'

Esther nodded. That made sense. The Freikorps were a German paramilitary group. Like the Irish republican movement, the organisation was made up of lots of independent units, but was much, much larger, and with even less central control than the Irish rebels. They tended to be staunch nationalists, though many were less idealistic and somewhat more right-wing than their Irish counterparts. Many were soldiers for hire, ex-military types turned mercenaries and 'adventurers'.

When Germany had been forced to give up much of its military, it had left a lot of bitter ex-soldiers out in the cold as they watched their country getting carved up and controlled by the war's victors. If the Freikorps were making moves to drive their enemies back out of Germany, a U-boat would be extremely useful, as would a truckload of chlorine gas. They had a reputation as a ruthlessly effective fighting force, and there were plenty of ex-navy sailors among them, including U-boat crews.

'How did the Irish get involved?' she asked.

'The deal was, the Irish help them get into Belfast and steal the submarine, and the Germans provide support for an *Irish* operation. They're planning a gas attack, but Nigel doesn't know where, or against whom. Faulkner hasn't kept him in the loop.'

'I don't understand. I've been trying to track down that gas. Why would Faulkner want me arrested?'

'Because you wouldn't stay out of it, even when he ordered you to.' The Sikh officer took another turn and gunned the engine on a long, straight stretch of coastal road. 'Faulkner's not trying to *stop* the Irish attack. He *wants* them to carry it out.'

Esther turned to stare at him, about to protest that this made no sense, and then it struck her.

'The peace process,' she said. 'He wants to sabotage the peace process. If the Irish launch a major attack on a British target, he thinks Lloyd George will pull out of the negotiations.'

'Yes,' Chowdhury said, nodding.

'And by accusing me of treason, Faulkner's discredited me. Anything . . . Anything I try to say will be treated with extreme suspicion.'

'Yes. I'm sorry. This is a foul thing he's done to you.'

'Does Nigel know who else in the service is involved?'

'He didn't say.'

She was already pondering the pernicious logic of it. With her father's influence, she was sure she could defend herself against this charge, but it would take time, and it would not prevent her arrest. The accusation was too serious. Faulkner just needed her out of the picture long enough for these events to unfold. No doubt he could brush it away later as a misunderstanding.

Edward Faulkner was an English supremacist and always had been. He considered the Irish to be an inferior race, and detested the way his Prime Minister, David Lloyd George, had deigned to acquiesce to their demands. In Faulkner's view, the wretches were right where they deserved to be, under the heel of the British Empire, and the republican rebels were little more than a stone in its shoe. He was offended by the obscenity of these 'thugs' being given the status of statesmen, sitting in Downing Street, discussing terms with the Prime Minister. If the Irish were not willing to submit to British rule, than they should face the full force of its military might. The army on the streets with artillery and tanks, warships in the harbours. . . whatever it took to quell the miscreants. Give an inch to one of them and you could start a chain of events that could collapse the Empire.

Esther and Chowdhury were both silent for some time after that. It started to rain, and she angled the top half the of the windscreen up so that her companion could see, though it meant the wind blew some of the rain in through the gap underneath. It was already dark and there were no streetlights this far out from the city centre, so even with the headlights, it was hard to see along the muddy, pockmarked road and now the rain made it worse.

'Where can I take you?' he asked.

For a moment, she was at a loss. She'd been following his lead, but it was clear that he'd been caught up in this with no more warning than she had. And she didn't have an answer. She was a British agent on the run from Crown forces in rebel country. She realised there was only one place to go that made sense.

'Stay on this road for a few more miles, then there'll be a turn to the right. I'll direct you. But we'll need to lose these bounders first,' she said, pointing her thumb back at the car that was following them, and he nodded.

'I am done with this country, I can't wait to get out of it,' Chowdhury muttered as he wiped some of the light spray from his face after another silence. 'The sun never shines here, and it can rain at any time, and everyone is so *white*. They hate everything British, and some of them have a special venom for those of us who are brown-skinned *and* British. We're taking a huge risk coming this far out of town, even with the truce. A lone soldier out with a woman, on a dark, isolated road? If we run into any rebels . . .' He shrugged helplessly. 'There wasn't even any point in my trying to disguise myself as a local was there? I mean . . . I can't do the accent.'

He looked over at her and burst out laughing, which lit up his face, and she couldn't help but smile back.

'Isn't a part of you interested in how this will all turn out?' she asked him. 'If Ireland can get its independence, don't you think India would try too?'

The lightness left his face.

'I am a loyal soldier, Miss Sinclair.'

'I'm sorry, I didn't mean . . .'

'I know what you meant, and you're right.' He shook his head. 'Britain will face a reckoning in India, have no doubt about that. I am afraid of what's coming. Back in 1916, during the rising in Dublin, you know that many of the soldiers deployed to quash the rebellion were Irish? They were shooting their own people.

'Last year, a group of Irishmen serving with the army in Jalandhar in the Punjab *mutinied* when they heard what was happening over here. The spirit of rebellion is spreading like a fire around the world. I served with men like Nigel Moore in the war. They are my brothers. I will never take up arms against them, but . . . but I will not serve in the British army in India. That's why I'm here. I asked to be transferred here because the brass wanted to send me back to India. And they said yes, because no officer in his right mind *wants* to serve in Ireland now.'

That made Esther think of something else.

'You're a sapper. Did you ever work with chlorine gas during the war?'

'Yes. It's dreadful stuff.'

'I agree. But if you were to deploy it for a terror attack,

how would you use it for best effect?'

The engineer chewed his lip, uncomfortable at having to contemplate the situation, but after a few moments, his face settled and became expressionless, the demeanour of a professional soldier.

'For best effect? For the greatest number of casualties? On the battlefield, our biggest challenge was the wind, so I'd use it in an enclosed environment, where a large number of the enemy were gathered, with no access to gas masks. Ideally, one where you could lock them in and seal the doors and windows to contain the gas.'

Esther nodded. Yes, that had been her thinking too. Somewhere like a moored submarine. That would have been a useful test. She was already trying to work out who and where the Irish group's target might be. It would have to be very high profile, given everything they were doing in preparation for it, and the stakes involved. She knew Faulkner could be cold blooded, but was he really willing to make that kind of sacrifice to prolong this horrid little war?

They had left the city behind and were still being followed, the pair of headlights a constant sight about two hundred yards behind them. A few minutes later, as Chowdhury was taking a long curve through a village, Esther pointed off to their right.

'Here! Pull in here now, and turn off the lights.'

He did as she directed, swinging the car into an empty stable yard, and Esther was already jumping out as he switched the lights off. There was a high pair of gates at the entrance and she pulled them shut even as the other car drove past. Peering through the gap in the gates, she guessed that they must have been questioning the sudden disappearance of their quarry, for they had slowed right down. The man in the passenger seat was lighting a cigarette as they rolled past, and it was just enough light to see his face. Esther cursed to herself.

It was 'Sergeant Dennehy', who was definitely *not* a member of the Dublin Metropolitan Police. Chowdhury was telling the truth. And Faulkner had been trying to take her out of the game from the day she'd got here. Was this the 'Dollmann' she was supposed to meet at the edge of the city? She assumed the other two men in the car were the same brutes he'd had with him last time.

The car slowed nearly to a halt, and she held her breath, drawing the gun from her pocket, but then the engine revved and they accelerated again. They must have assumed they'd fallen behind. She opened the gates again, and Chowdhury hurriedly exited the yard with the lights off, heading back in the opposite direction before switching them back on. She pointed him down another road, taking a new direction. There was no more sign of the other car.

They continued driving, the Sikh lieutenant cautious as Esther directed him along the uneven, rural roads, and a few hours later they arrived at Michael Regan's house.

Chapter 32
The Need for Proof

Akiko was flushed with suppressed intrigue and excitement to see Esther show up back at their house. It was after ten o'clock when the British agent arrived with an Indian officer wearing a turban. This only added to the thrill, as despite all the different types of people she had encountered on the family's sailing trips, Akiko had never met a Sikh in person before. She had so many questions she wanted to ask him. Papa and Mama were guarded, but polite to these two uninvited guests. The lieutenant declined an invitation to stay and have something to eat, and asked only for some petrol for his car. Papa fetched a can from the garage out the back. Once Lieutenant Chowdhury had drunk a cup of tea and refuelled his vehicle, he took his leave, after finally accepting a couple of apples for the road. Esther stayed. And she had a lot to tell them.

Wolfgang was called down to the large kitchen, where the family sat with Esther as she ate a reheated pork chop and some potatoes. The adults did not try and exclude Akiko and Liam, who listened intently to Englishwoman's explanation for why she was here, and why she needed their help.

Liam's expression was openly hostile. When Akiko and Wolfgang had told the others that Gorey had been part of the gas attack in Belfast, he'd refused to believe it at first, and said, even if it was true, that the poison gas was the kind of demonic weapon that *Germans and British* used, and that Gorey wouldn't have agreed to something like that. Now, here was this British agent showing up at their door, one who had lied her way in to their home and their trust before Michael had exiled her. To Liam, she was an enemy, and that was all there was to it. Akiko's feelings were more . . . complicated.

Esther understood that she was taking a risk, that Papa was not pleased to have her here, and was fearful that she would bring the Crown forces to his door. And yet, she was sure that her boss was conspiring to commit some atrocity, and whatever their differences, she was certain that Papa would share her determination that it had to be stopped. For the moment at least, he agreed to put those differences aside.

'Have you heard of these . . . these Freikorps?' Papa asked Wolfgang.

'*Ja.* They are a formidable organisation,' the German officer said, with a grimace. 'Professional, very well armed . . . they have half a million troops, perhaps more. They are an army without a nation. You would not want them as an enemy.'

Akiko expected that, after what Esther told them, Papa would share what they had learned from Wolfgang, which confirmed at least part of the woman's story:

That the hijacking had been carried out by a company of Germans, that they'd used gas, and they had been supported by an Irish group. But it seemed he wasn't quite ready to trust her yet.

'If Faulkner is so sure that this operation is going to happen,' Michael pressed their visitor, 'he must have a spy close to the leader of the Irish group. Is that the case?'

Esther looked uneasy now. Akiko supposed it must be a mortal sin for a spy to betray one of their own, but she gave a curt nod.

'We have to warn him, Michael!' Liam blurted out. 'If they've an informer, he needs to know!'

Papa motioned to him to hold his tongue for a moment.

'If Faulkner had a spy in the Irish company, it would be easy for him to slip them with information too. The kind Faulkner might *want* them to have,' he went on. 'It would make the spy look more credible, increase the group's trust in him, and help advance Faulkner's plans. He's manipulating Gorey for his own ends. This all fits.'

'*What* all fits?' Esther barked. 'You know something, don't you? I've risked my career, perhaps even my life by coming here, Michael! But this could be more important than our lives alone. If you know what's going on, for pity's sake, tell me! Do you understand what this could mean for your whole country? And for mine?'

'She could be lying,' Liam muttered. 'She could be lying about all of this. Michael, we can't trust a word this witch says.'

'I believe her!' Akiko piped up, and Esther flashed her a grateful smile.

Michael went to say something, then thought the better of it, shaking his head and turning away. But there was doubt in his eyes. Akiko had never seen her father look so troubled. In the end, however, it was Wolfgang who spoke up.

'We sailed from Belfast to Dublin in an Irish freighter. Akiko explored the ship, she took photographs.'

Akiko took this as her cue. She lunged for the manilla folder on the one of the dressers in the kitchen, and handed it to Wolfgang. He took out one of the photographic prints, and laid it on the table in front of the British agent.

'The man you see here is working on something called an ocular box. It's a component of the targeting periscope on a U-boat.'

Esther studied the photograph, which was slightly blurred and lacking contrast from the artificial light of what looked like a ship's engine room.

'A freighter? Which freighter? And are you certain this is an ocular box?'

'It could not be anything else,' Wolfgang said firmly. 'I spent years using one. It cannot be a coincidence that they have one on this ship. The U-boat in Belfast had a faulty targeting periscope. It was never replaced, because the vessel was going to be scrapped. This is a very specialized part, almost impossible to get in Britain. I know because we tried a few months ago. Very few people would have known about this. When the hijackers came to Belfast, they must have brought this replacement part with them. And they brought it, so that the U-boat could be made ready for combat.'

Esther took the folder from Akiko and looked through some of the other photographs.

'Did you take all of these, Aki?'

'Yes.'

'I'd like to . . .' Michael began.

'They're jolly good,' Esther went on. 'It's no easy task to get that kind of definition with indoor lighting. And no flash, I presume?'

'If we could . . .' Michael tried again.

'No. Do you really like them?' Akiko felt her heart lift.

'Of course! And what a sense of composition you have! Still using the Vest Pocket Kodak?'

'Yes, I love it!'

'And rightly so. Though we must look at getting you something more advanced. These are absolutely splendid.'

'Thank you!'

'I we could just . . .' Micheal tried for a third time.

'You must be ever so proud of her,' Esther said warmly to him and Midori. 'The girl is an artist with light.'

'We are *extremely* proud of her,' Michael said impatiently. 'But if we could get back to the matter in hand? This photograph proves that they had the kind of inside knowledge of this particular U-boat that could only have come from its crew or someone else in the Royal Navy . . . or perhaps supplied by British intelligence.'

'Yes, I suppose it does,' Esther said quietly. She held up the photo. 'What's the name of this ship? Do you know where it is now? If I could have it searched by the Navy, we might find this periscope part . . . perhaps other material proof too! I could blow this thing wide open!'

'Don't be naive, Esther,' Midori said sharply, speaking up for the first time since she had served Esther the food. Sitting at the opposite end of the table, she was looking uncharacteristically bitter. 'This man, Faulkner, has made a criminal of you. You are a lone, discredited woman in the company of Irish rebels. Do you know how many Irish women have ended up in prison for speaking up or getting in the way? Look what happened to you tonight! You will not be listened to. Women's voices are not heard. It is the same in my country. This is why I joined this fight. Even your father, a man with connections high in the government, cannot help a woman accused of treason. And if they catch you, you will be disposed of in a quiet cell somewhere – or worse. No, my dear, your fate is entwined with ours now.'

'You're right though, Esther, there is something serious being planned here,' Michael added. Seated beside his wife, he laid a hand on hers now. 'And I'll accept that there were Irish lads helping these Germans. You've just told us that you've been charged with treason for trying to expose this. I could take this story to the leadership in Dublin; they won't want anything threatening the peace talks, but . . . *poison gas?*

'If I accused our own people of this, and told them the information was coming from a British agent – especially an agent who was once welcomed into my home – it would be disputed. I could be branded as a traitor myself. The man who leads this group is a *hero* to our movement. I can't just take your word for it that there's some gas attack planned. Liam is not wrong;

you've proved yourself an imaginative liar, Esther. I need more proof than you showing up at this hour with a wild conspiracy.'

'At the moment, this wild conspiracy is all I have,' she retorted, throwing up her hands. 'And what you've just told me supports it. Midori's right – I'm *on the run*, Michael. My own people are after me. What proof can I give you?'

Papa's expression clouded, and Akiko could see something in it that might have been resolve or grief – or both. He looked at Mama, a question in his eyes, and she nodded, clasping his hand in hers.

'We need to take the *Subversive* out there, board the *Medusa* and search her,' he said at last. 'I need to find out for myself.'

'YES!' Akiko burst out, giving everyone a start, and even Liam snorted a laugh.

Michael gave a wry smile, then turned serious again as he addressed Wolfgang.

'I made a promise that you'd never have to be involved in this,' he said to the German.

'This concerns my boat, and my crew,' Wolfgang replied without hesitation. 'If it means a chance of justice for them, I will do whatever needs to be done.'

Michael nodded his thanks.

'Akiko, might I borrow your camera?' Esther said as she pushed her empty plate away. 'We'll need more than your father's word for this. I need evidence I can show.'

'You're not coming with us,' Michael told her.

'I can assure you, I am,' she retorted. 'We need to

convince *my* superiors as much as yours. We're in this together now, Michael, and you may as well accept it.'

Papa pressed his lips together, but then nodded in grudging agreement. He checked his watch and cast his eyes around the table.

'We need to catch the tide before it gets too low to take the boat out of the cave. Everyone get changed, get what you need, and be back here in fifteen minutes.'

As the others stood up and left, Midori did a familiar rotating gesture with her hand and Akiko turned around to let her okaasan braid her hair. She could not wear it loose on board the *Subversive*. Like her mother, she would wear the ama, the white pearl diver's headscarf.

'You're really going to let us come, Mama?' she asked, her voice nearly shaking with feverish anticipation.

'You are growing up, Akiko-chan, and we need a full crew,' her mother said as she started separating out strands of her hair. 'You know that my mother started training me as a diver when I was ten. I was working by the time I was your age, diving to fifty or sixty feet, around sharks and poison fish . . . But here, there are different risks we must take. I cannot spare you from the dangers of this world, my dear, so I must train you for them.'

Akiko could not keep the giddy smile from her face. Finally, *finally*, she was going to be a pirate.

Chapter 33
Pirates

Esther had never truly appreciated that a submarine was completely blind while it was fully submerged. This was only her second trip in one, and she'd been barely conscious the first time. Though she knew they needed to be close to the surface to use the periscope, and that it wasn't possible to see more than a few yards underwater, she'd never really put it together in her head what that meant in a practical sense.

After Michael guided the vessel out of the cave and beyond the treacherous currents of the Devil's Drain, he ordered Wolfgang to disengage the diesel motor and engage the electric one and told Akiko to angle the dive planes downward, which took them below periscope depth. And from that point on . . . they couldn't see where they were going.

Their only 'sense' was the pair of hydrophones, mounted on either side of the bow. Liam was kneeling beside Midori, who was teaching him how to identify different sounds, both of them wearing headphones plugged into the panel that connected to the specialised microphones. But the ocean was filled with noise, and if there was a rock sticking up from the seafloor ahead of them, or a ship sitting with its engines off and a fishing net or anchor chain stretching downwards, there would be no warning of it. They could only count on the accuracy of their sea charts and the hope that no silent vessel lay in their path. It was unnerving to think of what might happen, so Esther concentrated on the mission instead.

The only lights currently illuminating the *Subversive's* cabin were red, which would not affect the crew's night vision, but it was bright enough for her to study Akiko's photographs of the *Medusa*. The girl had sketched a rough layout of the ship too, to help Esther find her way around once she got on board.

'It'll be after midnight by the time we get there, so there will likely only be one or two crewmen on watch outside,' Michael had said. 'The ship is anchored, and most of the crew should either be asleep, or will have taken the chance to go on shore, so with some luck, the ones on watch won't be paying much attention to anything they can't see coming from a distance.'

Looking at the layout now, Esther was growing ever more skeptical of their chances.

'It's going to take a long time to search this whole boat,' she said. 'We're sure to run into someone.'

'We don't need to search from top to bottom,' he replied. 'There were only a few ships the movement used regularly for smuggling large loads. The *Medusa* was one of them. When they were figuring out how to build secret compartments into those ships, they asked the only marine engineer they had with the right kind of experience. I know where those compartments are. If your poison gas is on board, and there's as much of it as you say, there are only a few places they could be hiding it.'

The submarine had two sets of helm and throttle controls; one in the turret for maneuvering on the surface, and one at the periscope station, where he sat now, below and behind the turret. He guided them to the *Medusa's* position by following his route on a chart with the boat's compass and a watch, gauging the speed of the current and timing his turns precisely. Then, when he decided the time was right, he told Akiko to bring them up to periscope depth. She pulled back on the levers that controlled the hydroplanes, the little 'wings' on either side of the propellor. It was very, *very* strange to feel the deck tilting under their feet, bow up, as the vessel climbed up through the water, Akiko levelling it out when they were close enough to the surface to raise the periscope.

After rotating it to check the area in all directions, Michael motioned to Esther to take a look. Only visible as a dim, dark shape against the sky with few lights showing, Gorey's ship was still at anchor where Michael had first seen her that morning, about two hundred yards from their position. The ship's stern and port side were visible.

'It's odd that they only have the mast and navigation lights on,' he said. 'Still, it'll work in our favour.'

Midori took his position at the helm as he went forward. Unlike the freighter, their boat did not have enough chain to anchor in this depth of water, but it would make too much noise anyway, so they'd have to keep her running to hold her position, but that was fine. It was likely they'd have to make a quick getaway anyhow.

Turning a wheel on the diving controls, Akiko pumped compressed air into the ballast tanks, and the vessel rose to the surface. The planes were used to drive the boat up and down while they were moving forward underwater, but once the ballast tanks filled with air, the *Subversive* effectively became a surface vessel. It rose slowly, coming up out of the sea until the deck was above the waterline, the noise increasing noticeably as the water slopped around the hull. On the steel over their heads, Esther could hear a faint sizzling sound.

'Good, it's raining,' Michael said. 'That'll give them a reason to stay off the deck.'

Liam helped his uncle pull out a charcoal-coloured cylindrical pack that lay alongside the torpedo tube. It was taller than either of them, and just narrow enough to fit through the hatch in the turret. Akiko switched off the lights and Michael climbed up into the turret and twisted the lever to unlock the hatch. Esther noticed there was no squeak of metal, all the joints on board were well greased. The crew had to be able to work in silence. A dull grey light flooded in and he clambered out.

Liam pushed the cylindrical pack up through the hatch and Michael pulled it out. Then Wolfgang followed it up, dragging a hose that was connected to a part of the electric motor. After he'd gone up, Esther finally got to climb out on deck. The rain was heavy, but the sea had only a slight swell. She was dressed in more practical clothes that Midori had provided; dark grey sweater and trousers and soft-soled boots, with her hair pinned up under a black woollen hat. Michael wore similar garments, and also had a small backpack.

He had taken off the straps that bound the large pack, laid it on the deck and attached the hose to it. With a deep hum and a low hiss, a pump powered by the electric engine began to inflate the rubber boat. She had seen inflatable boats before, but few of this quality. Within three minutes, it was ready to lower into the water, a dinghy large enough to hold four or five people.

'Last chance to wait it out here,' Michael said to her in a hushed voice. 'Are you sure you're up for this?'

'Why are you even asking?' she replied.

He nodded and motioned to her to climb into the boat as he held it steady. Wolfgang passed him two paddles and some kind of jointed pole about five feet long, which he slipped into the boat before climbing in himself. Fitting the oars into the oarlocks, which Esther noted were padded with fabric to muffle any noise, he started rowing with smooth, silent motions, the boat gliding through the rain and darkness towards the *Medusa*.

Chapter 34

Distant Lights

Liam crouched on the narrow strip of steel deck, forward of the hatch, with his back to one of the snorkels, the air intake pipes that could be retracted into the hull. He was watching his uncle and the British agent crossing the stretch of water that separated the submarine from the freighter. He quickly lost sight of them. Despite the uneasiness he felt in working against Jim Gorey like this, he desperately wanted to be in on the action, but he knew the more people there were boarding the ship, the more likely it was that someone would spot them. He consoled himself that he still had an important role to play; the *Subversive* had to be ready to get underway as soon as they returned.

Wolfgang was squatting next to him. The German blew into his hands and rubbed them together, his eyes also fixed on the distant ship. Liam saw him frown, then he asked Midori to hand out the binoculars. There was a pair in a pouch mounted next to where she stood at the controls in the turret, and she passed them out to him. Wolfgang peered through them, and there was a twist in his mouth as if he was troubled by something.

'Midori, can you move us south a bit? Perhaps about twenty or thirty yards?'

The electric motor was still running quietly, holding them steady in the current, so Liam's aunt turned the bow and they drifted south, hardly making any wake, which would make them easier to see in the gloom. Wolfgang was looking through the binoculars again.

'There's something else there, beyond the ship,' he muttered. 'I can see something low near the stern, just picked out by the lights . . .'

As the submarine slowly changed its angle in relation to the ship, lying more astern of it now, Liam saw another hull on the far side of the *Medusa's*. It was large, but with a lower freeboard than the freighter, so most of it was hidden from sight behind the ship. Wolfgang was cursing under his breath.

'That's why they have hardly any lights on,' he rasped. 'That's my U-boat.'

Sure enough, as they came around slightly further, Liam could make out the silhouette of the bow, and the conning tower, just over the end of the stern, though even from the far side, the ship's outline would make it hard to see at any real distance. His first urge was to dive in and swim after Michael and Esther to warn them. They couldn't see it from the angle they were approaching . . . but sense prevailed. He couldn't catch up with them now, and they'd be certain to see the conning tower once they got up on deck.

With a bitter, sinking feeling, he had to admit to himself that this proved that the suspicions of the others were correct. Grim Jim Gorey was working with the Freikorps who'd hijacked the submarine in Belfast. Midori spoke down into the cabin, telling Akiko what they'd seen. Liam's cousin climbed up past her mother to have a look for herself.

'There's another boat out there,' Akiko murmured, pointing at a spot on the sea, about midway between the harbour and the freighter.

Barely visible against the black background of the coast, there were two pinprick lights, red and green. Navigation lights on either side of a boat's bow, and heading in their direction.

'Gott im Himmel, it's some more of the crew coming back!' Wolfgang growled. 'Michael and Esther won't see them either. They won't know they're coming.'

Liam only hesitated for a few seconds. He pulled off his shoes, jacket and hat and slid down the side of the hull into the water.

'Liam!' Midori whispered desperately. 'Liam, come back! You come back right now!'

But Liam was not listening. With slow, strong strokes and as little splashing as possible, he began to swim after the dinghy. It was hard to judge how far away the motorboat was, but he was confident he could reach the ship first, and he wasn't thinking much beyond that. There were going to be too many people moving around on that ship. He had no time. *He had no time.* If Jim Gorey found Michael sneaking on board his boat, in league with a British agent, it would mean a death sentence for both of them.

Men like his father and Gorey did not tolerate spies or traitors, and he doubted that the men of the Freikorps were any more forgiving. It took all his control not to swim as fast as he could and instead, to concentrate on staying quiet. It would take silence now, to keep them all alive.

Chapter 35

Nightmares

Michael pulled his paddle out of the water as the rubber boat touched the hull of the *Medusa*. On the floor of the boat was a rope attached to a device of his own design, a suction cup the size of a dinner plate, which could be attached or released with a short lever. He stuck it onto the painted iron wall in front of him, securing their dinghy to the ship. Then he pulled up the jointed pole that lay beside him. Esther watched with curiosity as he unfolded the parts, revealing that it was a boarding ladder formed of a single pole with the rungs on either side and a big hook on the top. It telescoped out to eight feet so, standing up in the boat, he was able to reach easily to the lowest part of the ship's gunwale above them, where he hooked it on. Rubber rings top and bottom stopped the metal ladder clinking against the hull.

With practised movements, he climbed up the side of the freighter and flinched, nearly letting out a cry of shock when the figure of a man leaned over to greet him. It was John Holland. Michael ground his teeth. This was no time for hallucinations.

'Are you all right?' Esther whispered from beneath

him. 'What happened?'

'Nothing. Nothing, it's fine,' he breathed.

Lifting his head slowly over the rail, he looked for any sign of those on watch. There was none, so he pulled himself over onto the deck. Holland tipped his hat to his friend and glanced down at Esther.

'This is a fascinating new development,' he commented.

Michael had to remind himself that he was the only one who could see or hear the dead inventor, and he must remember not to talk back to him. He scowled at the ghost before moving out of the way to let Esther step lightly onto the deck behind him. Michael knew that there were three places where large loads could be concealed within this tramp steamer's structure: One in the hold, one in the engine room, and the largest in the main passageway on the starboard side. He was about to wave Esther towards the nearest door when he realized there was something wrong with the shape of the looming cargo winch. There was something behind it. Moving slightly to the side for a different angle, his eyes widened and he gripped Esther's arm. Her equally startled reaction confirmed that it wasn't.

They were looking straight at the top of a conning tower, a rectangular shape with rounded edges, its intake pipes and periscope sticking up from the top. There was a submarine lying on the freighter's starboard side. The U-boat from Belfast was *right there* in front of them. They moved into the shadow of the winch that was used to lift cargo into the hold and gazed at the German vessel. There was no one in the tower or on the deck below, that they could see.

'She's a big brute, compared to my boats,' Holland muttered. 'More ship than submarine really, but impressive nonetheless. This changes things for you, Michael. The Germans will take that boat back to their country, but Gorey wants one of his own. And he won't make the same mistake that you and your American clods made with the *Fenian Ram*.' He paused, and then added: 'He will take your submarine from you . . . and he has the men who can train him how to use it.'

Michael was suppressing a growl, still trying to ignore the ghost of his old mentor, but he couldn't deny the truth of it. If Gorey wanted something, he was not inclined to let anyone stand in his way.

'So that's why they have all their lights off,' he said softly to Esther, gesturing towards the U-boat. 'From a distance, the two hulls would look like one silhouette. Well, that's one matter settled. But I still want to know if they have the gas on board.'

Esther nodded. She took Akiko's camera out of Michael's bag. It was wrapped in oil cloth. Unwrapping it, she opened it up and took some shots. He doubted they would come out in this light.

Then they made their way forward, past the large hatch that gave access to the stern hold, and in through the closest door. It opened onto a passageway and a stairwell. There were lights on here, and Michael waited just inside the door, listening intently. There was no sound of movement, so he took the steep, narrow iron steps down to the passageway below, with the

British agent and the inventor following him. Here, he stopped again, and searched around the painted metal floor until he found a hole a few inches from the wall, just big enough to stick his thumb through. Taking a right-angled piece of metal from his pocket, he inserted it, twisted and pulled. A section of floor about the size of a coffin lid lifted up. He gently leant it against the other wall, revealing what was inside.

The entire space below was filled with cylinders, each one roughly the size and shape of a large Thermos flask, with a thinner, shorter piece protruding from either end. One of those parts was an explosive charge. Each cylinder was a khaki colour, with a grass green band painted around one end to identify the contents. There were wads of fabric wedged in between the cylinders to cushion them and stop them moving around.

'These . . . these are Stokes mortar shells,' Esther said. 'That green band means they contain poison gas. They're not German, they're *British*.'

'You sound surprised,' he replied.

'They weren't named in the ledger. It only said 'chlorine gas shells'. I just assumed . . .'

'You assumed the missing nightmare weapons were *German*,' he grunted.

Esther winced and nodded. They both continued to stare. Michael did a rough count. The bombs were laid three deep, and six across, and if they ran the full length of this underfloor space – there were two more panels he could lift after this one – there could more than two hundred of these stored here. And there could be more in other parts of the ship. Esther took some shots with the camera. The definition would be poor in the passageway light, but it would be enough.

'You should take one, Michael,' Holland said. 'They won't believe you otherwise.'

Michael reluctantly agreed. He took off the pack and laid it on the floor. Then he carefully lifted out one of the shells. Some spare fabric had been left folded on top of the mortar bombs, and he wrapped the shell in the navy-coloured cloth. This and the photographs would be proof enough for the lads in Dublin. Jim Gorey was planning something that could prove a disaster for the peace process. He had to be stopped. Michael was down on one knee, sliding the bomb into the pack, when a hushed voice called out to them and nearly made him drop the shell.

'Michael!'

It was Liam, standing there at the foot of the steps in shirt and trousers, soaking wet and dripping all over the place. He must have swum over from the *Subversive*.

'Jesus Christ lad, what the blazes are you doing here?' Michael hissed.

'There's a boat on its way back, with a load more crew on board,' the boy told him. 'They'll be here any minute!'

Michael and Esther exchanged urgent glances. They were out of time. She wrapped up the camera and put it back in the pack, pressing it in on top of the shell, and he buckled down the flap. With Esther and Liam's help, he quietly lowered the steel panel into place over the hidden compartment and locked it again. He shrugged the pack onto his shoulders, and they were heading back along the passageway when there came the sound of feet on metal rungs and then someone came out of the door behind them that led to the engine room, a few paces away.

Joe Goat froze when he saw them, his mouth dropping open. Michael, Esther and Liam went stock still . . . and then Esther's hand whipped to the deep pocket of her trousers, she drew her automatic pistol and levelled it at the engineer. With a careful movement, Michael put a hand on her wrist, pushing the gun down.

'Joe,' he said, reaching out with the other hand. 'It's me. It's *Mick*. Mick Regan. Don't shout out. I just . . . I needed to know what was going on here.'

He couldn't tell if his old friend recognized him. Joe seemed paralyzed, unblinking. His intense stare was unnerving. John Holland was standing to one side of Joe, a frown on his face. With a solemn expression, he shook his head and tapped his temple.

'I can't go back to those days, Mick,' Joe Goat said at last, swallowing hard. 'I've left them behind.'

'What do you mean?'

'You keep tryin' to take me back there, but I'm not goin'.'

For a moment, Michael was confused . . . and then he understood. That was what Holland was getting at. Joe suffered from the same affliction that Michael endured. And suddenly he knew how to play this. He hoped the other two would keep their mouths shut.

'You were always one of my best, Joe. Always a man I could count on. I'm going back out to sea now, back into the deep.' Michael caught the hint of panic in Joe's expression, even as he ignored Esther's quizzical look. Hurriedly, he added as calmly as he could: 'But you don't have to come with me, son! You've done your time, and there's nothing more I could ask of you. You gave everything you could to the cause. You served us well. I'll leave you in peace, if that's what you want.'

'Yes!' Joe exclaimed. 'That's . . . that's what I want, Mick. I'm happy here. I just want to be left alone now. I don't want to go back to those days. I can't . . . I can't be doin' with all that. I'm done with hurtin' folk. It's not right. I keep hearin' them at night, and I can't be doin' with that now.'

'Of course not. That's all right, Joe. That's all right,' Michael replied with a reassuring tone. 'Off you go now. I'll let you be. I'll let you go and find some peace.'

Joe Goat nodded and gave a hesitant wave, backing away to the door behind him, and then swivelled and disappeared down into the engine room again. Michael turned to find Esther and Liam staring at him.

'He thought we were hallucinations,' he explained. 'Or at least . . . he wasn't sure. Joe's mind was broken by some of the things he did when he was with me. For that man, I'm just a whole load of bad memories.'

They crossed the deck to where the ladder was still hanging. They could hear a small motor near the bow of the ship now, and men's voices in the quiet of the night. Michael and his two companions descended the ladder, and he unhooked it and handed it to Liam to fold up. John Holland waved goodbye from up on the deck as Michael released the clamp and he and Esther started paddling away from the ship. There was a glow of light from the bow, and figures were starting to climb aboard on the other side, near the U-boat. Michael kept looking back for any sign that their piracy had been detected, but there was nothing.

When they reached the *Subversive*, the electric motor was still running. Michael left Liam and Wolfgang to pump the air out of the dinghy and pack it away as he watched the *Medusa* through the binoculars. As soon as the dinghy was away, they all scrambled below and he sealed the hatch. Even then, he watched through the periscope as Midori filled the ballast tanks and the submarine settled in the water, then with a push of the throttle, he started them forward and they began to dive as Akiko angled the planes down. He kept the speed low, to create as little wake as possible.

Michael thought he saw lights shining out over the water towards them as the periscope finally submerged, but the beams would not reach this far, and even if they decided to send their motorboat out to investigate, there would be nothing here to see by the time it got close.

The *Subversive* was gone.

Chapter 36
An Unpleasant Duty

Esther and Michael had shown the others the Stokes mortar bomb on the way back to the cave. The tide was low now, and that made maneuvering the *Subversive* into the cave more challenging, even with the calm weather, but it hardly distracted from the situation they now faced. Despite the low water, Michael made sure they turned the boat around and refuelled before leaving it.

He had decided he would take the first train in the morning to Dublin, bringing the shell and the photographs with him. Esther and Akiko developed the film and began making prints as soon as they got back to the house. But Michael wasn't sure who he could talk to. Liam listened to him discussing it with Midori in the living room. Though his uncle knew Michael Collins personally, the director of intelligence was in London, and would be difficult to reach, as was Arthur Griffith. It was possible that he could get a meeting with Éamon De Valera, the president himself, but he would have to go through others to reach him, any one of whom might be sympathetic to Jim Gorey.

'I've heard that the negotiators might be coming back

from London at the weekend,' Midori said. 'You could reach Collins then, if he's in Dublin.'

'We can't wait,' Michael said, shaking his head. 'We need to alert them as soon as possible. We don't know when Jim might make his move. No, I have to talk to Mulcahy, or even Brugha, God help me. Someone with the authority and the nerve to take on Gorey.'

Liam continued to listen with interest. Only two weeks before, he had known his uncle and aunt were supporters of the Irish cause, but thought it was only with their words and their money. Now, he was sitting here, listening to them talk about these revolutionary leaders as if they knew them personally, with the intent of informing on Grim Jim Gorey, one of the movement's greatest heroes. And Liam wasn't sure how he felt about that. Everything was so much more complicated than he'd once believed.

Esther and Akiko came downstairs, having finished making the photographic prints. Michael took the mortar bomb, still wrapped in the fabric, and placed it in his briefcase with the envelope of pictures. It was decided that he would get to Dublin as early as possible and make some telephone calls from there. He was sure he could reach someone of sufficient authority.

'Whatever Gorey has planned, it'll be against a major British target,' he said to the others. 'But that's only the first part of his plan. He wants to provoke retaliation. He's always understood the power of publicity, that the best weapon the *Irish* have is *British violence*, and the bloodier the better. Every atrocity the Brits commit brings more angry young men and women to the cause and wins us sympathy from other nations, the Americans especially. '

'I'd have to agree,' Esther said. 'The main reason our government has always resisted sending in the full force of the military is that it would be admitting it had lost control of Ireland. The Easter Rising taught us that. We'd make even more enemies here, and lose so much respect abroad – and all the other colonies would surely take note.'

'They're *already* taking note,' Liam grunted. 'Your empire's days are numbered, missus.'

'And the end can't come soon enough,' Michael said, throwing a sardonic glance at his nephew. 'But let's keep our eye on the ball here. My bet is the operation will be something up in the north. Jim was probably doing reconnaissance while he was up there. The border around the northern counties, the new parliament in Belfast . . . Gorey considers them obscenities – most of us do. He won't stand for seeing Ireland divided, and if the peace treaty is signed as it is, that border will become permanent. The northern counties will be cut off from the rest of the country.

'He wants to provoke a backlash, a violent reaction from the Crown forces, like the artillery bombardments and the executions after the Easter Rising. He wants to create martyrs. The more dead Irish bodies there are, the more we can show the British to be monsters, and get the Irish people fired up again. He thinks we've all lost our nerve, and wants a war to the end. For him, it's complete freedom or nothing at all. And there are many who'd agree with him, but it can't happen like *this*. There have to be limits to what we're willing to do.'

It was after two in the morning, but no one could sleep, so they all stayed up talking. Liam felt pent up, bursting with conflicting emotions he couldn't make sense of. He was worried that what they were doing was betraying the cause. How much violence was too much? How far should men like his father and Gorey be allowed to go? Ever since the fight in Belfast, Liam had been reliving the moment when Wolfgang had shot that man.

Did it matter what you used to kill or maim someone? His own father was happy to use guns or bombs, but he had faced poison gas attacks while serving with the army in France, and cursed whoever had created the stuff. Michael, who decided not to arm his submarine with torpedoes, had certainly shot men who stood between him and his objective. Wasn't it hypocritical to kill someone one way, and then to call another type of weapon monstrous? Forty children had died when the British had used artillery in Dublin during the Rising, but wouldn't the Irish have used heavy guns if they had them? How much violence was too much?

Liam couldn't come up with a good answer. He eventually left the room and went outside, sitting on the step of the porch, which was lit by a small lamp on the wall. He felt achy with tension and yet drained of energy.

It was still raining lightly, and the air was sharp and fresh. One of the dogs, Bran, came around from the back and slumped up beside him, damp and panting as if he'd been chasing a fox or a badger, which was a likely possibility. Liam absent-mindedly scratched between the wolfhound's ears, thinking over this strange day.

'Liam!' a voice called softly. He glanced out to his right, and spotted someone peering through a gap in the hedge. 'Liam, over here!'

It was his father. What was he doing here? Getting up, he walked wearily over to the hedge, where Lar was hiding, trying to stay out of sight of the house. Bran ran over to greet him, and Lar tried to shoo the big dog away. His left hand was tucked into his jacket pocket, helping take some weight off his injured shoulder.

'What are you doin', Da?' Liam asked. 'Sure, come on into the house and have a cup of tea. Everyone's still up.'

'I can't be seen here, son,' Lar replied. 'I came to leave a message, to warn yeh. Jim Gorey's put the word out on your uncle – out on all of yez. He's had someone watchin' yer house. He says yer harbourin' a British spy. Is that true, lad?'

'It's Esther Sinclair. She's been accused of treason by her own side, Da!' Liam hissed. 'She was tryin' to warn us. Listen Da, Gorey's workin' with some German fellas. He's planning a gas attack up the north.'

'Gas?'

'*Poison* gas! We sneaked onto his ship. We found chlorine gas shells. Hundreds of them!'

Lar's face stiffened, his eyes widening and, seeing his reaction, Liam was sure that though his father might have the highest respect for Gorey, he wouldn't stand for that abomination being unleashed in Ireland.

'Listen, he wants the submarine too,' Lar said. 'And if Mick doesn't give it to him, you can bet your arse he'll take it by force.'

Liam's eyes widened. If Gorey seized the submarine, he wouldn't need Michael or the rest of the family. That German U-boat crew could figure it out, and train his men how to use it. He was about to say something when they heard the mumble of distant engines, and they both looked out towards the road to see three pairs of headlights approaching. Three vehicles turned into the driveway, all of them filled with men. They spread out as they pulled up, all their headlights shining on the house, their glow sliced into streaks by the rain. The men got out and scattered wide, staying behind the lights, while one man walked forward. It was the tall, imposing figure of Grim Jim Gorey.

Michael came out onto the porch and Bran, always keen for attention from the head of the family, bounded over to him. Michael clicked his fingers and sent him inside, but Bran was a curious beast, and was keen to stick around and see what all the excitement was about, so he hung back by the door. Liam backed up and watched from the concealment of the hedge. No one had spotted him or his father yet.

'All right there, Jim,' Michael said. 'You've picked a strange hour for a visit.'

'I think you know why I'm here,' Gorey replied, touching the peak of his flat cap as he stopped a few yards back from the step of the porch. 'You've been doing some visitin' yourself. Joe Goat thought he was seeing things, the poor soul, only hallucinations don't leave a wet trail behind them when they walk. And they don't steal cargo.'

Liam winced. He'd been the one who'd entered the passageway on the ship, dripping water the whole way after his swim.

'Not sure what Joe's been saying,' Michael said, 'or what you're getting at. What cargo would that be? And why has it brought you here, with enough lads to storm Dublin Castle?'

'I didn't come here to debate yeh like some politician, Michael. Who else is in the house?'

'What business is it of yours?'

Gorey's long, furrowed face did not show any hostility as he dismissed Michael's objections with a simple shake of his head. Instead, he looked solemn, almost regretful. It was the expression of a man tasked with an unpleasant duty, but one that he was determined to carry out. He took a deep breath, glanced back at the men behind him, and shook his head again, brushing his hand over his thick moustache.

'Ah Michael,' he sighed. 'I know you were on the ship. And you know what I have to do about it. Why did you have to get the children involved?'

'That's what happens in war, isn't it? All the wrong people get caught up in it.' Michael responded. 'Things never go the way you plan. And whatever it is you're planning with that gas, the British are already on to you. Nobody will stand for this. You're crossing the line, Jim.'

'The Brits know what I *want* them to know,' Gorey snorted. 'And I'll decide where the line is. Now I've had a bellyful of your guff. But I'm willin' to let the young ones live, if you bring them out. We'll have to hide them away, but they'll *live*. That's the best I can offer yeh, Michael. You'd want that, wouldn't yeh? For them to have a chance?'

'You seem to have forgotten your manners, Jim, so let me put this to ya in terms you'll understand.' In a smooth, unhurried motion, Michael drew his .45 Colt from behind his back and aimed it at Gorey's chest. 'If you came here to threaten me or my family, ya'll catch the first bullet, and that's a promise. Take your lads and head on outta here.'

'I can't abide a traitor, you know that,' Gorey told him, unmoved by the threat. 'Send the children out, and whoever else is there, and let's get this done. Otherwise we'll have to burn them out.'

Lar pushed through the gap in the hedge, shoving Liam back into the shadows behind him.

'What the hell is all this?' he roared, making both of the other men look round. He had a Webley revolver raised in his right hand, and something else cupped in his left. 'That's you is it, Jim Gorey? Are we threatenin' and killin' children for the cause now, are we? Because that's not the fight *I* signed up for . . . and one of them is my *son*, yeh louser!'

It took a few seconds for Gorey to recognize who was speaking. When he realised who it was, he seemed taken aback, but only for a moment. He was now facing two guns from two different directions, and still he was not fazed by it.

'You're standing with him are you, Lar?' he said. 'It's weak-willed men like him, who'll make sure Ireland will always be Britain's dog!'

'I won't have anyone question my loyalty to my country, Gorey. Not even you.'

Then, without warning, Gorey dropped to the ground, and the instant he did, his men opened fire. Michael was forced to fire at the figures behind the headlights as he threw himself back through the door, nearly falling over the dog behind him as bullets gouged holes in the woodwork around him. And in the family's wolfhound. Bran let out a yelp, flinching and collapsing on the porch.

With tears in his eyes, Liam shouted for Bran, but then he too was forced to dive for cover as some of the shooters aimed in his direction. Seconds later, Lar was there with him, shoving him into the ditch behind the hedge.

'Bran! They killed our dog! *They killed Bran!*'

'Keep your head down!' Lar shouted over the noise. Shoving his gun into his pocket, he switched the grenade he was holding to his right hand, pulled the pin and hurled it at the cars, bellowing: 'Here, share that amongst yez!'

Some of the men took cover, but others were too slow. The blast sent shrapnel flying and caught the fuel tank of the middle car, which burst into flames. Lar was already dragging Liam out of the ditch and the two of them ran into the darkness, heading for the back of the house. They saw Michael come out the side door, and he waved to them to follow him. Liam was wondering why the others weren't with him, and then he copped to what had happened. Michael had been creating a diversion, distracting Gorey while everyone else escaped. They were well ahead, racing for the cave, and the submarine.

'Thank you for . . . for that, Lar,' Michael panted as they ran. 'They caught us . . . us off guard . . . They'd have taken me and Liam if . . . if you hadn't been there.'

'They might . . . take yeh . . . take yeh still,' Lar snapped at him. There was pain in his voice, and he was struggling to keep up with them. 'Shut yer trap and . . . and . . . and keep runnin'!'

Chapter 37
On the Run from Everyone

Michael could see that Lar was injured. He could not normally have stayed ahead of the younger, more athletic man, but now Liam's father was struggling to keep up. Had he been hit by one of Gorey's men, or was it something else? There was no time to worry about it now. They rushed through the darkness towards the Monterey Cypress that concealed the way down the cliff. Liam kept having to slow to wait for his father and uncle, and Michael urgently waved him on.

'Tell Midori to cast off,' he hissed. 'And be ready to go as soon as we get there!'

The boy raced off ahead. Treading through tufts of thrift and scurvygrass along the coastal path, Michael and Lar stooped low whenever the gorse bushes and high stands of nettles thinned out on the bank beside them, to avoid being silhouetted against the sky. Few enough people knew about the cave, and even fewer knew the way down to it, so once they reached the top of the climb, Michael was confident they could evade the men who were hunting them, even if some of them were locals. Gorey would find it eventually – he knew it had to be there – but the Selkies had always taken great pains to step along rocks to get around the tree, to avoid creating a visible trail to it.

They could still hear shouting and the odd gunshot, though nothing in their direction. Michael was looking back, thinking they might have lost their pursuers already, when one of Gorey's men came sprinting out of the gloom behind Lar. He had his pistol raised. Michael stopped dead on the spot. Grabbing Lar and shoving him aside, he brought his own gun up.

He and the other man fired at almost the same instant. His opponent's shot was rushed, taken on the run. Michael felt something thump him on his right side and though the impact turned him, he kept his automatic up and fired a second shot. It went wide, but the first one had taken the man square in the chest and he collapsed to the ground. Michael grunted, feeling a dull pain in his ribs. Lar put a hand on his shoulder and he nodded in response. The others would know where they were now.

The pain in his side was growing, and he knew it was going to get bad. Liam came back to them, and it was only when he lifted Michael's arm over his shoulders to support him that the agony struck like an axe and Michael had to clench his teeth hard to keep from screaming.

'B-b-broken ribs, I think,' he gasped. 'Let . . . let my arm down.'

'Can you climb?' Liam asked.

'I'll make it down, even if it kills me.'

It nearly did. They reached the fissure in the cliff where

they could clamber down the sandstone surface, wet now from the rain. Liam led the way, helping Michael place his feet, with Lar following. Every time Michael had to take his weight on his right side, the pain was excruciating. There was hardly any light at all in here. Twice, he slipped, and it was only Liam's support at his feet that kept him from falling. When they finally reached the bottom, Michael was barely in a fit state to make his way along the narrow ledge above the waterline to the cave. Eventually, they got inside, though he was sure he could hear others starting to make their way down the split in the cliff face.

'We can't let them . . . take . . . take the cave,' he growled to Lar. 'There are torpedoes in here. Explosives and . . . and weapons. I won't have that bastard getting his . . . getting his hands on any of it.'

'Don't you worry. I'll blow the place to kingdom come,' Lar assured him.

Working their way onto the wooden boards of the dock, Michael had to lean on Liam to make it to the end of the jetty, where the *Subversive* was waiting. Wolfgang already had the diesel motor running. Akiko was in the turret, waving at them to hurry. Liam turned to look back, and saw that Lar had stopped by one of the storage racks, where he was opening a box of grenades.

'Da, come on! You have to get in!'

'You go on, Liam. I'm not comin' with yeh. I've a job to do here.'

'What the hell are yeh talkin' about? We're not leavin' you!'

Lar gave him a twisted grin.

'You won't be lockin' me inside that tin can, son! I'd rather be shot. Don't you worry about me, I'll be fine.'

'Then I'm stayin' with you!'

'You are in me arse, sonny. Michael, you be sure he gets on board.'

'Da, please! *Please!*' His voice was frantic now. 'It'll be all right. Please come with us!'

'Listen to your father,' Michael said, his voice strained, his chest tight with pain. The right side of his shirt was drenched in blood. 'We have *no time*, Liam. The longer we wait, the more we're risking everyone's lives.' He dragged at the boy's arm. 'Get on the boat! Liam! *Gorey's coming!* We have to go!'

And that was the end of it. Liam's face was a conflicted grimace, but he climbed down into the turret and helped Michael down after him. Akiko was sitting at the plane controls, while Midori was ready at the ballast valves. Wolfgang was out of sight of the turret ladder, down by the engines in the stern. Esther was standing off to one side, stooping slightly as she hung onto the mount for one of the high pressure air cylinders.

Michael reached over his head and swung the hatch down, yanking the lever over to clamp it closed. The movement caused the broken ends of his rib to grate together again, and he whimpered in agony.

'Wait. Wait! What about Lar?' Akiko asked. 'Why are we leaving Lar?'

'We'd never get him on board,' Michael told her. 'He couldn't bear it. He's got severe claustrophobia. Have some faith. The man's a born survivor. Here, did you bring that bag?'

Akiko pointed to his briefcase, which still held the mortar shell and the photographs. Michael nodded and, peering through the deadlights in the turret, he opened up the throttle and engine rumbled louder inside the steel hull. He steered the vessel down the narrow tunnel towards the mouth of the cave. He saw Gorey and some of his men working their way along the wall. They were shouting as he cruised past them, though he could barely hear them. There was a loud, sharp, metallic bang as something struck the hull, and then another.

'They're shooting at us!' Esther exclaimed. 'Can those rounds penetrate the hull?'

'The air intakes and periscope are retracted,' he said. 'She's built to withstand the pressure two hundred and fifty feet down. She can take a few bullets.'

Even so, he had to wonder if the rounds were doing any damage as the ricocheted off the thick steel plate. Any flaw in the hull could quickly become a leak under enough pressure, and he wasn't sure how bulletproof the small, glass deadlights might be. With the bow lined up to exit the cave mouth, he risked a glance back. Gorey's men had turned their attention to Lar, who was shooting back. Michael muttered a curse as he saw Liam's father jerk backwards and topple into the water. And he saw no more of him after that. Had he managed to rig the grenades to go off, and set off the rest of the explosives in the cave? Michael guided the submarine out of the cave, bracing himself for an explosion that never came. Gorey's company had captured the cave, and everything in it.

'Take us down,' Michael wheezed.

Wolfgang switched the gears, disengaging the diesel and engaging the electric motor. Michael motioned to Midori, who quickly took the other helm, behind the periscope, and as she got her hands to it, his legs buckled under him. He'd have fallen off the turret platform if Liam and Esther hadn't caught him and lowered him to the floor. The only reason he didn't shriek in pain was that he was barely conscious.

Akiko was at the diving controls. She twisted the ballast tank valves open, flooding them with water. As the hull gained weight and settled lower in the water, she angled the submarine downwards, the propellor pushed the vessel into the depths and the sea sounds of the surface faded away. They were safe . . . for now. Michael let himself lie still in a blurry daze of pain as Esther cut off his shirt to examine his wound and start dressing it.

'He's going to need a doctor. Maybe a surgeon,' he heard her say. 'My God, we're on the run from everyone now. Where . . . Where are we going to go?'

'Dublin,' he gasped. 'We have to go to Dublin.'

Midori uttered her response in Japanese, and Michael was glad none of the others, including Akiko, would understand that particular obscenity. But his wife knew he was right. They had no other choice but to try and reach the rebel leadership before Gorey could convince them the Regans were all traitors – and the Tipperary man already had a head-start.

As unconsciousness crept over Michael's senses, he could hear Liam crying for his father.

Chapter 38

His Place in Time

Michael struggled to understand what was going on. He was underwater, and at times he seemed to be on board a submarine, while at others he was swimming with Midori in Tokyo Bay. He was in Japan, and he had fallen in love, both with this fierce, quiet woman and with the world she was showing him beneath the waves. He was a confident swimmer, but compared to her, he moved in the water with all the grace of a dairy cow. Kicking ahead of him, she pointed out oysters that looked like discarded dragon scales, sea cucumbers like huge caterpillars, the gaping maw of a giant clam.

He had worked on submarines for much of his life, but had been so obsessed with the engineering challenges, he'd given little thought to that vast, alien world waiting to be explored. He was starting to realize that he had rarely taken time to appreciate the beauty of the environment he was so intent on conquering. He was savouring it now, having put so much distance between him and the hostile politics that had consumed his life.

'You're in a bad way, Michael.'

He opened his eyes. Had they not been open before?

He was lying on the deck of the submarine again. John Holland was standing over him. Was he back in the States already? When had he left Japan? Had he *stolen* this boat? No, he was getting confused again. The theft of the *Fenian Ram* had happened a long time ago, when he was little more than a boy, long before Japan. The memory of that first betrayal revived the guilt over the hurt he had caused his old friend. No, this was the *Subversive* – *his* boat – and someone else was trying to steal it from *him*. Who was it? His mind was too muddled. He seemed to have lost his place in time. Was it the British and their spies in America? No, that wasn't right either.

At the start of the new century, while still in the process of selling their first submarines to the US Navy, Holland's firm, the Electric Boat Company, sold their designs to *Britain*. John Philip Holland's original dream had been to create a weapon that would help Ireland take on the Royal Navy, but his business partners, the money men, had taken over the company. They took a less idealistic view of this new weapon of theirs, and in a cruelly ironic twist, it was the *British* who would prowl Ireland's coasts with the Irish inventor's sea devils.

'I was gripped by a passion for the science, so I let Frost and Rice control the money,' Holland sighed, as he knelt down now, by Michael's side. 'And they ended up controlling *everything*. They fooled me into signing over my patents and drove me out of my own company. They even stopped me from using *my own name* for my work. I just wanted to build my boats, and eventually, their lawyers even blocked me from doing that.'

'I warned you,' Michael said in a gurgling growl. '*I warned you* about them.'

'Yes. Yes, you did. And I'm sorry I didn't listen,' Holland replied with regret. 'I was slow to understand the strangely unpatriotic heart that beats in the breast of a corporation.'

'Who's he talking to?' he heard Akiko say, which was wrong, because his daughter wasn't born yet.

'He's seeing ghosts again,' Midori's voice replied.

His wife knew about his hallucinations of course, he couldn't hide that from her, though she did not know how common they were becoming.

Seeing the Royal Navy start to build its own Holland submarines had been a bitter blow for Michael. During one of the many arguments he and John had after that, and in a moment of spite, he told Holland that he had helped steal the *Fenian Ram* all those years before. The words that followed brought both men to tears. The company needed someone to travel to Japan, to supervise the building of some new boats. The day after that argument, Michael accepted the role. He felt he had betrayed Ireland, and hated himself for it. He wanted to get away from the men who had placed him in this position, Holland included.

He met Midori in 1905, while he was working with her father at the Yokosuka Naval Arsenal. They were building Holland boats for the Imperial Japanese Navy and he was training their engineers and crews. It was an eye-opening experience, both at work and outside of it.

Those Japanese lads had approaches to engineering he'd never seen anywhere else, and made improvements he and Holland hadn't even considered, particularly in enhancing the speed of the boats.

And on his days off, he would swim with Midori and her sisters, and they would show him the wild world beneath the surface of the sea. Within a few months, he had asked Midori to marry him. Years later, her father would help him build the *Subversive*.

The *Subversive*. How was he lying on his back in his submarine now, when he'd been swimming only moments before? He was getting confused again. He had to watch that. If you were going to take to the sea, you needed your wits about you.

'You're safe, Papa,' Akiko said, from somewhere in the future. 'You're hurt, but we're here with you. We're going to get help for you.'

Was that part of his hallucination? Did he have a daughter now? He found himself swimming again, following his wife's lithe form along the seabed in the clear water near the shoreline in Tokyo Bay, taking in the wonders around him. It was an experience he hoped to one day share with his children.

Holland's main competitor in America, Simon Lake, was designing submarines to *explore* the ocean rather than go to war in it. Lake's latest vessel, though it was less developed than Holland's, had a chamber to enable a diver to enter and exit the boat under the water. Michael was finally starting to understand the extraordinary opportunities this would create. But there would always be more money for war than for exploration.

The swimming was getting harder now. It hurt to breathe, he felt so weak, and Midori began to speed away from him, disappearing into the blue expanse.

'I can't swim that fast, my darling,' he rasped. 'Come back! I love you!'

'He's delirious,' he heard his wife say, with characteristic bluntness. 'It might just be the pain and exhaustion, or the wound may be infected. His lungs are still clear, by the sounds of it.'

'Is he going to be all right?' Akiko's voice asked.

'We've done what we can, my petal. He needs a doctor.'

He was thrashing, desperate to reach the surface. Above him, he could see bodies floating in the water, limp and lifeless, moving with the waves. His face broke the surface to find he was surrounded by the dead; some drowned, others shot or burned. The mass of corpses extended out in every direction. He could see no way to get free of them.

He was trying to get a breath in, but his chest spasmed, causing a stabbing pain in his right side. Someone was trying to steal his boat. They were going to hurt his family. His arms and legs flailed on the steel deck, and friendly hands tried to hold him still, in case he made his injury worse.

Even as Michael built submarines for Japan, and as he was falling in love with a Japanese woman, he knew that the Electric Boat Company had sold one of its boats to Russia too, and was building more for them. While Japan was *at war* with Russia. In the end, selling weapons to both sides of a war was more hypocrisy than Michael could take. It was the kind of practise that would only guarantee more wars to come.

It wasn't just the British and the other colonisers who bled nations dry. The world was in the grip of the capitalists, the profiteering warmongers, and if you didn't have money, that world would eat you up. And so Michael Regan, the committed socialist, vowed that he would become *rich*, but on his own terms. He would not build weapons for the money men. He was done with Holland and the Electric Boat Company. But before he left, there was one last thing he needed.

'I want to build a submarine, John,' he said to his mentor. 'For *our* people. I'll find the money for it. Forget what the company is doing. I want the boat *you* would make, if you could. Give me the designs. It might be the last one of yours that ever gets built now, so let's make it count. Let's do everything we can to give our country a fighting chance. Will you do it, John?'

He went still, barely able to open his eyes, listening, hoping for a response. His body felt as if it was floating, limp and inert, like one of those corpses in the sea.

'And we did it, didn't we, Michael? But the fight's over now,' John replied at last, still kneeling over him. The inventor looked older now, more feeble, as he had towards the end, when his health had started to fail him. 'I think you've caused enough hurt. We both have. It's time to find a better purpose for this monster we've created.'

Chapter 39
Navigating the Hazards

They had travelled through the night, cruising beneath the surface of the sea, following the coast north from Cork, and fatigue was starting to tell. Even Michael had finally settled into a deep sleep after a feverish few hours, reliving old nightmares.

Navigating a busy port always offered challenges, but sneaking in underwater in a submarine before dawn was an entirely different level of difficulty. If they used the periscope, they took the chance of being spotted, especially if they were moving at any speed, because of its thin white wake. If they didn't, they were effectively blind, trusting to their chart of the seabed, with Midori listening to the feed from the hydrophones for any vessels around them. They risked collision with any boat that didn't have its engine running, or was moving under sail, making it all but undetectable.

Now, with her hands on the levers for the planes, making the boat dive or rise according to Wolfgang's directions, Akiko gazed at the complicated engineering all around her, anxiously trying to guess what lay beyond the hull. Only her father had taken the *Subversive* into Dublin Bay before, and he was in no fit state to stand, let alone control a submarine.

Wolfgang was at the helm behind the periscope, tense and sweating as they entered the bay, approaching the mouth of the Liffey, between the Poolbeg Lighthouse on the Great South Wall on their left, and the North Bull lighthouse out to their right. They moved at a snail's pace, getting as close as they dared before raising the 'scope. The mouth of the river was notorious for its sand banks, whose shapes could change over time, making parts of it treacherously shallow and difficult to chart. Wolfgang got the boat past the lighthouses before he decided they could risk going no further.

Emptying the ballast tanks, they surfaced and Wolfgang climbed into the turret and opened the hatch, looking around before he waved the others up. The dinghy was hauled out onto the deck and inflated. Michael was woken, and was in better fettle, able to make it up the ladder himself. Akiko was going ashore with her parents. They had two missions: their first was to find a doctor for Michael, their second to try and reach someone in the republican leadership who could stop Gorey. With Midori's Cumann na mBan contacts, it was felt that she had the best chance of finding medical help. And if Michael didn't recover, it was agreed that a woman and a girl would be considered less of a threat, and might be able to get closer to the republican command.

Wolfgang took his shirt off, giving it to Michael to replace the one that had been cut off to treat his wound. With Michael, his briefcase and a satchel stowed in the boat, Liam, Esther and Wolfgang climbed back down through the hatch. Akiko and Midori pushed off, and with the hum of her motor and a bubbling hiss, the *Subversive* submerged, descending to rest close to the sandy seabed, where she dropped anchor, and would stay until nightfall.

Mother and daughter rowed upstream, wearily straining against the current, until they reached the port, where Regan Marine Engineering had a small dock and boathouse maintained for their Dublin office. Midori had brought the keys for both the boathouse and the office, and once the dinghy was stored away, Akiko and her mother helped Michael walk to the office, which was in a two storey brown-brick building just off the quays. It was a Saturday, and the staff weren't expected in that morning. It wasn't a big place, a few rooms with cream-coloured walls spread over two floors, but its windows had a good view onto the street at the front and the alley at the back, and there was a telephone line. They settled Michael upstairs in the manager's office. Though it was a bland, utilitarian room, it had a small sofa. Midori opened a drawer in the manager's desk and pulled out another bunch of keys.

'There's a store room at the end of the hall,' she told Akiko, throwing them to her. 'It'll be locked. We need to change your father's dressings. We need bandages, iodine and whatever painkillers you can find. Look around for any food and drink too. We don't know how long we'll be here.'

Midori sat down at the telephone and lifted the receiver.

She glanced up to see Akiko was still hovering there, hoping to hear some of the call.

'Do as you're told, girl! No dilly-dallying now!'

The windowless store room was locked with good reason. It was better stocked with medical supplies than the office of an engineering business had any right to be, though of course, Akiko knew now that all of this was preparation for revolutionary activities, not the treatment of work-related injuries in the office. She pulled out dressings, bandages, iodine and even a small bottle of morphine. Her parents had been teaching her to treat injuries since she was very young, and she had belatedly accepted why that was. There were also some blankets, cans and jars of food, water canteens, sheets of coded information, as well as maps of the port and the city beyond, and charts of the river and the bay. Everything a good rebel pirate would need, apart from weapons.

Her okaasan was still on the telephone when she came back into the office. Akiko put down everything else, and read the label on the bottle of painkiller. Under her father's direction, she used the eye-dropper in the bottle to measure out the dose of morphine onto a teaspoon.

'Careful now. Often, the only difference between medicine and poison is the size of the dose,' he told her, his voice weak and hoarse. He gave her a pained grin. 'Huh! In that respect, it is much like a revolution.'

She got busy changing his dressing, noticing that there was reddening around the edges of the entry and exit wounds in his side that suggested an infection was setting in. The drug was taking effect however, and it wasn't long before he was looking more comfortable, more like himself again, if a little drowsy.

'This is a good lesson, my girl,' her father said. 'There will be times when trouble arises and there is no one else to turn to for help. And you need to be prepared for those times.'

A few minutes later, when Midori hung up the receiver, her face was taut, pensive, and at first, she didn't say anything. Then, she took a deep breath.

'I had to try four different people, Gorey's already started turning everyone against us. Kitty's going to see if she can reach Kathleen Lynn. She served as a medic during the Rising, and she knows a lot of the right people too. It's going to be difficult getting a hold of anyone. The negotiators are on their way back from London. De Valera has called a meeting of the Cabinet for this morning at the Mansion House. Griffith and Collins are to return to London tonight. The Prime Minister of Northern Ireland is raising hell, and the British are insisting the treaty must be signed by Tuesday, but half the Cabinet is refusing to accept the terms. Some are saying it's a surrender, a complete betrayal of Ireland.'

This was not a surprise. Unlike its population as a whole, Ireland's new government was made up almost entirely of revolutionaries; many of whom had taken an active part in the war against Britain. The treaty, like any agreement between two warring sides, had some bitter compromises, and though everyone had their hopes pinned on it, some of the Irish viewed anything less than complete independence as a failure.

'That's all the fuel Gorey needs,' Michael snorted. 'In his mind, someone "betraying Ireland" gives him a license to do anything in response. It justifies any act of violence. This is a man who was shaped by the battles of the Great War – he sees bloodshed as the only way to get things done. Nothing would make him happier than to see the negotiations collapse.' He shook his head. 'If the leaders are all meeting, then you're right; it means . . . it means that everyone we know with the authority to take on Gorey is going to be here in Dublin, but we can't get to them. The building will be under heavy guard, and they're going to be arguing it out all day.'

'So you can go up there and just wait until they're finished, and talk to someone when they come out?' Akiko said.

'No, we can't,' Midori replied. 'The man you shot, Michael – he's dead. Gorey's spreading the word that you killed one of his men to protect a British spy.'

'Well . . . that's not untrue, I suppose.'

'He also claims the *British* have supplied *us* with poison gas. He wants us all rounded up. He's accusing us of treason and murder. If we show up at the Mansion House, or if we approach the wrong person, we could be shot or captured before we got close. And let's be honest with ourselves; we have no way of proving our innocence.'

'We'll have to wait until we can reach one of them . . . one of them . . . at home,' Michael said. He put a hand to his brow. 'That drug is making me sleepy. I need to lie down.'

He stretched out on the sofa, and within moments,

he had fallen asleep again. Akiko was feeling on edge, not knowing if she wanted to stand or sit. A gramophone was one of the few home comforts in the office, on a table in the corner. The record sitting on the turntable was a John McCormack song; *When You Look In the Heart of a Rose.* It was a popular and gentle piece which normally put her in a good mood. She lifted the needle onto the disc and set it playing, letting herself drift away with the slightly crackly recording.

It failed to have any effect on her okaasan, however. Midori was leaning against the wall, lost in thought. Akiko moved closer to the window, gazing out on the road and the building belonging to a shipping business that stood on the opposite side. Her mother's tension was putting her on edge too, and she studied the people passing by. Work started early in the port. There was a young man who had just arrived at the corner who caught her eye. He stood there, apparently waiting for something, and for some reason he reminded her of Gorey's lad Seán, who'd been watching them outside the pub in Belfast. He had the same loitering look about him. As Akiko watched, two more men joined him. The first one pointed at the Regan building. He'd spotted Akiko in the window.

'Mama,' she said, her throat tight as she pulled back.

Midori lifted the needle off the record, silencing the gramophone, and crossed the room, but stood well back from the window, following her daughter's gaze. The three men began striding in their direction.

'Gorey must have sent them to watch this place. We

can't fight them. More will come once they know we're here,' Midori said, taking her husband's automatic from her satchel. 'Aki, I'm going to try and draw them away. You need to get your father out of here.'

'But Mama, I–.'

'Don't argue, there isn't time. Do as I say now.'

And then she was hurrying downstairs to the reception and the front door. She stepped out and closed it after her. Through the window, Akiko saw the men's reaction as they recognised the distinctive Asian features of Michael Regan's wife, and shouted at her to stay where she was. She drew the gun and fired a single shot over their heads, and then started running in the opposite direction. They were young lads, fresh-faced and impulsive, and they immediately sprinted after her, but halfway up the road, that first one she'd seen slowed and stopped, and looked back towards the office door. He turned around.

There was no time to worry about what was going to happen to her mother. There was no way to get Papa out in time. Akiko still had the bunch of keys, and she was about to go and lock the front door, before she realized that this would only slow the fellow down. He could still break in through a window, or call for others to help him. She had to deal with him herself. She did not have a gun, and this lad looked head and shoulders taller than her and about twice her weight.

She rushed over and picked up the gramophone. Coming out of the room, she locked *that* door, and then ran to the store room, putting the machine on the floor at the back. She set it playing again and draped a blanket over the funnel-shaped horn. The music was muffled, but still audible enough. Downstairs, the front door was thrown open, and she heard the sound of his boots on the floorboards.

She put the keys in the keyhole on the outside of the door, and stepped into the office beside the store room, closing the door over, to leave the narrowest crack to peer through. The intruder was searching the rooms downstairs. Akiko made a few heavy footsteps of her own, and that brought him charging up the stairs.

The young man had a knife and, big and aggressive as he was, he looked almost as scared as he was excited. He was frowning, confused, hearing the singing, but not seeing any obvious source. Glancing around warily, he approached the store room. He lunged inside, and she slipped out into the corridor. She heard the music grow slightly louder as the blanket was lifted off the gramophone. The man was looking back in shock as she reached out, slammed the door shut on him, and locked it.

It was a good solid door, and though he threw himself against it, roaring curses and kicking at it, she was confident it would hold him long enough. She hurried back and released her father from the locked office. He had been woken by the noise, but was still groggy.

They packed the morphine, a couple of water canteens and the cans of food she'd brought down into the two bags, and headed downstairs and out onto the street. Instinctively, they moved with the heaviest flow of people, drifting towards the city.

'They'll be looking for us everywhere,' Akiko said. 'Papa? Where can we go?'

'I think I know what we need to do,' Michael said, his left hand pressed to his injured right side. 'But you're not going to like it.'

Chapter 40
The Target

It was Liam's turn on the hydrophones. With no way of seeing around them, the only warning they would have of danger would be what they could hear through the water. Wolfgang was confident that most larger ships would pass wide of them, staying in the deepest part of the channel, but they couldn't be sure that a ship with a very deep draught wouldn't drift off centre and, at low tide, that might cause it to run over the top of the submarine. If there was any threat of that, they had to be able to move, and quickly.

With the headphones on, he kept his eyes closed most of the time, listening to the different sounds in the water and trying to identify each one, and gauge its speed and direction; the chugging drone of engines, the churning of propellors, the white noise of water against a moving metal or wooden hull, the slapping of waves against a stationary one.

Long, monotonous hours had passed. A glance at the clock told him it was quarter to seven in the evening, which was five minutes since he'd last looked. The *Subversive* was held in place by its anchor, the electric motor was off; they were trying to eke as much life as possible out of the bank of batteries that lay under the deck, so they only had one light on over the middle of the cabin. If the batteries' charge got too low, they'd have to surface and start the diesel engine to charge them again.

Wolfgang had spent some of the time drilling Liam on his knowledge of the engines and the ballast system, and training Esther on some of the submarine's basic controls. Now the Englishwoman was sitting on the deck opposite Wolfgang, the two of them playing poker. They chatted in German sometimes, and Liam wished they'd stick to English. He could speak Irish and a little French, but not German, and it made him feel all the more isolated.

He was already anxious, and was beginning to get claustrophobic, stuck down here, sealed inside this chilly, clammy steel can, anchored above a sand bank under the weight of the sea. His father was probably dead, and they were being hunted by one of the most dangerous men in Ireland. And even now, Grim Jim Gorey would be doing his best to turn the whole country against them.

'There's something about all this that bothers me,' Esther said then, slipping back into English, presumably to include Liam in the conversation, and he lifted one side of his headset. She threw her cards down and leaned back on her hands. 'Edward Faulkner is a calculating swine, make no mistake about it, but he is a deeply *patriotic* calculating swine. I simply cannot see him standing by while Irish terrorists attack a major British target, even if it serves his purposes.

'He was never overly concerned when it was local Irish

targets, policemen or officials being attacked, but he couldn't bear for Britain to look weak in the face of an Irish assault. And it seems certain that whatever Gorey has planned, he's very intent on making international headlines. The target is likely to be something of great importance, something very public.'

'When him and his lads showed up at the house last night, Michael told Gorey the Brits were on to him, and he didn't seem surprised,' Liam replied. 'It was like he didn't care. He said "the British know what I want them to know". Maybe Faulkner's not as clued in as he thinks.'

'If they knew they had a spy in their midst, they might only have fed him what they wanted him to know,' Esther mused. 'That would be a clever move to throw us off. Sorry . . . not *us*.' She gestured at those present. 'I mean the intelligence services.'

'Having trouble picking sides now?' Liam needled her.

'I'm on the side that objects to *mass murder*,' she shot back, though he knew he'd scored a hit.

'Well, we're glad you've finally had a change of heart, missus. Took you long enough.'

'Oh, do spare me your cutting wit . . .'

'Perhaps Faulkner *does* know what the target is, but it isn't important to him,' Wolfgang cut in, before the argument could really kick off. 'Michael thinks this is about Northern Ireland. Could it be something up there? Something *Irish* that is also a symbol of British power?'

'You mean like the whole of the bloody north?' Liam snorted, folding his arms.

'You're really not helping,' Esther replied.

'Could it be the government in Northern Ireland, perhaps?' Wolfgang suggested. 'What's his name . . . Craig, their Prime Minister? They certainly hate him enough.'

'No, Faulkner wouldn't allow—,' Esther began, and then stopped as Liam waved at them both to be quiet.

He was hearing something on the hydrophones. A faint knocking noise . . . TAP-TAP-TAP . . . TAP-TAP . . . TAP-TAP-TAP . . . It repeated like that, three taps, then two, then three again.

'It's them,' he said. 'They're back.'

This was the agreed signal from Michael and the others. On the surface somewhere above the submerged boat, they'd put one oar in the water and were banging the other oar against it. It was after sunset, so hopefully it would be dark enough that the submarine could surface without being spotted. Wolfgang motioned to Liam to take over at the motor and Esther to take control of the planes. Swinging the boat around to free the the anchor and winch it in, he took it up to periscope depth and raised it to look around before finally surfacing. The dinghy was about twenty yards away, and only Akiko was on board. They quickly deflated and loaded the dinghy, and within five minutes, they'd submerged again, settling back close to the seabed.

Akiko was cold, scared and seemed to be maintaining her composure through sheer force of will. She told them what had happened at the office, that she didn't know where her mother was, how the only people who could help them were in the meeting at the Mansion House, and that she and her father had spent much of the day in the National Library, keeping a low profile as they waited for the meeting to finish.

'You've played an absolute blinder, Aki,' Esther said. 'But where is your father now?

'In the end, Papa thought the only way to be sure he could reach someone who'd listen was to catch Michael Collins and Arthur Griffith when they got on the mail boat this evening, on their way back to London,' Akiko told them. She realized she was still clutching her satchel, and laid it down on the deck. 'He's gone to Kingstown. He gave me the mortar bomb to bring back, because he didn't want the bodyguards thinking he was a threat if they searched him. He figured that if he was on the ship with them, he couldn't be dragged off somewhere without Collins knowing. But if he is, at least we'd still be free to tell the truth if Gorey manages to pull off his attack.'

Though it wasn't great news, it did at least offer hope. With Michael departing for Britain on the ship, there was nothing else for them to do at that moment except try and find out what had happened to Midori, and find a safe harbour for the *Subversive*. There were no easy answers for either question, but the safe harbour had to take priority. It was clear they couldn't stay here much longer. They needed to surface at some point to recharge the submarine's batteries with the diesel engine and replenish their supply of air. Before long, they would need to refuel too.

As they sat discussing their options, Liam took the mortar shell out of the satchel, still wrapped in the navy-coloured fabric. He'd never had a chance to examine it, and like most boys his age, he couldn't resist the opportunity to take a proper look at a real live bomb. The fabric was actually a sailor's jumper, and something on it caught his attention. He laid the shell on the deck to unfold the jumper and hold it up. The deck was at an incline, the bow slightly lower than the stern, and the mortar round began to roll, and he had to snatch it up before it banged into something. The others all looked sharply at him, alarm in their eyes.

'Do. Not. Play. With. The. Poison. Gas. Bomb,' Esther growled at him.

'This is a piece of a sailor's uniform,' he said, ignoring her. 'Look, what are these from?'

There were yellow letters embroidered into the collar: 'Property of LNWR'. Esther came over and took the jumper from him. Her features creased into a frown.

'It's . . . They stand for the "London & North Western Railway",' she said. 'It's the company that runs the mail boats between Britain and Ireland.'

'You mean . . . like the ones from Kingstown to Holyhead?' Akiko asked.

'Why would Gorey have one of their uniforms?' Wolfgang wondered aloud. 'Is he going to attack one of the mail boats? Is that his target?'

'No,' Esther said, shaking her head, her gaze focussed on something beyond the hull of the submarine. 'No, I think . . . I think he's targeting someone *on* the mail boat. The Irish negotiators. Gorey's not attacking a symbol of British rule, he's *executing traitors*. He wants to wreck the peace talks and get back to an all-out war on

Britain. In an enclosed area like a ship's passageway, with the doors locked at either end, the effects of the gas would be horrendous. That's why Faulkner is going to let it happen, he wants the same thing. He despises the idea of having to bargain with these men. He wants Britain to use all its force to put Ireland back in its place.'

'That doesn't make any sense,' Akiko objected. 'The stupidest thing the British ever did was execute the leaders after the Easter Rising. It turned the whole of Ireland against them. If Gorey kills Collins and the others, the Irish will . . . they'd *hate* him for it.'

'They won't know,' Esther said. 'That's what Faulkner doesn't realize. I didn't know the gas shells were British, and I bet *he* doesn't either. But they're easy to identify. The world's press are watching these negotiations, and the two sides barely trust each other as it is. He only needs to detonate one or two of the bombs, and leave one that doesn't go off. Then they claim the whole thing was a British intelligence operation. It would create enough anger and confusion that there'd be no chance of any peace talks again for years.'

'But they're on a *ship*,' Liam pointed out. 'By the time Collins and them are on board, the boat'll be ready to leave. Where can Gorey's lot escape to? They'd be caught, and then everyone would know who they were.'

'No, they wouldn't be caught,' Wolfgang spoke up. 'They could carry out the perfect escape.'

The others turned to look at him.

'They have a submarine,' he said simply. 'Think about what Michael used to do. If they time the rendezvous correctly, they could just jump overboard and be picked up by the U-boat. They'd be gone in minutes, disappearing beneath the sea. No pursuit would be possible.'

'Okaasan said the Irish leaders had to meet today because the treaty has be signed in the next few days,' Akiko said. 'That's why Papa's hoping to catch Collins and the others on the mail boat. The deal's almost done. They're going back to London tonight, as soon as the meeting's over.'

'Which means, if Gorey wants to stop the treaty being signed,' Esther added, gazing at the embroidered letters on the sailor's uniform, 'then he has to carry out his attack *tonight*.'

Chapter 41
The Sentence for Treason

The mail service between Britain and Ireland ran like clockwork. The mail trains came right out onto Carlisle Pier to stop alongside the ship, sheltered by a large steel-framed station roof, and schedules were coordinated so that the trains and ships met with as little delay as possible. The same service also handled deliveries of the daily newspapers, and each of the mail boats doing the round trip even had a sorting office on board, so that post coming into Kingstown was separated by county into sacks by the time the ship docked. Interruptions to the service were treated with the utmost seriousness, and a hefty fine was imposed for each minute the mail was delayed.

The *Hibernia*'s hull was painted black, with a white superstructure and two red and black funnels. Little more than a year old, she looked impressively modern, with sweeping lines that spoke of power and speed. The treaty negotiators were held until the last minute by their hostile meeting that evening with the Cabinet, and barely made it to the ship in time. The captain, bound by his ruthless schedule, was reluctant to wait, even for these famous and important figures. Their tardiness was fortunate for

Michael, as it meant the delegates' team of bodyguards were not there to look over the other passengers who gathered on the pier. He was able to board without incident, his fedora hat low over his eyes, just one face among many.

When the exhausted negotiators did finally arrive, their bodyguards had to wave aside journalists who shouted questions and took photographs, wanting to know the latest decisions that had been made. Of course, they were told nothing. Michael could only see Griffith and Collins; the others in the party must not be sailing on this ship. He had considered going to the newsmen with the photographs he was carrying in his briefcase, but many of them were republican sympathisers, and might wait to hear Gorey's side, or question the story long enough for him to pull off his attack before they published. No, it had to be these two, men he knew and trusted.

Michael watched the small group from the deck, careful not to catch anyone's eye. He wanted to make sure the vessel was well underway before he went looking for their attention. They were protected by serious men, and he wasn't sure who he could reason with. He spotted the tall, vigorous figure of Ned Broy, the former police detective, walking ahead of Collins. The man who had served as a spy in the heart of G-Division. Watching from the rear of the group was Emmet Dalton; a younger, debonair fellow with a toothbrush moustache and the bearing of a cultured military man. He had distinguished himself as an officer in the British Army during some of the worst fighting of the Great War, before coming home and joining the rebellion.

Both were perceptive, intelligent and even-minded, and he thought he had a good chance with them. The party would be booked into the first class cabins, and he was about to go in and intercept them, when he saw someone greet them at the gangway leading to the door onto the ship. It was Jim Gorey himself, grinning and shaking everyone's hands. Michael pulled in and leaned his back against the rail. What was Gorey doing here? Had he guessed that Michael would be on board? It seemed too much of a stretch. Was this some kind of last minute attempt to sway the opinions of the delegates? To ask them not to sign? That too, was hard to believe. From their conversation outside Belfast, it was clear Gorey had lost all faith in these negotiations. He had read the draft treaty and dismissed it out of hand. It was not in his nature to waste time on anything he considered a lost cause.

Michael could imagine what it had been like at that meeting of the leaders today. Gorey might be more extreme in his methods than others, but his grievances were real, and were shared by many in the movement. Michael felt a profound sadness come over him. Here they all were, people who had fought for the same cause, and even as the British Empire was finally about to surrender most of its control over their country, the Irish looked fit to tear into each other over the details. There were too many conflicting views of what Ireland's future should look like. Even if this treaty passed, he knew it would be a long time before the country truly found peace.

What *was* Gorey doing here? Michael pressed a heel to his brow and shook his head. How was he going to deal with this? The pain in his side was becoming intense again, making it difficult to think clearly, and moving around made it worse. He needed to take some more of the painkiller, but it wasn't yet time for another dose, and it would cloud his mind even more.

Having watched for the negotiators and their security, he was puzzled by the lack of anyone surveilling them on the pier. There were normally British intelligence agents hanging around like flies as soon as the delegates came anywhere near the ship, and Michael had been picking out undercover agents since his days working for Holland. If there were any here now, they were successfully keeping a low profile. Perhaps they'd been pulled back, now that the deal was all but done.

The *Hibernia* would not be delayed. Michael pictured the second officer reporting to the captain that all was ready as the gangways were pulled back onto the pier, the heavy lines were cast off, the third bell was rung and a long, echoing blast of the whistle was blown. The lever was thrown on the telegraph, signalling to the engine room to stand by, and then the captain gave the order to let go and turn ahead. As the massive engines were given more power, a slight tremble went through the ship, and she pulled back away from the pier, her propellors churning up the sea at her stern. She started out of the harbour, and once she'd passed the breakwater, the captain ordered full speed ahead, and the ship, one of the fastest ferry services in the world, was soon accelerating up to twenty knots, out into the darkness of the Irish Sea.

It was starting to rain and the passengers who had been out on deck to watch the departure began to make their way inside. Michael decided there was nothing for it but to head down to the delegates' cabins and try to make his case, even if it meant confronting Gorey while he did so. He went inside, heading for the first class passageway. A young man in a seaman's uniform was striding in the opposite direction, a faint smirk on his face, a satchel tucked under his arm, and he touched his hat in greeting as he drew close, their eyes met for a moment, before the fellow's widened in recognition and quickly pulled away. Michael reached out and grabbed his arm.

'Well there, Seán. Didn't know you'd joined the crew. Lookin' for a change of pace, were ya?'

The young man, the same one from Gorey's company who'd followed the Regans in Belfast, jerked away reflexively, but Michael held on, despite the pain that sawed through his ribs. Then he reached for the satchel as he heard the clink of metal, feeling the shapes of two flask-sized cylindrical shapes within. Wrenching free, Seán shoved the older man aside and ran to the end of the passageway and through the door that led to the deck. The impact sent a scorching pain through Michael's injured ribs, and he slumped against the wall.

'Jesus,' he gasped, wheezing as he clutched his injured ribs. 'Jesus Christ.'

This was Gorey's target. The delegates. Why hadn't he seen it earlier? All they had to do was set the bombs to detonate – a grenade in the bag with them would do it – then throw the bag in and lock the doors at either end of this passageway. And it explained the complete absence of British agents. If the Irish wanted to murder their own people, Faulkner saw no reason to leave his own men in harm's way.

Michael had to move. *He had to move.* He had dropped his briefcase and, wincing in agony as he stooped to pick it up, he started staggering down the passageway. He didn't believe that even the most fanatical republicans would support this, and yet Michael had no doubt that Gorey was willing to kill these men. The logic was simple; the veteran rebel saw the treaty as a betrayal of Ireland, and for a man who'd learned his trade on the murderous battlefields in France, there could only be one sentence for treason. But how could he justify the damage it would do to the cause? How did he expect to get away with it?

Pushing those thoughts aside, Michael focussed on finding Griffith and Collins. Other people passed him in the passageway, regarding this sweating, grimacing, unsteady man with expressions that varied from concern to aversion. A cabin door opened ahead of him and he could hear voices from within; he recognized one of them as Collins' jovial tone. Finally, he'd reached them.

Then Grim Jim Gorey stepped out and closed the door behind him.

It took only an instant for the other man to register who this was in front of him, and Michael's weakened state, and he acted without hesitation. Michael went to shout and Gorey jabbed him twice in the chest, crippling him with pain and driving the wind out of him.

'Mick! Isn't this a small world? Sure, what are the chances, eh?'

Pulling Michael's arm over his shoulder to support his weight, he held him tightly, making getting his breath back even more difficult, and with his free hand, Gorey pulled his Mauser machine pistol from his jacket pocket. Lifting it up under Michael's coat, he muttered:

'You shut yer trap and walk with me now, or I'll paint the wall with yeh, sunshine.'

With their bodies so close together, the gun was mostly concealed by the coat, and Michael could barely wheeze, let alone cry for help. As they made their way out to the main deck, Gorey was making apologetic shrugs to people and saying things like: 'Sorry folks, he always gets seasick when he's had a few pints.' The rain had driven everyone else inside, and as they reached the rail, Gorey bent him over it, pushing the barrel of the gun harder into his ribs.

'You've done me a favour, truth be told,' he said, his voice rough, but still low. He looked at his wristwatch. 'Y'see, I need them to cut the engines in a few minutes, as the job's gettin' done, so my lads can make their getaway. D'yeh know how you get a ship this big to *stop suddenly*, out here in the middle of the sea?' He leaned in closer to Michael's ear. 'You shout "*Man overboard!*".

'Now, I was just gonna have one of the lads *lie* about it. Tell the crew there was someone in the water, but now I have *you*, Mick! You're goin' to be my man overboard. Don't you worry though, I'll be stickin' around to make sure the story's told right. You'll die a hero, shot while trying to stop the British agents who planted the . . . What in the name o' God is that?'

His glare had strayed out into the gloom beyond the ship. Still struggling to breathe, Michael gazed down at the much smaller craft rocking around in the *Hibernia*'s wake, the hatch in its turret open. And he was almost as confounded as Gorey.

'That,' he mumbled, 'is my bloody submarine.'

Chapter 42
A Close Thing

Kingstown lay on the south edge of Dublin Bay, a few miles across from Dublin Port and the mouth of the Liffey. It would have been an easy sail in a surface boat, but in a submarine trying to stay undetected, the heavy traffic crossing the bay meant the chances of a collision forced them to pick their way carefully past the other vessels, using the periscope as little as possible.

They had intended for Esther and Wolfgang to go ashore at the harbour and find Michael, to warn him, or if they couldn't find him on the pier, to warn the authorities before the ship could leave. When they realized that they weren't going to make it ashore before the *Hibernia* departed, they tried to radio the vessel, only to discover their radio did not work. It was such a basic mistake: They had rarely needed to radio anyone before this, and hadn't noticed the problem with the antenna. In the time it would take them to row to shore and find someone with a working radio, Gorey might already have carried out his attack.

Their only hope was to intercept the ship as it left the harbour. Even this posed a major challenge. Underwater, the *Subversive* might have a hope of keeping up with the steamer, as long as it hadn't reached its maximum speed of twenty-five knots, but on the surface, the submarine, shaped for the depths, would soon be left behind.

With the electric motor going all out and the periscope raised, Wolfgang found the lights of the ship and angled the boat across the bay on an intercept course. The sea was calm enough that they weren't being thrown about much by waves, but the *Hibernia* was accelerating, and as they closed in, the much smaller craft began bounce around sickeningly in the ship's wake, making it ever more difficult to maintain her speed.

To preserve their night vision, they only had the red lights on. Liam was standing by the ballast valves, and he waited anxiously for Wolfgang's signal. The moment they surfaced, they'd be much more affected by the turbulence and would start to slow down, so they'd have to time it just right. They were barely keeping up as it was. Akiko was sitting beside him at the hydroplane controls. Esther stood ready under the turret, holding herself steady with one hand, the boarding ladder held in her other. As the *Subversive* rocked and jolted, they could hear the rumble of the *Hibernia*'s huge engines and the churning of the propellors, even through the steel hull. And the noise was getting louder.

'All right . . . stand by . . .' Wolfgang said. 'Now! *Up ten degrees*! Blow ballast!'

Akiko tilted the boat upwards, Liam blew the ballast, and they came up hard, breaking the surface little more than five yards off the ship's port side, just short of the bow. They immediately lost some speed, and as they dropped back, the ride got rougher. With his heart pumping like the *Hibernia*'s pistons, Liam darted past Esther and up into the turret. Pulling the lever to unlock the hatch, he pushed it open and scrambled out. Esther followed him, passing out the ladder before climbing out herself.

Akiko took the helm from Wolfgang, who moved up into the turret, which gave him a better view of the ship than the periscope.

'I have the helm!' he barked.

'You have the helm!' she repeated, letting go of her wheel as he took over again.

Now they were riding in a surface vessel, an *awkwardly-shaped* surface vessel, built to tunnel through the water, not skim across it, with hardly any keel to keep her stable, and a now open hatch only a few feet above the waterline. Spray was being thrown off the bow into Wolfgang's face as he steered the boat in as close as he dared to the side of the *Hibernia*. If they collided with the side of the ship, it could be disastrous. Unlike bigger submarines, the *Subversive* did not have separate internal compartments to help her stay afloat if she was damaged. One buckled plate or one split in the hull could send this steel and iron machine to the bottom.

Esther kept her balance with difficulty on the narrow, wet, rocking deck. She was hesitating, the ladder fully extended, waiting for a better chance to hook it onto the rail, but they were drifting back towards the *Hibernia*'s stern and, certain that they were going to miss their chance, Liam snatched the ladder from her and lunged up at the rail above them. He lost his balance, and would have fallen between the hulls of the ship and the submarine if the ladder's hook had not caught.

He dangled precariously above the frothing water for a moment, and then he managed to haul himself up and get his feet on the rungs. Clambering up, he gripped the rail as Esther made her jump, more deliberate than his, more coordinated, but still a close thing, her feet scrabbling on the wet hull before finding the ladder. She pulled herself up until her head was about level with his stomach.

'Good God, boy. No . . . no one could ever . . . ever question your nerve,' she panted.

Wolfgang had steered a little wider, and was coaxing some extra speed out of the *Subversive* as he drew clear of the worst of the wake. Liam climbed over the rail, breathing hard, and Esther followed, her right hand clutching his shoulder as she pulled her gun from her jacket pocket with left.

'Liam,' she muttered. 'Hold it.'

Not ten yards away, Liam's uncle was staggering up to the rail, and half-dragging, half-supporting him, with a Mauser machine pistol jammed into his side, was Grim Jim Gorey. As they reached the rail, Gorey was talking, though Liam couldn't hear what he was saying over the noise of the ship. There was agony written on Michael's face, and his hands gripped the rail like claws. Liam crept closer, still unnoticed, as he heard Gorey say:

'. . . Don't you worry though, I'll be stickin' around to make sure the story's told right. You'll die a hero, shot while trying to stop the British agents who planted the . . . What in the name o' God is that?'

And now both men were staring down, transfixed by the incongruous sight of a small, grey submarine racing alongside the steamer.

'Liam, move aside,' Esther told him, waiting to raise her gun.

He ignored her, still edging closer, weighing up his chances of leaping at Gorey without getting his uncle shot. Gorey's attention was still fixed on the *Subversive*.

'That's a cryin' shame now,' the veteran rebel said.

Letting go of Michael, he pulled a Mills bomb from his pocket and tugged out the pin, the lever still held in place by his grip. Liam felt a thump in his heart, gazing from the grenade to the open hatch on the submarine and back again. He couldn't stop it. He was too far from the men to stop it.

'God, Jim . . . please. My children,' Michael begged, grasping for the other man's arm, only to have the butt of the Mauser slam against his temple. His knees crumpling, he hung on to the rail. His voice broke in a sob: 'Jim, please!'

'That was always your problem, Mick,' Gorey declared. 'You lacked the balls for a real fight.'

Michael finally saw Liam standing there, and gave him a sad, bitter smile. As Gorey stepped up to the rail and swung back his arm to toss the grenade, Michael threw himself onto the arm, smacking the bomb out of Gorey's hand. It dropped to the deck at their feet, the lever springing off, triggering the four-second fuse.

'How's your balls now?' Michael snarled with a savage grin, as he clung onto Gorey's arm.

With a desperate cry, Gorey kicked the grenade down the deck and tore free, hurling himself backwards and slamming Michael against the rail. Liam and Esther dropped flat on the deck as the bomb detonated fifty feet away. Liam felt the violent jolt of the blast go through him, and in the seconds afterwards, it was as if he'd been punched in the chest and on the ears. He could feel smaller pains in different parts of his body now, where he must have been hit by shrapnel or debris.

By the time he was able to get himself onto his hands and knees, there were people rushing out onto the deck, crewmen and passengers. He had been between Esther and the blast, and she was already up, but still unsteady on her feet. Over the whiny ringing in his ears, he could hear her calling to one of Collins' men.

'Look to your charges, boys! Jim Gorey's out to kill you all. His men have chlorine gas bombs. You need to get up high, out in the open, and keep everyone away from you.'

'That's absurd!' one of them snapped back.

'Absurd it may be, but it's a fact.' She gestured to the blast and shrapnel damage around them. 'And even if you don't believe, me, you can believe this: Keep your men safe!'

Though the bodyguards' reaction was suspicious, incredulous, they couldn't deny there was a threat at hand, and they had a job to do. Liam could only hope they didn't allow themselves to be cornered down a passageway, but as he sat there trying to get his senses back in order, he cast his eyes around for Michael, growing ever more frantic when he couldn't see him. There was no sign of Gorey either. He grabbed the rail and pulled himself up, leaning against it to steady himself. Michael had been against the rail when the grenade went off. Looking back into the gloom, along the ship's wake, Liam saw a dark shape bobbing in the foam. It looked like a body, face down in the water.

'MAN OVERBOARD!' he bellowed, and without another thought, vaulted over the rail.

There was a long drop into the dark, churning sea and the shock of the cold hit him hard, but he had his hand clamped over his mouth and nose, suppressing the irresistible reflex to inhale, his chest spasming as he plunged deep. Kicking to the surface, it took a minute to gasp in some tight breaths and regain his coordination before looking around. Orientating himself with the ship, he stared back along the vessel's wake, searching, searching for any sign of his uncle. The ship's whistle was blowing. Hopefully, they'd be stopping and were lowering boats.

It was a cloudy night, the visibility made worse by drizzle, and beyond the light from the ship, there was a black emptiness, broken only by the faint glow of the foamy wake and the tips of the waves. He couldn't see anything. Please, he thought, his breaths coming in sobs. I'll find you. Please be alive. He couldn't bear to lose his father *and* his uncle in the space of a day. It was too much for him to bear.

'Michael!' he yelled, when he could draw in enough

air for it. 'Michael, where are yeh? MICHAEL!'

Someone was swimming towards him. He twisted round to see Esther had jumped in too, and she was pushing a life ring in front of her. Treading water, Liam looked back along the ship's path. He was sure he'd seen a body when he'd looked down from the deck . . . He started swimming, getting seawater in his mouth as he shouted for his uncle, and Esther joined in. Their voices sounded weak and tinny in the void. The cold dug into Liam, making his limbs stiff and his movements awkward, but he kept going.

There was no reply from out in the darkness. There was no sign of Michael at all.

Chapter 43

The Hunter in the Dark

As soon as Liam and Esther had boarded the *Hibernia*, Wolfgang pulled the submarine back to a safer distance, but they were going to quickly fall behind. Akiko had switched off the red lights in the cabin. With the hatch open, the glow might make the boat's low, slate-grey hull more visible in the gloom. The fewer people who saw her, the better.

Finding her way around by torchlight, Akiko jumped down to the engine deck, and pulled the levers to start up the diesel engine, stamped on a pedal and pulled another lever to disengage the electric motor, then pushed forward the one that shifted the diesel into gear, so that it was now driving the propshaft. They'd been running on the batteries for almost the entire time since leaving Cork and there was hardly any power left in them. Now, while they were on the surface and the boat could 'breathe' through its intakes and exhaust, they needed to run the diesel and recharge the batteries.

Even over the sound of the engine, she heard a loud bang from the direction of the steamer.

'I need your eyes up here, Aki!' Wolfgang called.

He stepped down and to the side just long enough for her to climb past him through the turret with a pair of binoculars.

'There was an explosion,' he said, raising his head back up and pointing at the ship. 'A grenade, I think. I didn't see any gas. At least one person was blown overboard, and someone else jumped in after them . . . possibly a third one too. They'll be in the water aft of the ship.'

The *Hibernia*'s whistle was blowing, and her engines had slowed. A wall of light in the darkness, she was still moving, veering hard to port to pull her propellors away from the people in the water and come about to where they'd fallen in. There were already men starting to lower two of the boats on this side. As Wolfgang kept an eye on what was happening on the *Hibernia*, Akiko scanned the sea for the swimmers. The first one she spotted was a woman – Could it be Esther? – made more visible by the red and white life ring she was pushing. Ahead of her, further from the ship, was someone else, too far and too low to make out clearly, but from the swimming style, she guessed it was Liam. There was only one reason she could think of why he'd be swimming *away* from the mail boat.

'I think Liam's gone in after somebody,' she said. 'I can't see anyone else . . . I doubt *he* can either. We should get over there.'

Wolfgang nodded, and turned about, setting a new course in the direction she'd indicated. They were only a minute or two away. Liam was still swimming, with no obvious target in view. Akiko tried to ignore the chilling sensation that was trying to creep over her. She hadn't seen her father on the deck of the *Hibernia*, but that didn't mean anything. And Liam . . . Liam was always looking for a chance to be heroic. He'd swim out into that darkness to save anyone – a complete stranger. It didn't have to be someone he knew. Still, she could tell he was tiring already, probably drained by the cold, and she shook her head in dismay.

'He's going to . . . Wait. What's that?'

A light had caught her eye. She swung her gaze a few degrees to the left, closer to the steamer. Further out, beyond the trail of disturbed water left by the ship. There . . . a pinpoint of light that could only mean another craft was out there in the night. A tiny light, perhaps just a torch. Lowering her binoculars slightly, she could see the splashing of five more people in the sea. They must have fallen or jumped from the other side of the ship as it was slowing. They too were swimming away from the ship, all of them in the same direction. She looked back at the light, shifting the dial to tighten the focus, and her breath caught in her chest. There, only fifty or sixty yards from the *Hibernia*'s wake, its conning tower barely visible in the single light on the vessel's deck, was the sleek, predatory form of a much larger submarine.

'Wolfgang, it's your U-boat! Gorey and his men are escaping to it, just like you said!'

As she watched, they reached the submarine and climbed up using a rope ladder that had been laid down the sloping steel hull. One of them took much longer to get there and struggled to get up, needing help to make it onto the deck. From the way he moved, he appeared to be injured. Akiko couldn't keep her eyes trained on the U-boat, as she had to sweep back and find Esther and Liam. Guiding Wolfgang towards them until he was able to see them himself, she took a glance back at the U-boat, and saw that it was submerging. Good. Let them go. She had more immediate concerns.

The *Subversive* drew alongside Esther first, and Akiko threw her a rope, helping the British agent drag herself up onto the deck, still clinging to the *Hibernia*'s life ring. Then they caught up with Liam, and he climbed up more reluctantly, jerking free of their hands once he was on board, still looking out and around him.

'Michael . . . Michael's still out there,' he panted, slumping down on the wet steel plate. 'I can't . . . I can't see him, Aki. He was knocked overboard by the explosion. I can't find him.'

'*What?*' Akiko gasped, grabbing his shoulder. 'What did you say?'

She too cast her gaze out over the dark sea. The water here was slowly settling, but there were still traces of the turbulence left by the ship. A nauseating wave of fear came over her, and shudders ran through her body.

'Papa!' she cried. Then, in desperation, she screamed as loud as her lungs could muster: 'PAPA! OTOSAN, WHERE ARE YOU?!'

She and Liam both called out for him, over and over again, and with the noise they were making, they didn't hear Wolfgang at first.

'. . . *Gott im Himmel*, will you get down and hold on!

Akiko, Liam, shut up!'

It was only when they felt the boat suddenly accelerate and make a hard turn to starboard, nearly throwing them off their feet, that they finally fell quiet enough to hear him, and now Esther was shouting at them too. She was pointing to where the U-boat had disappeared.

'Torpedo! It's a *torpedo*!' she yelled as Wolfgang hauled on the helm, the throttle wide open. 'Get down! Hold on!'

And then the two cousins saw it; a faint line of white, disturbed water, speeding in their direction, the only sign that there was a self-propelled bomb beneath the surface, more than ten feet long, racing towards them, faster than the *Subversive*, faster than any vessel. Capable of sinking a battleship, it could completely destroy the small submarine. Wolfgang was swinging the boat around, trying to steer her out of the line of fire. They had seconds left. Akiko was lying down, facing Liam, her jaws clenched shut, hands gripping the edges of the deck. She could see her own terror reflected in his expression.

The torpedo missed them by a few yards, with a faint, high-pitched hiss. Wolfgang was already waving to them.

'*Get in, get in, get in!*' he shouted. 'We have to dive!'

'But Papa . . . !' Akiko cried.

'You're no good to him dead! The ship has sent boats out to search, now *get below!*'

Thirty seconds later, they were all inside and Wolfgang was sealing the hatch. Esther turned the red lights back on. Wolfgang pointed Liam to the planes controls, Akiko to the ballast valves, and he took the helm at the periscope station. They wasted no time, and a minute later, the

Subversive was diving away from the surface. Akiko was crying, aghast that she'd been forced to abandon her father in the sea. Esther tried to reassure her:

'The ship's men will find him – and they're better suited for a search than we are.'

'Akiko, on the hydrophones please,' Wolfgang said softly. 'We need to know where that U-boat is.' He looked at Esther. 'What happened on the ship? The gas attack?'

'Scuppered,' she replied. 'We were able to warn the bodyguards. There was no gas released before Gorey and the others jumped overboard on the other side of the boat. I don't know what happened after that – I followed Liam into the water.'

They levelled the submarine out at a depth of a hundred and fifty feet, and they all felt able to breathe freely again.

'Are we safe now?' Esther asked.

'For the moment,' the German said, with a grimace. 'We're a very small target, almost impossible to hit while submerged, but . . .'

'But what?'

'It depends on how badly they want us dead,' he said.

Liam gave a snort of disgust. He was still at the planes controls, shivering intensely, his drenched clothes dripping on the deck. He was covered in spots of blood, peppered with small wounds from the grenade's shrapnel. It was probably only the cold that stopped him from bleeding more, from feeling more. Esther had some too. They'd have to dress those soon. Esther, who was also suffering from her swim, dug two towels out of a storage locker, tossed one to Liam, who quickly wrapped himself up in it.

'We wr . . . wrecked their whole plan,' he rasped, huddled in the folds. 'And Gorey strikes me as a . . . as a fella who'd hold a grudge. I don't think thuh . . . they'll let us go. They'll sink us if they can.'

The others reluctantly nodded in agreement. Akiko spoke up then, saying she could hear the U-boat, moving slowly off their stern. The bearing was constant, suggesting that it was following them.

'Do you think they'll take another shot?' she asked.

'No, it would be a waste of a torpedo.' Wolfgang shook his head. 'They can only shoot in a straight line, and that's hard enough to do at sea if a target is moving on the surface, with no depth to estimate, where you can line your sights up on it. However, if it is their intent to hunt us down, then they can.

'Their range is greater than ours, they know we have no weapons and they must know we've been hiding, submerged for most of the last day, so our batteries are nearly drained. We can't stay down much longer. We can outrun the U-boat over a short distance, but not their torpedoes, and if they catch us on the surface, they can sight on us.' He gestured at the gauges in front of him. 'With the power we have left, we might make it a couple of kilometers . . . I mean a mile or so, but they could hear our propellor noise, and track us, as they're doing now.

'Our other option is to stop here, stay quiet, and hope they don't wait us out. Again, time is on their side. We're more than a mile from the *Hibernia* now. They only have to wait with their periscope up until we're forced to surface, and they can see us. They're armed and we're not.' He gave a sour smile and shook his head. 'It is a painful irony.'

'What do you mean?' Akiko piped up.

'The U-boat had no torpedoes on board when it was hijacked. I think they must have taken the ones from the cave. The ones Michael chose not to use.'

That caused them all to fall silent for a minute.

'What . . . what are we going to do?' Liam said at last. 'The batteries are going to die soon. We can't just wait around. We have to do something.'

'We could *ram* them,' Akiko declared.

'Oh, please . . .' Esther blurted, out as she began towelling her hair.

'No. No, she is right.' Wolfgang raised his eyebrows, nodding. 'We could ram them.'

'Have you lost your minds?' Esther exclaimed, pausing to look from one to the other. 'You can't be serious!'

'We're twice as fast as them, and we can turn in half the distance,' Wolfgang pointed out.

'I'm rather more concerned by the idea of *crashing our little ship into a larger ship*,' she protested, her free hand gesturing at their surroundings, 'given that we're halfway sunk already.'

'A submarine is a *boat*, not a ship.'

'I hardly think the distinction matters at the moment!'

'Holland designed his boats back before torpedoes worked very well,' Akiko told them. 'His early boat was called the *Fenian Ram* for a reason. Back in the day, before people even called these things "submarines", they were called "wrecking boats", because they were meant to be able to charge into the hull of a ship. Holland even crashed into a wooden pier once, by accident. He smashed the pier, and the boat came off just fine.'

'But this isn't some wooden pier, or some nineteenth century tub,' Esther pressed them. 'You're talking about driving us into a modern steel hull, built to be as strong as this one.'

'It could work, if we hit them at the right point in that hull,' Wolfgang insisted. 'We're not trying to sink them, we just need to show them we can bite. The commander of that boat is coming after us because there is no cost to him – he thinks we're helpless. But I don't think he'll persist if it risks damaging his vessel, no matter what Gorey wants.' He cast his gaze around, resting it finally on Esther. 'If we're going to survive this day, we have to show them that if they come after us, they'll pay a high price. He has to think we're that crazy.'

'But that means we have to *be* that crazy!'

Closing her eyes, Esther took a deep breath and then nodded curtly, though she looked sick with fear. Liam didn't look much better, and Akiko was feeling it too. The *Subversive* couldn't take much damage to its hull. As Esther had said, a submarine was halfway sunk already. One bad crack could send them to the bottom of the sea.

Wolfgang stopped the motor, silencing the vessel, and stepped over to take Akiko's position. Pulling a chart of the currents in the area from a locker near the helm, he unrolled it and sat down at the hydrophone station to study it.

Then, putting the headset on, he took a stopwatch from his pocket.

'We have only enough power to try this once,' he said quietly, closing his eyes to concentrate on the sounds the microphones on the hull were picking up. 'And we have to hit them just right. I need you to follow my directions precisely.

'They cannot hear us now. I think they will be above us, submerged, but at periscope depth, watching for us to surface. They are still aft of us . . . wait. Yes . . . here they come . . . About two hundred and fifty yards and closing.'

It wasn't long before they all heard the dull, chugging rumble of the larger submarine's twin propellors as it passed overhead, also running on its electric motors. Though the motors ran quietly, the propellor sound was threatening, impressing upon them the hard fact that they were dealing with a more powerful vessel, one built for modern warfare.

As the muted thunder passed them, Wolfgang started his stopwatch, still keeping his eyes closed. From this point on, it was all about time, speed and distance.

'We are off their stern now. They can't hear us over their own noise. Akiko, engine ahead two thirds. Come right to one-six-zero.'

'Ahead two thirds, aye. Coming right to one-six-zero.'

'Liam, planes up ten degrees, make your depth . . . forty feet.'

Liam too, acknowledged the command, and the *Subversive* came up to their enemy's estimated depth. Akiko brought them onto the new bearing, watching as the former U-boat commander opened his eyes to do some quick calculations with a pencil on the chart, plotting a course that would take them out away from the other boat, and then curve back to intercept it.

'Esther, stand by at the ballast valves,' he said. 'We might need to surface in a hurry.'

Then he was focussing his attention on the sounds again, and Akiko imagined the U-boat ahead of them, off their port bow, as the smaller, faster submarine began racing out wide to get some distance between the two of them. As they drew level with the U-boat, Wolfgang checked his stopwatch and told Akiko to adjust their course so that the two vessels were travelling parallel to one another, with little more than a hundred yards between them.

'They'll be able to hear us by now. Let us see what they'll do . . .'

He stiffened, then stayed very still, as if any movement might drown out the feed from the headphones. He lifted a hand, his mouth opened slightly . . . 'They're slowing. They think we're making a run for it. They want to pull back, get in behind us . . .'

Akiko could see it now, the U-boat captain, probably with Gorey standing next to him, vengeful and hungry for the kill, hearing their prey out to starboard, ordering their engines to slow so that the *Subversive* would sweep on past, and they could fall in behind again and hound the smaller submarine until her batteries died and she was forced to surface.

But slowing down would make the U-boat an easier target. Wolfgang glanced down at his stopwatch and jabbed a hand towards Akiko:

'Left full rudder! Turn . . . turn to eight-zero! Full speed ahead! FULL SPEED, NOW!'

'Full speed, aye!' she called back.

She spun the helm and pushed the throttle lever all the way forward. The deep thrum of the electric motor rose to a louder, sonorous scream, throbbing with power. Her eyes fixed on the compass as the *Subversive* surged forward, making a tight turn to the left, bringing them onto the new bearing . . . and a collision course with the side of the other submarine.

'Bearing, eight-zero.'

'Akiko, follow my hand!' Wolfgang told her. 'Liam, planes down five degrees.'

'Five degrees down, aye.'

Wolfgang was staring into space now, not seeing anything except the U-boat's track, drawing on all of his experience of hunting ships during the Great War to try and judge its exact position. His hand was stretched out in front of him, and as he shifted it slightly right, slightly left, small, urgent movements, Akiko adjusted the helm to follow it. She could feel the vibrations from the engine through the hull, tickling her feet, running through her body, as the acceleration drained the last of their battery power in this one final burst of speed.

'They know,' Wolfgang growled, with a maniacal smile. '*They know we're coming*! But it's too late, you schweine! It's too late. BRACE! BRACE FOR IMPACT!'

Akiko hunched down, gripping the spokes of the helm, leaning her shoulder into it, her eyes squeezed closed.

Picturing the U-boat as it loomed before them, closer, closer, *closer*, she thought she could hear its propellors in those last few seconds . . .

The impact was sudden and terrifying, slamming her against the helm with the ear-pounding, explosive sound of smashing machinery and buckling steel plate. There was a teeth-aching grind of metal against metal, pipes split, spraying the cabin with water, and most of the bulbs burst, plunging them into darkness.

'Liam, planes up twenty degrees!' Wolfgang shouted. 'Esther! Esther, blow ballast! Blow the ballast now! Dump everything!'

They were still scraping past the U-boat with a horrible grating sound, having hit the larger vessel side-on. Akiko guessed the *Subversive* was dragging her hull over the other boat's sloping side, and was grinding along the aft part of its conning tower.

There came the loud, rushing hiss of the ballast water being driven from the tanks as air was pumped in, and the *Subversive* jolted again under their feet, lurching upwards this time, reaching for the surface.

There was still water gushing in from half a dozen leaks, the propshaft was making a nasty screeching sound and Liam said the planes weren't responding properly. Akiko could smell smoke from somewhere. One red light was still working, and Esther switched on the remaining white lights so that they could see what was going on.

The equipment around them had taken a severe blow, but the hull seemed intact. Wolfgang was shutting some of the valves, cutting off the worst of the leaks. He had pulled his headset off, but even over the other sounds, they could all hear noises beyond the hull.

It was the nightmarish sound of a vessel sinking, pulled down into the depths. Rushes of air bubbles, the groaning of metal under stress, the sudden crack and boom of bulkheads collapsing under the sea's pressure.

'I think we broke through the wall of their control room . . . or the engine room,' Wolfgang said in a near whisper, his face tense with suppressed emotions. 'She's going down so fast! We probably damaged the conning tower too.'

Akiko listened, her heart thudding as if it too would burst under the pressure. By the time the *Subversive* broke the surface, she was crying. They had survived, they had won, but she was sick to her stomach at what they had *done* to win. Liam was still sitting by the planes controls, wrapped in the towel, a haunted uncertainty in his eyes, as if he was still grasping the scale of the violence he'd just been part of. He was trembling, and she was sure it wasn't from the chill of his wet clothes. Despite clinging to one of the hand-holds, Esther had fallen during the crash and, putting her hand to her face, her fingers smeared a trickle of blood that ran down her forehead. From her rueful expression, Akiko guessed that it was not a serious injury.

Wolfgang climbed up the ladder, opened the hatch, and hauled himself out. Fresh air flooded in, and Akiko closed her eyes and took deep breaths of it. She followed it up through the hatch. The expanse of opaque water made the U-boat's fate feel all the more final, and she turned her thoughts away from the new, steel-plated graveyard on the seabed below them.

The bow of the *Subversive* was crumpled and dented, with deep scrapes along her starboard side. They were ugly wounds, but she could tell they were not fatal. Wolfgang was shining a torch around the waterline, though there were no obvious air bubbles rising anywhere from splits in the hull. In the darkness off their stern, Akiko could make out the distant lights of the *Hibernia*, its crew no doubt still looking for the people who had gone overboard – including her otosan. She sat down on the deck, and even as the sea air revived her spirits, for it always did, she felt the first real stirrings of grief, and she was certain, in that moment, that she would never see her father again.

She was wiping her eyes as Liam clambered up through the hatch and crouched beside her, wrapping his arms around her, and despite his wet clothes, she was grateful for the embrace. He was still bleeding from a dozen small wounds, reminding her that, in all the mayhem, they had not been dressed. Huge problems could so often drown out smaller, but still important ones.

What had gone through Jim Gorey's mind in his last moments? She wondered if it had been just blind terror, or bitterness at his failure or rage at those who had killed him . . . Had there been pride too? Had he convinced himself that he was dying for Ireland, as so many men dreamed of doing? She decided then, that there had been quite enough dying for Ireland, and it was time to put an end to it, though the fight was far from over. There were corpses on the seafloor because of her, and she recognised that she was at a crucial point in her life, sitting here on this cold metal deck, feeling the motion of the waves though the hull. Because she had survived this day, when others hadn't, she felt compelled to make something of this life from this point forward. She resolved to have an effect on the world.

Her father and mother had dreamed that she would grow up free, in a fairer, more just society, and she would to help make that happen. So she would not die for Ireland, but she would *live* for it, for her home, and the people she loved. She turned her head to look into Liam's face. His attention was fixed on the ship in the distance.

'Things are going to change,' he said, as if reading her thoughts.

'Only if we change them. Come on, let's get you patched up,' she replied. She pulled free of his arms and stood up, gazing west to a coast that was hidden from view. Then, to Wolfgang and Esther too, who were both on the deck behind them, she added: 'We need to get back and fix up our boat. We still have a lot to do.'

And minutes later, they were underway again, setting off for home under the cover of darkness in their battered submarine. Because they still had a lot to do.

Chapter 44
A Well Ordered Narrative

Sitting in Edward Faulkner's office once more, Esther lounged back in the comfortable swivel chair, legs crossed as she faced him across the desk. After her father had spoken to a few of his friends in government, challenging the paltry evidence against his daughter, the warrant for her arrest had eventually been withdrawn, explained away as an unfortunate administrative error.

Faulkner was in no position to press the matter. Esther had not been surprised when she was summoned to a meeting with him, and though she felt some apprehension, she knew this arch puppetmaster had found himself tangled in his own strings. His superior, Winston Churchill, was one of the men who had negotiated the treaty with the Irish, and if he ever found out about Faulkner's involvement in what had become known as 'the Irish Mail Boat Incident', he could kiss goodbye to any chance of retiring with a knighthood. Indeed, that retirement might come a great deal sooner than he'd intended. A long stay in a prison cell might not be out of the question.

However, if there was one thing that Edward Faulkner excelled at, it was ensuring that someone else always paid the price for his sins. And if Esther had one objective in this meeting, it was to make sure it wouldn't be *her*. The cad was more than capable of evading her father's influence if he set his mind to it.

She had her own cards to play. Faulkner knew she had no material proof either, that he had conspired in the poison gas attack, which was why she had refrained from making any accusations . . . for now. Like a venomous snake, he was most dangerous when threatened, but she knew enough to make life very uncomfortable for him too, if he backed her into a corner. This was the game they had to play here and now: to see if one or other was going to bite, and how hard.

'What I'd like to establish today,' Faulkner said, lighting a cigarillo after a brief exchange of pleasantries, 'is a well ordered narrative of events. I've read your report, of course, but I just wanted to . . . to *clarify* things – before I close the file, you understand.'

'But of course,' Esther replied, giving him a reassuring smile. 'One must strive for clarity in all administrative matters. Clarity and truth. They are pillars of the service, don't you think? That *arrest warrant*, for instance . . .'

'A most regrettable mistake,' Faulkner said earnestly. 'I offer my most heartfelt apologies. That was Dollman exceeding his brief, for which he has already been given a dressing down. I can assure you that his next role will provide him with significantly less opportunity to interfere with the work of other, more diligent agents.'

'Oh, has he been reassigned?'

'He's currently on his way to a very lonely lighthouse

on one of the lesser Falkland Islands.'

Even though she was sure Dollmann had only been following orders, Esther could muster little sympathy. In her experience, the men who were chosen for this kind of dirty work against their fellow agents tended to be of a particular character.

'Back to the matter at hand,' Faulkner continued, exhaling smoke. 'The narrative. You were investigating Michael Regan and his family, and on the evening in question, I'm told his entire household was on the run from republican gunmen, at least partly because of their association with *you*. One informer even places you at their home the night before, though it's not clear how you got out to that godforsaken spot – it wasn't in the car you'd hired in Cork.'

Esther was careful not to react. Was this the same informer who'd infiltrated Gorey's company? If so, had they been on board the *Hibernia*? Had they identified her, or had they gone down with the U-boat? The irony was, what she was doing now was tantamount to treason, and that arrest warrant was part of the reason for it. She had avoided any mention of the Regans' submarine in her report. And failure to alert her superiors to the existence of a republican submarine operating in the Irish Sea was a grievous offense.

But the Regans had saved her from drowning and had let her live despite the fact that she knew about the *Subversive,* potentially at the cost of their freedom, or even their lives. They had protected her from Gorey and risked their lives again to stop a poison gas attack that members of her own service had conspired in. At every step in this affair, Faulkner had sought to deceive, obstruct and endanger her, while the Regans had acted with honour and courage. And she believed them when they swore that they would take no more part in any violence. She could not, in all conscience, turn them in now.

'. . . Then the family was forced to flee from the house when James Gorey and his murder gang showed up and shot the place all to hell,' Faulkner went on. 'They were aided in their escape by the republican leader, Lawrence O'Leary, who was shot and fell into the sea. He is presumed dead.'

Esther didn't correct him on that either, but Liam's father had survived, against all the odds, with a few more bullet wounds to add to his collection. She was certain that Lar would be joining the growing number of Irish rebels who considered the compromise treaty a betrayal of the Irish republic, and were declaring that the fight was still on.

Ireland's troubles were not over by a long way.

'They made their way to Dublin – again, we're not sure how – where Midori Regan attempted to get medical help for her husband, who'd been wounded in the attack,' Faulkner said. 'They were also seeking protection from Gorey, and hoped to contact senior figures in the movement. And indeed, Regan himself was on the mail boat when it sailed, presumably to petition Griffith and Collins, both of whom he knew personally. So . . . were you in the house when all the shooting was going on?'

'Yes I was,' Esther replied. 'And it's true about Gorey.

He tried to kill us all that night, even the children. Michael had contacted me and told me he had learned of Gorey's intention to launch a gas attack. He assumed the target would be British, and meant to stop it. He also tipped me off about the arrest warrant you'd issued–.'

'That *Dollman* had issued . . .'

'Yes, so you've said. Anyhow, Gorey and his gang showed up before I could get through to you about it, and I escaped with the family and travelled to Dublin. By car. Michael had one waiting some way from the house for just this kind of emergency.'

'A resourceful man.'

'Yes he was.'

'He "was", you say. So you're certain that he was killed on the ship? Even though you claim you weren't on board?'

Esther remembered the stunning force of the blast from the grenade. She had minor wounds all down her left side from it, though none showed on her face, and Michael had been standing much, much closer and was already injured before the explosion blew him overboard. She remembered the abyss of black water, Akiko's and Liam's despair. And how Midori's usual stoicism had collapsed when they'd told her after she'd finally found them. No, Michael Regan was gone, though they might never find the body. His death had been like much of his life; consequential, violent and hidden from view.

'I spent the next couple of days with his grieving family, Edward – hiding from the authorities until I could clear my name. They have no hope that he survived. And you *know* I wasn't on board the ship. The police questioned everyone who disembarked at Holyhead. I'm sure you read their report even before I could. Though it's curious that there were apparently no intelligence agents on board. Why was that?'

Faulkner waved the matter away like the smoke from his cigarillo.

'It was a question of manpower,' he said breezily. 'The treaty was all but complete and they were needed elsewhere. With the benefit of hindsight, it was a complacent decision – very embarrassing for the agent in charge.'

Not for *you*, of course, Esther thought. Never for you.

'It's just that some of the witnesses mention a young Englishwoman who warned the Irish bodyguards about Gorey's attack,' he pressed her. 'The police were unable to identify her among the passengers. They say she saved the day, and yet no one has come forward to take the credit. She might even have been one of those who jumped overboard.'

There it was; the question. The one piece that he couldn't make fit. It made him doubt his ability to manipulate the situation, and *that* was Esther's winning card. She shrugged.

'Perhaps this girl *was* on the ship at Holyhead, but she's the shy sort,' she suggested. 'Women are so often overlooked.'

'Perhaps. But how would she have known about the plot, do you think?'

'You're asking me to speculate. She might have seen something on the ship, or heard something . . . It could have been anything. The statements from the witnesses are all quite confused. Gracious, I mean, nobody's even sure how many people went overboard! From what I read, it varies from three to eight. And none were retrieved! It's a wonder the police could make any sense of it all.

'All of which is to say, Edward,' Esther added, meeting his gaze, 'that we might never know what she knows.'

'Mmm. Quite.' Faulkner regarded her through the faint cloud of vapour. 'There was the U-boat too, of course. It seems Gorey and some of his people managed to escape on board the dratted thing. There's no telling where they'll turn up – probably in Germany somewhere – but we've seized their ship, the *Medusa*. We found where those chlorine bombs were concealed, right where you said. One of our chemists confirmed traces of them, but they're gone now, probably on the U-boat. Although . . . I presume you read what a couple of the witnesses claimed, that there was a second, smaller craft out there, on the other side of the ship? Perhaps it even picked up the Englishwoman, and one or two of the other swimmers? What do you make of that?'

He said it casually enough, with a hint that he knew more than he was letting on, but Esther decided he was fishing, and ignored it.

'I have nothing to add, Edward. As I've already pointed out, I wasn't there.'

He was quiet then, casting a lingering look at her, then staring at the ceiling over her head for an uncomfortably long time. At last, he sniffed, cleared his throat, stabbed the stub of the cigarillo out in the ashtray on his desk and arched an eyebrow.

'How are you feeling, anyhow?' he asked, with a markedly more chipper tone. 'Champing at the bit? Given the . . . admirable judgement you've shown in how you've handled all this, I'm compelled to put in a good word for you. We need more women like you in the field. Though you might be ready to try somewhere more exotic than our muddy little neighbour, perhaps? So . . . are you keen to get back in the action?'

She chewed her lip and then nodded, not quite managing to hide her eagerness. He turned to look at the large map of the British Empire that dominated the wall beside the door. Red-topped pins marked areas of concern. There were a lot of those pins.

'Now that the wretched Irish have wormed their way out of our grip, half the bloody empire's getting ideas above their station. The rabble have been roused, my dear. There are revolts kicking up all over the place, and we need feet on the ground. India? Egypt? Turkey? What takes your fancy?'

Esther had once been in awe of the spread of countries under British control, a range of territory that reached around the globe. Now, she saw these places in a new light; appreciating each one's intent to express its own culture, its own character. She relished the way each one offered different possibilities. She gazed up at the map with an unfamiliar, exhilarating kind of hunger, one whose nature she was only starting to understand. It was the Regans' influence, of course.

Esther was developing a taste for revolution.

Dedication

The older I get, the less I'm inclined to think violence is a solution to anything, and that in general it tends to make things worse, so my feelings about the events of, and many of the people involved in, Ireland's War of Independence and subsequent Civil War are complicated. The violence of those times has led to a legacy of division and conflict that lasts in Ireland to this day. But there is no question that the men in power in Britain at the time, with their oppression, racism, violence and theft of resources, created a situation where many of those struggling to win Ireland's independence felt they were left with no choice. They had to use force – and in as many different and inventive ways as possible. I often find myself wondering what views I might have held, and what role I might have played, if I'd grown up in that environment, under the rule of a coloniser.

Like all revolutions, the final result failed to live up to the high ideals of of its early dreamers. Beyond achieving a free Ireland, there was a lot of disagreement over what form that new state should take. Visions of a progressive, egalitarian and united society were muddied; as the Anglo-Irish Treaty led to the Civil War, and eventually to a republic on a divided island, those who were not abandoned in the northern counties found themselves living in a socially conservative state characterised by religious control, misogyny and huge levels of emigration.

The bloodshed had another effect, blotting out all the other actions that led to Ireland's independence. The men (and it was almost entirely men) who took violent action are granted most of history's attention, despite the fact that many of them, like my grandfather, would never speak about that violence afterwards, even to their families. They made headlines and contributed to the immortal symbols of the martyrs, and yet there were so many other factors in this revolution; political campaigns, publishing, the fundraising, the rekindling of the language, intelligence-gathering, labour strikes, arts, culture and sport, the women's rights movement . . . the thousands of different acts of civil disobedience, those who provided refuge and supplies, the passive resistance, the protests and acts of support, all of which contributed to the modern republic Ireland is today.

So this book is dedicated to everyone who did their part, whether you were a politician or a chambermaid, a fighter or a teacher or a homemaker, a farm worker or a sailor, whether you gave money or food or medical attention, whether you walked out on strike with your fellow workers or stayed in the office late, mining police files for the valuable intelligence they contained. To all the writers, speakers and scholars, the artists and musicians, the smugglers and thieves, the printers, secretaries and clerks, the spies, the vandals and messengers, to those who kept their secrets and those who refused to be silenced, I am grateful to you all for this country I call my home.

Acknowledgements

I can't remember when I first learned about John Philip Holland and the three submarines he built for the Irish republican movement, but it was an idea that soon took root in my imagination, and I knew I was going to have to write a story about it someday. It ended up becoming not so much about Holland himself, but a lens for me to explore what is arguably the most impactful period in modern Irish history. It is one of the conflicted pleasures of historical fiction (even alternate history when you want to keep it reasonably accurate) that you can barely write a few lines without having to go and check something. You also have to remind yourself constantly that just because *you* find something fascinating, that's not an automatic reason to include it in the book. You must spare the reader your rabbit holes.

But there are some particular sources I found valuable. The best references I found on Michael's mentor were *John P. Holland 1841–1914: Inventor of the Modern Submarine* by Richard Knowles Morris and *Going Deep: John Philip Holland and the Invention of The Attack Submarine* by Lawrence Goldstone. Both take a comprehensive look at the man and his work.

Ireland is awash with reference material on the War of Independence and the Civil War, and I'm sure my story will not help the ongoing arguments about who was right or wrong in the end, and whether it should still continue to shape our country now. One book I want to pick out is *We Go Into Action Today at Noon* by Eamon Duggan, which I found useful not only for its close-in descriptions of events, but also the language and terms the people used in that time and place. In a similar way, *The Riddle of the Sands* by Erskine Childers, credited as being one of the earliest spy novels, gave me an insight into sailing and navigating the coast in that period, and the language to go with it. An extraordinary character in his own right, Childers was an Englishman whose love for the British Empire would eventually sour to the point where he joined the ranks of Ireland's most passionate and anti-British revolutionaries.

Colum Kenny's *Midnight in London: The Anglo-Irish Treaty Crisis 1921* is a short book that captures the last stages of the negotiations of the Treaty and the incredible pressure the Irish team was under to deliver a workable compromise between the demands of hardened guerilla fighters and those of an imperial government used to getting its own way. The *History Ireland* podcast offers well informed insight into different aspects of the two wars, and is an easy way in for anyone looking for detailed breakdowns of the subject. *In the Waves: My Quest to Solve the Mystery of a Civil War Submarine,* by Rachel Lance, is a forensically detailed investigation into the fate of the 'Fish Boat', the tiny Confederate submarine later named the *HL Hunley*. I found this quite late in my work, but it tells us a lot about the scientific and engineering challenges faced by some of the early pioneers of the submarine, and is well worth a read if you're interested in the subject.

The *Subversive* is based on a mix of different Holland

designs – there was a lot of variation – and I modernised it to fit the era, but the US Navy's *Plunger* class and the Royal Navy's *Holland* class were my starting points. If you're more specifically interested in the Holland subs – they do seem to have captured people's imaginations – there are now all sorts of engineering breakdowns, and amazing 3D rendered and animated models online.

It's worth noting that the basic shape of today's modern military submarines ended up having more in common with the original form of those early Holland designs, abandoning many of the surface-ship-like characteristics of vessels from the first half of the 20th century, once they became capable of spending most of their time submerged. The low profile form adopted by many of today's 'narco subs' used by drug traffickers, also bear a striking resemblance to Holland's vessels, created over a century ago.

Making a living as a writer and illustrator is a strange, unstable and challenging existence, and I'm grateful for the support and encouragement of friends and family, and to the wider community I have the pleasure to be part of, in Ireland and online.

And finally, I'd like to offer a huge thanks to the Arts Council of Ireland, which provided a bursary to support the research and writing of this book.

Oisín McGann

STEEL-PLATE SUBVERSIVE

Oisín McGann